Embers of
the Earth

ALSO BY ROBERT BALMANNO

September Snow
{Book One of the BLESSINGS OF GAIA SERIES}

Runes of Iona
[Book Two of the BLESSINGS OF GAIA SERIES]

Embers of the Earth

Book Three of the Four-Book Series
THE BLESSINGS OF GAIA QUARTET

▶▶▶▶

Robert Balmanno

A Caveat Lector Book

REGENT PRESS
Berkeley, California

Copyright © 2016 by Robert Balmanno

All rights reserved under International and Pan-American Copyright Conventions. No part of this book may be used or reproduced in any manner whatsoever without the written permission of the Publisher, except in the case of brief quotations embodied in critical articles and reviews.

This is a work of fiction. Any resemblances between characters, names, places, or incidents described here and any actual such, living or dead, known or imagined, are coincidental.

ISBN 13: 978-1-58790-333-5
ISBN 10: 1-58790-333-4

Library of Congress Control Number: 2015914775

First Edition

0 1 2 3 4 5 6 7 8 9 10

Cover design/photos by S. R. Hinrichs

Manufactured in the United States of America

REGENT PRESS
www.regentpress.net
regentpress@mindspring.com

to Richard Primont

Chronology

1963 – "The Curmudgeon," poet and bon vivant, is born.
1970 – Earth Day, on April 22, is first celebrated.
1971 – William Golding (winner of Noble prize for literature in 1989), meets with British scientist James Lovelock in a pub in a village in Britain and suggests alternative title — using Greek goddess's name Gaia — as title for Lovelock's paper. The concept of Gaia goes on to spawn scientific analytical worldviews, and general belief systems.
1972 – James Lovelock publishes paper: *The Gaia Hypothesis*.
1973 – Orsen Pipes, author, is born.
1979 – James Lovelock publishes the book: *The Theory of Gaia*.
1993 – Regis Snow is born.
1994 – In the Twenty-fifth year celebration of the First Earth Day, Tom Novak is born.
2022 CE/AD – September Snow is born.
2040 to 2051 AD – A massive war rages worldwide, posthumously named: "The Eleven-Years-War," five years after signing of armistice. One and one-half billion humans die.
2051 AD – The Age of Gaia is proclaimed by a small but growing conglomeration of Gaia-Domes, inaugurating a new calendar — Gaia Year One — and a "New Era of World Peace."
2051 to 2060 AD – Due to the effects of "The Eleven-Years-War," ozone layer is destroyed. Simultaneously, human caused climate change and global warming, already dangerous for growing portions of the world's population, steeply accelerates.
2052 AD (Gaia Year One) – Kull is born.

2054 AD (Gaia Year Three) – Lloyd Thompson the fourth, Special Magister in the Gaia Domes, is born.

2057 AD (Gaia Year Six) – Iona, daughter of September Snow, is born.

2060 AD (Gaia Year Nine) – Regis Snow, husband of September, chief executive scientist for the Gaia-Domes, is executed for treason.

2060 AD (Gaia Year Nine) – After fighting secretly for half a dozen years, September Snow formally declares war on the Gaia-Domes.

2062 AD (Gaia Year Eleven) – Orsen Pipes commits suicide.

2063 AD (Gaia Year Twelve) – Tom Novak for the first time meets September Snow.

2063 AD (Gaia Year Twelve) – "The Curmudgeon," age 100, buries in a valley in Antarctica important archival documents intended for a chance discovery by people in the future.

2070 AD (Gaia Year Nineteen) – At the age of thirteen, daughter of September, Iona, is directed to make a perilous journey across the Forbidden Zone.

2070 AD (Gaia Year Twenty) – September Snow's group successfully destroys the nuclear-powered wind machine network. Also, September is captured and executed.

2075 AD (Gaia Year Twenty-Five) – Kull and Iona are united, beginning a lifelong journey together.

2064 to 2075 AD (Gaia Year Fourteen to Gaia Year Twenty-Five) – Tom Novak, one of the few survivors of the first series of rebel wars, hides in desert as recluse and hermit.

2097 AD (Gaia Year Forty-Six) – Iona and Kull lead a new army that defeats the Gaia-Domes in the field, then migrates and settles in the Western Quadrant, on the Colorado Plateau. They become a rebel group known as "The Unseeing Watchfulness of Gaia."

2097 AD (Gaia Year Forty-Six) – In captivity in the Gaia-Domes, Tom Novak dies.

2101 AD (Gaia Year Fifty) – Lloyd Thompson, acting as ad-hoc ambassador for the Gaia-Domes, meets on the Colorado Plateau with Iona, spiritual, religious, and political leader of the forces of "The Unseeing Watchfulness of Gaia," to negotiate peace.

2102 AD (Gaia Year Fifty-One) – Ambrosia, youngest and last of the Original Twelve Leaders of the Unseeng Watchfulness of Gaia to survive, gives birth to a baby girl, Perum.

2133 AD (Gaia Year Eight-Two) – In a secret place in the desert of Nevada, Kull dies.

2134 AD (Gaia Year Eighty-Three) – In the same place, a year later, Iona dies.

2142 AD (Gaia Year Ninety) – Lloyd Thompson, Special Magister, three months before expiring, buries in his garden, for purposes of being found in the distant future, his own secret set of memoirs and documents. Lloyd's garden is located in the shadow of the most important Gaia-Dome in Manhattan, in the old remnants of New York.

2200 AD (Gaia Year One Hundred and Forty-Eight) – From a height of eight-and-a-half to nine billion people in the early 2040's, the world population drops to 250 million and continues to drop another 50 million during the next two centuries. Then the population stabilizes and slowly grows back.

Chapter One

In the YEAR GAIA 519 A.G. – After Gaia – (2570 A.D.)

PALLAS WAS ONLY THREE YEARS AWAY from achieving his official age of maturity. He was 100 days shy of his eighteenth birthday, causing him to be caught in that nethermost point where boyhood had ended, but manhood had not begun.

He had received the preliminary rights of adulthood: travel, self-reward, body control, but not the most important one: clemency from three more years of being subjugated by his father.

Alongside the trail, Pallas came across a Gaia ring. The ring consisted in 979 one-quarter-inch wide, identical-size pebbles placed in a circle. The ground within the circle had been hollowed out, tamped down, and smoothed. The ring had been created for purposes of conducting certain religious rites. Pallas stepped into it. He drew himself up.

He faced west.

He enunciated the words, speaking in a low-timbre, drum-beat, rote-learned fashion: "What should I plant? Should it be corn or manioc? Should it be squash or pumpkin? Should it be lentils or beans?"

Facing south, Pallas positioned himself again. Bowing, he said: "What quarter should the moon be to propitiate a favorable planting?" To the east he pivoted, bowing, "Will the crops take root?" To the north he pivoted, bowing, "Will the crops wither?" Pausing, he pivoted once more, this time west again. He bowed. "Even before the bounty is harvested, will I still be alive? Will my clan not perish? Will *all the people*—as human beings—survive?"

He paused. Another rotation. One more pivot. He looked straight up, as if he were gazing at a fixed point in the sky. He smiled and said, his eyes disoriented for a moment by a bright, glimmering shimmer of refracting sunlight, "Through all this process, will Gaia protect me?"

Twelve Questions. Pallas kneeled on the ground. He grasped his arms around his chest, as if he were fending off bitter cold. But Pallas was in the middle of the desert. It was 99 degrees Fahrenheit. He closed his eyes. He did not move. Several seconds lapsed. Following standard procedure, he brought his forefinger and thumb to his forehead, then he brought his two digits together to touch his lips, his chest, his abdomen. In an act of complete supplication, he got on his hands and knees and let his forehead touch the ground: once, twice, thrice.

Rising on his haunches, Pallas bent slightly forward. He considered it a noble honor to recite the ritualized prayers institutionalized by the Obsidian Order, the religious order Pallas had joined under duress. A draconian punishment would have been administered by his father, had he not submitted.

That decision occurred when Pallas was seven. Seven years later (celebrating his "first and provisional level" of maturity), he had been placed under an obligation of the Obsidian Order to recite prayers whenever he reached what he interpreted to be a gateway.

And in all honesty Pallas thought he had reached one. All signs were clear. The discovery of a bleached-white spinal column of a horse, loose scattering of ribs, angle joints, leg bones, most noticeably, the jawbone—of the decomposed horse, lying alongside the trail.

Pallas also spotted two skinny funnel sand-stacks, commonly known as devil dusters, 500-feet tall, twisting, swerving, moving on parallel lines, three miles away. They were the end products of a distant and deteriorating windstorm; now the stacks were more modest in breadth and depth, but still fairly tall. Another sign.

Taking in five consecutive hurried breaths, through both mouth and nostrils, Pallas detected a pungent scent of sagebrush, with a skimpy overlay of pinon: a tempting fruity nut smell, filling him with a craving in the form of a deeply urgent gastronomical desire.

Unlike the source of sagebrush, which was located almost literally at his feet, the pinon "nutriment" smell was born on a wind traveling a great distance: pangs of hunger—gentle yet firm, or more touching, or more pronounced, or *in extremis*, extremely lugubrious—caused Pallas's sense of smell to roar, independent of the degree to which he was experiencing hunger.

Pallas had a weakness for pinon nuts. But because his sense of hunger was only moderate, with an application of restraint, he tried to stifle the urge.

Pallas needed to focus on *something*, to keep his mind away from the fruity nut smell. His taste buds and his only quarter-filled, churning stomach were still, oh weakness!, in play.

To the rescue, a one-of-a-kind, exceptional phenomenon came into view.

Like a hawk, peering up gimlet-eyed under his combination hat-visor, Pallas detected (at 10:00 o'clock) a 40th-of-an-inch-wide nascent crescent moon, looking like a brief, tiny hair-line fracture. *It looked so strangely alien and unworldly.* The thin wedge looked so unnatural it was as if it had been painted just above the horizon of the day's sky, a thin-curved line.

The discovery made Pallas feel content, filling him with a sense of religious resolve. All was right with the world.

The moon reminded him he had important duties to be thinking about. He had no time to pursue a diversionary path in search of some distant pinon trees and some ethereal pinon nuts.

Having risen three hours earlier above the horizon's rim, opposite from the moon, the sun was already beating down in the mid-morning air. In the hot desert air—if he were caught in an ozone layer *"risk hole"*—there lurked the potential for a severe bearing down of hazardous, death-causing radiation rays. But Pallas was comforted by his possession of a combination hat-visor, effective for protection.

Pallas's skin was mahogany in color. He was lean, very thin, yet in tip-top condition, in admirable shape. Pallas's hair was shoulder-length and lanky. A prickly goatee graced his chin.

His eyes, however, had a depressing feature. Albeit they were spellbinding and hypnotic to some people who gaped at them—this was true for both friends and strangers alike, they were also defective-looking. They were what were called "milk holes." Their centers were non-irises (technically they were white-covered, thinly covered irises) and tiny pin-size pupils. Pallas's detractors labeled his eyes pejoratively "snake eyes" or "dead eyes." They had a chilling, ghost-like appeal, but if seen in a more sympathetic light, they made Pallas look solemn, pious, even religious. Pallas's looks were otherwise boringly normal—in conformity with the people he lived with—but for his eyes! For some, they were difficult. Pallas tried to compensate. He groomed himself. *In areas of appearances, Pallas thought: "If only I could blend in, there's nothing I can do about these sad-looking orifices in my face, yet my dearest of dearest, my Telia, refers to them lovingly as: 'My darling eyes, my gorgeous eyes, my two beautifuls. With her saying that, could they be so bad? No! Only some—my enemies—find my eyes so offensive, so base, as to push them beyond the constraints of the merely envious or the truly coldhearted."*

Pallas dressed in two layers of clothing. With two long lengths of fabric, one eight feet long, the other ten, both white in color, Pallas wrapped himself in a "neck-to-toe" covering.

Sun-poisoning, a savage scourge which hampered humankind for 525 years, since the age of Gaia was declared, when the ozone layer was destroyed, was no longer a grave threat. Over a period of 100 years, much of the ozone layer had been restored, especially at the equator and in the temperate parts of North and South

Hemispheres. The polar and sub-polar regions were the last places on Earth that were still categorically extremely dangerous in terms of contracting sun poisoning.

Also, four widely spread volcanoes erupted beginning in 410 A.G. (After Gaia.) Following these four, a huge volcano exploded at Sumatra 19 years later. Then there were eruptions at Yellowstone, in the Hawaiian Islands, in Iceland, 24—30—39 years, respectively, after that. Collectively these volatile events had much to do with the Earth cooling. (Aerosols produced from the volcanic eruptions deflected solar heat in 59 of those 65 years. So, at least in the short run, they severely reversed trends of global warming.) But with the ozone layer, Pallas still had to be cautious. Even after a sixty-year period of ozone layer restoration he could still fall into a dreaded "dead zone" without realizing it, especially in the midst of the unpopulated desert.

Of all the threats in the desert Pallas's elders had taught him to be wary of, inadvertently stumbling into an ozone layer hole was the most important; the second being attacked by cannibals. These diminutive, ghoulish figures, 3' 6" to 4' 6" tall, were common enough, and plentiful in most parts of the world 85 years earlier. Cannibals were increasingly rare in Pallas's day but still existed, particularly in the dry, under-populated zones.

In their heyday, old-style cannibals feasted on the sun poisoned, the diseased, the wounded, the bodily *well disposed* (regularly functioning bodies owned by normal people who were—alas— "inconsolable to life's hope"). During the darkest days of the deepest and most severe environmental devastation, pickings for cannibals were plentiful. But conditions changed. Over time, people became healthier and stronger. By virtue of these reduced opportunities, these same-species devourers had their work cut out for them.

Cannibals of later date were known to stalk their victims for days—even up to ten days at a time. They traveled in groups—*or wolf packs*—consisting of two alpha males, with a third or fourth weaker cannibal straggling farther behind, often bringing up the rear. They usually kept a safe distance from their larger-in-size prey, sometimes as far as ten miles, until an hour or two before "the strike," which usually occurred sometime between one and six in the morning.

After crossing a considerable part of the Nevadan alkaline desert, Pallas looked up at the 9,500-foot-high mountain range, with the snow-capped, lone mountain 2,000 feet higher, perched in the middle. Rising out of a sea of sand, the improbable oasis was on the outskirts of nowhere, a pocket-size mountain enclave in the middle of the desert.

As a child, Pallas was somewhat free-spirited, at least in the sense he took well to solo-ventured traveling. On one occasion, at age fourteen, he traveled 185 miles in order to visit his Uncle Xandry, who was "on-day" dying from a twenty-eight-year-long case of sun poisoning.

Even though Pallas had never been in the desert this far west before, he knew from maps shown to him that Iona's shrine lay on a hill beneath the single mountain, about thirty miles away.

Pallas recited a prayer he had composed to himself that had nothing to do with the rites, procedures, or protocols of the Obsidian Order.

Had Pallas's father known of this *heretical prayer*, he would have whipped his "too-smart-for-his-own-good" son right down to the bone to teach him a lesson. He would have used a strong whip for good measure, for composing the awful prayer in the first place and then having the audacity and idiocy to recite it aloud. *Who did he think he was, anyway?*

Knowing the effects of a penitential, blood-letting punishment, Pallas told no one of the prayer, not even his most trusted friend and confident, Matthew. Matthew, three years older than Pallas, and during their childhood, benefactor-as-an-older-brother protector of Pallas, would never have betrayed his friend. But Pallas, ever vigilant, kept the prayer to himself. Even though times were changing in The New Rebel Bands Of Gaia, known seventy-five years before as The Unseeing Watchfulness of Gaia, he had to be careful.

Knowing another human didn't lurk within seventy miles, Pallas shouted out the words:

September Snow did not die
In an anonymous ditch
On a strange, immutably dark road
Forsaken by all the people, castaway by all the world
Under an ozone-depleted firmament
In a death-knelled environment
On a cruel rock: beyond hope of being repaired Earth:
Mocked by indifference: the universe non-sentient, non-alive.
No! No!
Hail Gaia! Hail Truth! Hail the pinnacles of both paradigms.
For are these two seemingly unrelated IDEAS not the same?

As Pallas recited his self-made prayer, he was struck by a sense of calm, by an even more profound sense of inner solace.

Pallas sighed. He thought he had completed his obligations, ritually of course, to the Obsidian Order, but more importantly—sincerely—to himself. His prayer, although he wanted to call it something more powerful: A POEM, satisfied his personal obligation. That Pallas equated Gaia with nothing more than an idea, like truth was an idea, was a breach in the principle of a religious theology that had been established many years before Pallas's birth.

But that's what Pallas hoped he believed in his heart of hearts: Truth *and* Gaia.

He soldiered on his first solo journey, his initiate's maiden voyage, to the shrine of Iona. Enormous trust had been placed in him that he had been allowed to make the journey, not just a rare privilege but an almost unheard of gift to have been extended to a seventeen-year-old boy.

Pallas had been brilliant at school. He was a superbly gifted person. He was blessed with rare intellectual qualities. By the time he was twelve his teachers knew he was being groomed for higher things. He was allowed to skip three years of memorization and rote exercise; he'd have skipped one or two more years had his teachers thought it wouldn't have placed him at too great a disadvantage relative to the size of his classmates.

Pallas graduated star master of the 52nd class of 519 A.G. He became the highest ranked initiate to join the religious order. His language skills ran circles around all, elderly and young.

One thing troubled Pallas greatly. He was appalled that his fellow students had to develop basic literacy skills by studying truncated screeds or cut-in-half parables. Many ancient texts existed only in crude fragments completed between 360 and 370 A.G., in a primitive ten-letter runic alphabet, or in a slightly more complicated thirteen-letter runic alphabet introduced in 498 A.G. by a dubious, often sodden foreign monk. In either case these tools were hopeless for honing language skills, engaging in serious discourse, or deliberating on critical thought.

In early Sixth Century After Gaia (A.G.), the Gaia religion had become a mixture of factual historical events and colorful legends. After 397 years of living in the darkness of caves, the New Rebels had views that had been first created for survival purposes, but morphed into doctrines that were taken over by the authority of the Obsidian Order to lend purposefulness, dedication, and meaningfulness to all the brethren of the religious order, and also to all the members of the community at large. In 519 A.G., the Gaia religion was crude and superstitious; yet in places *highly sophisticated*, a hooded mantle from a receding, and far intellectually superior past.

"Oh, I have come so close," Pallas said to himself, beneath his breath. He had walked another sixteen miles since his last prayer.

The thought of his being fourteen miles from the shrine filled him with a feeling of exhilaration.

The alkaline desert soon gave way to a thin but well-shaded, high alpine valley that ran just below the jut of the mountain crest.

Pallas was almost there. He was within reach.

When Pallas closed his eyes, he thought he sensed Iona's presence. But Pallas had enough practical grounding to know that spiritual attachments could be the result of an over-expansive exuberance. An over-heated imagination was a drawback. He had to be careful. A healthy dose of skepticism was a good and necessary antidote for irresponsible elation.

Pallas was non-conformist in his behavior, idiosyncratic in his thought processes, but he was a firm follower of September Snow and Iona. For all Pallas's adolescent rebellion against the Obsidian Order over minor issues—maybe over a few targeted major issues as well—he still believed in the basic tenets of The Blessings of Gaia. He believed in Gaia.

And so it was that Pallas had gotten a sanction from the supreme, titular head of the Obsidian Order, Naxos Sparrus, to make this fabulous trip, without the accompaniment of a more experienced chaperoning monk. He had, however, a mission.

(Pallas could not forget Naxos's hidden agenda. Naxos had his own reasons for being an enabler of Pallas's voyage. Pallas knew what Naxos expected. He had no intention of fumbling this once-in-a-lifetime opportunity. Pallas knew exactly what was at stake.)

Pallas was clear-headed, sharp-minded, and physically tough. He was gold.

As he entered the canyon itself, he at last found himself cloaked in gentle, pleasant shade. Did he sense the spirit of Iona, as mysterious as that might have been? Or did he sense the presence of them, the sinister, the shadowy figures of apparition that had been dogging him since he had quit the last outpost at Deseret, a good distance into his journey?

Was he being tracked at a safe distance by a small handful of cannibals?

Pallas could not shake the shadowy substance of this mental intrusion, this aberration. He couldn't remove from his thinking this sixth sense—this sense of foreboding.

But he also hungered for positive feeling. He tried to alleviate his anxiety. He began by meditating on the mightiness—the past glories, the small humilities—of Iona's sainthood.

How to conduct one's life with nobility, sanctity, simplicity, and virtue; these had been established, burnt into Pallas's brain, by the highest role-model possible. That role model was exemplified perfectly by the life of Iona. Sweet, virtuous, noble Saint Iona.

Iona had been reputed to have breathed her last moment of life near the top of the sacred "lone, snow-crested mountain in the middle of the desert," in 86 A.G. During the times of the "last, old" generation, a powerful controversy brewed and spread concerning the specifics of the circumstances surrounding Iona's demise. The issues implicit in this controversy smacked of heresy. The small shrine to Iona, built of softer stones but also of granite, and the placement of the inscribed runic stone nearby, close to the mountaintop, had been a foundation stone for the controversy. (Some believers were seriously questioning if Iona died, as her mother, Supreme goddess September Snow, according to well-established fact, never experienced human death, but instead, was elevated, borne up in a mysterious fashion, to a higher realm.)

Naxos's predecessor in the leadership of the Obsidian Order, Andromenus—*Andromenus the Good*—nearing the age of 94, hoped to please, or at least appease, all the warring factions of the population by simply fudging the controversial issue.

Naxos would have none of that backsliding. Obtaining power at last, Naxos, the hardliner, wanted to squelch the controversy, nip any and all possible heresies in the bud.

With Andromenus dead at 94 (after serving selflessly for forty-three years), Naxos, at the age of 44—proud, ambitious, devoted (in his own way), and unflaggingly hardworking, consolidated his newly acquired leadership of the Obsidian Order.

In the evolving control of the higher body: The New Rebels Of Gaia, the head of the Obsidian Order always ranked at least fourth in the hierarchy of the civilian structure; but sometimes third, with influence and ranking.

In special circumstances, which occurred only about once every 150 years, when there had been an eruption of a major internal religious dispute, or there had been an external war to be waged, such as the devastating wars of 258 A.G., the head of the Obsidian Order had been honored with the highly cherished second seat, a sort of *primacy* vice presidency.

Naxos wanted to achieve something akin to that historical marker, if not for himself, then at least for the power and the glory of the Order.

Upon seeing his opportunity for the main chance, in his fourth official statement, Naxos wanted to set the underpinnings for the creation of one of those once-every-six-lifetimes circumstances, by, among other things, personally sanctioning Pallas's sacred pilgrimage.

Chapter Two

TOO SELF-ABSORBED to worry about cannibals, Pallas reached Iona's shrine. The sacred, lone, snow-crested mountain, located in the middle of the desert, loomed high overhead. The shrine stood near the entrance to a small cave at 9,500 feet. Surrounding Pallas were patches of snow in the deeper folds of the earth, tiny pockets found only on the north side of the hill.

At the entrance to the cave, Pallas saw and read the brief inscription on the runic stone. What was so controversial about the runic lettering on the stone anyway? It simply read: "Iona spent the last five years of her life here with Kull, her cohort. Iona was the supreme follower of Gaia. She understood Gaia as well as anyone could. She faced the inexplicable mysteries of the world, just like everyone else faced them."

At the end, almost as an afterthought, the final words were: "Iona did not die." Or, in an alternative interpretation: "Iona did not perish." Or the inscription could have been read as: "Iona did not submit." If the final word in the inscription was "submit," the carver could have readily intended it to have meant: "succumb." Eight out of nine readers would have interpreted the passage on the stone as "Iona did not die," in any event.

Pallas nodded his head. It was a ten-letter runic meta-alphabet. The carver had not relied on rounded letters, rather she used straight slashes and slanted hash-marks, primitive letteration.

Had any faithful followers expressed this sentiment before? Surely in the course of 500 years, adherents expressed it. Probably most people, all fervent followers of Gaia, had said something akin. At some point, they were likely to have voiced the idea in their informal prayers. Certainly before the time of "THE CANON OF THE 100," the acknowledged, vetted, and acceptable prayers—accepted by all in the community, but not without *an initial unsuccessful outburst of opposition*—had been firmly established by the Obsidian Order in 465 A.G.

There was a difference in the one stone: no one carved those exact words on any of the other runic stones. If only the message had stopped before the carver had inscribed those last four words: (Iona did not die); THERE WOULD BE NO CONTROVERSY!

Pallas thought of the official pronouncement of *Andromenus the Good* on the subject of the old runic stones that bore no date markings. "Of course the sculptors gave them no date markings. Statements inscribed on them were intended to be inviolate and eternal. No subsequent human volition was ever to hold any justification for a desecration, for an intervention."

Intervention then? Pallas's job was his undisclosed mission. Desecration was the pretext of his journey. Pallas's mind became so deeply clouded he tried to close it off. He tried to cut out all interfering thoughts, yet how could he close his mind from all possibilities of thinking, and by thinking, all opportunities for doubt?

The most recent runic stones were the only ones that had dates stamped on them. The dates were 448, 450, 468, 470 A.G. Unlike the twelve original runic stones, representing in legend the original "Twelve Wise Ones," the latter *four* hadn't "aged" long enough. (Pallas remembered that Andromenus had been a twelve-year-old shepherd boy, living near the top of the highest mountain in the realm, subsisting on a diet of pine needles, pine nuts, goat's milk, and, on occasion, goat's cheese, before the earliest "dated" runic stone had been cut.)

All of the "latter" runic stones, therefore, had been created during living memory.

Earlier dateless runic stones, all of them 350 years old at least—a few of them even perhaps as old as 425 and 450 years, were considered infallible, and therefore sacrosanct.

Pallas was staring at one of the two most famous runic stones of them all, one representing the personage of Elsie, the other representing the personage of Dominic, the first two of the original Twelve Wise Ones, who had been anointed by Iona herself.

The other famous runic stone was kept in a glass case in Escalante in the mission center of the Obsidian Order. Pallas knew the words chiseled on the second-oldest runic stone from memory. They were reputed to have been given by Tom Novak (teacher and mentor of Iona) to Iona, written in his hand on animal skin, when he had been teaching Iona the Pre-Gaia language by drawing letters of the alphabet in sand with a stick. "All history is philosophy, and all philosophy is religion, all religion is literature, and all literature is art, all art is music, painting, dancing, and all music, painting, dancing are the heart, brain, hand of man and woman, through all of time."

What scandalous words! If it wasn't for the fact they'd been reputed to have been written by Tom, and given to Iona in a highly religious ceremony, the use of the words would have been forbidden. But they were sacred. Perhaps Tom was not a true believer in Gaia after all! Tom was blessed, but he was also a product of a corrupt and impure time, a pre-Gaia time. The words were written on an old runic stone. Let the contradiction stand—so the old religious pundits ruled.

Try as he may, Pallas couldn't stop thinking, he couldn't prevent himself from remembering when *Andromenus the Good* had been head of the Obsidian Order. Andromenus had a solution. His solution always involved possibility and pluralism.

Naxos, brand-new to power, wanted something different. He

wanted that which mirrored the sharpness of the obsidian blade. From the body of the community, he wanted to cut out all harmful thinking, as if evil thoughts could be likened to cancerous sores. In an action analogous to the performance of a surgeon's knife, he wanted precision. He hated the fuzzy and the dull. Most of all, he hated heresy. He saw it as his ultimate mission to stamp it out.

Facing the entrance to the 20-foot-high by 20-foot-wide shrine, Pallas threw his body hard onto the ground. He lay motionless. He did not stir. With his arms and his legs fully outstretched, he prayed to the memory of the deeds and thoughts of Iona.

In his agitated, and too often unfocused and wandering mind, Pallas sought from her inspiration and guidance. He took the task before him as one that was weighty and somber. It affected lives, perhaps many lives, and it would affect these lives for many years to come.

For Pallas, the conflict was not over the profane pursuits of transitory back-door politics or intrigue-driven power grabs—the world of Naxos. It was over something far more enduring.

Beads of sweat formed on Pallas's cheeks and forehead. For two hours, he prayed. He hoped he might be able to follow Iona's footsteps. He hoped he could be guided by her sayings, by her teachings, but most of all by her love. In the twists and turns of his uncertainty, Pallas craved knowing what was the righteous direction to take.

Chapter Three

PALLAS ENTERED IONA'S SHRINE. It wasn't what he expected it to be. There were four granite uprights, a roof made out of shale, four thin stone walls, a slick marble floor. No place for votive lamps, no place to lay down offerings (Pallas was glad for the absence of offerings), no chairs or benches, no altar for sacrifice (again, Pallas was grateful for the simplicity and the correctness), not even a place for prayer. It was just a place of shelter against the wind. A shrine simple. A place for Iona alone.

A place of austerity. Architecture that was tactfully done. An impressive piece of work. Absolutely nothing inside that could have been viewed as being even remotely heretical or suspect. Pallas felt relief at the correctness of it all.

Pallas had two secret missions assigned to him.

He had to find the grave of Kull. That was easy enough to do. It had been marked by a long flinty slice of stone 430 years before. But the grave, even the loose bones, of Iona had never been found. With the rise of this new cult, this had given credibility to the notion that since Iona's remains had never been located, perhaps she had never died a natural death.

Pallas's assignment was to search around to see if he could find Iona's grave, or at least some sort of indication of her remains. Well, she had died alone, that much was certain. So no one could have buried her and therefore of course no one could have known the exact location of her death. (Kull, preceding Iona in death by a year, had been buried by Iona.) He checked the cave where Kull and she had been reputed to have lived. He poked around but found nothing.

Altogether, Pallas knew that this was an absurd assignment. And for people to think that just because Iona's remains could not be found that therefore she might not have died represented the height of folly, stupidity, a brazen form of superstition. He saw the assignment as a huge waste of time.

But Pallas was disciplined and he also saw himself as a responsible follower of Gaia. He took his assignments from the Obsidian Order seriously. He looked around, poking here and there, broke the earth with his digging stick in a few places, surveyed the slopes around the shrine, canvassed a perimeter within three miles of the old dwelling cave, checked the bottom of ravines, turned rocks over along the lower points of the creekside (those were the places where an animal might have dragged Iona's remains), went through the motions. There was no scientific or forensic way of doing this, but he did his best anyway. An order given was an order taken.

The second assignment was harder. It may or may not have gone against Pallas's conscience, but it definitely went against his conviction that one should preserve antiquities, regardless of their putative value.

Naxos had ordered Pallas to efface the last four words on the runic stone, "Iona did not die." Of course Iona had died. Iona was a saint. Pallas had no problem with this. But although this action may have represented the destruction of a falsity, as a cultural artifact the runic stone was, nevertheless, a "truth." It was the second oldest runic stone in existence, if not the oldest. In a way, it was tampering with the evidence, too.

Pallas took out his blacksmith's file. The lettering was etched lightly in the stone. Pallas could see the lettering with his eyes, he could also *feel* the lettering with his fingers. With marble, especially with imperfect slabs, there were the unique striations in the stone, the slight pittings of age. He filed away at the lettering. After all, it was just four words. He wanted to do it carefully, so he took his time to complete the task. In twenty-five years time, with normal aging, no one could ever have been able to tell that the letters had been there in the first place.

"There, that isn't so bad," Pallas said to himself, appraising the effectiveness of his work.

Pallas knew that this conspiracy, if erasing four words from an old runic stone was such an elevated thing as a *conspiracy*, created a special bond between Naxos and himself.

Before Pallas's departure, Naxos had taken him aside and said to him, "Don't worry, it won't be hard, you'll be saving Gaia. You know what the ultimate truth is. Protecting *that truth* is our mission. That's what was done in the days of September Snow and Iona. Don't deceive yourself into thinking that they didn't take bold actions to secure the growth of Gaia. The continuation of their vision is why we've been entrusted with Gaia today. Enabling the survival of Gaia is our sacred mission, *our only mission*. You're not falsifying the truth, you're redacting it."

The Obsidian Order had always emphasized discipline and obedience. Now secrecy was added to the mix.

Pallas had no idea what Naxos had said to his father to finally get him to stop beating his son after nearly a dozen years of beatings, but it had succeeded where everything else failed. Pallas's father never so much as touched a hair on his son's head after he had been spoken to. Naxos was formidable in this way. He had a more forceful means of coercion at his disposal of course, but he also appeared to be outwardly the most mild and persuasive man Pallas had ever met.

Aside from possibly Naxos himself, Pallas was the closest thing that there was to being a scholar in the Obsidian Order. In his own independent studies of original texts, when he had been given the rare privilege of conducting such studies, he had discovered that neither September Snow nor Iona ever said a word about the *growth* of Gaia. From the point of view of human intervention, they always insisted on limiting human action to the *restoration* of an orderly and balanced planet. Gaia was supposed to proceed in its own way, at its own pace and heal itself.

But Pallas kept his mouth shut. He kept his thoughts to himself. He knew how dangerous it was to spar with Naxos Sparrus.

Before departing the mountain, Pallas looked back. Thinking about the questionable handiwork of his erasing the four words on the rune stone, he muttered to himself, "Here I go again, keeping a secret."

He paused. "But this time I'm doing it for the most powerful man in the Obsidian Order, Naxos Sparrus. Indeed, together, it's our silence." Pallas paused. "Oh my goodness!"

Pallas bit his lower lip. Blood trickled down his chin. Mightily, he chose to suppress the inappropriate urge to laugh. Like the urge to snigger at a name-giving party, or to display a smart-aleck impertinence at a military flag-raising ceremony, or to giggle nervously at a ritual shrine funeral, Pallas persuaded himself not to give in to a tension-reducing laugh. He suppressed his all-too-human need. He was embarrassed at his temptation. He knew that there was no room for levity, however fleeting, over grave and serious matters.

From his childhood memories, Pallas had also been inculcated in the notion of a primitive religious propriety. The powers of September Snow and Iona were, alas, awesome and sacrosanct.

Chapter Four

IT WAS ONLY AFTER PALLAS retraced his route east by traveling thirty miles back across the alkaline desert that he realized his suspicions had been correct all along: a coven of cannibals had been pursuing him.

Pallas found the remains of one. His reaction was immediate and conclusive: it was an obvious case of "inside butchery." He examined the evidence. The mutant creature had been dishonored. All that was left were the bones, some of the head (eyes and fleshy parts of the face had been gouged out), and entrails (which had curiously not been eaten, indeed, had been left untouched). The largest bones had been cracked open to extract nutritious marrow.

In a perfunctory way, Pallas had been trained to reconstruct crime scenes, but with the attacks of cannibals having become increasingly rare over the previous four or five decades, the past reconstructions had been either scenes of battles between "normal" humans, or aftermaths of attacks by higher level predator animals. With that limited background, Pallas tried to piece together events from evidence. His curiosity could only barely outmatch and trump his profound sense of repulsion and nausea at the dreadfulness of the act.

Still holding his nose, Pallas concluded his study.

He could immediately see that there were hacking scars—slashing marks—that had been cut across the largest of the bones. The cannibals who had done the work possessed some knives, and perhaps even a small axe.

Images of mayhem flooded into Pallas's mind. He couldn't stop himself from reenacting the probable events in his head.

Perhaps the slain one had been the weakest in the group. Or perhaps he had gotten sick. Or perhaps he had fallen behind, developed a limp, or some other ambulatory hindrance.

Perhaps the others had drawn lots and just fell on him in a frenzy of ravenous hunger. All of them could have been close to starvation. He may have been just the unlucky one in the draw.

Perhaps the victim had never been in the group at all. He could have been a straggler, or, more accurately, a scavenger of scavengers, waiting in the shadows to scoop up the leftovers after the others had left. And when the larger group discovered him following them, they turned around, traveled the few miles necessary, and pounced.

Pallas had his file, and he had his knife, a very sharp one, but he did not carry with him an old fashioned ballistic gun, much less a sophisticated laser gun. Pallas's father would have insisted that Pallas carry a gun with him on such a journey, to be on the safe side, but Pallas no longer listened to his father. To Pallas's chagrin, and to his regret, Pallas realized that he may have *not* brought a gun just to spite his father!

Pallas realized he must take great care that night. He must sleep lightly and be watchful.

For all of Pallas's abilities, protecting himself while asleep was not one of his strengths.

The first night, Pallas managed to be careful. He slept lightly. But doing so left him fatigued, irritable, and much in need of rest. He knew that with time he wouldn't be able to keep the regimen.

On the second night, just before dawn, Pallas fell into a fairly deep sleep.

But Pallas had several defenses. First, no single cannibal on his own could overcome a normal male human being. Pallas would have outweighed and far out-muscled a cannibal. (That's why cannibals always attacked in groups, usually in groups of three or four.)

Pallas's knife, of course, was his second defense. He slept with it clasped in his hand. He had a third defense. He slept next to a blazing fire.

And strangely, he had a fourth defense. There was a pot of water, still hot, part way to boiling, on the fire.

The cannibal attack occurred just before dawn. Pallas thought he was dreaming. One of the cannibals tried to grasp his arm and chest, but Pallas woke quickly. A wave of stench, a horrible miasma of smell, seemed to cover him. With his left hand Pallas instinctively tried to protect his vulnerable spot: his neck. Aiming for the neck, the cannibal bit deeply into Pallas's hand. With his right hand Pallas plunged his knife deep into the intruder's throat. He finished the thrusting motion and tossed the 85-pound creature to his side.

The second attacker came at him with a knife and slashed his entire left side, causing Pallas to drop his knife. With blood dripping from his bitten hand, Pallas clasped a piece of wood from the fire and swung it hard. The fire at the end of the piece of wood did nothing but momentarily disorient the attacker, but the second blow was so powerful it knocked the cannibal senseless.

The third attacker jumped from behind and tried to rise up on Pallas's shoulders, but he was too listless or enfeebled to do so. Pallas wheeled around and dropped to his knees. He grabbed the pot of water by its handle and hit the attacker on the head with it. The spraying water missed the attacker completely, in fact some of the water scalded Pallas's wrist and arm, but the pot hit the attacker squarely on the head, knocking him out.

Pallas recovered his knife and slit the throats of the two unconscious attackers.

Only after Pallas realized he was no longer in danger did he begin to retch. The cannibals' offensive smell permeated the ground around him. The stench was absolutely unbearable.

Pallas rested for a moment. He then saw that he was bleeding. He looked at his hand. It had been bitten badly. There were deeply indented teeth marks, it really hurt, but there wasn't much blood. Then he felt his side. He realized that that wound was deeper. At the sight of so much blood, he almost panicked. He found the deepest part of the wound, the entry point of a knife just below the ribcage, where the blood was rushing out. Grabbing a piece of wood from the fire, lying back, without even looking, gritting his teeth, he cauterized the wound with the embered end of the stick.

He "rolled" the fire over the wound, back and forth. He was impervious to the pain (or maybe he was so close to shock, he operated on adrenalin). Strangely, the smell of his own burning flesh didn't seem to bother him much.

As much as he absolutely hated and detested his father, Pallas realized—just before he came close to passing out—that it had been his father who taught him how to execute this emergency procedure. His father had used it to save his younger brother's life after he had been attacked by a mountain lion. Without thinking about it, on autopilot, Pallas had performed it on himself.

Pallas shivered. It wasn't from the cold he shivered. It was from his injuries. Having bound up the cauterized wound on his side with loose wrappings of cloth, tying the ends together with his teeth, he lay on the ground in a moment of calm. But he had to make sure that the bleeding under his ribcage had stopped. When he realized that it had slowed to a trickle, by feeling with his hand on the cloth in search of a growing circle of dampness, he then allowed himself to drift into sleep. And what a strange, deep sleep it was.

Chapter Five

WHEN PALLAS AWOKE, all he wanted to do was pack up and leave. He knew that the ethical thing to do—the moral and *correct* thing to do—would be to bury the cannibals. In spite of their deformity and degeneration, they deserved a decent Gaia burial. But he didn't have half the strength to dig a hole, having no access to a small shovel, just his trusty digger stick.

Furthermore, Pallas had to figure out an alternative route, or he wouldn't survive the journey across the desert, not in the crippled state he was in. Without his wound properly healed, he knew he'd never make it back to Deseret, a distance of almost 300 miles.

Like a burst of illumination, an idea for his potential salvation came to Pallas. He knew there was a family living forty miles to the north. Information about the family had been given to him before the start of his journey, in the event of an unexpected emergency. In fact, this family, along with a host of others, had been especially chosen by the authorities of The New Rebels of Gaia from those willing to make a move to a remote resettlement site for purposes of facilitating safer long-distance routes for Gaia sojourners. The New Rebels of Gaia subsidized the families, and gave them further inducements to make the move.

Pallas knew if he could make it *there*, that would be his survival. He scanned the horizon. He plotted his route north.

Before his departure, Pallas took one more somber look at the bodies of the *cannibals*. He realized it was a misnomer to call them cannibals. Cannibal was a hopelessly antiquated term. They had been breeding apart from the main human gene pool for too many centuries to be humans. Arguably, they belonged in the animal kingdom, the end product of an extraordinarily bizarre human devolution. Yet they didn't like eating the "soft parts," the innards, the stomach, the intestines, parts of human anatomy that coyotes, wolves, and lions enjoyed devouring the most. Did that strange instance of fastidiousness and selectiveness link them to humans?

In death they seemed so small, so piteously hideous, in spite of their almost quaint humpbacked, curved-spine deformities, and so harmless. One of them could not have weighed more than 70 pounds. The other two were only slightly larger. No wonder, as a group, they were close to extinction! Twenty years after the time of the Eleven-Years-War (2040 to 2051 A.D.), and the environmental collapse which subsequently occurred, the "scavenger-cannibals" represented 15 percent of the total adult human population. Over a period of the next 15 generations, during the height of the dark ages, in an era of great eco-dislocation and devastation, they were continuously a force to be reckoned with.

Five hundred years of trans-mutation had narrowed the prospects of the heirs of these original cannibals for finding a niche in an ever-changing world. The environment was improving. It was as if it were millions and millions of years in the past and cannibals (or whatever you wanted to call them) were the last dinosaurs astride the terrestrial plane, and an asteroid was on the verge of completely obliterating them.

Pallas noticed that his cauterized wound had started bleeding again. He focused all his energies on the state of his injury. He could have been sucked into a bottomless pit of consternation, or succumbed to a self-anguishing anxiety, but he wouldn't allow himself the luxury of turning his fear into panic. Instead, he remained calm. Death might take him away one way or another, but Pallas wasn't going to go easily into the night. No time for second guessing. His only chance of survival was to make it—either crawling or walking—to the outpost family farm before his water ran out.

He devised a plan. He would walk five miles, rest for an hour, or for however long it took to revitalize his strength, and walk another five miles, so on and so forth, breaking his trip into eight equal segments. To conserve water, he would allow himself only a half pint of water during each segment of the trip, no matter how hot the sun beat down, or how thirsty he became. He lacked the strength to carry two water bags, so contented himself with one, containing four pints.

Pallas ripped the last yard of cloth from his toga to make longer and wider strips of bandage for his wound, applying the strips by wrapping them snugly around his midsection.

Pallas didn't think as he did this, he just kept busy. It was as if he were preparing for battle, except the desert was the war, and walking a span of it for forty miles was the battlefield. Pallas ordinarily detested military metaphors, especially when they were inappropriate—and they almost always were inappropriate—but in this case the metaphor was relevant.

Pallas discarded all unnecessary possessions. He allowed himself the toga, his shoes, and the critical combination hat-visor. From a string attached to his right shoulder, hung a small pouch of manioc mush. He slung the water bag over the shoulder that was on the opposite side of his wound.

Stripped down to the bare minimum, he lit out for the north.

The first six segments went extremely well. The first thirty miles worked. After each five mile walk his wound would start bleeding again, but if he stopped long enough it would temporarily repair itself. But after several stops the wound suddenly tore and began bleeding badly. He came to a full stop. He was in such a perturbed state that he drank all that remained of his water supply. He had apparently taken off his combination hat-visor at one of his previous stops and had failed to put it back on.

Pallas did everything he could to rebind the wound, but now he could not walk anymore.

Against his better judgment, and seemingly against his will, Pallas fell asleep. He slept a long time. When he woke, he had revived a little, but he was still unable to walk. He was experiencing a powerful thirst, but his water bag was empty.

Everything looked so strange around him, as if he were looking at the ground through a darkened lens. He also realized that, oddly, he didn't need his visor cap. It was as if a tree had sprouted up over night and was now shading him.

At first there was nothing to see. Then Pallas felt a certain weariness that told him something was in the air. Then he heard thunder, a distant rumble here and there, but he couldn't tell where it was coming from. All of a sudden the mountain that was a little more than five miles away seemed strangely near. There wasn't a breath of wind, yet dense cold air piled up in the sky. Changes in the weather were coming fast. The mountain almost vanished behind a wall of haze. Clouds rushed in from all sides, but there was no wind. There was more thunder now, and everything around looked eerie and otherworldly.

Pallas waited. Then suddenly the sky erupted. At first it was almost a release. A storm seemed to come out of nowhere, descending on the valley. There was thunder and lightning all around. The rain clattered down in huge drops, smacking the dry dirt and sand with loud-sounding thuds. The storm seemed to have been trapped between Pallas and the mountainside, and thunderclaps echoed and reverberated off the mountain. The wind buffeted from every angle. And when the storm finally moved away, leaving in its wake a clear sky, Pallas could hardly remember where those thunderclouds were, let alone which thunderclap belonged to which flash of lightning.

Pallas only had to reach over with his hand to find a puddle of water next to him.

Without even turning on his side, he was able to refresh himself by lifting with his hand water from the puddle. "Like manna from heaven," he said as he drank his fill. "Praise be to God," he said.

Such odd-sounding phrases. Where'd they come from? They'd just popped into his head.

Surely the phrases were not part of the Gaia religion. Maybe they were utterances he had picked up randomly from a foreigner, or from a stranger, or from an ancient grandmother of the wife of a stranger perhaps—someone who had made an incomplete or improper transition from an older religion, before Gaia.

Pallas hadn't a clue what "manna" meant. Bread? "God," of course, was an avatar, a relic from the past, a phenomenon of superstition from the time of violent ecological destruction and world-wide fratricidal mayhem when seven to eight billion people died. When the planet was supposed to have been a safe haven for all of humankind, *but proved not to be.*

Pallas knew he should have offered a proper prayer of thanks to Gaia, but he was too exhausted to remember the phrases. Religion seemed so irrelevant to him at the moment, as if all religion in all its forms was an unnecessary relic from the past. He began to fall into unconsciousness, but he brought himself right back up. He quickly abandoned these treasonous, blasphemous, heretical thoughts.

Pallas pulled his toga up and covered his eyes and once he had secured the covering, he fell asleep.

Standing over him was a thin figure. The hot sun was beating down. The figure had a severe, weather-beaten face and was so wispy and emaciated that Pallas couldn't be sure of the gender. But the long strands of lank, dirty-blond hair suggested it might be female. The age was indeterminate, somewhere between the end of childhood and the beginning of adulthood.

"Aren't you from HQ?" the figure asked in a squeaky voice. She must have been a girl, Pallas thought.

"What do you mean HQ?"

"Headquarters of the New Rebels?"

Pallas nodded.

"You're far from the pilgrimage trail. It's dangerous here. Why are you traveling alone?"

"I'm thirsty," Pallas replied. "I'm injured. Badly."

"Our farm is eight miles away. Can you walk it?"

"Huh?"

Impatiently, she stared down at Pallas. "Can you walk it unassisted?"

"A short distance perhaps. I'm bleeding. I've already bled a great deal. I'm so...*thirsty*."

The girl noticed the blood seeping from Pallas's torn and soiled bandages. He could raise himself only with difficulty, barely lifting his back and shoulders.

"Don't move," the girl said. She examined Pallas's wound. Her fingertips were delicate and deft.

"Goodness," the girl said. "This is terrible. They really got you. But you're not going to die."

Pallas tried to hazard a smile, but what he managed was far from convincing.

"All your walking has more than aggravated your wound. You should have stopped and let nature take its course. Eventually you would have been able to move without tearing yourself apart."

Pallas wanted to object. He thought of talking about the cannibals' attack, but instead he remained silent. He didn't see the point of providing more information than was necessary.

"We'll bring the buckboard up," the girl said. "You've no business traveling alone, not in this territory, not with thieves or bandits about. There are even cannibals." A look of gloom covered her face. "Lucky for you we still have a broken-down horse to transport you."

Pallas wanted to say that he didn't fear thieves because he didn't carry valuables. But what of his body, what of his water? Were they not valuable?

The girl disappeared. A few hours later she returned with a man on a buckboard. The girl was walking in front, leading the scrawniest, most emaciated specimen of a pygmy pony Pallas had ever laid his eyes on. The man was the girl's father. He was probably middle-aged, but the way he handled himself made him appear older. The lines on his face were deeply etched. His full, massive beard, reaching down past his chest, was streaked in gray. The thin thatch of hair on his head, closely cropped around the ears, was snowy white. But the look of his hands suggested someone younger. His fingers were subtle and delicate. Pallas had seen before how the desert speeded up a person's aging process. The girl's father could have aged 20 years, perhaps even 25 years, before his time.

Pallas noticed that both daughter and father were not wearing protective visors. Then Pallas remembered he didn't have his visor either. The two lifted Pallas carefully on the back of the buckboard. The man didn't have to whip the pony in order to get it to move, but he did have to flick the whip over its head to get it to respond.

The pygmy pony pulled, but he had to flex his muscles with a grim determination. It was as if the owner knew the animal would work and strain under the threat of the lash. It was a pitiful sight. But Pallas was on his back in the buckboard, unable to watch the animal being forced to pull the weight of his body.

Pallas wished he had something more than a handful of manioc mush to feed the horse. What further proof did he need of the family's miserable circumstances, Pallas wondered?

Chapter Six

PALLAS MUST HAVE PASSED OUT along the way to the family's homestead. He couldn't recall any details of the trip. He lifted his blanket and examined his bandages. They had been changed and were surprisingly clean. He was lying on a stiff, short canvas cot, located off the alcove from the main room of the house.

The dwelling was made of sun-dried brick. There were no flagstones, the floor was beaten down earth, scraped clean. The roof consisted of reeds overlaid with mud. The walls were exposed clay. On one wall hung an elk skull. There was no chimney, no windows, just a hole in the roof. The open hearth in the middle of the room emitted smoke. There were more layers of soot on the rafters, from previous fires that had been banked too high (the place was a definite firetrap). A ramshackle door to the outside had been left ajar to help circulate air. Mud-dabbing wasps could have made a home for their mud hives in the ceiling reeds (Pallas had seen that before), but probably hadn't only because of the preponderance of smoke.

From across the room Pallas could make out a family of three seated at several rows of thin planks lying parallel to each other on a pair of puny barrels, making a makeshift table. Their heads were bent in prayer. At the end of one of the planks was a guttering candle. Because of the smoke, the light emitted by some candles in the scullery and the two candles flickering on the earth beside Pallas's cot made the room barely visible. Pallas thought he was in a dream.

The father said, "We thank Gaia for our meal. We thank the Blessings of Gaia."

Mother and daughter dutifully nodded. "Amen."

Pallas recognized the prayer as standard Gaia issue.

Then the father began reciting the fourth canto of a sophisticated and esoteric poem. It was a soul-stirring interpretation of a work of poetry from the times of old. Few people had heard of the poem, much less knew how to recite it. There was not a single written version of the 2,500 word poem in existence. Secretly, it had been passed down orally from one generation to the next. The controversial contents of the poem supposedly drew on the originality of the thought processes of Tom Novak, a hermit, when he had reputedly been acting as chief protector, teacher, and mentor to Iona when she was a young girl, sometime between the years 2063 A.D. and 2071 A.D. (or between Year Gaia 12 and Year Gaia 20).

The title of the poem was: "Pre-Gaia, The Collective Souls' Torture As The Best Mind In The World Was In A State Of Shock."

The poem represented an extraordinary erudition on the part of the father, and his recital took Pallas by surprise. Pallas knew only two eccentric elders, one named Malmud, the other Aeon, who knew the poem by heart. In spite of its cryptic origins and obscurity, Pallas knew the poem himself. He cherished it. He was fascinated by the story, truncated or no, that had been passed down from a lost era, the time before Iona. From an intellectual point of view, Pallas thought the most interesting part was the fourth canto—where Tom's feelings of doubt in the very existence of Gaia soared to the highest levels.

After he completed the fourth canto, the father recognized that Pallas had awoken. Pallas had propped himself up with a thin ledge of a pillow, and was staring at the family from across the room.

"So you've decided to return to the world of the living," the father observed. He clapped his hands in merriment. "My daughter is a great nurse, isn't she? You have her to thank for your recovery.

You've been asleep for a long time. I emphasize the words: more or less. You probably don't even know that my daughter has been feeding you spoonfuls of broth. Did you know that you talk to yourself in your sleep? You're a real motor-mouth. You conduct entire conversations with your eyes closed."

"I thank you for saving my life," Pallas said, addressing the daughter. "Especially, I thank your daughter for rescuing me," he then added, speaking directly to the father.

"You should be thankful," the father nodded. "If it wasn't for my daughter, you'd be a stringy piece of meat for birds to pick on. When they were done, what would be left? Bones?"

"What is your daughter's name?"

"Myrina."

"Myrina," Pallas repeated. "And what is your name?"

"Raine," the father nodded. "And my wife's name is Bhamini."

Pallas nodded in recognition to Raine's wife. "I can tell that you're followers of Gaia. You're brethren of the truth."

"Of course. And you're from the *what*? The inner sanctum?"

"What?" Pallas asked in a puzzled voice. He looked astonished. He was completely baffled. He felt slightly insulted. "What are you talking about? What do you mean? Inner sanctum? The only inner sanctum I know exists in the Gaia-Domes. The people in the Gaia-Domes are murderers. Centuries ago, they practically committed genocide. They came dangerously close to killing off all of the inhabitants, certainly all the ancestors of the New Rebels, who lived outside the domes. It was only September Snow who intervened. It was only she who stopped the grandmagisters of the Gaia-Domes from taking complete command of the devastated planet. If it wasn't for her sacrifices, none of us would be alive today. If it wasn't for the sanctity of September Snow, there would be no hope today. If it wasn't for September Snow's bounty and benefice, we would be living on a barren planet."

"You needn't be so sensitive," Raine said smiling. "Don't be so defensive. You're among friends."

"I observe," Pallas said, "you're not filled with the usual terrors and superstitions that afflict the minds of simple farmers."

"Amen," Raine said smiling. "I hope not."

"I aspire to being a scholar too," Pallas said. "It's true. If the opportunity should present itself. Now there's hope of that happening. Things are changing. Oh, even as we are speaking! The venerable Andromenus is dead. A new leader of the Obsidian Order has been anointed."

"Well, that's all well and good, but there's something else," Raine said.

"What?"

"Something else you repeated in your sleep, I'm afraid."

"Really?"

"She didn't die. Clean slate. Falling into this vacuum...like I fall...into an abyss. You repeated those words. This was followed by great tossing and turning. You repeated the words over and over. Or variations thereof. Were you fearful of falling off a cliff? You were feverish."

Pallas struggled. For once in his life he was at a loss for words. "I...I..." He hesitated.

Raine probed deeper. "Who didn't die? This mystery? This vacuum you referred to? What is this vacuum? You must be pretty lucid when you're dreaming. You sure are lucid when you talk in your sleep. Was it *Iona* who didn't die? Was that what you meant?"

Pallas turned pale. He murmured, "Never mind, please. Drop this matter, will you?"

"Is your life now a clean slate?" Raine asked. "Maybe that's what you meant!"

Pallas's face darkened. "My life? A clean slate? Hardly. If anything, the opposite's true." Pallas looked unsettled. Raine looked embarrassed, as if he had probed too deeply.

"Forgive me," Raine said, turning away. "It's not my place to meddle. It's none of my business to delve." Raine offered up a prayer to Gaia. He asked Gaia to intercede on behalf of Pallas's success. He wanted to do anything he could to change the subject.

Pallas realized in a moment of illumination that he had his interlocutor pegged. The Obsidian Order held sway in the center of things, but the further you traveled from the center, the more the power was watered down. In the outer-reaches, the Obsidian Order had less firm a grip. On the fringes of the outer-reaches, the Obsidian Order had virtually no power at all. But the Obsidian Order had few worries about this. With notoriously few exceptions, the fringe was populated with illiterates and fiercely primitive farmers. In some ways, they were the rejects of the settlements, in spite of the inducements for resettlement that had been extended to them.

But Pallas could see that Raine and his family were different. They existed on a different plane.

Pallas made several obvious but crucial observations. True, Raine's family lived on the fringe. They were very poor, but they were hardly what anyone could call rejects, and they were far from being primitive.

Pallas realized one of the candles on the earth beside his cot was dead. The other candle shot up briefly, flamed for an instant, then sputtered out, leaving him in growing darkness.

Pallas was on the verge of falling asleep. He felt safe and secure under the protection of Raine's family. He didn't feel that he had to keep his guard up.

Raine's wife, Bhamini, mumbled to her husband, "I can't believe Andromenus is dead. He'd been the leader of the Obsidian Order for over forty years. With him gone, what will happen?"

"Don't worry, it's been too long. It's been 23 years. They've forgotten us. We are not important to anyone anymore. Let old dogs lie. I'm sure that's what they're thinking. We're dust, we're nothing—if they ever thought about us, well, they're not thinking about us."

Pallas fell into a deep sleep. When he awoke many hours later, Raine was all solicitations and smiles. "No talking in your sleep this time. Before it must have been the fever talking."

"No talking this time?" Pallas asked. "Quiet? Completely?"

"Like a church-mouse. Monastically quiet."

It was as if Raine understood. He didn't want to bring up the subject of Pallas's mumblings in his sleep again. And Pallas *had* stopped talking in his sleep fortunately.

Pallas did not hide the fact that he felt deeply relieved to hear the news.

He asked Raine to bring in his daughter, Myrina, so that he could thank her properly for saving his life. Raine fetched his daughter. She stood still in the center of the room. Her eyes were downcast, her head hanging down.

"Why is she so quiet?" Pallas asked Raine. "She stares at me so blankly. She doesn't speak?"

"She's naturally taciturn," Raine replied. "Well, she's meek." Addressing his daughter, Raine said, "Why don't you say something nice to our guest, Myrina?"

Myrina cleared her throat. At first she appeared tongue-tied, but then she found her voice. "We can't repair the Earth, sir. But we can repair each other. We can't heal the planet, kind stranger, but we can, at least, heal the sick. We can also bind up the wounds of the injured. Perhaps also aid those who suffer from brokenness." She clapped her hands together. "Earth, Gaia, is the common parent of all humankind. Let us not spare truth. Let us allow it to sound loud and true. Let us praise her for a restored health."

Raine looked bemused by his daughter's words, as if affected by an odd combination: *pride and meekness*. "From the mouth of babes, dearest me," Raine nodded.

Pallas thought Myrina's words were beautiful. Wisdom pearls, gems of poetry—superior to the words of a common Gaia prayer. In so many ways, superior to his own meager poems.

Pallas and Raine spoke for the rest of the afternoon and for the next few days. It had been many years since Raine had had an opportunity to talk about the oral traditions with someone who was as knowledgeable about them as Pallas clearly was. Raine was enjoying the great ebb and flow, the give and take, of a learned discussion. At certain points in their dialogue, Raine became animated.

Raine was a far cry from Pallas's boring and predictable teachers. Stumbling upon Raine was like scratching a cheek in the dark cavern of a coalmine, only to discover that the cause of the cut was the surface of a finely sharpened diamond. A cunning narrative teller, a born story teller, Raine was a sober tease, like some teacher who was discreetly, yet adamantly, anti-didactic. Pallas realized that Raine cared fervently about the truth. He was struggling mightily to grasp the basic seedbeds of a world tragedy that had unfolded centuries before, and he would not debase himself by being duped by comforting myths and childish fantasies. Pallas had no doubts how intelligent Raine was. It was truly fascinating for Pallas to behold.

"You're a dissident, aren't you," Pallas said at last. "Don't deny it. I know you are. One of those people whispered about. Long ago. In my school, I've heard stories—rumors—about people like you. You recited the fourth canto of Pre-Gaia, The Collective Soul's...et cetera, the night I regained consciousness. Remember? That's when I realized you're different. The poem? Yes, I know it. 'Course I do. *The poem.* So you couldn't be more educated than you are. Do you have reservations about the reliability of the Oral Traditions?"

Raine's eyes shot up. With firmness, he declared, "I've reservations about everything." He spoke in a proud voice. He throbbed with animation. "I studied the written, the vetted oral, and the orals that didn't make the grade. Not like a parrot, not like a cipher, no, but with open and searching eyes."

"Reservations about both the written and oral?" Pallas asked. "Both? Reservations? Everything? Why didn't they simply kill you? Be done with it? I know how ruthless the gatekeepers can be. Ho! I know who they are!"

"They couldn't," Raine replied. "No. No matter how extreme was our heresy, no matter how blatant were our infractions against the orthodoxies, no executions. No. They couldn't. It would have been impossible. To snuff us out would have been to make the New Rebels, and more specifically, the Obsidian Order, just as bad as the leaders of the Gaia-Domes. They never would have agreed to that. Besides, they had another choice. Exile. Did not September Snow smile upon the compassionate? Did not September Snow always shine upon those who were merciful? There were other options. And we had Andromenus to protect us. The little that he could do, he did."

"What advice would you give me?" Pallas asked.

"Learn from experience. Keep your head low. The world is changing. Change with it."

"If you had to do it over again, would you choose the same?" Pallas asked. "Would you have made a different decision? Would you have taken a different path than exile?"

"I don't know. I hope you don't have to make the decisions I've made. No doubt you'll have to turn your back on a past that is familiar. Undoubtedly, you'll face trials of your own. I don't wish my fate to be your fate. Gaia grant you the grace of a different road."

Pallas rested for eighteen more days. His wounds healed. He got his strength back. He started to walk around. His condition improved. He was ready to leave.

The family decided to hold a dinner to commemorate the unexpected set of events that had caused Pallas to show up at their homestead's doorstep. The celebratory dinner was also arranged to mark his departure.

They arranged the dinner carefully. Even though it was supposed to have been a celebration, the dinner was partaken in glumness. Pallas could sense sadness. During the course of his recovery, Pallas had grown fond of the family. But he was already late in returning home. Naxos was waiting for him.

Pallas realized the price Raine and his family paid for their exile was far dearer and more extreme than he had at first thought.

Chapter Seven

PALLAS RETURNED HOME. He experienced no extraordinary ordeals along the route. Not a single cannibal came within a hundred miles of him. He covered at least twenty miles, sometimes as many as thirty miles, each day of travel. The superficial wound to his hand and the more threatening wound to his side were both mending according to a natural rhythm, as long as he walked in a careful fashion, without extreme bending or stretching. He even managed to take two days off, "throwing a blister-mender." He rested two days next to a shaded pool of dark, cool, cavern-fed water, in a deep fold of a 6,000-foot-high crag in Western-central Utah.

Coming down the hill, near the bottom, Pallas stopped to take another rest. Poised on a rock next to him, was a lizard. What a delight! In spite of centuries of eco-devastation and destruction, this represented a piece of anecdotal evidence that the natural flora and fauna were returning. Enchanted by its fluid bodily motions, Pallas watched the lizard doing "push-ups."

Pallas made it back to his home in just fifteen days. However, when he stepped into the main square of the town of Escalante, what he saw caught him by surprise.

A large throng of men were jostling each other in the public area. Among them were individuals he clearly recognized. One of the apparent instigators of the menacing-looking crowd, haranguing them with a blood-curdling speech, was his next-door neighbor.

With wild gesticulations, his neighbor was whipping the crowd into a frenzy. "They're murderers. They destroyed my wife's family, which made her an orphan when she was just a three-year-old girl. One hundred and thirty-three years ago, they destroyed the villages of Sarlinia and Kit, killing over 4,000. Before that, they wiped out even more villages. All around the world, in every corner of the planet, they tried to commit genocide. They blew up my great-grandfather in 422 A.G. with a plasma bomb just because his sheep strayed too near their territorial boundaries. They've always been butchers and monsters. Death to them all. Death is too good for them!"

Oh, Pallas had seen this before. A murder committed 500 years in the past was felt no less seriously—and taken no less to heart—than a murder committed the day before, especially in the mind of a vengeful farmer.

Pallas looked in the direction of his parent's house. He witnessed three men running in the middle of the road. They were bearing multiple coils of rope, draped around their shoulders, as if they were so many banners and flags. When these three reached the congregated crowd, it was as if they had been swallowed up by the larger group. The crowd then moved like a giant ameba, moving alternately snake-like and then crab-like, in the direction of two large oaks that were located in the very center of the square.

At first view Pallas thought the spectacle had started out as a public celebration gone bad, but he realized that no religious holiday had been scheduled, and therefore something else was happening. If he looked more closely, there seemed to be a strange and giddy anxiety, mixed with a sense of menace, about the crowd. Pallas then realized something else far more foreboding and unusual was occurring.

Men in the center of the crowd were on the verge of lynching a small handful of robust, rotund-looking middle-age men they had taken prisoner—men who were clearly frightened beyond their wits. They were all dressed in the robes of Gaia-Domes officials. These people had always been the ancient enemies of the New

Rebels. Wearing foreign-looking clothes, these outlanders appeared out-of-place.

Pallas did not doubt that they were Gaia-Dome officials. There didn't seem to be any lower-level Gaia-Domers among them. Lower-level personnel had in the past wandered into town, but only did so when they were dressed in the disguise of common laborers or manque sojourners. Knowing how unwelcome their visit was, and how dangerous it would be if their true identity had been discovered, they always kept a low profile, often dashing into town just long enough to purchase bits of scarce food items. And they never lingered longer than necessary. In contrast, these were high-echelon officials, mainly sub-magisters and magisters.

Pallas had been trained to know what Gaia-Dome uniforms looked like. He even thought he detected the green and purple robe of a Grandmagister. All that was missing was the tall, two-foot-high bejeweled white hat to make the Grandmagister's outfit complete.

Hemmed in like cattle, pressed together as if in a killing pen, there were six of them.

Pallas speculated about what had happened. Where had these outlanders come from? Obviously from a Gaia-Dome. But the closest Gaia-Dome, 250 miles away, had been dismantled seventeen years before. Along the entire eastern frontier, separating the New Rebels from the Gaia-Domes, practically all of the Gaia-Domes had been dismantled during the preceding 40 years. Rumors had it that Gaia-Domes had been collapsing one by one all over the world. Why live under the protection of a Gaia-Dome when the ozone layer had returned?

Living in the same world as the Gaia-Domes for almost 500 years, and the Gaia-Domes having most of the advantages up until the previous 50 years, no one seemed to notice that the domes had no reason to exist when their roofs were no longer necessary. Just as the cannibals were on the verge of extinction, so the inhabitants of the Gaia-Domes were on the edge of either coming out and adapting to the rapidly changing conditions of the world, or of facing the fate of fading away, just as their obsolete world was fading away.

September Snow and Iona had been right in their predictions. It was the prophesy of extreme dexterity and brilliant adaptability of the Unseeing Watchfulness of Gaia—renamed later the New Rebels—that saved them from their own destruction. And although the New Rebels never defeated the Gaia-Domes from a military point-of-view (only once had their ancestors actually defeated the Gaia-Domes in a conventional military stand-off, which occurred in 46 A.G.), they had—*apparently*—accomplished the next best thing, they had outlasted them. The patience of the New Rebels had proven more powerful than the technological superiority of the Gaia-Dome civilization. It had just taken more than 480 years for that patience to achieve fruition. It had taken so long that the New Rebels weren't even aware yet of where they stood in the current order of the world.

A shot rang out.

One of the Gaia-Dome officials was down. To get a better view, Pallas climbed a small tree, nestling himself in the crock of its largest, most stable limb. He was now only 100 feet from the edge of the group. From his improved vantage point, Pallas could see it was a Grandmagister who had been shot. The Grandmagister was on his hands and knees, on all fours, probing the ground with his fingers, apparently searching for a pair of eyeglasses that had fallen. From the blood trickling down the side of the Grandmagister's face, Pallas could see that the shot had only grazed his temple. He somehow managed to retrieve his eyeglasses. He gave a momentary shout. In the search for his eyeglasses the Grandmagister also found his big bejeweled white hat. Like a fool he heaved the stiff cloth-hat back onto the crown of his head. What was he thinking? Whereas in the Gaia-Domes the hat represented the highest acclamation of authority, here it was like issuing a calling card to be lynched first. He was completely oblivious to the danger he was in.

Pallas could see that it was the crowd's intention to lynch all six of the officials. That was the meaning of the rope. Wasn't anybody going to stop them? Pallas surveyed the entire square. Where was the constabulary? There wasn't a policeman in sight. The forces of law and order were conspicuously absent.

And where, Pallas wondered, was the Obsidian Order? (In many ways, they were much more powerful than the forces of the police.) Since the Obsidian Order had only recently declared their opposition to any mob-like behavior occurring anywhere in public places, Pallas thought that they would have tried to put an end to this. For all intents and purposes, the Obsidian Order had appointed themselves the hidden persuaders and the morality-police of the New Rebels.

The only persons attempting to thwart the crowd from committing acts of murder were three skinny initiates from the Forandi Order.

Against this maddened crowd, Pallas could see that they didn't stand a chance.

The three were repulsed from coming anywhere near the center of the group. With every attempt to push inside, they were pushed back. Someone launched a punch that landed on the face of one of them. Finally threatened at gunpoint, they were escorted out of the square by a small group of self-appointed vigilantes.

Oh my goodness, Pallas thought, this angry crowd really meant business.

As had always been his nature, Pallas stood apart, resolutely separate. Viewing from the outside had always been his favorite stance at public events.

Pallas wondered where the Gaia-Dome officials had come from? They had obviously not wandered into town. From a Gaia-Dome in Denver, perhaps? If so, things had really changed. The original Gaia-Dome in Denver had been abandoned and dismantled six years earlier. Another candidate was the small garrison town at Omaha. No, that didn't seem likely. The other possibility was the small Gaia-Dome in Kansas City. No, these Gaia-Dome officials were from some large dome.

Where were they from then? And how had they arrived? Transported by a helioplane? Transported by a *crashed* helioplane?

Someone shouted, "St. Louis!" Someone else shouted, "Chicago!" Someone even murmured "New York."

St. Louis! Chicago! New York! Were they from St. Louis or Chicago or New York Pallas wondered? Had the entire Gaia-Dome world collapsed overnight?

The head of the Obsidian Order, Naxos, was reputed to have been familiar with, and on actual speaking terms with, some of the Gaia-Dome officials. In spite of their status as enemies, if he had known they were coming he might have been able to grant them diplomatic immunity, safeguards, protection, even security.

Pallas left the scene in a state of disgust, only to return an hour later when his curiosity had gotten the better of him. When he did return, the six Gaia-Dome officials were hanging by their necks, in groups of three, from the lowest bows of the oak trees. Of the six, only the Grandmagister still had his hat on. Everyone else had left. The square looked deserted, as if it were a ghost town.

Axiomatically, all acts of murder were horrible, Pallas knew. But he also knew, only too well, that way too many murderers were capable of seeming to be perfectly normal and ordinary. That was why Pallas had resolved to keep himself separate from the vigilantes.

The next day, Naxos called Pallas into his office.

Naxos greeted Pallas at the door. Naxos had craggy good looks. But he went out of his way to try to make himself appear dull and unnoticeable. There was nothing about his appearance that suggested the aura of the angelic, the otherworldly, or the religious. Naxos was simply a diligent and highly skillful administrator.

Smiling warmly, Naxos took Pallas's hand in his own. He decided to extend all of the old-fashioned courtesies. He enthused, "Ah, welcome, Pallas Missette. You're back! I trust you had a safe voyage."

"Why do you ask?"

Naxos smiled again, this time wanly. "You surprised me though, you know. After all, you are three weeks late in your return." The comment was not intended as a rebuke. Naxos was just stating a fact.

"A minor incident occurred which threw my plans a bit awry," Pallas said. "Everything went okay, though. All we talked about was accomplished. You have my assurances on that score."

"Good," Naxos nodded. He looked mollified. "Then we needn't go into details, do we?"

"No, we don't." Pallas politely put his hand up. "However, I do wonder sir, why you insisted on including in my mission the search for Iona's grave."

"Iona's grave? I almost forgot."

"In all these years, nobody ever found her remains. During the entire time I was working on it, I was wondering why you needed that assignment done? At the risk of speaking out of turn, it was a hopeless and futile task, a complete waste of time. There is no grave of Iona."

Naxos was of two minds when he considered his response. He could have lied. After all, he was Pallas's superior. His explanation would not have been challenged. That would have been the easiest course to take. Or he could tell the truth. But that would reveal more about his thought processes than he wished to reveal.

He was talking to Pallas, so he opted to tell the truth. He realized it would leave a better impression.

"It was ridiculous—and futile, I know. You're right. I gave you that mission because I wanted to keep your over-active brain preoccupied. I didn't want you to have too much time on your hands for idle reflection. I wanted to minimize the occasion for second thoughts about the important task, the task we shall not elaborate on. Let's just call it the business of 'tapping the stone.' I manipulated you. I won't apologize for it. I did it for a reason. Success is its own justification."

Pallas wouldn't have been satisfied with any reply Naxos gave, he was only testing him. Pallas found Naxos's response sufficient only because it had the appearance of being *seemingly* transparent. That's all he expected.

"Fine by me," Pallas said. He quickly changed the subject. "Why were those men murdered in the square last night?"

"Oh that! Heavens above! Gaia! That horror!" Naxos looked concerned. Then he groaned. He was clearly embarrassed now. "We should have interfered. We should have stopped it. How do you prevent a crowd from engaging in acts of bestiality? A senseless group, filled with irrational impulses, egged on and driven by powerful urges of bloodlust and revenge? Perhaps you have a chance of reasoning with a single person. Good luck. Can you reason with a mob? How? With a sweetened honey pot of perfumed reason and high-sounding platitudes? You try it. I'd like to be there when you do. We were cowards, yes. But we were taken by surprise, too."

"In all this business, where were the police?" Pallas asked. "There wasn't a single policeman in sight. The crowd went crazy. All semblance of law and order broke down. It made me embarrassed to think I'm a part of this so-called community."

"Like us, the constabulary was frightened. It was a huge embarrassment. I admit it. Nothing like this has happened before. Unprecedented. We'll do better next time. If there is a next time."

Pallas eyes shot up. He gave Naxos a withering glance that abruptly morphed into a more inquisitive glow. Naxos shot back as if communication had occurred without words. "Now don't go looking at me like that, Pallas, I know how insolent you can be. The least we can say is that the police are not in the position to suppress the crowd either. Have you ever thought about that? Have you ever thought about that trade off? All actions we take are hemmed in and circumscribed by limitations imposed upon us by the exigencies of the world. I've been in office for only four and a half months now. Things don't change overnight."

"Oh," Pallas said. This was his weakness. Pallas was flattered and complimented whenever Naxos treated him as if he were a colleague. Naxos was practically the only adult who treated him as if he were an equal. Here he was being treated with such confidence and trust! Pallas had to use all of his powers to prevent the temptation from over-powering him, of allowing Naxos's attention and solicitude to go to his head.

For a brief moment, Naxos dropped his guard, then resumed his normal reserve. "Frankly, I'm sorry about the lost opportunity. We could have gotten a treasure trove of intelligence from them if we had had a chance to interview the Grandmagister. There was a Grandmagister among them! Imagine the flow of information. He was in our hands. Gone. Those wretched beasts."

"I'm mystified," Pallas said. "Confused, rather. Where did they come from? It's as if they dropped into our laps from outer space. And how did they fall into our hands so easily?"

"It is as if they did drop from outer space," Naxos confirmed. "They're from Buenos Aires, Argentina. That much we now know. The southern core of South America's Gaia-Dome system has collapsed."

"How did they end up here, of all places?" Pallas asked.

"The helioplane they were traveling in strayed off course. They had technical difficulties. How far is it from here to Buenos Aires, Argentina? 5,000 miles? 7,500 miles? All I know is that it is a long way. We can't even figure out where they were headed when they crashed in a cornfield a few miles outside of town. Even before they knew what was going to happen to them, they were already frightened to death. The last refugees from another collapsed Gaia-Dome system. All lost."

Pallas was about to smile in a mischievous fashion. But instead he exercised self-restraint and maintained an expression of caution and neutrality.

"I have something special for you, you know," Naxos said. "There is no point in me keeping it a secret any longer. It's a reward for all your hard work. You have done so well, I have something that is going to make you happy. Oh, you're going to be so very pleased with me."

Pallas's face lit up. "A horse, saddle, gun, holster. You're making me a knight!"

"Even though you are near to being of age, it doesn't mean you are at liberty to act like a complete idiot," Naxos replied in a mild voice. "You, a military man, of all things. Astride a horse. Horses are expensive. Outfitting a horse? Ruinous! Your father couldn't afford any such thing. Making you a knight would be the most absurd thing I could ever do."

Pallas regretted the immature and inappropriate remark.

"Look at you!" Naxos asked. "What a reputation your generation has. Elders call you the spoiled generation. Elders maintain you're hopeless. They say we've coddled you! They claim we treated you with excessive indulgence. Maybe they're right."

"They also say that we should be beaten within an inch of our lives whenever we commit a tiny transgression," Pallas said. "We're also expected to follow in lockstep, as if we're incapable of being able to think for ourselves."

"Your father did that. I was opposed to that."

"I know, and I am thankful to you, but we're not spoiled," Pallas insisted. "We're responsible. We just have an attitude. How would you like it if you were taught every day of your life that your great-great-great-great-great-grandparents' experience—is the be-all and end-all of your future? Would that fill you with joy? Make you love your prospects?"

"Don't make me regret my decision," Naxos said. "I've monitored your education. I know what you've dreamt of." He paused. "I know what you're capable of."

Pallas had noticed—it was for him an almost universal observation—adults always seemed to know best how to conceal their awkwardness in even the most perplexing of situations. "I apologize for my remarks, Naxos. I need to remind myself that I am inexperienced in the ways of the world."

"Nonsense!" Naxos said with a touch of annoyance. "Listen to me. We are going to send you to Europe. Only you are going alone.

It's going to be a long voyage. You are to be the first to be sent on such a mission. You are going to learn letters—real letters. You are going to learn how to read and write. They will teach you true scholarship. You are going to bring back to us true literacy, a new alphabet to use, not a bunch of primitive runic letterings, but the basis for a whole new educational system. We are going to let you study with the Oggaci!"

The words just tumbled out in quick order. Pallas could only mumble a humbled reply: "I am truly honored...But I a...And I a...a...in the past, what you're proposing has been seen as an object of precariousness. A great danger. An even graver peril." Pallas thought: For centuries, perhaps with compelling and honorable reasons, the New Rebels had always feared the threatening allure of the foreigner, not just the foreigner, *but all ideas foreign in context and content.* With literacy came other things. With literacy came unexpected things.

"What are you so afraid of?" Naxos asked in a surprised voice. "Do you not welcome this opportunity? I don't understand. I expected you to be overjoyed."

"I am pleased," Pallas said. "But would it not be better if I was sent to a still functioning Gaia-Dome? They are thoroughly corrupt, that's true, but they have learned men who know some things about the past that we should be aware of."

"In the past, when they were all powerful, the Gaia-Domes were perceived as being our enemies," Naxos said. "They are still perceived as being our enemies. They may still have a trick or two up their sleeves. The committee would never agree to that. No, no one would trust you if you came back from the Gaia-Domes. Angry folks would string you up by your neck. You can learn more from the Oggaci anyway and learn it more quickly." Naxos looked at Pallas carefully.

"We have, at last, after much delay, the final approval of the committee. I'm your sole sponsor. You're to be responsible only to me. I have been pushing this since I was named supreme head of the Obsidian Order. You're going to Europe. There's more. Imagine being able to recite the essence of original texts like an unrivaled master. Imagine there would be no more accumulation of human error, human folly, and trivialization caused by centuries of imperfect oral transmission. Imagine, in the future, scholars being able to cite passages that are unblemished, more importantly, passages that are unsurpassed in beauty of diction, grandeur of thought, and articulation of spirit. IMAGINE THIS HAPPENING BECAUSE OF YOU! Don't abuse me by saying, you're not intrigued? Upon your return, you'll not just be the stellar marking point, you'll be the gold standard for all education. You're going to bring back to us something which we have had missing for 500 years. A written language."

"Very well," Pallas said. "To the Oggaci. To Europe."

Hidden inside, Pallas was bursting with happiness.

Naxos took a piece of overused vellum from the sleeve of his coat. Placing it on his nightstand, he straightened it out. "Listen to this, Pallas. This is why I'm doing this. Here is a script left by an inhabitant of a collapsing Gaia-Dome. It was written with the luxury of a full alphabet. This is the script: 'We are vegetating in a ghost town, without the benefit of electricity or gas, without water. We are forced to think of personal hygiene as a luxury and hot meals as abstract concepts. We are living like ghosts in a vast field of ruins... A city where nothing works, apart from Wallscreen, that still beams in and out, still controls our lives.'" Naxos quit reading and peered at Pallas. "A dull, ignorant, pie-eyed monk, using our primitive runic alphabet, translated this passage as: 'Time is hard. Place is hard. Life's painful. It's impossible. I don't wish to live anymore. There are piles of brick. I smell bad. I stink. There's no food. There's no water. Cracked walls.'"

"Do you see my point?" Naxos asked. "Our runic alphabet is absurd. It's for children and hopelessly subservient adults who are incapable of becoming whole adults. We are ignorant. We must change."

"How long will I be gone?" Pallas asked.

"You'll be gone for a long time. Twelve years, at least."

The length of time staggered Pallas. He closed his eyes. "When

I return, people will not remember who I am."

"You exaggerate. People will remember."

"I am a bit frightened too," Pallas said. But he smiled. "I'm also content."

"You should be," Naxos said. "You are going to do something that has never been done before. Think of it. You'll be a pioneer. You should be proud."

"But why didn't you decide to send an older person instead?" Pallas asked. "Why don't you send someone whom you hold in higher regard, someone whom you can place greater trust in?"

"It's going to be twelve, hard, grueling years," Naxos smiled. "We want someone strong. We need a young person who will hold up under the strain. And I do hold you in the highest regard. We need someone who will not be too old later, when we need to establish the foundation for our future. We have it all planned out. I trust you. Think about it. You'll be thirty years old, when you return."

"I'm speechless," Pallas said.

"You must never forget Pallas, Gaia—our sacred Earth—is ultimately our teacher, not the Obsidian Order. Man was created from Gaia—the Earth. Gaia the Earth—will always help man."

With a gesture of his hands raised over Pallas's head, Naxos gave Pallas the standard Gaia blessing. Pallas dutifully knelt in front of Naxos to receive the blessing. In his delivery, Naxos tried to sound spiritual and pious, but all he managed to accomplish was to sound like a self-serving administrator.

In his official Obsidian Order functions, Naxos was embarrassed to admit he looked like he was just mindlessly going through the motions, his delivery lacking in fervor or credibility. *No spark of emotion, no feeling of sincerity, certainly no passion, just the routine mouthing of the formulaic.* On certain platforms, he wasn't the greatest of actors.

Pallas tried his best to look like he took Naxos's blessing as if it were given in a heartfelt fashion. But Pallas could see through Naxos's duplicity. He had already done his bidding. He had accomplished Naxos's dirty work. He had erased the message on the stone, scratched out the lettering as he promised he'd do. And he knew now, there was no turning back.

"I will pray for you as I will pray for myself," Pallas said. "How do you plan to treat those who adhere to the heretical belief that Iona is a goddess? What is your plan? How will you break them of their idiocy?"

"I'll use firmness," Naxos said. "But I'll also exercise patience. In our zeal, we'll not break the sacred laws. We'll not kill them. Education is by far the better course to take, not the employment of violence. But we must remain firm. With the task you've accomplished, you've helped us in this endeavor. Mark my words, Pallas, we shall stamp out this heresy."

Pallas rejoiced. He was going to go forward. He was going to travel to the other side of the world. For twelve years, he would be on his own. He was going to achieve something that he had only dreamed of. He'd be the first of the New Rebels to visit the world of Europe.

But first he had to break the news to his father. And he had to give his goodbyes to his mother. And he needed to tell Telia, his sweetheart, about the news. And not least of all, there was much advice he needed to receive from Matthew. Not least of all, he had to be sure to talk to Matthew.

Chapter Eight

PALLAS'S FATHER'S REACTION was swift. He was filled with hatred and seething with anger. At one point Pallas thought his father was bent on giving him a thrashing. But although his fists were clenched and his face was flushed the color of purple, he stopped short of attacking. Instead he sputtered, "I despise you. I spit on the notion of calling you my son. You're useless. You're a complete loss. No denying it, you'll become a scribbler—*or worse.*" For good measure, his father then turned his back on Pallas.

"But Naxos Sparrus is sponsoring me," Pallas protested. "He thinks that this is the best thing that could happen to me. I'm going places, Father. Without a doubt, this is the greatest opportunity to fall upon anyone of my generation. All my peers are jealous of my great luck!"

Pallas's father turned and stared at Pallas. "Jealous of you? You? Your luck? You're a worm. Well, if you have Naxos Sparrus to speak for you, you surely don't need me, do you? Now go. Get out of my sight." He looked fierce and vengeful. But as contradictory as it seemed, he also looked strangely broken and defeated.

Pallas was relieved. The storm had broken. He thought he had gotten off easy. The task of breaking the news to his father had gone better than he feared. In the end, Pallas's father looked so defeated that Pallas almost felt sorry for him. This was not what Pallas desired.

He only wanted his father to be neutralized, pacified, sidetracked, out of the way.

"I'm just an ignorant farmer anyway." Pallas's father said. His voice softened. "Be sure to tell your mother that you're leaving. How long will you be gone?"

"At least twelve years, Father."

"An eternity. Maybe you'll be swallowed up by the ocean. Maybe strange beasts will devour you. Maybe foreigners will cut you up and serve you as if you were a cutlet. Maybe there's no point in saying anything to your mother." Then, in a dejected voice, he added, "Naxos paid a visit four weeks ago. He got to me before you came back from your pilgrimage. He gave me a good talking to. He gave me my marching orders on all this education business—all this traveling to the other side of the world. I've been told in no uncertain terms how to conduct myself. You don't have to worry about me. I love Gaia. I love our religion. I will faithfully serve our religion. Like any other good, devoted Gaia follower."

"Thank you, Father," Pallas said. Pallas even bowed to his father like a dutiful son.

Pallas had no choice. More than anything else, he wanted to visit Telia. But he had to do so on the sly. If Pallas's father knew that he was going to see her, he would be in trouble. Pallas's father disapproved of Telia. Moreover, he detested her family. There was something about Telia's parents that made them suspect in the eyes of many in the New Rebel realm. Like other sub-sectarians, Telia's family attempted to protect their tradition by a strategy known as *rumitquan*, meaning to hide one's inner core beliefs from the prying eyes of outsiders to avoid persecution.

But Pallas loved Telia more than anyone else in the universe.

Through his brother, Pallas sent a message that they were to meet in an alleyway in the middle of the night. When they met, Telia flung her arms around Pallas's neck. Pallas spied over Telia's shoulder to make sure no one was watching them. Between the dark, twisted, narrow, barely lit streets, Pallas saw a silhouette of a figure lurching back and forth, heading in the direction of the south end of town. Pallas guessed it was a drunkard, careening wildly from the effects of a serious bender. From the corner of his eye, Pallas also noticed two boys. They were passing in the opposite direction, north. Pallas assumed they were shepherds up extra early because they wanted to get their flock to the best pastures before the other shepherds arose. Snows and rains had been better than average that year and eager shepherds would have wanted a head start. Between the ages of eight and twelve, Pallas had worked as an assistant to a shepherd's mate.

Only after the boys and the drunk finally disappeared was Pallas satisfied all was safe. Only then did he fully return Telia's embrace. He planted a kiss on her lips.

Oh, Pallas and Telia, they were so much in love.

Pallas had been infatuated with Telia in a puppy love sort of way since the age of eight, though it must be said Telia never offered a single gesture of affection to Pallas in their youth, and was more Escalante Tomboyish than anyone. A pail of pig slop she dumped on Pallas's head might have been a harbinger for a sensible boy, but as a sentimentalist Pallas was always trying to get at the heart of something that frequently didn't have a heart. Later, at age fourteen, Telia figured that Pallas suffered from an acute malady called unrealistic fantasy, though at that age she couldn't have called it by its more accurate description: romanticism. Matthew figured out Pallas from the start: stern and dreary yet incurably dreamy, stubborn and driven yet visionary, cautious and thoughtful yet unrealistic. In other words, romantic. Naxos in his way figured out a key to understanding Pallas too: he had a belief that he could, single-handedly, *change* the world. All those brains, but where was the pragmatism? Where was the skepticism? Indeed, where was the common sense?

Between Pallas and Telia, bit by bit, after some "stiff-arming" by Telia, in slow stages, a spark turned into flame, which then turned into a fire. Telia's resistance began to subside. At the age sixteen-and-a-half, her resistance broke. What turned Telia around was her discovery that there was an inextricable part of Pallas's romanticism that was premised not on *a mere acceptance of asceticism*, but also on a *full-fledged embrace of absolute asceticism*—when connected to a higher idea. What idea? A calling. Pallas's calling? Pursuit of truth. How romantic!

Pallas had been seduced by Telia early on. Pallas was a year older than Telia and by nature circumspect and cautious; Telia by contrast was free-spirited and spontaneous, and sometimes a huge risk-taker. She took joy in risk. That was the basis of Telia's seductive charm. Pallas also loved the fact that Telia had a secret. He was romantic about all parts of her—*everything*.

An example of Telia's risk-taking? When she was thirteen-and-a-half, she hid three runaway outcasts in her family's farm-crib. Telia's parents protested at first, but as always eventually caved in to her strong will. Pallas knew that Telia's action was dangerous, but since he knew there was no stopping her, he adopted an air of stoic resignation and grew to actively support her. Telia nursed the runaways' wounds. She surreptitiously fed them for four weeks straight. During the entire time, she protected them until they were strong enough to escape. She got away with this illegality, but if she had been caught by the authorities she would have been sentenced to hard labor as an indentured servant to a prosperous, tithe-paying farmer. After completing her sentence, she probably would have been forced to marry the farmer, whether he had been a widower or not. She would have been prohibited from engaging in long-distance travel. She would have been placed on a community watch list for fifteen years. Whether or not she had been forced to marry the farmer, she would have been banned from marrying Pallas.

Having reached her majority, Telia was ready to go with Pallas anywhere. She hated the coding system, the primitiveness, and the cultural restrictions imposed on everyone in Escalante.

Freeing themselves from the embrace, Telia used her strong fingers to smooth out the wrinkles on Pallas's tunic. She placed her fingers to Pallas's lips. "Is Naxos going to dress you in gorgeous, lavish robes, so you can preen and prance about the slick heads of town like an elevated scribe? *Which is what you want?* What will Naxos call you? Something suitable. Pallas the superiorly blest? Pallas the marked one? Pallas the brilliant? Pallas the super-educated?"

"Stop it. Your sarcasm is duly noted. Have you heard the news?"

"No." Without skipping a beat, Telia blurted out, "When are you going to marry me? Then we can run away together. Leave this accursed place that my parents have chosen to die in."

Pallas nodded, then tilted his head to his side. "We've talked of this before. Where will we go? The Gaia-Domes are collapsing. When they are gone, and the Gaia-Dome armies are nothing, there won't be a plausible enemy to defend the land against. Then everything will change. You want to go heedlessly into the wild? You want to live on the frontier? I've been there. Not a pretty sight. Your urgency to get away is understandable, but your impulse to escape is driven by unreasonable enthusiasms rather than by discretion and planning. If we followed your instincts all the time, out of the frying pan, into the fire."

"Frying pan? We've been cooked before. I'm not afraid of fire."

"I know you're not. That's what I've come to talk to you about." Pallas lowered his voice to a whisper. "That's why I insisted we meet in the dead of night. By the way, I love you. I adore you. I approve of your sarcasm. I do wish to marry you. I'm anxious to do so. *But not today.*"

Telia broke into a broad smile. "Well? What are you waiting for? Your father's approval? He'd kill you first rather than allow you to marry me. And you may stoop to allow Naxos to manipulate you, but you'd never permit him to interfere with your wedding." Telia snorted. She let out a petulant laugh. "Liars! They're all a bunch of hypocrites!"

Nimbly, Telia squirreled around, standing back to back, at Pallas's back. Before he could stop her, she interlocked Pallas's arms with her own.

"No, no, no, don't...," Pallas cried in anguish. "No, Telia, darling, please. Don't. Not now!"

Telia grinned. She giggled. She had done this trick before. She executed what she called a "windmill," a maneuver taught to her by a circus performer. This was not your garden variety form of acrobatics. It was gravity-defying. Stage one of the act was the "send-off." First, Telia forced Pallas to stretch out his arms, to the snapping point. This would allow Telia to snap back at the right moment, propelling her, like a human sling-shot. Stage two was where Telia used Pallas's back as a platform, causing Pallas to bend *forward more*, while extending his arms *backward*. Stage three was the trickiest part. This was where Telia rocked back, propelling herself over Pallas's back and lowered head, flying over his head and flipping herself. At the end of the flip, the two of them would be facing each other, Telia's eyes staring at the cartilage notch above Pallas's sternum at the bottom of his neck. The danger was mitigated by the fact that Telia was extraordinarily light, weighing just 90 pounds, and was only 4' 11." But Pallas had to break their hold at just the right instant, as Telia flew overhead, or he would injure his back, his neck, his wrists, *or her wrists*. Performing the trick required trust.

Somehow, once more, too close to the opportunity of a mistake leading to an occurrence of a horrible accident in Pallas's opinion, the trick worked.

Extremely relieved at having completed it, Pallas said, "Change of plans. One day you'll injure me—then I won't be able to do anything for you. You're a real ball-buster, you know that?"

Telia smiled. "Why don't you like having fun once in a while? You're too responsible, too gloomy, and you're too damn serious for your own good. You're such a killjoy."

But in spite of his anger, Pallas still held Telia close. He hugged her closer. He placed his hand delicately on the side of her head. In response, Telia looked up into his eyes. He told her about his conversation with Naxos. He told her about his trip to the other side of the world. Telia sensed a feeling of exhilaration and delight in Pallas's voice and marveled at his gestures.

Then Pallas's conversation took a more soberly turn. "To be honest, I'm a little scared. I'll be facing the unknown. All my life, I've wanted this; exploring the unknown, eliminating—at least pushing farther out—the boundaries of knowledge! Now it's finally happening! But I expected it'd last four years, five years, six years at most, not twelve. The proposition I had in mind to submit to you is the hardest thing I've ever asked you. You are, of course, under no obligation, you understand, regardless of our past affiliations..."

"*Affiliations?*" Telia asked mockingly, laughing. She had a provocative way of repeating words with which she disagreed. "You mean like your tribal affiliations?"

Pallas continued, "You're free to answer my question any way you wish."

"Why ask the obvious? Spit it out. Naxos is a dimpled-chin beast. Getting away from him is the best thing that could ever happen to you, did you know that? And I don't suppose you'll miss your father. Twelve years? You wouldn't miss this place if it was 100,000 years."

"You'll wait for me?"

For all Telia's directness and candor, it took her some time to come up with a snappy reply.

"You expect me to marry an old widower, because he can put a roof over my head? I have no honor because my family has no honor. It's my duty that my family has a secret. My family has no past tribal affiliation. My ancestors, then outsiders, joined The Unseeing Watchfulness of Gaia 425 years after Iona was born! We're latecomers, my grandparents wandered into a New Rebel settlement when they were young. Need I remind you there was a world in existence before there was Gaia. The Gaia-Domes have already obliterated all knowledge and memory of that. If given half the chance, the Obsidian Order would in all likelihood follow suit. Now that would be a sight, those two in league together. How scary could that be? I've been placed under severe pains never to disclose my family's secret truth. To be unmarried is a social and religious disgrace, and is there anything in the world a family resents more than an unmarried daughter? That is, if you accept the mores of our society. But my family doesn't. They hold fast to something different. Even if it means risking becoming complete outcasts, they will always hold fast to the heritage of their earliest beliefs. I'll wait for you forever."

"Well, it's twelve years," Pallas said. "Which is practically the same as forever."

"The only thing the Obsidian Order is good at is taking our money and requisitioning our corn. You might as well get something from them in return."

"Besides your biting sarcasm, there's something else I love you for," Pallas said.

"And what is that, my love? My adherence to obedience? My ability to stay submissive? Why is September Snow a goddess? Why is Iona only a saint? Because the original adherents of the Unseeing Watchfulness of Gaia knew so little about September Snow and what they did know was only second hand. But what they knew about Iona was first hand. She was too human—too…un-divine. It is only because the Obsidian Order has staked their authority on the doctrine of September Snow being a goddess, and Iona being *merely* a saint, that it is really such a big deal. Otherwise, who cares? And so big a deal, it's enough to put someone into exile, if they even so much as question the doctrine. What does a goddess have to do with Gaia anyway? Nothing. Gaia has nothing to do with the supernatural and it has practically nothing to do with the human race. Is there such a thing as the human race? Where did that come from? Not from Gaia. Gaia is Earth. Science! Does anyone question that? Of course not!" Telia emitted a full-throated laugh.

"I know you," Pallas fumed. "I'm going to ignore your heresy. You just like to provoke me. You'll say anything to get a reaction. No," Pallas continued, "I love you for your practicality."

This was so unexpected, so counterintuitive, and unlike Pallas, it took Telia by surprise. Grabbing Pallas by the shoulders (she was so short she had to reach up almost a foot), she flung him back and forth, controlling him like a rag doll. Pallas had gone conveniently limp. Then she shook him energetically. She stared fiercely into his eyes. She slapped him across the face. "I'm practical? Then get your head out of the clouds! For once! See the world for what it is!"

Pallas took the blow in stride. He offered no resistance. He didn't even wince. Instead, he offered a self-mocking, sheepish grin. "Will you always be sending me up to my worst fates with a good love tap for good measure?" he asked.

"Not to worry," Telia said in a tender, calming voice, "I'll *always* be keeping the watch."

Telia smiled deviously. It wasn't the kind of smile of a full-fledged woman, but that of a young girl—or better yet, a fearless boy. Her devious smile then morphed into a determined smile. It was the kind of smile she'd use when facing an opponent during a competitive game. Tilting her head a little, teasing, she displayed the toughness that Pallas absolutely adored.

"I'll do more than the watch. I'll keep you on the right track. I'll be your guide."

"Gaia!" Pallas shouted, grinning like a fool. "Such luck!"

"Shhh," Telia said. "We are surrounded by spies. With all your shouting, you'll wake the dead. You want to continue your existence, zombie-like, among the brain-dead?" Telia may have still been a child-woman age-wise—but she had the self-possession of someone many decades older. She was a worldly-wise, preternatural spectator of all the comings and goings of Escalante.

Pallas and Telia had so many inner secrets they kept between themselves. As they embraced, they were seized by an uncontrollable, euphoric vitality.

Matthew was special and one of a kind. His oddity was that he had a Christian name, a rarity in the world of Gaia. His ancestors had arrived from the Far East 250 years after the founding of Gaia. Although they were nominally Gaian, they had stubbornly held to their outdated Christian beliefs. Matthew's superiors in the Forandi Order had been more or less accepting of Matthew's grandfather's stubbornly-held Christian heritage, but Matthew's parents and Matthew himself had sincerely converted to Gaia.

In terms of ethical certitude and altruistic rectitude, Matthew was as close to embodying pure moral virtues as anyone in Escalante. Once Pallas playfully charged Matthew: "Your grandfather may have been a degenerate Christian, and you may, in some ways, be a covert one, but that's not the same thing as being Christ-like!"

"I'll remind you, Pallas, being a follower of Gaia does not give one the right to think one is Iona-like, much less September Snow-like! Your worship of Telia—your love—is too obvious."

"You're too clever by half. That'll be your downfall. But I love you for it."

"Those poems you keep so guardedly inside, will you ever give me the pleasure of reciting one to me?"

"No," Pallas said. "They're my secrets. I'll never allow anyone to hear them."

"To be held inside," Matthew bowed, "for an eternity. I also hold certain things dearly. Let us honor them. Let us never allow anyone to pry them away from us!"

"Amen," Pallas said.

If there was anyone who could resist the three-part temptations of power, wealth, and acclamations of notoriety, it was Matthew. By virtue of these allegedly "Gaia-given" attributes, Matthew was Pallas's alter ego and his conscience. Matthew believed that Gaia, like God, was good, and therefore, for that reason, he also had to be good. It was a simple deduction. In this, and in so many other ways, Matthew was simple and direct.

Pallas had knocked twice at Matthew's door. Matthew had been seated on his cot in his small monk-cell: five feet long by six feet wide, a room barely large enough to hold a low-slung cot made of two-inch and three-inch wide tree limbs, twisted, with the bark still on it, darkened by age, the color of teak, lashed together by primitive, wiry ropes. The bed was sixty-five years old. There was also a wobbly eighteen-inch high, three-legged milking stool shoved in the corner of the room. Finally, there was a wicker basket hanging from the ceiling, holding a mixture of herbs, dried corn, dried fig. There was also a residue of over-ripened cabbage leaves, and a stale odor of garlic, proving that at least some meals had been prepared in the room. Pallas, strangely, had always associated this "odor of Matthew" with the Spartan-like maintenance of pure physical health.

Matthew opened the door a crack. Under the shade of his white cowl, Pallas could barely make out Matthew's long, lined, thin-nosed face. Smiling dimly, Matthew shoved the door open wider. He pushed his cowl back from the top of his head. Recognizing his visitor, he smiled broadly. He threw his arms around Pallas's neck. "Let us bear down all sorrow," Matthew said, using the most famous of all Gaian greetings. He kissed Pallas gently on each cheek.

"Let us, Gaia be pleased, bear down all sorrows, Pallas," Matthew repeated formally.

Pallas told Matthew about his trip to Europe. He told Matthew about Naxos's role in organizing the trip. He asked Matthew for his advice.

"Don't think twice about it. Don't hesitate. Go."

"That easily? Wouldn't that result in my compromising my beliefs in poetry and truth?"

"Poetry and truth are all nonsense! Don't even think about it. Go. You'll never have an opportunity like this again."

But Pallas looked conflicted. Although Matthew could see that Pallas was thrilled and overjoyed at the prospect for travel and seemingly limitless education, he had lingering doubts.

"Look, Pallas," Matthew said, "religion is not theology, but the way people treat each other. The Forandi Order doesn't need to know anymore truths than what we already know. But you are different, Pallas. Go and find more truths. Go and find new truths, truths that have not yet been discovered. For you, there is a battle raging between the opposite forces of tradition and reason. For you, there will be fear and doubt nagging you at every step. That's what makes you so powerful. *That inner uncertainty!*"

"Really?"

"The future doesn't care what we think. It will be as kind or as cruel as it chooses to be."

"No," Pallas said. He gave Matthew a mirthless, hopeless smile. "No, don't say that."

Matthew spoke with a note of great confidence. "No, no, no, rest assured. I believe I'll still be alive. You are also likely to be alive. There is reason, there is purpose, we are destined to see each other again. You'll see."

"You sure?"

"The Forandi Order is the court jester to a stifled world. What was the world like 500 years ago? No one knows. How can we know? What was the world like 1,000 years ago? No one knows. How can we know? How can we stem the tide into the future? I am a Christian in name only. I am not a Christian. I am a follower of Gaia. But I am suspect. So I speak only to you."

"You place too great a burden on my meager means," Pallas said. "You place too much hope on my modest abilities. I'm destined to be a messenger only. Only a messenger—*Matthew!*"

Matthew's face looked pure and angelic, but his voice sounded foreboding. "Was September Snow destined to become what she was, or did she become what she was because she chose to be a goddess? Was Iona something different from just a saint?"

"Don't play games with me," Pallas hissed. "A messenger only."

A Forandi monk, younger than Matthew, arrived at Matthew's door. He knocked lightly and beckoned Matthew to join him. He whispered into Matthew's ear. Matthew nodded. He smiled at the monk. Then he nodded to Pallas. He looked to Pallas for understanding. Pallas assented.

"You know what you're doing, and what you're doing is the right thing," Matthew said.

The only sound in Pallas's ears was the sound of the leather of Matthew's sandals slapping on stone as Matthew wandered back to his superior's cell.

Pallas made one last visit. He went to see his ailing mother. She was a simple woman, unlettered and uneducated. She smiled at Pallas. She made it clear as she beamed at him that she was proud. Even though she did not understand what this unique education was going to entail, she was happy he had been given a once-in-a-lifetime opportunity.

"Your father hated you because he was jealous of you. Always the brightest! You were always the brightest! To admit that would have meant that he had to admit to his own failure. You were a constant reminder of his own dismal deficiency." Mother's wit combined with common sense: It was only in his mother's presence that Pallas felt genuine meekness and humility.

"He was so strange to me."

"I'm sorry he was so cruel."

Pallas asked his mother for her blessing.

She gave it to him.

Pallas raised his tunic to his neck, exposing his mid-section. He showed his mother the long scar of the wound below his ribcage.

"That's recent," she said, pressing her fingers to Pallas's scar. She looked away.

"I have not shown this to anyone, Mother. Not even to Telia. I only wanted to show it to you."

"I am sick. You will not see me upon your return, my son. Gaia go with you." She stared off into the distance.

Pallas kissed his mother on her forehead. Pallas knew he had to be tough. He knew his mother would no longer be alive when he returned from his voyage.

"Good bye, Mrs. Missette," Pallas said. He moistened his index finger with his mouth. He dabbed the finger on his mother's cheek along with a glob of saliva, initiating a gesture from his childhood. It was something he did when he was a frightened four-year-old and a distraught five-year-old—at a time when his mother had been his sole protector. But his mother remained passive. Pallas thought that repeating the gesture might bring her back to an earlier time, but to no avail. He felt foolish.

She continued to stare into space. Pallas took his mother in his arms and held her. He rocked her back and forth. "You saved me, you saved me, for almost three years, when you were able to. But then you couldn't save me anymore." He kissed her on the forehead again.

In the middle of the night, after grabbing his last belongings, Pallas ran into his brother. Pallas said, "You're up late. By the way, I am thankful to you again for tracking Telia down and acting as my messenger."

Pallas's brother appeared neither happy nor sad, just resigned. "You are my older brother. I will do as you order me to do. Only don't ask me again. You'll only get me into trouble. If Father had found out, he'd beat me."

"I am finished with our father," Pallas said.

"Submit."

"Easy for you to say. Father loves you."

"Father loves you, too. In your case, it comes out in a strange way. Alright, in a peculiarly twisted and perverse way. Submit."

"I'll never submit."

"It would be easier for all of us if you did."

"I'll never submit. We shall not speak about this again," Pallas said. "I will not submit myself to parental authority. I don't have to anymore."

Naxos had arranged passage. With an eastern caravan, Pallas traveled across country. Even though the caravan had been granted an international writ of neutrality, they kept as far away from the Gaia-Domes as possible. The Gaia-Domes had a reputation for doing nasty things to outsiders just out of spite. They knew their end was drawing near, but that only made them more cruel, less reflective, more destructive. They lashed out with their decaying technology, a technology that was the only thing seemingly within their grasp and under their control.

The caravan traveled without incident. Every year, travel was becoming easier. Two hundred years before, they made the trip only once every decade. At least one time in three, the journey ended in failure. Several discouraging trips in a row, one after another, could destroy a caravan operation. The journeys were costly and dangerous. Cannibals preyed on them, Gaia-Domes attacked them, goods were shoddy and in low demand. Forty years ago, they'd been barely able to shave the travel time in half. Twenty years after that, they'd been able to halve it again. By the time Pallas was born, they had improved their track record to make one trip a year. They kept improving, and as they did, they prospered. Wants were multiplied, tastes were refined, trade flourished, and hundreds of industries from earthenware to metal to alchemy sprang into existence. A journey of 2,150 miles. Pallas got to the coast in a record eight weeks time! And the road was clear.

Along the way, Pallas came across an old Gaia-Dome scroll in a market stall at a crossroads. The content of the scroll was apparently a chest-thumping panegyric, useless and sort of bizarre, but the writing, because it used a full alphabet, was thrilling and marvelous. Pallas was able to get the proprietor to teach him twelve letters that were not in the 13-letter runic alphabet he knew. That, along with the faded illustration on the cover, enabled Pallas to figure out a portion of the title of the scroll.

It read: "How we made rebel [untranslatable word] ready for ?*their?* winding cloth."

Or an alternative reading was: "How we made a rebel [untranslatable word, perhaps]: *army?* — ready for its winding cloth."

The scroll was in poor condition. The title was as far as Pallas could read. Before he got to the East coast, it fell apart in his hands. Pallas felt cheated. He sulked, believing that he had not received his money's worth. Unlike in practically every corner of the domain of the New Rebels, where the inhabitants were inspired *to do good*, or at least at a minimum were driven by fear of being punished *to do good*, east of the Rocky Mountains, there were confidence men, highwaymen, bagmen, flimflam men, bushwhackers, swindlers, all eager to prey on the foolish, the naive, and the easily bamboozled. Pallas was thankful to Gaia he had the protection of the caravan, and the knowledge and wisdom of the caravan leader, to keep him from straying into the back-eddies and undertows of the road.

Chapter Nine

MAKING GOOD TIME, the caravan arrived just at the doorstep of the Eastern Sea.

At the last minute there was a change of plans. The leader of the caravan thought that getting to Pallas's ocean-going ship would have involved some surreptitious maneuvering to keep the caravan from entangling with forces of the Gaia-Domes. But when they got near the coast, they learned that the Gaia-Domes of New York City had been abandoned only two months before. Instead of crossing from the mainland to the western end of Long Island at night, they decided to do a little investigation of the recently depopulated island of Manhattan.

Instead of skulking around the boundaries of the domain of the Gaia-Domes, as had been the caravan leader's safe practice in the past, the two of them commandeered a small boat on the western shore of the Hudson River, and then boldly crossed over to Manhattan in broad daylight (something the caravan leader had never risked before). The southern tip of Manhattan had been submerged for nearly four centuries, after a 14 to 20-foot rise in the level of the oceans, but most of the rest of the island, aside from the low-lying areas adjacent to the Hudson and East Rivers, had survived intact above the new water line. Most of the area between the old and new waterline had been converted into swampland, or at extremely low tides, mud flats.

Crossing through knee-high stagnant water choked with salt-grass and thickets, the caravan leader and Pallas finally arrived on dry land. There they followed well traveled slender footpaths between the crumbling mounts of iron, pulverized concrete and cement, between rusty girders of steel resembling twisted tails, some lying snake-like on the ground, others coiled like tentacles, bent at right angles, jutting into the air. A few of the smaller, older buildings were half standing, half fallen. Pallas could see the inner pillars standing through the decaying walls.

Because the place had not seen the likes of pilferers for so long, Pallas regarded the excursion as a unique experience. For him, the ruins of Manhattan were a labyrinth. Among the ruins, a question arose in the back of Pallas's mind. Where had the inhabitants gone?

He could decipher that in spite of the debris and rubble there had been streets that had been laid out on a grid, at perfect right angles. He found a partially hidden sign, lying in a pile of rubble. Pallas, with some effort, tugged the sign out of the dust. It was creased in the middle, resembling a butterfly. As best he could, he flattened it out. On a three foot high block of concrete, he tipped it up. He stepped back for a better view. Now he could see it clearly. He wanted to decipher it. He waved over the caravan leader, then slowly read the wording: "No U Turn." He knew what the word "no" meant, he could figure out what "turn" meant, but the "U" baffled him. A symbol of what? A sign about a place? A sign about a state of mind? A sign about a direction? The word "turn" suggested a direction. But what direction? Why a sanction against "U"? What was "U?"

Pallas scratched his head, looking puzzled. The caravan leader waved his hands over his head in protest. "Curses. You invite me over for this! Garbage! Why show me this?" He was beside himself. "Gibberish! Debris! Digging in the past is for idiots! People who lived in the dead zones those long eons ago were ogres. Violators of truth. Idiots! Why not drop a bomb on the place. Blow it to smithereens." He fumed and raged. "Building stock pens, or at least grazing pastures, over this despoiled cesspool, *now that would be a positive use of land.*"

But the caravan leader's displeasure didn't dent Pallas's curiosity. If he had the time, he would have tried to decode the lettering even further. It was a challenging enigma.

From the debris of massive buildings Pallas could see the butts of piping, evidence to him that there had been indoor sanitation systems in the buildings. Pallas thought to himself: violators maybe, not ogres. Escalante was only beginning to experience the rewards of indoor plumbing. Naxos's most recent house had piped-in water. He knew the Gaia-Domes were known for their water taps and what they called "flush commodes." In one pool of debris, Pallas fished out a kettle, a broken bottle, and a tin can. In what appeared to have once been a gutter next to a road abutment, Pallas found two "plastic-material" objects. One was a comb, prongs bent badly, two-inches long, barely a quarter-inch wide. A comb for a doll? The other was a doll. Using his tunic's sleeve, Pallas wiped away the dirt. It was a figure of a boy with yellow spiked hair and blue tight, hip-hugging trousers: blue, yellow, face and hands pale pink. There was a devilish gleam in the eyes of the doll. The artifact was made of plastic. Pallas was aware that plastic lasted longer than cloth, was more durable than earthenware, less delicate than glass. But what did the artifact signify? He showed the caravan leader the figurine and asked him what he made of it.

"Evil worship," the caravan leader pronounced sternly. "Devil doll. Throw it away. Quickly. Don't hold it any longer! Drop it. Offer a prayer to Gaia. Clean your hands afterwards."

Pallas dropped the doll. He wiped his hands thoroughly on his tunic afterwards.

But it was larger objects that commanded Pallas's greatest attention. Pallas found them, big as glacial rocks, on the edges of broken pavement. These objects struck Pallas as immutable, yet surreal. To be sure, Pallas had seen several of these "rocks" before. One that had been converted—back home—into a huge flower pot. A top committee member's wife made a flower arrangement out of the hoodless front, the concaved middle, with the roof removed, and the trunk with the lid opened. New Rebels had come from miles around to view the flower arrangement. But these "rocks" were *what*? There were relatively few of them in the vicinity of the Colorado plateau. New Rebels didn't waste time trying to figure out what they once had been 550 years before. They had been inexplicable crumpled pieces of mangled metal.

But on the island of Manhattan, there were hundreds of them. *In fact, Pallas calculated there must have been thousands.* Sometimes there were as many as six placed in a row, some with spaces of five feet between them. End to end, they made Pallas think of dogcarts, buggies, or even, wagon conveyances (without horses.) They were approximately eight to ten feet long by six feet wide, but only barely four feet tall, most with their tops compressed. When Pallas asked the caravan leader what they were, the caravan leader replied, "*Cars.*"

"They don't look like it now, but they were once gleaming boxes of metal and glistening chrome," the caravan leader explained. "Legend has it that they used to race at speeds of 120 miles per hour. Transport. Moved on tires. They carried people to and fro. There were bubble cars of course, the Gaia-Domes built them later, but there were only a tiny number of them constructed. The vast majority of these rust buckets were from very olden times."

"I don't get it?" Pallas asked bewildered. "Where'd they come from?"

"A factory. That's where they were made."

"A factory? You mean like an apple or pear warehouse? A tannery? A cloth dryer?"

"No! *Large factory!* Like a Gaia-Dome factory! Machine-makers making machines."

"How'd these rocks work?"

The caravan leader pointed down at the bottom of the scrunched objects. "You can't see them now, but do you see those one-inch-thick patches of black that look like pads on the bottom of the four corners of the metal box? They don't look like it now, but they were once tires. A car had four of them."

"You mean they were...*what*...? Wheels?"

"Unlike our wheels, the outer rims were made of a thing called rubber. *Tires.* Like on a helioplane. The tire was much smaller than the tire on a Gaia-Dome helioplane. It was made of rubber in the form of a tube and the tube was inflated with air. And the tube and the rubber and the air constituted a wheel, and the metal moved on the wheel."

"The car flew?"

"Gaia! Don't be ridiculous. I said *like* a helioplane. Not as a helioplane. Cars traveled on ground."

"Oh," Pallas said. "Then they were pulled by something? A horse? An ox? Animal traction?"

The caravan leader's temper flared. He was on the verge of getting upset. "Your brain? Keep asking me questions like this, Pallas, and people will assume you're a moron. A car had a thing called an engine. Gears. Stuff. You know. Innards. Put your mind on that. Someone tried to explain the devil of an *engine* to me once, but I didn't get it. Wait till you see the ship you'll be traveling on. That'll help you understand. It'll give you a hint. Believe it, your ship has an engine too! One that operates! One that works! One that functions!"

When Pallas asked the caravan leader where all the debris had fallen from, he replied, "Originally, there were skyscrapers built by an ancient civilization. When the civilization collapsed, these towers were abandoned. Uninhabited, they sprouted vines and vegetation, making them resemble gargantuan beanpoles. Eventually, of course, they toppled down. Ever since, they have been lying in ruins, the concrete crumbling, the iron rusting. Some of the older, smaller buildings were left; they'd been built stronger. Some day, perhaps a thousand years from now, all this garbage will be broken down and recomposed by the Earth again. Or so I'm told. Back to forest. Back to pasture."

As they traveled across the central spine of Manhattan, Pallas got an excellent view of the debris. The recently abandoned Gaia-Domes were in good shape. Pallas counted thirty of them. Most of them were small, but a few were large, two were *gigantic*. The few that were close by looked like massive mushrooms, blocking the rays of the sun. They were impressive, but there was no human activity around them whatsoever. There was a pall of gloom around them. Manhattan resembled a ghost town, twice-over, twice-removed.

Having double-tracked back over the island to the Hudson, they took the boat back to the mainland shore. They rejoined the caravan. The caravan leader decided to escort Pallas personally to the ship.

With the exit of the Gaia-Dome magisters and their forces, the ship was still waiting at the harbor at Rockaway Bay. The captain greeted them at the dock. He then escorted them to a hut onshore to have a drink. There the captain explained to the caravan leader that the Gaia-Domes' demise had been too abrupt and unexpected, there had not been enough time for the captain and the crew to move to the better anchorage in the Hudson or the East River estuaries. Since they were ready to disembark anyway, they had decided to stay put for now. In the future, however, the captain planned to move his docking operation to Manhattan, not sure yet whether to anchor the operation on the south end of the East River, or the south end of the Hudson River.

The captain and the caravan leader made it clear to Pallas that he was not invited to join them. So when they set off for the hut, Pallas got on the ship. Prior to his arrival at the Hudson, Pallas had never seen a boat more than 25 feet long, much less a ship. But from what he had been told, he imagined it was something propelled by wind, had sails, had masts, and was made of wood. But what he saw was a squat black thing that looked different from what he'd imagined.

Instead, what he saw was a state-of-the-art independent rider. It was dirty and ugly, a coal-driven steamer. It was a "new" ship, put together from cannibalized parts of older ships.

Pallas hated the ship. It was 95-feet long, made largely from iron. There was already a horrible, black smoke belching from its single smokestack Leaning over the gunwale, taking in the harbor of upper Rockaway Bay, he met a member of the crew who couldn't have been more than a few years older than himself.

"I'm a second engineer," the crewmember said in an unsteady, uncertain voice.

"You don't say."

"I do. Well, I was just a crew member until late last night." Aside from the stubble on his chin, he looked like a cherub. "Second engineer died. In his sleep. Upon throwing his carcass over the side, they appointed me his replacement."

"Cause of death?"

"Old age. Plus sun poisoning. He may have been only 40, but he looked like he was over 70. His skin had blotches on it and had the look of old, tanned leather."

"Where I come from, except for the old, who are actually approaching the age of 70, we hardly see the effects of sun poisoning these days."

"He served in the polar regions where the threat from sun poisoning is still dangerous. He served 250 miles from the polar cap for twelve years, with forays to the polar cap itself, where there's no ice for five months of the year. Good pay, early death."

"Good point. And who is the first engineer?"

"You don't want to know him." In only slight caricature, he mimicked the first engineer as a drooling drunkard, staggering uneasily, clutching an imaginary bottle. "He's a heavy boozer."

"And what about the captain? I just got a glimpse of him when I came in."

"He's fine. Pretends to hate everyone, but underneath it all he's true and blue. Tough, stern, courageous, knows his job. Lucky to have him. I'd follow him anywhere."

"And why are we sailing in—what do you call it— 'a coal steamer?'"

The second engineer broke into a wide smile. "Coal abounds! Huge holds of it! Just for the taking! Lying in abandoned coal-tips and slag heaps. Easy to pick up. Left here from the old days. They say there's enough coal to last forever. All you have to do is cart it down to the sea."

"What happened to the Gaia-Domes of New York City? I heard they were once great and formidable!"

"Gone!" The second engineer exclaimed. "All of a sudden! Right up to the last minute, broadcasting messages threatening impending destruction to all possible enemies, real or imagined. Then, now we know, now we know—last gasps, last gasps—then SILENCE! They exited. You don't want to go anywhere near 22 miles inland from a place that was once called Norfolk, or 32 miles inland from a place that was once called St. Augustine—in a place that was once called Florida, some parts of which are now submerged, or have been turned into patches of broad swampland. Eastern seaboard's been consolidated."

Pallas looked like he was impressed, but he was also confused. "I thought we were going to sail? Is this the way to go? Where I come from nobody knows that a contraption called a coal steamer exists. Is it safe?"

The second engineer looked confident. "Of course it's safe."

"This contraption—this *ship?*" Pallas asked. "Does it have an... *engine?*" Pallas didn't want to sound stupid or ignorant. He hoped the question suggested he was knowledgeable and competent in the ways of the world.

Just before the second engineer was ready to reply, something intervened. Suddenly a swarm of midges came out of nowhere and surrounded the deck. The two men were completely inundated. The swarm was thick and impenetrable. For fear of swallowing some of them, Pallas didn't open his mouth. The minute insects became aggressive. But they didn't sting. They formed a coat on Pallas's face and arms. He frantically batted his face with his hands, stirring them up, then in a panic he swung his arms widely in concentric circles. They would form, fly off, then reform. Thirty seconds later, the midges, as if they represented a single organism, as if they were a single entity 150-feet wide and 75-feet thick, rose up, seeming to levitate, and then swept across the sky, looking like a dark, impenetrable cloud.

"What was that?" Pallas screamed, in between hastily drawn gulps of air. He had held his breath for thirty seconds. With palpitations of the heart, Pallas felt possessed, affected by a mild panic attack. "That's the strangest thing I've ever seen in my life!"

"Midges. Sometimes they sting. But where do they come from?" The second engineer shrugged his shoulders. "Search me. Don't know. You're lucky."

"Why am I lucky?" Pallas asked, beginning to calm down, but still in a disturbed frame of mind.

"They didn't sting. They didn't stay too long either. They flew away."

"Where I come from," Pallas said, "flying insects—midges…? They're unheard of."

"They come in waves," the second engineer said. "Arrive in late July, in August." He looked around with a wave of concern. "This is the second largest swarm I've ever seen. My father said they were never seen when he was a child. Only ten years ago, no, five! Five years ago, swarms were less than one-fifth that size. The Gaia-Domes of New York City collapse, and the midges appear en masse for the first time. Funny, isn't it? What were we talking about?"

"Never mind," Pallas said.

The caravan leader and the captain emerged from the hut. The caravan leader waved goodbye at Pallas and shouted to him: "Good luck to you."

The captain went back into the hut. He emerged three hours later. As soon as he came on board the ship he went straight to his cabin and slammed the door behind him. He did not emerge until another day and another night had passed.

A day later, the captain came out. He assembled the crew and they set off. The captain looked independent and strong, badger-like, as if he had been dragged from his bed against his will and had been stuffed into ill-fitting clothes. *You might have respected him, or you might not have respected him, but you certainly feared him. He had a mysterious quality, like an agent of the unknowable.* But by the look of the crew, Pallas believed that they grudgingly respected him.

Taking short, slow steps, the captain came up to Pallas. He eyed him suspiciously.

"I'm not a flogging captain, but I've sailed under some who were. You look like a child. Your billy-goat goatee doesn't fool me at all. How old are you? You're the passenger, right?"

"Yes."

"You're our sole and only passenger, right?"

"Yes."

"On a ship? Ever kept watch before?"

"No," Pallas said.

"Worked as a stevedore?"

"No."

"Worked in a scullery?"

"No."

"Tended the sick and dying?"

"No."

"Ever had the opportunity to fight against pirates?"

"No."

"What good are you to me then?" the captain asked.

"This is the first time I've been on a ship," Pallas said. "Where I come from, we're nearly a thousand miles from the nearest ocean."

"Ever shoveled coal?" the captain asked smiling. "Tended a boiler? You are going to do both. No one is idle on my ship. Because if you don't I'll have you emptying slop buckets and scrubbing the privy."

Without hesitation, Pallas saluted the captain. "Aye, sir! Your command is my pleasure!"

Looking satisfied, slightly amused, the captain turned away from Pallas. But he turned back quickly and issued orders. "Tomorrow morning, you'll begin your first shift. But you're still our passenger. If it pleases me, you'll be my guest at my table. You'll work 12 hours, but only every other day. Between shifts, I might even let you take some meals with me. You're from the New Rebel territory of the great interior, right?"

"Yes I am!"

"Good," the captain replied. He followed that by a rude gesture made with his fingers under his nose. "New Rebels. Superstitious. Dirty. Uneducated. Obsessed with religion. Country I've never been to. No coastal cities near by. With the partial collapse of the Gaia-Domes, especially in the interior, I'm surprised you barbarians haven't made it to both coasts of the continent by now. Why haven't you expanded? My great-grandfather told me that you once ate maggots. He said you used your own excrement to catch the little fellows. Do you still practice that art? You'll teach me a thing or two about your homeland, stuff I don't know. Agreed?"

"I'd be honored to. I'll teach you whatever you wish. Of course. There are at least two dozen things we ate *first*, before we resorted to eating maggots, and one of those includes dirt."

A grin graced the captain's lips. "I've eaten dirt before. I'm not proud. To keep me in good humor will be your job. If you succeed, crew will be thankful. If you don't, I'll have you shoveling coal every day till your hands crack. You'll open the stoker door to the boiler so many times your face will turn a beet red. I'll have you pitching slop buckets on every deck."

"At your service," Pallas said in an earnest voice. "I'm not afraid of work."

"That'll please me. As with everyone else, I reward honesty and diligence."

"Your orders are my command, sir," Pallas said.

Once they had an opportunity to be seated in the captain's cabin in a state of tranquility and privacy, Pallas soon discovered he was able to display his gift for gab. He found the captain a pushover. In his private collection, the captain had several clay jars of sweet wine, from, of all places, Chile, Turkey, and the southern tip of Africa (he'd traveled everywhere). On occasion, the captain would share a taste of his wine with Pallas. Pallas came to acquire a taste for it, especially the wine from Turkey. The thing that the captain liked most about Pallas was his poetry. And this surprised the captain to no end, since he didn't know anything about poetry. But Pallas had such a special gift, it sneaked up and overwhelmed the captain.

Pallas recited a line from a subversive poem. It was from the ancient Greek poet, Pindar. "Oh my soul, do not aspire to immortal life, but exhaust the limits of the possible."

"Now where did you hear that?" the captain asked, astonished. "That's poetry. That's truly amazing. And you learned it in such a primitive place."

"Well, I didn't pick it up from my father, that's for sure. I didn't pick it up from my teachers either, all of them backward and befuddled. I look for poetry wherever I can find it."

The captain shook his head. "'Exhaust the limits of the possible.' Hard to improve on that. I'm sure you're clever, but how did you come to know that?"

"Even the most primitive and isolated people in the world have tiny philosophical treasures bequeathed to them that have been filtered down from the distant past. These jewels are few and hard to come by. A mendicant with five-foot long, stringy braids of hair, practically naked, with his body painted in dried mud and feathers, was passing through Escalante. His visit was an extreme rarity. He didn't stay long. Before he left, he taught me that one."

"Amazing," the captain said.

"Where I come from, most people cannot read, and there is little to read. No women can read. And yet, on this Earth, poetry—I've been told—existed before writing. That is why we know that poetry is bread, and must be shared by everyone, for literates and illiterates alike. Where I come from, we do not recite poetry."

"Why not?"

Pallas clamped his hand hard on his mouth. He pretended to suffocate. After pretending his air supply had been shut off, he relaxed his grip and smiled. "Problem with poetry's content. We can't say just anything we want. Yet I believe in poetry."

"Well," the captain said, shaking his head, "September Snow may be the greatest goddess in all of creation—as your people preached for centuries—but, in your travels, you may learn more things, and greater things, than what your mendicant taught you, I'd imagine."

The captain and Pallas got along famously. After they got to know each other a little, Pallas asked the captain his opinion on a host of questions. As his confidence grew, Pallas drew the captain out. He even asked the captain his opinion on controversial subjects—subjects he wouldn't have dreamed of broaching in the confines of the territories of the New Rebels. One of the first he asked about was the breakdown and collapse of the order of the Gaia-Domes.

The captain leaned back in his chair and smiled. In a ponderous voice, he said, "Well, that's a touchy subject, isn't it? Few people know this, so I'm going to take my time to explain it to you, what I know. There were a few pieces of knowledge from the distant past that were passed on from parent to child. Eventually, indirectly, my great-great-great-grandfather passed this information on to me. He taught those pieces of knowledge to his daughter or son, who in turn taught those things to his daughter or son, so on and so forth. Get my drift? See where I'm headed?"

"I think so," Pallas nodded.

"However, I must exercise caution. I might find myself interjecting something that may interfere with another's—shall we say—sensitivities. *Your* religious sensitivities, for example. There are people in the Gaia-Domes who would torture me, then summarily shoot me, for enunciating the views I'm about to express. And you may not take kindly to the ideas either."

Pallas smiled with genuine warmth. He appreciated the captain's predicament "Fear not. Feel safe to say whatever you wish. This conversation is rare. It is a highly valued breath of fresh air. You need not worry about my religious sensitivities, I'm already *far, far* away from home. I don't think I'm looking through my window anymore. I've stepped through a trap door."

"What?" the captain asked. "Door?" He looked puzzled. He didn't understand. But he continued.

"Right, then. Where to begin? To answer your question now, we must go back to the beginning. I'm talking about 550 years ago. Back then, there were things called nations. These nations collapsed. Communities fragmented under the weight of internal chaos and the increasingly dramatic changes caused by global warming, untenable wars, and economic despair. Some retreated into a survivalist mode, a form of primitive tribalism, without linking themselves to the concentric circles of a wider community. This retreat exposed the helpless. The bulwark that separated those who remained human and those who by necessity turned into savages was removed."

The captain paused.

"The powerful and the wealthy, who successfully convinced us that we no longer possessed the capacity to understand the revealed truths presented to us, or to fight back against the chaos caused by war and devastating environmental collapse, used their resources to create privileged little islands where they could have access to security and goods denied to everyone else. They created Gaia-Domes. As long as those outside the Gaia-Domes were frightened and bewildered, suffering from advanced states of ignorance, fed by the Gaia-Dome's propaganda machine that sent them reeling into forms of near-dementia, they existed in a state of torpor and repression. Do you know why *that* happened?"

Pallas shook his head.

"The point is that at some point the magisters who ran the Gaia-Domes woke up to the fact that they pretty much controlled everything. *Everything that mattered, anyway.* But they had a fatal weakness that revealed itself only centuries later. Complacency. That turned out to be their flaw. They'd been on top too long, unchallenged. They were in a corrupting state of privileged power. They were too used to pushing their weight around without fear of pushback. Even as late as eighty years ago, no adversary touched them. If there was a threat, they simply exterminated it. Their domes were glittering, their helioplanes splendid, their fire-power insurmountable. But the magisters became too set in their ways. In the last fifty years, the only thing the Gaia-Dome armies were good at was serving guard duty. The dogs still had bark, but they'd lost their ability to bite."

The captain paused.

"Remember, Pallas, when the environment collapsed, they were the only ones left who held the remnants of the old culture. Oh, there were a few independent outposts in Greenland, New Zealand, and the Falkland Islands—my great-great-grandfather was from a Falkland island. Once there had been eight and half billion people, some say nine billion! Two hundred and fifty years later, there were less than 300 million. After the environmental collapse, the oceans had risen anywhere from three to six feet. Later, another 14 to 20 feet! One by one, a dozen massive ice sheets fell into the ocean. Most of the coastal regions were flooded. As my father had been, I'm a man of the sea. I've been told that two out of three people in the world once lived within 50 miles of the world's coasts. There was a country that was called Bangladesh—well, over a period of 100 years, half of it sunk beneath the waves. A series of islands in the Pacific Ocean and the Indian Ocean disappeared without a trace."

The captain threw his hands in the air. "Why did our global civilization have to collapse? Was the deadly transition to the Gaia-Domes necessary? I was told that at one time, the last few years before the huge world-wide war commenced...what? What did they call it? Yes. The Eleven-Years-War! They experienced huge extremes in weather swings. They just sat around and watched what they called movies.

Old stuff. Went into the interior. Went into their heads. Made them feel safe? Natural? The really big climate change didn't occur until several decades later. Decades after the end of the Eleven-Years-War. Then there was the loss of the ozone layer."

The captain paused. "A couple of generations ago, the New Rebels were eating dirt and maggots. Now, there are a half a dozen places on the Earth where they are growing grapes and making wine out of its pulp. They put the lovely elixir into clay jars, figured out a way to hermetically seal the lids, and sold the dew to strangers on the other side of the ocean. One hundred and fifty years ago, such a ridiculous thing could not have been dreamed. Fifty years ago, could such a thing have been possible? No. But today, albeit on a small scale, we're doing it. Tomorrow, we'll be trading food across the ocean. The day after tomorrow, we'll be trading precious metals, other things, things I can't imagine."

"Which leads me to one more thing," the captain added, as if struck by a powerful afterthought. "It's a mystery to me why your people never took advantage of your unique situation. If there was any group in the world that was not affected by the rise of the oceans, it was yours. Instead, your people withdrew further into the interior. Instead of reaching out and acquiring better farmland, for example, or opening up the possibilities of long-distance trade, you burrowed your heads in the sand. I don't understand it."

"Our total insulation, our absolute separateness, our immersion into our own high desert, was our salvation," Pallas explained. "That's the one thing that September Snow taught us. A few isolated groups, small groups, could exist here and there. We knew that. But there were thousands of us. We survived the dark times by living in caves, under rock bridges, and under crop overhangs. We survived because we lived where nobody else would live. We took one of the harshest places on Earth and made it work for us. Self-reliance and hard work, they were the two virtues that set the foundation for our future and for our survival."

The captain sighed. "In my opinion, that's about to change.

Because of the dwindling number of Gaia-Domes left, well, their days are numbered. They're doomed."

Although it proved to be one of the smoothest crossings the crew had ever made, Pallas was seasick on several occasions. Even though the weather was clement almost during the entire journey, Pallas did not take to the Eastern Sea. In fact, he didn't like the ocean except when it was in a dead calm, or there was a slight breeze. The captain was surprised to find that Pallas was, nonetheless, extremely competent at shoveling coal, and worked diligently with enthusiasm. The captain offered Pallas a job for the return trip (or any trip), but Pallas respectfully declined.

A representative from the Oggaci was waiting for him when he stepped on the dock at Calais. The young man reminded Pallas very much of his old friend Matthew. However, his dress was strange and foreign-looking. He wore a thick and heavy woolen cloak. The hemline of the cloak came down past the mid-calf of his legs. He wore a large, elegant, blue and gold-colored brooch pinned to his upper-right-hand shoulder. On his head he wore a hat, festive with some plumage, the feathers of a raven. His heavy leather boots, well-formed and sturdy, came up to his mid-calves. His hair was blonde, more light-colored than straw, long in front, covering part of his forehead and falling over his eyes. But the back of his neck was shaved, and the back of his head, right up even with his eyes, was shaved too. He wore an expensive-looking "hoody" made of black and gray fur that made his shoulders look bulkier and more powerful than they actually were. To Pallas, he looked like a sturdy, inner-strengthened, well-traveled fellow, with only a slight whiff of the urbane and the diplomatic.

The stranger smiled silently at Pallas. He did not introduce himself. He just took Pallas's bag, so different from the way in which a New Rebel greeted a co-religionist upon his first arrival.

In a hushed voice, with an absolute minimal exchange of words, Pallas learned that they were going to have to make their way to the Oggaci stronghold, in the northern rim of the Alps, by traveling on foot, but this news pleased Pallas.

When they got on the road and had traveled a short distance, Pallas's guide explained to him that the Gaia-Domes were apparently still active in the Mediterranean, at the western end and the eastern end, but not in the center, and therefore the southern ports were still dangerous. But the forces of the Gaia-Domes had been pushed out of northern Europe, especially north of the Appennini mountains in Italy. In the interior, they had been expelled completely from the former countries of France, Germany, Britain, Spain (except Granada), the Scandinavian countries, the central and northern parts of Portugal, and most of the Balkans, more than a century before. The central and southern parts of Italy had been turned into a neutral zone.

Pallas was anxious to begin his education.

Chapter Ten

TRAMPING ACROSS the windswept plains of northeastern France, and crossing over the borderland into what had formerly been Belgium, the two of them finally emerged into a sparsely wooded region. After walking 50 miles deep into the forest, seeing a delicate spiderweb strung between closely spaced fir trees, glittering with dew, inspired in Pallas a sense of wonder.

Forty miles farther into the same forest, Pallas spotted the most spectacular spiderweb he had ever seen in his life. What a thrill he experienced! Almost three feet in breadth and three feet in length, with silver—and, in places in the light, also *blue*—lustrous threads, the web had a cross-dabbled orange-yellow-mauve leaf lodged in one corner, signifying the advent of autumn. The sheer intricateness of the spiderweb, *and its magnificent size*, caused Pallas's heart to beat faster. If there was anything that pointed to renewal of the health of Gaia, it was this marvelous creation. If only on a spiritual level, the spiderweb filled Pallas with awe, joy, a quivering sense of mystery. Maybe that was the true meaning of Gaia. Not history or disputatious controversies over long-lost acts of goddesses and/or humans—September Snow, Iona, Tom Novak, the Gaia-Domes, the power of the magisters, the knowledge of the special magisters, the awesome glory of the grandmagisters—they were all buried deep, deep in the unreachable past. But rather the sheer exuberance of nature, unblemished by human touch...*the return of Gaia TODAY.*

For several more days they traveled southeast, then they headed due south.

This was a countryside vastly different from what Pallas had been accustomed to back home. But Pallas took this change in weather and terrain as a helpful restorative. The rainfall was plentiful. The water table was high, the soil well-saturated. Even though the planting and harvesting of crops was not as punishingly difficult as it was on the land of the high Colorado plateau, he could see that this land was grossly under populated. This was all the more strange to Pallas because there were only a few, isolated places where he detected any sort of acidification of the soil, the telltale blackened, exposed ground with little vegetation. But even in the places where the soil was excellent and fine, there were few people.

The farmers still lived in crude huts, often in miserable isolation. As a people, they were timid, fearful, and utterly lacking in confidence. A paranoid and xenophobic clamp seemed to descend to constrain the circulatory systems of their hearts and minds. Stricken by the unexpected arrival of strangers and outsiders, the population was repelled, and felt compelled to run and hide. People lived in tiny settlements, and they kept to themselves.

Where people did appear, Pallas noticed that both men and women wore uniformly plain white cloth hats, lacking beaks or face shading. He asked his companion if people in the region always wore such simple headgear. The response given was that the practice had only begun thirty years before. Before that, people were required to wear protective visors to ward off sun poisoning. But sun poisoning was no longer a threat here. It was then explained to Pallas that people in general were resistant to change, but that the new headgear was a change that was embraced with enthusiasm.

As they traveled farther south, they seldom interacted with anybody on the road. But they came upon one intersection that was choked with horse-drawn carts. There Pallas noticed a Gaia sign in the dirt, similar to the Gaia signs popular in his homeland. It consisted of two large bones from a large bird, perhaps a crow or raven, a jaybird or magpie. (If those bones could not be found, then the bones of a gull or mallard would do.) The bones were stretched out from end to end, with feathers hanging down at opposite ends. It was the Universal Sign of Gaia.

"Where I come from, this is a sign to September Snow," Pallas said.

"As it is here!" his guide replied with alacrity. "As it is here, too!"

"They worship September Snow here as well?"

"Yes. She is worshiped everywhere. She traveled all over the world before she saved us, then she was taken away from us."

"We worship her as the supreme goddess," Pallas said with a note of pride.

"We worship her too. Sometimes as a goddess. But we don't ever call her *supreme*."

"No difference, no difference at all," Pallus said in a low-key, non-argumentative voice. "No reason to quibble over petty, small details. The trivial should not rule."

"You're one of the lucky ones, did you know that?"

Pallas was grateful for an opportunity to talk on a matter of substance. "How's that?"

"The New Rebels of the new world have sole claim to having the daughter of September Snow, Iona, as their founder. Do you know how lucky you are? By virtue of that, you are paramount of all the true Gaia groups."

"That may or may not be true," Pallas said in a modest voice, "but we still need to learn from others."

"There are so few of us," Pallas's guide said, bowing deeply. "But we are willing to help."

"What is your name?"

"Excuse me. I am Aeon. We normally engage in a set ceremony before we exchange names. Usually we wait until the seventh or eighth day after an initial meeting. It's an archaic practice, but it is steeped in a time-honored tradition, and we observe it. But you have different customs from us. It's been four days since we've first met. I'll meet you half way."

"I'm Pallas."

"Of course. We know. We were told that you were coming a year ago."

"That long ago?"

"Arrangements had been made in advance. In spite of your extraordinary youth, you are thought of most highly by the people from whence you came."

"What is the ceremony for exchanging names?"

"Oh that!" Aeon said in a friendly way. "We clasp hands—like this—and say to each other, 'Give sorrow its due.' Or we say, 'Give sorrow its words.'" Aeon grasped Pallas's hand at the wrist.

"But we say something similar," Pallas said with enthusiasm. "We say, 'Let us bear down all sorrow.' I think it amounts to the same thing."

Aeon smiled in appreciation. "Yes, indeed, I think it is the same thing. 'Let us bear down all sorrow.' I like the sound of it! Looking at this ravaged planet, it doesn't matter where you live, we have—all of us, everywhere—so much to be sorrowful about. It is as if there has been an accumulation of five centuries of sorrow, a room filled, and yet filled again, with blood."

"As we believe too," Pallas said, nodding, "as we think as well." He paused, looking puzzled. "But why wait seven or eight days before making an exchange? True, you knew my name, but you didn't tell me you did, and you didn't give me your name. Isn't that awkward, or doesn't it create an atmosphere of artificiality? What do you say to the companion you're traveling with, *'Hey you?'*"

Aeon laughed. "We wait to see what the intentions of the stranger are. We wait to see if the stranger tries to kill us before we have time to learn his name. As an act of self-defense, killing a stranger whose name we don't know is easier for us to do than killing a stranger whose name we do know. Without a name, the stranger doesn't exist. That's our custom. People are afraid of strangers. We live in fear. Maybe you do, too. And we stay put. It is not often we have occasion to meet a stranger. Among the Oggaci, I am different. I travel. I'm the exception to the rule. To explain this, of course, is difficult. But I'm trying to explain it to you now, as you are no longer a stranger."

"Is it *that* dangerous to travel in this area?" Pallas asked. "So far, it doesn't seem that horrible."

"Of course, not to worry," Aeon said. Pallas felt a profound sense of confidence in Aeon. He wasn't experiencing even a smallish degree of apprehension or anguish.

"I know the way," Aeon said with certitude.

At one point, after marching deep into the middle of the night, they hastily made camp beside a swift-moving, cold stream. They built a small fire. They kept it lit throughout the night. Pallas fell asleep immediately and slept soundly through most of the night. Then Aeon heard a stirring in the distance. He rose to his feet quickly—so quickly that it startled Pallas from his sleep. Pallas glared up at his companion. Aeon was wielding a large, heavy club, his eyes were bulging out, and his hair was standing on end. It was as if he were anticipating a wave of encroachers to descend on them. "What's the matter?" Pallas whispered.

"Shhh," Aeon said. "I heard something," He placed his fingers to his lips.

"This forest is frightening," Pallas said in protest, huddling in his blanket against the cold. "Where I come from, it's harder to sneak up on someone because we are not surrounded by so many trees. How can you see *anything* in this impenetrable forest?"

Aeon chuckled. He loosened the grip on his club. From the light of the fire, Pallas could see the muscles in Aeon's arms relax. Aeon sat down on a green, mossy wooden bough. He smiled. "A friend of mine was attacked in this neck of the forest years ago. Everything's fine. I'm just a little jumpy. People never enter this dense forest, especially at night. If anything, we are more likely to be attacked by a pack of hungry wolves than by a band of brigands. Go back to sleep. I'll keep watch for the rest of the night. Dawn will be breaking soon."

But Pallas couldn't get back to sleep. Instead of being comforted by Aeon's words, the word "wolves" set off a panic button in his head.

Pallas lay on the ground. Disturbing thoughts and trenchant images flooded his mind. These images raced to and fro in a compressed jumble of impressions. Pallas thought back to the time of his childhood. Images of confrontations with wild animals flitted into his consciousness. As hard as he tried, Pallas was unable to suppress them. His first image had occurred when he had been barely six years old. They were not about wolves, but their cousins, coyotes. Oh, the memory, the *suppressed animus...*

One time in his early childhood, because Pallas had not washed the wooden soup bowls and wooden spoons immediately after a family meal, his father yanked him up by the arm so aggressively it nearly dislocated Pallas's shoulder. His father dragged him like a rag doll to his bedroom. He beat him with a strap. Aside from a casual swipe here, or an unusual slap there, it was Pallas's first savage beating at his father's hands. Being a vulnerable and unprotected child, Pallas now felt the strange contradiction of having done something wrong, but also of having been treated unjustly and unfairly—harboring both the sin and the dispensation of the sin simultaneously in a confused jumble.

"But what have I done, Father?" Pallas pleaded as he was being beaten. "I was going to wash the bowls. I promised. I promised. What am I doing wrong?" He received no reply.

His father raised his hand to the roof, in prayer, but then, brought it down in wrath. He gave his son a serious kick. "What have you done? You're born. That's enough. Find your nesting spot, you spod. (The word spod, in Cundi, was slang for a poor spawn.) Go to sleep."

Unable to resolve this contradiction, Pallas, just six years old, was unable to sleep. He tossed and turned. He finally gave up trying to sleep. He sneaked out of the house, taking a night-walk. It was late at night, the dead of night, three hours before the sun would rise. He walked with steely intent, direction, earnestness—yet paradoxically he also walked in a kind of a daze. Before he knew it, he had walked two miles, so far from the edge of town that the tiny circle of haze given off by the few public torches and candles still burning at that hour emitted no light. *He had of course not done this before.* He had been in such a state of anguish and discombobulation that he had not thought to bring a light with him and was just barely able to see by the light of the stars and a half moon. Then, as he stood in a small clearing, the moon dipped down to the lip of the horizon, and in two minutes flat, as he watched in a combination of wonderment and foreboding, it sank below the dark outline of trees, disappearing. Then suddenly, with the partial moon gone, there was even greater darkness. Pallas stopped. He took ten steps forward, and as he did, his ears were assaulted by a din. He figured out the cause of the uproar immediately.

It was the sound of coyotes: braying, yelping, howling, sometimes in unison, sometimes in a cacophony of disunity, a bloodcurdling audio equivalent of uncontrollable rage. Judging by the sound alone, Pallas presumed that there were several coyotes in the group. But how far away were they? As close as 150 feet, or maybe as far as 175 yards. There were five or six coyotes, or perhaps as many as nine or ten. (Coyotes were known to amplify their voices to make their numbers seem larger than they were.) The noise was coming from below. Pallas reached out, which was the only thing that kept him from slamming into a chest-high over-crop of rocks directly in front of him, forming a ledge. It was dark, he couldn't see. He realized the coyotes must have detected him not by sight, but by smell.

There were tiny drops of blood trickling down his back and crotch, from his father's beating. Could they have smelled it? Within four seconds, five seconds, six seconds at most, the noise grew more deafening, more sinister, louder, but he wasn't sure. The darkness was playing tricks, causing audio distortions. How could Pallas—so young, inexperienced, and naive—enveloped by a blanket of almost total darkness, judge distances by *sound*?

Either the coyotes were screaming and yipping at a higher pitch, or they were moving, circling. Fortunately they had to climb, not descend, giving Pallas a little breathing room. Pallas couldn't tell which it was, but he feared the latter. He was alone. He was six-years-old. He had no light. He had no weapon, not even a stick. It was absolutely dark. *It was the coyotes' world he had thoughtlessly encroached upon.* There were only two choices: fight or flight.

Pallas turned abruptly and ran.

Aside from the elders' warnings and remonstrations, he didn't know yet from his own experiences that the safety of the human world radiated only short distances out from the town, then nature took over. But he had learned the lesson now. He ran. Within twenty seconds he gained traction on a stretch of gravel, causing him to rejoice that he might be opening a distance between himself and his pursuers. But after he had covered 250 yards, and miraculously kept himself from tripping or stumbling, the screeching, yelping, howling, yipping abruptly stopped. It didn't taper off, it just stopped.

Encrusted with fear, Pallas's heart beat fiercely. But he thought the danger was past. He knew he was no longer being pursued, he just *knew* it.

The very young of the New Rebels grew up fast. Pallas's instincts knew what his mind refused to admit. His body shook. Terrors were alive in him, of a devouring. There was not only the sheer panic from the assault alone. He imagined his flesh being torn to pieces, but there was also the ultimate humiliation of being eaten and being passed out as coyote excrement. The New Rebels knew *shame*, that's why they were fiercely devoted to the sanctity of burying their dead, specifically to prevent disinterment by animals. These were the hobgoblins that stirred in Pallas's mind, but they finally passed. The wild animals had departed.

Forty minutes later, at a quick walking pace, Pallas returned home. His adrenalin was so pumped up that at reaching his "nesting spot"—a thin wad of discarded wool and a jumble of soiled cotton clumps in the corner in the dark, next to the place where his father kept a corn crib and hung tobacco leaves for drying—he couldn't get back to sleep. Listening to his own breathing slowing, his own confused and irritated sighs, it hit him like a sledgehammer. To have been called a *spod* by his own father, Pallas thought, that was the lowest. HIS OWN SON?

Pallas slept where the family's pet dog used to sleep before she died from a bloody bowel eruption. Pallas's father had named the dog Ugly, thinking that a watch dog named Ugly would be better at its job. But better than what? Better than Ferocious? Better than Fighter? Pallas wouldn't be given a proper sleeping arrangement until his twelfth birthday. To be sure, children of Escalante slept on floors, on stairs, on landings, that was normal. But sleeping on a cold, dusty storage floor, that was only common for the children of the poorest families.

Pallas didn't tell his father what had transpired on his night-walk for the simple reason that he feared he'd be beaten again. He didn't tell his mother for fear that he'd not be seen as a "man." But, the very next day, he told his friend Matthew. He showed Matthew the wounds from the punishment his father had inflicted on him.

Matthew reached out to Pallas. He gave him support. Matthew told him that the next time his father beat him, he could come and stay with him. Matthew promised he'd protect him. Although only three years older than Pallas, Matthew was strong and courageous, and Pallas knew that *he meant what he said, and he would keep his word, and he was a true friend!*

Pallas's mind returned to the forest in Europe, where he presently lay. That was his first memory of animal threats. Pallas remembered that only ten months before some half-starved coyotes attacked a three-and-a-half year old boy, who'd been left unattended, dragging, mauling, ripping him apart.

But wolves, even a lone wolf, were more dangerous than a pack of coyotes. Back home, coyotes ruled the high desert. Wolves, however, were only found in the mountains above 7,000 feet, roaming all the way up past the timber line. With the exception of bears and mountain lions, timber wolves were the supreme beasts when it came to threats to humankind.

Pallas's second memory of the attacking wolf was even more powerful.

As he lay on the ground in the forest in Europe, his thoughts raced back to the second incident. As he thought, this different set of disturbing images overtook him. At that time, he had been twelve years old. The images were so powerful, Pallas felt as if they telegraphed events that had just occurred. He had been working as an assistant to a shepherd who was only twelve years his senior. Oh, this memory was so much more bleak he had suppressed it, but now it came surging back, as if the floodgates of his imagination had been forced open. Pallas didn't want to remember the phantasmagoria of disturbing images, but he couldn't stop them from replaying in his mind. *Over and over again they played.*

Pallas had to tell Aeon what happened. He had to relate the story to Aeon. He rose from the ground, blurting out the beginnings of the story, the narrative just gushing out.

Aeon grabbed Pallas's shoulder, patting his back, saying in comforting words, "Go on, Pallas. Tell me now. Take your time. Easy now. Easy does it. Tell me the story. Tell me all of it."

The shepherd and Pallas had ascended with the flock to 8,500 feet. A sudden storm had come in and forced them to spend the night near the exposed mountaintop. Just after the break of dawn, a lone wolf attacked. Pallas, with almost all of the flock, was halfway down the hill, and the shepherd was still on the mountain crest, recovering three stray sheep. As Pallas ran up the hill to help the shepherd, the shepherd waved him off. "Protect the flock! Take these three with you. *I'll send them down. No problem. They've already smelled danger. I'll hold him off!*"

With resolve, in a rush of adrenaline, Pallas ignored his orders. He bolted past the sheep who were descending fast in the opposite direction, their eyes wild with panic (they may have been independent-minded strays once, but like rebels everywhere, any imminent signs of danger caused them to want to return desperately to the protection and safety of the larger group).

Without thought, on automatic pilot, Pallas was ready to enact the role of hero. But the shepherd fiercely waved him off. He heard the shepherd scream: "Stand down. I command. Take'im back. Save the flock. Flock's your mission. Obey my orders!!"

Upon his superior's command, Pallas turned. Sulking, he skulked down the hill, corralling the three formerly strayed sheep, jumping seven feet down into a deep ravine, in the side of the hill, where they cowered. He remembered the importance of always following orders.

But the shepherd didn't survive the attack. When a day later Pallas led a search party back up the hill, all they found was the body of the shepherd with his bowels ripped open and his face mauled. He was missing an eye, his nose was gone. His hands were crushed (consumed?), wrists nibbled to nubs. There were brown-colored blood-clots, looking like liver spots, on the skin of his arms. Lying on the grass were slivers of undigested shredded bone matter, his former fingers?

And what did Pallas remember about the self-sacrificing and altruistic shepherd, a man who was only 24 years old? Pallas remembered that he had been a deep and profound believer in Gaia, that he had been a fierce devotee to the cult of Iona, that he had no education, that he was functionally illiterate, that he had to use an x when he was directed to sign his name, that he was a man of severe, piously held religious beliefs. And when Pallas thought of the power of Gaia as a religious belief, especially in the ennobling light of the sacrifice, he found himself only then able to get back to sleep. Oh, the superstitious aspects of Gaia still had a powerful grip on Pallas, in spite of his conceited sense of intellectual pride, in spite of his sense of entitlement to mental dexterity and cerebral acuity. Only when he thought of the power of the great sacrifice that the young shepherd had made, and what that great sacrifice symbolized, was Pallas able to sleep. *And also, only after he told the story to Aeon.*

After hearing Pallas's story, Aeon nodded. "We know the forest. We hunt in it. The most powerful stories are about wolves. My grandfather taught me that wolves are the only predators who'll kill for the sheer joy of it. They eat their prey while the animal is still alive. They've been known to chew fetuses out of cows. If you fear for something, Pallas, talk." Aeon smiled. "Talk to me. Talk always keeps us human. If you are unable to sleep, do that. *I'll watch your back. I'll stand guard over you as you talk.*"

Only after being able to relate the lone wolf attack story that occurred six years before, on the lonely mountain on the Colorado plateau, to Aeon, did Pallas manage to get back to sleep.

But Pallas had to remind himself, that the replaying of his past experiences occurred too often, and that they were *too often* more vivid than the present. He had to ask himself, "am I now a different person, unable to entirely reinhabit the past, unable to step into the same river twice?"

Aeon and Pallas continued on their trek. They followed a circuitous route that took them closer to their destination. They continued to travel 50 miles east, then another 100 miles south. At that point, they changed direction and headed back west. They hugged the edge of the mountains which represented the boundary of the Alps.

Finally they made it to the settlement of the Oggaci, located next to a large alpine lake.

Chapter Eleven

PALLAS WAS GREETED by Chief Mantou. He was built like a tree, tall and broad. He had a whitish beard, peppered with gray, bushy, twenty-two inches long. However, unlike the other male Oggaci, including Aeon, who shaved the back of their necks *and* the back of their heads, Mantou's entire head was shaven clean. He had a broad and strangely sympathetic face, and powerful arms with golden bracelets and silver amulets clasped around his enormous biceps. His entire body, including his shaved head, was tattooed—the bonus of having boxes of stories—stories painted in black, purplish-pink, lavender, magenta. When Mantou smiled (especially when he smiled), he looked tough and cruel, an impression he cultivated, just in case he had to face down a determinedly murderous adversary.

Some of the tattoos were elaborate and poignant. The tattoos were not just decorative, they told stories—some moving and bizarre. Mantou was like a walking picture book. Even on his head there were little boxes of stories, displaying odd things, myths of Gaia.

When Mantou turned, there was displayed on his back a portrait of September Snow. September's arms were extended, giving a blessing. Tongues of fire were flitting about her head. It looked like there were beams of light shooting from September's eyes—to strike the viewer.

Portrait of a goddess? Pallas hadn't seen one so colorful before.

As Mantou addressed Pallas, he was smiling. He appeared to be quite proud of the body art. Pallas wondered if there were other stories or portraits that lay veiled beneath the sweep of Mantou's beard. If his chest, stomach, and upper abdomen were laid bare, what would be revealed? Eruptions of devastating wars? Sweeps of disease? Collapse of the ozone layer? Five-to-seven degree Fahrenheit rises in temperature? Rise of Gaia-Domes? Accounts of Iona's feats? *What a specimen!*

Pallas believed that Mantou must have been between 45 to 50 years old—that old-young look. He guessed that men, even those twenty years younger than he, could not match Mantou's strength. It didn't take powers of deduction for Pallas to know that the chief was an important warrior, undoubtedly highly esteemed, not just by his family and clan, but by the entire tribe.

After a ritual-filled introduction, an elaborate drinking ceremony that involved carved ram's horns as drinking cups and a fierce interplay of back-slapping (the chieftain even once pinched Pallas's cheek in an affectionate, avuncular sort of way), Mantou seemed to become mesmerized by Pallas's ghostly, milky-white, pin-pupil eyes.

Displaying an utter lack of decency *or* diplomacy, Mantou put the question indelicately to Pallas: "Legend has it that you New Rebels were born of monkeys in the wombs of demons."

Pallas gasped, then laughed. Could evidence of such mind-boggling ignorance be the cause of insult? It wasn't his skin color, his hair, the shape of his skull; no, it wasn't those attributes, the demon bit was PALLAS'S EYES!

"Pesky sun-poisoning could have passed to me from the genes of my great-great-great-great-great-grandparents," Pallas said. "Some of my people think that, from a genetic point of view, our family has been lucky!"

Pallas paused. "Thinking on the subject, if you live permanently in the forest you may not be affected too adversely by sun poisoning. If your ancestors before you lived in the forest, your genetic inheritance may also be free from a large amount of damage."

Mantou seemed placated by Pallas's explanation. "You are welcome here. An interchange of cousins across the big waters is a good thing." Mantou could not have come up with the last statement on his own. Pallas assumed Aeon had planted the words in the obstinate man's head.

Aeon capped the meeting with a display of bonhomie. "The dark days that followed the dawn of Gaia have been difficult. We have all been hardened. As our brothers from across the sea have asserted, we proclaim it ourselves: *Let us bear down sorrows, we are brothers, we are brothers always, we are brothers forever, let us bear down sorrows.*"

"Amen," Pallas said, nodding. "Give sorrow its due. Give sorrow its words. But life is so much better now."

Aeon took Pallas to a hut. "This is where you'll be staying from here on out."

Simple and austere, with a Spartan mat for sleeping, a simple planked floor, a tiny table and chair, puny windows glazed over and not allowing much light to enter, it was a hut ascetic but commodious enough, not too different from the huts Pallas had known back home. Pallas felt relieved and happy at seeing his living arrangements. From Pallas's perspective, to have privacy, to have a place of his own, even if it were a small hut, was a privilege and a luxury.

In a conspiratorial way, Aeon took Pallas aside and whispered, "We have our brawlers and bullies here too, just like I'm sure you have back home. But, in all honesty, without them we would not have survived the long, black nights of the dark centuries. Some of them, mind you, had been mean-spirited, dangerous, hard to control. However, Mantou is different. In spite of his savage veneer, and his seemingly simple-minded manner, he is a gentle giant. He would never harm anybody. We are certain of this. We love him dearly."

"But what if he were confronted with a savage, neighboring, attacking tribe?"

"That's different, of course, he'd massacre them all," Aeon said in a matter-of-fact voice.

"I see," Pallas said, unable to hide his disappointment.

"Something is troubling you?" Aeon asked.

"I thought you people were different. I thought that an alphabet, a written language, learning and scholarship, would signify that you, as a people, didn't have to live in a state of mortal danger, that you were well protected."

"We are," Aeon said. "But we're a simple people. The level of danger is not so great to be sure, but it is ever-present. Would you like to see the reason why, over the generations and most difficult years, we were able to preserve an alphabet, a written language, and some of the learning and scholarship from the past?"

"Yes," Pallas said, "to know the reason why you're so different! That would be great to know. I am here to learn as much as I can. I'm privileged to know anything you have to offer."

"Well, let's go, I'll show you," Aeon said. "In the morning, I'll take you to see one of our most hallowed spots." Aeon thought for a moment and added, "The sharing of knowledge is important. You might not know which roots to dig up during a famine, but if your Grandma does, her childhood memories may save an entire village when hard times strike. Remember. This is important. We're a simple people."

Pallas slept well that night, even though he was in a new environment. Later, he wondered why. It was because he was free from the fear of someone shaking him out of a slumber in the middle of the night and senselessly beating him.

Aeon came in early in the morning to pick Pallas up.

Two miles from the strongly fortified, fenced-in settlement that Pallas guessed had a population of about 1,200 people, they came upon a huge, broad bog. On the edge of the soggy, unstable ground, even without stepping into it, Pallas knew that it was a scary place. Looking into the bog, with fog rising up from the surface,

Pallas estimated that 95 percent of the bog's surface was very shallow water.

Aeon said: "Thousands died, cannibals, mutants, thieves, brigands, over the past 500 years. They died trying to cross this bog to get to the island in the middle. During the worst years of chaos and destruction, when the threats from the outside were great, this island was our sanctuary. This was where our tribe hid. It's also where—in strong, waterproof leather pouches—we hid documents from pre-Gaia times, documents that provided us with the rudiments for learning a sophisticated written language, the twenty-six point alphabet of the Latinate."

Pallas was enthralled with what Aeon was saying.

"Come, I'll show you the island," Aeon said. "Do not stray from the path I delineate. Not even so much as a foot. This is a dangerous place. Follow me."

Aeon led the way. Pallas followed, step by step. They threaded their way through the thickets of grass, reeds, and weeds. If Pallas diverted from the path, even just a few inches, he found himself sinking, foot by foot, into a quicksand-like ooze. If Aeon had not been there to step back and pull him out, Pallas would have sunk, perhaps stuck forever. Pallas knew there would have been no way to extract himself under his own power. There was nothing to grab on to, to give him leverage, except for Aeon's arms.

As they penetrated farther into the bog, surrounding them were places where there were remnants of skulls and bones, half-exposed, half-sunk, where hapless travelers from the past, not knowing the way, must have sunk into an abyss, unable to free themselves. There were places where Aeon and Pallas had to jump three feet of open water to get to the next piece of solid ground.

In one place, they had to get a running start and jump a four-foot broad stretch of open water.

After they made the jump, Aeon turned to Pallas and said, laughing "This is the spot where few encroachers are able to exploit. The water's only three-feet deep, but the mud, deep below, is incredibly porous. If you're caught, you'll sink to your waist. During the rainy season, and at least for six months after the rainy season ends, there's no escaping this bog. There are probably over 500 bodies lying in this bog alone. If you consider all of the bog's area, on all sides, one can only speculate, but there are probably countless thousands of bodies buried." Even Aeon's long-term familiarity with the stretch of bog did not stop him from feeling a sense of awe. "This is the moat that nature had bestowed upon us."

Aeon showed Pallas the island. It wasn't very large, barely comprising three acres. There was a fortification located at the highest point. Aeon gave Pallas a tour of the first primitive fort, built in 86 A.G., with its base of wooden spikes arranged in a rectangular fashion sticking out below the single parapet that protected the elevated stronghold. He then showed Pallas the more elaborate fortress that replaced the old fort 100 years later, located just 200 feet below the island's heights. It was windowless and had walls seven feet high. The Oggaci returned to the mainland when conditions improved and became safer, in 488 A.G.

After that, the Oggaci renamed the fortress "the nut," where they stored nuts, multiple types, but mostly walnuts. (The Oggaci had been great harvesters of walnuts, just as the New Rebels had been, over the centuries, enthusiastic harvesters of pinon nuts.) On occasion they stored fruits as well. They also stockpiled auxiliary military arms in the nut. Aeon showed Pallas the small room where the written documents, the written alphabet, and the written narratives had been archived for 500 years. Arranged along the walls of the dimly-lit room were creaky, dusty bookshelves, some of which were in need of repair, some of which had completely fallen apart.

"Without this legacy from the past, which we've protected with our lives, we'd be dirt," Aeon said.

"Now, understand this, Pallas, I'm busy," Aeon continued. "I have pressing duties. I have absorbing responsibilities. I've only recently been named to the council. For that reason, and for other reasons, I won't be able to spend any time with you as you learn the alphabet, as you master the old written language, or as you explore our many, many books. We've assigned several scholars to help you in that endeavor. There's one scholar I know you're going to like in particular. Of course, there'll be plenty of time and opportunity for us to get together, to see each other, to attend special dinners. To be sure, we'll stay in touch, but I won't be there for your studies. Maybe I'll be able to escort you out to the island a few more times, but then you'll be on your own. Understand?"

"Of course," Pallas replied.

Chapter Twelve

BY THE CLOSE OF THE second winter at the Oggaci settlement, Pallas's skin became slightly paler, but he was still much darker-skinned compared to his hosts. No amount of absence of sunlight was going to change that, *that was the natural shade of Pallas's skin.* But Pallas wore his hair in the manner of the Oggaci, and he dressed exactly like them. He managed to fit in well among his new brethren, even though no one else possessed the look of milky-white, seemingly pupil-less, "blemished" eyes.

Within the first six months of his stay, Pallas learned five things about the Oggaci. They practiced better dentistry than the New Rebels—their tools were only slightly more sophisticated, but their techniques were far superior. They took better care of their horses than the New Rebels ever did. The imbibing of alcohol among the Oggaci was accepted and more tolerated than with the New Rebels, but the Oggaci exercised greater self-restraint in drinking. They used copious amounts of garlic in their cooking, encouraging better health and discouraging the spread of dysentery. Most importantly, the younger women of the Oggaci had an almost pathologically intense fear of foreign men.

Over the last point, Pallas didn't seem to care as much as he could have. He was still profoundly in love with his childhood sweetheart, Telia. Also, his studies were the most vital and most important aspect of his life.

Pallas excelled in the pursuit of learning. He had a complete grasp of the alphabet after two weeks. His reading skills were perfected within six months. Moreover, after almost eight years of 12 to14 hours of disciplined study per day, Pallas never took a break from his studies except to observe Oggaci religious holidays, his skills grew to where he was reading brilliantly, writing fluently, and eventually those writing skills became increasingly sophisticated.

Only a tiny fraction of the Oggaci population had learned to read. A smaller number had learned to write. The Oggaci saw their mission as being the protectors of the old written Latinate alphabet of 26 letters. Fundamentally, the Oggaci were mere preservationists.

Pallas's reputation for writing spread. People spoke of him with awe, and thought of him as more of a bookish freak than a foreigner. His skin tone didn't seem to matter much, but they spoke fervently about his exotic eyes. Maybe his reputation had something to do with him having come from a far-away place, where Iona had actually lived! To be the sole representative of the New Rebels, the community that Iona had founded!!

The curious traveled distances just to catch a glimpse of the boy wonder.

Pallas had accomplished this feat of brilliance and erudition by the age of 26.

By the age of 29, Pallas was rated as the best overall prose writer among the Oggaci, superior to all but their greatest epic poet, Ulm. Ulm, of course, had been a genius. He wrote his revered and renowned poetry when he was quite young, a boy of 16 when he started, completing his collection of poetry when he died at the age of 21. But Pallas was seen as far outstripping the Oggaci's greatest prose writer, Ingeline.

So for the Oggaci, their hoarded documents showed a picture of what life was like before the Gaia-Domes. But as valuable as that was, the information was limited. The more recent documents, added by the tiny number of Oggaci scholars, dealt with issues of survival, but none with romance, history, or legend (except for Ulm's poetry).

There were no documents, not one that dealt with the beginnings of Gaia, none that covered the critical period from 2045 to 2070 A.D., (or -6 to 19 A.G.) except for five that had been taken from the Gaia-Domes and were considered tainted and factually deviant. There were no documents from the period extending from year Gaia 1 to year Gaia 313, at which time there emerged the first survival chronicles by Ingeline.

One year after beginning his studies, Pallas dragged Aeon out and interrogated him as to how they had saved so many books from deterioration. He thought that it was a miracle that so many books had not been destroyed by mildew or just spoilage from routine exposure to air and moisture. He had noticed that some of the books were written on mediocre paper. The paper in those instances had yellowed, even browned, but though the pages had curled and cracked they were still, more or less, intact and readable. Amazingly, some of the books had colored pictures inside. They too had been preserved, although some of the color photographs were tinged with yellow, or had faded beige.

"Many of the books we allow you to use we've preserved in pouches almost all their lives," Aeon explained. "We only bring them out for brief intervals, for a week, once every 70 or 100 years."

More and more, Pallas realized that the preservation of the books had less to do with their intrinsic value and more to do with the fact that their preservation was for the Oggaci something bordering on a mystical cult, a sort of book fetish.

Aeon continued. "Of the few books from the past that had greater use we made copies and kept the originals in their pouches. But we've lost some of the work in our collection over the years. Some you are able to read only because no one has looked at them for one or two generations. It's like a bone yard."

"Why do you let me read them any time I want?" Pallas asked. "Why do you give me access to your entire collection—privileges you don't give to others. Not even to the elders."

"You're our guest," Aeon explained. "Enjoy!" He lowered his

voice. He took Pallas aside. "Truthfully, maybe you'll do something with the knowledge that we can't dream of doing. That's the true glory of your being an outsider. This is our way of celebrating your being with us."

This made Pallas think that he had to work more diligently at his studies. From that point on, he never took his privileges for granted.

The Oggaci had become so proud of Pallas that they made a copy of their alphabet, handcrafted, written on brilliant parchment paper. But that didn't take long to produce, it consisted of only one page. They also made copies of their most revered post-Gaia narratives, the poetry of Ulm and the prose of Ingeline, also handcrafted, the lettering treated with the greatest care, the product of four years of labor by their most renowned scribe, and gave them to him.

Pallas accepted the documents with pride and honor. But who was going to write the document that was going to cover the missing 324 years?

People thought that Pallas had acquired a certain magical charm. He knew now what must be done. Among the six "scholars," grandiose term for readers, all of them elderly, Pallas's favorite was Cacttus. He was old, reputedly 80. He had dark, ringlet eyes, and tuffs of hair growing from his ear orifices. Pallas called him "the raccoon," partly because of his looks, partly because he could ferret out the most preposterously obscure works. (Pallas found some books undecipherable, the pictures "explained" more than did the text.) In spite of Cacttus's clownish looks, and irreverent way of looking at the world, he had a deep and penetrating mind. He shared with Pallas an archival treasure trove of books from the 1920s to the early 2040s.

The first one Cacttus showed Pallas was a copy of "Baedeker's Travel Guide to England, Scotland, and Wales." It had supposedly been used by Adolf Hitler to choose the Luftwaffe's bombing sites during World War II. "Can't vouchsafe *this particular copy* touched Hitler's evil, desperate hands," Cacttus said dryly. "But he used Baedeker to pick British bombing sites, we know that for a fact. This copy is dated 1935. Book must've been like the one Hitler used.

Maybe so? Maybe not? We keep it as a keepsake. Tiny bits of history—funny bits of history."

The second book Cacttus showed Pallas was called "The Acolyte of St. Justin's." It was a novel that had nothing to do with religion, but rather with the son of a provincial financial family in what was called the "Eastern Establishment," centered in and around New York City in 1942. The main character, a boy, attended an exclusive private school (named St. Justin's, of course) which was connected to an obscure protestant religious sect, whose only goal Pallas could fathom was to teach these non-ardent, bored students how to achieve business success later in life. Cacttus said, "As you see, writing 650 years ago, as compared to just 540 years ago, was all over the map."

Cacttus also showed Pallas a third book which included a photograph of a row of cans.

"What's that?" Pallas's asked. "I've seen tin cans before. In the ruins. That's art?"

"That's Andy Warhol."

Intermittently, Pallas shared with Cacttus his study of what he called "The Narcissistic Eras." Cacttus believed these periods could have been broken down into three parts: Narcissistic Period One (1962 to 1982), Narcissistic and Self-Inflationary Period Two (1994 to 2019), Narcissistic, Self-Inflationary, and Voyeuristic Period Three (beginning in 2027, but cut short by the outbreak of the Eleven-Years-War).

Cacttus also taught Pallas how to find material written by shockingly open religious agnostics and atheists from the last three decades of the Twentieth Century, and from the first three decades of the Twenty-First. Pallas feared Naxos would have been upset had he known that aside from Cacttus and the five "scholars," Pallas had to teach himself. One exception was the Encyclopedia Britannia—published first in 1769, followed by 244 consecutive years of periodical republishing. A last print copy was reputed to have been published in 2010 A.D., later updates were kept almost exclusively in electronic memory banks—*all lost!!* The Oggaci's archives held two volumes of this 16 volume set, published in 2004, and rescued 98 years later. Volume 1 covered letters A and B, and Volume 14 covered P, Q, and part of R. Both volumes suffered severe water damage, suggesting what fate befell the other 14 volumes.

From this Pallas was able to put together a picture of Aristotle, Francis Bacon, Plato, and Jean-Jacque Rousseau. Pallas found these historical personages edifying and educational, but also, paradoxically, conundrum-like: minds the products of such bafflingly incomprehensible times.

The Oggaci provided an alphabet and documents to read, but other than that, they were just as primitive as the New Rebels, hardly a loadstone for advanced education. Most of the books Cacttus showed Pallas were trite, or filled with trivia.

Cacttus grew suddenly super-serious. "Study this time. Get to the problem underlying the symptoms. There was one particularly singular event that occurred one hundred years prior to the time September Snow and Tom met. It was the greatest of all the events prior to that meeting."

"What? The greatest of all the events?" Pallas asked. "What was that?"

"You must understand the context. The world was torn between two camps—two military, economic, and political camps. In one camp were the Russians, alongside their satellites. They launched Sputnik. By this act, there was fear in the West that the Russian Communists might win the Cold War, win the Arms Race, both conventional and nuclear, because of the Russian's reputation for advancing science, especially their progress in space science and technology."

"So what happened to assuage their adversaries' fear?" Pallas asked.

"Color."

"What?"

"Color. TV. It was introduced in America in 1963 with the first screening of a TV show called Bonanza. When Americans on main street watched that color TV set in TV shop windows for the first time, they knew instinctively that they had a fighting chance, indeed, a better than fighter chance, of finally prevailing in the Cold War, of beating the Russians. Ordinary folks slept better, more restful, in their beds. Underground fall-out shelters were looked upon as less necessary, less *de rigueur*. Many people knew in their gut that Communism was going to be defeated, it was only a waiting game, only a matter of time. America—indeed, the West in general—would finally win out."

"That happened with color TV?" Pallas asked. "That happened with the *technology* of color TV?"

"More or less," Cacttus replied, smiling.

"That simple?"

"Yes. It was always the technology, 650 years ago, 550 years ago, 450 years ago, 400 years ago, even 250 years ago, that meant that some social order was superior to another social order. At least that's the lesson the books from the past taught me."

"Color TV?"

"When Americans saw that color TV, it was like an icon from the darkest days of the Middle Ages. They knew they would be king, one hundred years into the future. Like some RFID dial, 50 years into the future after the color TV, that TV radiated the imagination!"

"But all that unquestioning faith in technology ended up resulting in the ascendancy of the Gaia-Domes?!" Pallas sputtered, half in the form of question, half as tentative statement.

"Yes," Cacttus said. "It was the *faith*—quite literally—of an unspoken form of religion. The endgame of hardened technology, unfettered by loftier values, unmitigated by normative inhibition, unchallenged by intuition, untested by instinct—that was the Gaia-Domes. They had to have gotten started somehow, hadn't they? They didn't just shoot up overnight, like a spreading bed of mushrooms. Well, that, as it were, is a tentative theory of mine."

"If you say so," Pallas said, gritting his shining teeth.

Pallas completed ten years of study. Book-wise, he learned everything there was to learn. He told Aeon that the idea of returning home earlier than he'd planned appealed to him.

"I knew this day would come," Aeon said. "I've anticipated it. Naxos made it clear from the start you were to stay twelve years and not longer, baring an emergency. I anticipated it. A boat can be easily arranged. You can return home any time you wish. It doesn't matter to us what you decide to do with your last year here. However, we could go on a special trip to Skellig Michael, and the other Skellig, in the northern sea, beyond the distant islands."

"A trip by land?" Pallas objected. "Or, allow me to understand, a real sea voyage?"

Aeon corrected himself. "It will be a longer trip by land. Then a shorter trip by sea."

The idea of traveling by sea gave Pallas the willies. He didn't like traveling by sea.

Strangely, Pallas had not thought much about returning home during the previous three years. He had become so acclimated to living with the Oggaci, experiencing homesickness at first, home was all he thought about when he first arrived. But the idea of returning home suddenly sprang upon him. It had been such a long time. The winters were so long among the Oggaci in the foothills of the northern Alps, winter seemed to last from early October to late May. Aside from a month of autumn, and a month of spring, in between, it was only during the three short months of summer that Aeon's face and skin turned red in the sun, his hair "dingy"—for a short while—but otherwise, it was a clime that was cold, dark, and in winter, icy white. And yet Pallas's skin stayed dark. (For him, it was a metaphor that he could never turn into something totally different from what he was.) Only on rare occasions, when he caught himself staring into his reflection in a pool of water, or caught a glimmer of himself in a mirror, did he remember how much he had forgotten. The person who looked back at him seemed so strange. Pallas thought about Telia at these times, and how much, over the years, he had missed her. He was not ashamed that he didn't think too much about his family, and he felt no homesickness for Escalante. Naxos? He could have waited another ten years to see Naxos. And the same held true with regards to the other members of the Obsidian Order. At 29 years old, Pallas had matured beyond the need to impress others. He had no need to show off to his teachers his "awe-inspiring, sweeping" command of an alphabet, and a brand-new written language. Fantasies, which had been the cornerstone for his sense of injured self-worth and pride, of coming back home to the primitive New Rebels with his new-found language—to show off!—and his wisdom and power of his knowledge—to impress!—had now become a triviality. Now that he actually *possessed* these rare skills, it didn't seem to matter much to him if other people knew he possessed them. Ten years among the Oggaci had given Pallas a broader perspective. Yet, he also missed Matthew—dear, sweet, Matthew. He wondered if Matthew's prediction was going to hold true, and whether his friend was still alive. He wondered if Matthew wondered if Pallas was still alive? And then he wondered, putting off the dreaded thought for as long as he could, if Telia wondered if Pallas were still alive? Did she still care? Were they still in love? Where was she? Was she still at home safe? Questions and uncertainties from his past flooded into his mind.

As if emerging from a dream-like state, Pallas shook himself free from his doubts. He returned to his conversation with Aeon. He asked, "Skelligs? Skellig Michael! They are rocks. At least, they sound like rocks."

"They are!" Aeon exclaimed. He bloomed with bursting delight. "They *are* rocks! They are tiny islands, pinpricks, like pimples, jutting out, located seven miles off the Kerry coast of a very large island, located north of Brittany in France, off the west coast of the island of Britain."

"The bigger island?" Pallas asked. "You mean Ireland?"

"Yes, of course. Farther out at sea. You know it?"

"Of course not, " Pallas replied grumpily. "But I've heard of it. You have a document that was dated 2003 A.D. that spends six of its 300 pages, *Frommer's Guide To Europe* I believe, discussing a place called Ireland." Pallas cracked a smile. He thought of another piece in the archives dated 2007 A.D., a pictorial displaying women wearing odd garments, a stripe of cloth across the waistband and a minimal stripe covering the breasts—"bikini." It was found in a volume selling beer, an odd inclusion in the canon if there ever was one. Teasingly, Cacttus had introduced both "illicit" books to Pallas.

Aeon laughed at Pallas's encyclopedic memory of their 275 pieces of 550-to-600-year-old book and magazine specimens. Aeon went on. "Well, next to Ireland, they are very tiny islands indeed, not on any maps, located off the southwest coast. I'll have to break my oath to the Oggaci if I bring you to see them. It will be our own little secret. And I'll have to break my word of honor to the head of your Obsidian Order, Naxos Sparrus. For the sake of obtaining a little more knowledge, do you wish to go?"

"Break your word of honor to Naxos?" Pallas asked. "Let's go. But what would I do there? More importantly, what would I *learn* there?" The somber and responsible side of Pallas took over. "If I can't justify the trip from the point of view of educational opportunities, I can't allow myself to go."

"People can tell you stories. Not just stories, special stories— passed down orally—about September Snow and Iona. They know things about Regis Snow, the husband of September and the biological father of Iona, that I can't even guess at. Most importantly, they know a great deal about Iona's teacher Tom Novak. These are the descendants of the people who survived from the order of the Shangri La, the lost remnants of the Post-Literate Oral Preservation Society, a clandestine group which the Gaia-Domes thought they had completely obliterated in 2070 A.D. But a tiny off-shoot of the group survived. How they traveled from a hidden 13,800-foot-high valley in the Himalayas to a tiny island off the coast of Ireland, I don't know. Helioplanes, old style, that could travel as if by feats of magic at 1,200 miles per hour, those must have had something to do with it. You think September Snow was a goddess? She set the original group up when she was a young woman.. Then she moved the few survivors of the offshoot a few years after her daughter Iona had been settled. They worshiped her in a manner of speaking, but not as a goddess."

"Really now." Pallas nodded his head sheepishly, skeptically. "I see. You don't say!" At first Pallas thought Aeon might have been pulling his leg, taking advantage of his inexperience and credulity. But the more he thought about it, the more the idea appealed to him. "You're serious then, you're not kidding?" Pallas asked, shaking his head. Pallas thought about the limitations of his so-called New Rebel education. "How do you know about this place? We don't know anything about this business, where I come from. Goodness, this could be a goldmine."

"I agree about its potential significance," Aeon said in a soft, plain voice. "Pallas, it is a goldmine. And we *can* make this trip! I thought you'd be more than interested." Aoen displayed his enthusiasm with a shout, then a long drawn out cheer, then he hushed himself. Then Aeon gave Pallas a conspiratorial smile. And a wink. "As far as I know, people who run the Gaia-Domes, don't know anything about the existence of these strange, withdrawn, withered creatures, thin as rails, hunch-backed, wearing filthy rags or at best, threadbare robes, flagellating themselves, conducting sentences of penance among themselves. Nor do the scholars in the Gaia-Domes know anything about the nature of the esoteric knowledge these monks have held secretly for 550 years. Oh, they're so isolated! You realize Naxos would have me skinned alive, smothered in honey, and then buried up to my neck on an anthill, if he knew I was taking you anywhere near this place, don't you? Yes, I'll be putting your mortal soul in danger. Exposure to this group could make you question your cherished beliefs. Heresies abound. You think you know who September Snow is? Think you do? Wait and see. You don't know anything."

"Why are you telling me this?" Pallas asked. "Why risk such danger? Why are you willing to take such inappropriate risks just for the sake of my own edification?"

Aeon studied Pallas's face carefully, searching for inner doubts, vulnerability, hesitation, but he didn't detect any of those things, just curiosity—a normal and healthy curiosity.

Contrariwise, Pallas felt he was in a state of thrall or rapture, on the edge of something important

"Because," Aeon said in a low voice, "perhaps in the near future, Pallas, I think it just might be possible that you may end up being the historian, the only historian, for the rest of the world, about the past, to the rest of the world, about their future, that's why. And in preparation for this role, perhaps there are some things you need to know. This is important."

"We should not get ahead of ourselves now," Pallas said. "I know my people. They are not so generous about intrusions from the outside world, even if intrusions are brought to them by one of their own."

Aeon laughed. "Maybe so. You know your people better than I do. But maybe, with Naxos's help, they'll agree to allow you to become a story-teller. And who knows where that will lead? They didn't send you here just to admire the sights and scenery. I can guess that much."

Chapter Thirteen

IT TOOK MORE THAN A MONTH to put together all the provisions to make the trip. If it wasn't one thing, it was another. There were constant setbacks, something was always going wrong. First, there weren't enough trading goods to make the venture look credible, and when there were, there were not enough earthenware pots and too many metal pans. Aeon loaded up the earthenware. Oggaci craftsmanship in earthenware was impeccable. But he threw all the metal pans into a heap on the ground.

(The Oggaci's experiments in metallurgy had been hit or miss. Metal pans came out brittle or snapped into broken pieces at just a slight touch. Besides, why perfect the art of making metal articles when it was cheaper and far easier to barter them from the other tribes, in exchange for walnuts, or protective gear and leather pouches, or for the odd trinket of an ancient book?)

Besides earthenware, Aeon thought they should stick to furs and pelts. Skins were highly prized and the Oggaci had a long-time, excellent reputation for leather work.

Finally, they had accumulated a small wagon full of goods, including some tradable grains and, of course, the Oggaci's prize-winning walnuts. Aeon refused to take along any gold, or silver, or precious or semi-precious stones that would only encourage thieves along the road. Aeon was insistent on not canceling the trip. No matter what the setbacks, nothing could change his mind; he was determined.

Finally, Aeon and Pallas commenced their journey. As a cover story they told others they were en route to a trade fair in Paris. Aeon thought they might go there anyway, it was only 100 miles out of their way.

The first 90 miles of the journey went fine. Then, before they got to Longeau, things didn't go right. They were held up on the road and forced to give away some goods, just for the privilege of being allowed to pass. The thieves weren't particularly heavily armed, but there were more than a dozen of them. They had the strangely mixed aura of derring-do *and* desperation. Fifty miles farther on, in a darker forest, they were met by a band of even more sophisticated and much more heavily armed thieves. These bandits stripped them of everything: their horses, their remaining provisions, even their personal clothing. It wasn't just goods and horses they were after. They were contemptuous, laughing in Aeon and Pallas's faces as they forced them to remove every stitch of their clothing, leaving them behind with nothing except an empty wagon and the bridle reins to pull it. The chief of the thieves took out a walnut from a confiscated bag, spat a spray of spit into Pallas's face, then cracked the walnut on Pallas's head. Picking out the flesh of the cracked walnut, nibbling on the flesh, he smiled broadly. After he finished, he tossed the shards of the empty walnut shell over his shoulder. He shouted and his cadres began to ride away. He followed in languorous pursuit.

"We haven't made it even a third of the way to the sea," Pallas complained to Aeon, "and look what's happened. My head hurts. Your walnuts can give a person a concussion."

Pallas was shocked by Aeon's reaction. Not only was he not perturbed, he was a portrait of equanimity. "No worries," Aeon said. "I've seen worse...*far* worse. It's happened before. One of the risks of the trade, but it's alright." He inhaled deeply, braving a confident smile.

"You say it's okay," Pallas groused, "but small wonder there's such sparse commerce on the road. How can anybody do business?" With only the wagon left, they physically pulled it, step by step, like a pair of horses in harness. "No wonder everybody wants to stay put," Pallas continued, "and big surprise the world is mired in the deluge of such primitive barbarity, just like this wagon is mired in the mud of this tractionless sludge. And my head really, *really* hurts. It's not your head that hurts. Mine does!"

"Stop grousing," Aeon said. "There's a town not far from here."

The only thing that saved them was Aeon's excellent contacts in the small towns, what few towns there were. Pulling the empty wagon, they walked the five miles, completely in the nude. Although winter had ended, it was still chilly, the skies were rent with clouds, occasionally causing a downpour. Almost in comic relief, Pallas tried to wrap poplar boughs around his body for modesty and warmth, but all he managed to do was stain his skin with sap. Aeon slapped Pallas vigorously on the back and said in a voice brimming with laughter, "We'll have to preserve you in amber to keep you from rubbing sap on your back." At a small town, they exchanged the wagon for clothes and plenty of food. They were provided with a place to stay. At first the townspeople were going to put them up in an emptied, roof-covered animal pen, but Aeon convinced them of how important and illustrious he was among the Oggaci, so they changed their minds and let them stay in a small, plain cottage.

It was only in the small towns, not in the depopulated countryside, that they were able to find help, replace stolen clothes, refurnish supplies, and scavenge for food. Aeon was able to do this only because he was able to introduce to his new acquaintances, or to his old friends from previous trips, a startlingly bold and revolutionary concept: credit. *"Can we borrow this cloak? Could we borrow these pairs of shoes? We're bereft. From what we take, we'll repay you double, even triple, on our next trip. Let us have this five-pound sack of grain now...next year, we'll return the favor. We'll double the grain. We'll throw in a goose. The word of the Oggaci is honor-bound. Your man Cerberos is going to Langres to deliver goods anyhow. How splendid. Well then, can we ride up on the wagon with him?"*

They bartered and borrowed their way across the width of

France. Getting rid of the wagon actually made it easier for them to travel. They could get off the main road and travel on paths where they were less conspicuous. But they kept getting robbed now and then. The lighter they traveled the better, but then they had nothing to barter with when they got to a town and so they had to borrow. Except when they were escorted, conditions were hazardous. Once they were escorted all the way from the south of Troyes to Orleans, and then part of the way to Bennes, and no one ever touched them. But that was the exception.

Aeon's original plan failed. The cover of conducting a trading exposition had devolved into a farce. Aeon and Pallas looked like a pair of indigent misfits trekking across a blighted landscape. When they were robbed they were sometimes also strip-searched, in an effort to find gold or silver or other valuables. Aeon had seen deplorable conditions on the road before, but none that were so low and calamitous. It was as if the old system had broken down—Aeon was beginning to doubt if *any* system had ever been in place—so deplorable was their lot. But they managed to make it across France. Once they got to a boat at the far end of Brittany (a boat that Aeon had arranged years in advance, paying for the entire boat, crew, and all its provisions) that would take them to the west coast of Ireland, they were safe.

It was as if the fates had done everything possible to prevent them from completing their task. But in spite of their bad luck, Aeon kept egging Pallas on. He did everything possible to ensure that Pallas's spirits didn't flag. "Cheer up," Aeon beseeched, "we'll make it!" Whenever Pallas looked at Aeon sideways, Aeon nagged Pallas onward. "Fear not," he pleaded, "we'll succeed!"

When they were all alone in the forest, Pallas said to Aeon, "You know, when I first met you, you lied to me."

Aeon gave Pallas a cross-eyed skeptical look. "Really! Is that so? Really? Refresh my memory. I am dubious."

"It happened a few days after we first met in Calais," Pallas said in a calm voice. "You wouldn't give me your name. The explanation you gave to me at the time was that you traveled with a stranger for up to seven days before you volunteered your own name. *Of course you already knew my name.* You said it was a caution. You lied to me. Gullible as I was, I believed you. I have seen you give your name to strangers on numerous occasions. In Longres, in Travares, just yesterday on the road. You volunteered it. He didn't even have to ask for it. Hell, we couldn't have traveled 100 miles if you hadn't told everyone your name was Aeon. You never could have sold the wagon if you hadn't. Why did you deceive me when you first met me?"

Aeon shrugged his shoulders. A denial was impossible. Having gotten to know Pallas so well, and his obsession with the truth, Aeon decided to own up to it. He looked Pallas squarely in the eye. "That was ten years ago, brother. Sometimes we have to tell lies. We often tell our kinfolk *never* to trust outsiders, and that is the truth. As you can see, the world is a scary place. That's why we made up the business of never revealing names until after we've known a stranger for a long time. But you're right, I don't observe our custom myself. If I had, I never would have been able to travel the way I have been able to. I told you then that I was one of the few of the Oggaci who ever traveled. That was true then, it's true now. And I have been honest with you. I promise I'll always be honest with you. Those eleven years gone, you were from a place so far away and threatening, you were afraid of me, but equally, I was afraid of *you!* I know you don't believe that. But it's true. The land of the New Rebels was like a mythical place to us, a land of unicorns and man-horses, half-beast and half-human, eight-foot-high hairy beasts with moss-like feet and blood-red claws, with claws longer and more powerful than that of bears, who craved human flesh. Without supporting facts, without knowledge on the ground, especially about faraway places, we become slaves to our own imaginations. I feared you might end up slitting my throat in the middle of the night."

Pallas accepted Aeon's explanation. "It's in the past. I have forgotten that the Cundi tribe, *my tribe*, can be very frightening too. I won't mention it again."

The memory of the lying episode made Pallas realize, in a fuller and clearer vision, he needed to repeat his commitment to returning home to the Colorado plateau no later than a year hence. Had he forgotten his initial reasons for coming to live among the Oggaci? Had he forgotten the mission Naxos had spelled out for him? Had he forgotten his undying love for Telia? It was a wake up call, reminding him that he couldn't live among the Oggaci forever, even though Aeon was his friend.

Once they had gotten under sail, things at last did take a turn for the better. But when they got to the island of Ireland, Pallas saw that conditions were even worse than in France: more poverty, more grimness, more darkness, more hopelessness. There were no roads, only paths, and most of these paths were not well-trodden. They were robbed again, but this time only their food was taken, a shivering man said he had to stoop to thievery to feed his starving family, but their provisions and clothes were not touched. Aeon and Pallas could have stopped the thief, overpowered him, but they felt such sorrow for him that they literally *gave* the food to him. When they made it to Kerry, there were more privations and desolation. When they finally arrived on the island of Skellig Michael, Pallas was thunderstruck at the difference of the place.

"Yes, it's practically impossible to get to this place," Aeon said. "but once you get here, it's truly amazing." The island was almost entirely vertical, 715 feet to the summit. But the few places where there was level ground, those parts were covered by beehive-shaped stone buildings and a small walled-in garden. Some of the buildings dated back 2,000 years. Monks also lived in caves, cut into the sides of cliffs. There were a number of old stone Celtic crosses on the island, some reputed to be 1,900 years old. All Pallas had to do was close his eyes and imagine himself being returned to a Dark-Age era settlement of ancient Christianity, rather than living in a dark-age era reality of the Age of Gaia.

In some places, monks used ropes and pulleys to get from one place to another. In other places, steps had been carved directly into the rock. On Skellig Michael proper, there were forty-five stunted-looking male inhabitants of varying ages. On a nearby smaller island, Little Skellig, there were six scrawny men. On another island, much farther away, an island that was even smaller, there were two miserable-looking creatures who only barely resembled boys coming out of adolescence.

"Why live in a place that is so harsh, a rock so impossible to live on?" Pallas asked Aeon.

"They do it by choice," Aeon replied. "At least here, monks are safe. Since they have nothing of material worth, why bother disturbing them? Why molest them? The only others they have to share the islands with are birds." Pallas looked up and saw a wave of gannets, their wings extended: They were resting and rising on the Eastern Sea wind.

The monks looked strange, even more bizarre than Pallas had expected. Thirty of them wore threadbare robes, but the rest were dressed in rags. Pallas had been warned to expect the shabby apparel, but almost all of them looked like they were in a state of near-starvation. These were not just impoverished, ill-clothed people, they were quite literally human wrecks. Their frames were skin and bones. Some had ghastly unshorn fingernails, of which they were perversely proud. Worse still were their toenails, brown or black in color, curling, twisting, curling, three or four times. When the youngest in the group smiled fiendishly at Pallas—was it hunger alone that brought on such a macabre smile? Pallas half-expected a pair of horns to sprout spontaneously from his head! Their otherwise fair skin was blackened from not bathing in years. They wore their hair several feet long, stringy, snarled, unkempt, never having seen a comb. With some effort, Pallas got used to their skeleton frames.

The island provided very little in the way of food: seaweed, birds' eggs, fish from the sea, a few vegetables from the garden. And they were able to bring in from the mainland barely enough flour to make a few bits of bread every once in a while. But even when there was more food, they still restricted themselves to just one or two tiny meals a day. They fasted completely twelve days out of each month!

The most important thing they had in common was their fellowship. The food was equally shared. Pallas learned later that the wearing of the threadbare robes was rotated once every six months, so that all had a chance to wear the better clothing.

And they shared something else: a deep burning desire to keep alive, in their minds, certain records that were given to them by September Snow herself.

As a preliminary, the first half day was spent touring the island, a tour that took a total of fifty-five minutes. The rest of the day was spent resting. The next day Aeon and Pallas learned the origins of the order and the history of the island. Pallas found the talk mostly boring, but out of courtesy he listened intently. Christian monks had spent many years living on the island, more years than the Gaia people had inhabited it. Pallas thought that Matthew might have enjoyed listening to the stories and history about the pre-Gaia Christian past of Skellig.

Finally, in the end, Pallas asked diplomatically if he could learn about September Snow.

"Oh, you have to talk to Angus the Elder about that," his guide replied. "He has the best memory. He lives on the smaller rock."

"Little Skellig?" Pallas asked nervously.

"Yes, I'm afraid. Right across the way."

Pallas looked out at sea. A half mile away, he saw another rock sticking out of the water. That meant a trip to a second island.

Sailing over in a small boat to Little Skellig, Pallas got to see three more monks (out of six) who wore threadbare robes, the rest wearing deplorable-looking tattered rags. Pallas was going to see the oldest member in the group, but he had to go up to him. Angus was infirm. He could not come down from his cell unassisted. Pallas had to climb up steep steps in the rock to get to the monk's cell, a tiny cell that had been carved into the highest portion of the rock. From a limited fare of dreadful food—a foul-smelling pasty substance made of seaweed, and occasionally a bird's egg—Pallas was already feeling lightheaded and dizzy. The day before, he had whispered to Aeon, "Let's stay three days, okay? I don't like staying here. Plenty of time to get the information I need, right? Surely long enough for us to register to these courageous people our courtesy, our thanks, our polite behavior. These people are so non-threatening, so non-hostile, so non-dangerous, all the same, they *scare* me. They are so famished."

Angus the Elder had long hair. He sported a wild beard. He was wearing nothing but a flimsy loincloth. Lying on a stone pallet, he looked decrepit. Thanks to an old back injury, he was hunched over. It was obvious that his daily meal had to be brought to him.

Inadvertently, the old monk groaned.

Pallas didn't beat around the bush. He introduced himself. Straight away, he asked the monk to tell him his version of the story of September Snow.

"Oh that," the old monk said. "That one. *That burning question.* That's the one that unfailingly gets me into trouble." He puckered his lips, then he ran his tongue over his teeth, as if in skepticism of being able to entertain yet another visitor.

"Let's get started." Pallas interrupted. "Was she a goddess?"

Angus the Elder laughed, then sputtered. He leaned over the edge of his pallet and spit. He looked up. "September Snow never saw herself as a goddess. None of the people, friends, enemies, neutrals, independents, all of her followers, all of her most *devoted, fervent followers*, not one time, saw her as a goddess. She started out as a calm, dignified and highly educated woman, who had in her possession great privileges, who had been ranked high in the hierarchy of the Gaia-Dome system. Originally yes, she lived in the Gaia-Domes. Indeed, for a brief period of time, she was the leader of the Gaia-Domes' propaganda operations, which even before her rebellion, morphed into a very nasty 'thought police.' Yes, the Gaia-Dome system, over a period of two decades, evolved into a fundamentally tyrannical and oppressive system. Her husband, Regis Snow, had been chief scientist of this system. But in the face of a growing oppression, Regis Snow rebelled against it. The Gaia-Dome authorities executed him. September Snow then took over the rebellion. That's the essence of the story, that and her martyrdom. Now her daughter, Iona, came a little later. It wasn't until 90 years later, after the death of September Snow, and about 40 years after the death of Iona, that September Snow began to be seen as a goddess, and her daughter Iona turned into a saint. That was the New Rebels handiwork, although, of course, the roots go back to when they were still called 'THE UNSEEING WATCHFULNESS OF GAIA.' Am I going too fast? Are you following me?"

"Of course I'm following you," Pallas said impatiently. "You're speaking blasphemy of course. The most egregious form of heresy. You're a heretic. You say September was martyred?"

"Blasphemy, hmm," Angus the Elder said. "Heresy. Perhaps blasphemy, heresy, and truth are all the same thing." He clucked with his tongue. "September was martyred. *Unceremoniously put to death.*"

"You should burn in hell for saying this," Pallas said. "Even the most tolerant Oggaci would clap you in irons. Although you might humor what passes as a scholar in the Gaia-Domes. After all, they refuse to admit that September Snow existed. Or that Iona was born. Claiming September Snow is not a goddess, and Iona not a saint, well, at least they'd see that as a step in the right direction. What you preach could give comfort to our enemy."

"Friends, enemies, enemies, friends," Angus the Elder said in a soft voice. He tugged on his beard, sighing deeply. "I've always felt the powerful urge of the Earth to tell me what I need to know. I don't need the skills of a so-called *theologian* to tell me that." He shook his head. "I am in no fear."

The old monk was nonplussed by Pallas's accusations of impropriety and disrespect. "They say Christians were once believers in nonsense, too. Oh yes! Hell-fire, sin, prophesies of impending doom. Revelation, apocalypse, end times, cults sprouting up through human history, sometimes powerful cults. And they never got over it." He laughed. He bellowed out a funeral dirge, filled with guttural stops, swooping sighs and moans, trying to keep the beat by tapping his side with the thumping ham of his hand. The tune lasted a full minute and a half. Near the end, Angus the Elder emitted a cackling laugh. His face relaxed. "Want to learn something?"

From Pallas's perspective, with his fiercely wild hair and gaunt, old face *Angus the Elder looked like a crazy man but that had been far from the truth.* From the point of view of showmanship, it was as if Angus was displaying a self-parodying caricature of himself, as if it were a role he was expected to play, his eyes gleaming hauntingly.

"I'm insane, you know," Angus said at last. "Don't judge me, at least not hastily. If you want to talk, you'll have to give me credit for being rational. Otherwise, what follows will sound absurd."

Pallas had become angry with Angus the Elder's initial words about Gaia, but he was also happy. Strangely angry. Flummoxed. Sweetly happy. He had never felt such powerful contradictory sensations at exactly the same time before. He blushed.

"Not used to a *real* give and take?" Angus the Elder asked. "Something unaccustomed? But you'll get used to it. It'll grow on you. In the beginning, Gaia was not a religion. It was a spirituality, yes, but it also had a secular perspective. It had a strong, active scientific component. Human beings were not seen as *separate* from the environment, they were seen as *part* of the environment. That was the whole point of Gaia. The survival of human beings required it, but it took a long time to convince the whole world of that truth. There were agreements, disagreements, debates. Diverse and divergent perspectives were openly expressed. They were not seen as heresies or blasphemies, they were seen as just that, *perspectives*. September Snow entertained different points of view. Different and contradictory ideas were allowed to be debated. Tom Novak, who was the teacher of Iona, never believed in Gaia. People think that that was because he was of the older generation, the man was born in the 1990s A.D. He must have been too old to see all of what Gaia became, but there could have been other reasons too."

"What are you saying?"

"I'm not saying anything," Angus said. "When they started dating these runic stones, was that when all these new theological pronouncements began creeping in?"

"I don't know," Pallas said. "I don't know anything about that. We were never given the wherewithal to attach a critical study to our own core beliefs. That was never on our syllabus of study."

Angus shrugged his shoulders, as if aping the mannerisms of a ponderous skeptic.

Pallas nodded his head, asking for Angus the Elder to continue. He gulped. "I'm not afraid to hear what you have to say. It happened so long ago. I'd almost forgotten. I was a seven-year-old boy when my father delivered me into the arms of the Obsidian Order. Initially, I didn't want anything to do with the organization. My father threatened to flay the skin off my legs and arms if I didn't accede. So I did. I've never forgiven my father his harshness and cruelty."

"You're not afraid then, I see," Angus the Elder nodded. "Good. *Good*. Then I'll teach."

Pallas stayed with the old monk for three whole days. During that time, they both subsisted on a diet of seaweed paste and bird's egg soup. Aeon had been right to assume that the experience would have a huge impact on Pallas. The experience turned him into a changed man.

And what Pallas learned about September Snow, Iona, Regis Snow, and Tom Novak—things that he had never dreamed of being true before—was astonishing.

Pallas knew for a fact that the new knowledge was something that he had to keep hidden inside himself under a pain of death. No, it was only the Gaia-Domes who put you to death. When he got back home, Pallas knew it was something he had to keep hidden under a pain of exile—permanent exile—the New Rebels' form of death.

But the New Rebels had been right! And the Gaia-Domes had been wrong. The New Rebels carried a truth, a truth of sorts, the most important truth, some of the truth, but not all of it.

The last thing Angus the Elder said to Pallas struck him the hardest. It hit him like a thunderbolt. "The only reason anybody cares about September Snow is that she is a goddess."

"What?" Pallas exclaimed. He shook his head in disbelief. "After all the things you said!"

Angus smiled. "It's true. Our group, after living for 520 years on nothing but hopeless dreams, surrounded by the sea, with only our faith to buoy us up, why would anybody want to know the true story of September Snow? If she wasn't a goddess? As time passes, our message becomes more distant and muddled. The original truth was that September Snow was NOT a goddess. That is our truth. But too much time has passed. The only reason that truth continues to exist, even for us, is because she *is* a goddess."

Pallas brought his hands together, clenching them. "So much of what I've been told has been lies. So many of them! Should we allow our lives to be racked by lies? By terrors? I love Telia. Why does she and her family have to be so apprehensive about being persecuted?"

"That's life," Angus the Elder said abruptly. "But there are different kinds of truths, Pallas. There are different kinds of lies, too. We must choose our battles carefully. I don't know anything about this girl you call Telia, or her family, but I'll wager she's going to face the same world you'll face."

"A primitive world constantly twisting lies into truth," Pallas said. "Through disingenuousness, through manipulation, no?" He folded his arms, shaking his head. "No, it's totally unacceptable. I won't bend my knee to this invisible wall of forgery and fraud forever."

Angus smiled. "Words of youth. Youth talking. Sounds nice all the same." Angus was pleased to hear Pallas questioning authority. "I'm touched. Do you know who Kull was? He was a real live historical figure. Just like Tom was. Did you know that? No, it's too complicated, I won't explain everything that he meant to Iona. I'm sorry I mentioned it. It's going to be too hard for you to find the truth, isn't it? Though I think I've set your mind adrift on the subject, haven't I? Well, that's for the good. Yes, yes, I'm sorry to say, it's going to be very hard for you."

Pallas knew about Kull. He had learned about him through a prominent Oral Tradition. But, of course, Pallas didn't know *everything* about him. Kull had been a cohort of Iona. "Eleven years ago, I was on a pilgrimage. I saw the markings of Kull's grave on a sacred mountain in the middle of the desert. I know who he was. But there are still some lingering doubts, especially about his dealings with the sub-Magister Clive. Where did all that stuff take place? I'm trying to remember. Oh yes! On the island of St. Helena, an island in the southern part of the Eastern Sea."

"Stay focused. It's not the *sacred* mountain in the middle of the desert, Pallas, it's just a *mountain*, only a place, like five other peaks, like ten or twenty other high places in the desert."

"I saw the markings of his grave on a mountain in the desert," Pallas said, correcting himself.

"That's better," Angus the Elder exclaimed. "Don't be so dejected. That's all you need to know. You'll do fine. And you have your Telia to help you, too. Oh I can tell, she is going to mean so much to you!"

Pallas needed to go home. He needed to be careful. If chosen by Naxos, he needed to write the best he could. That was his most important mission. *But he needed to be careful, tread carefully. The structure of his fundamental beliefs could have been disintegrating—collapsing—as he was thinking. Pallas realized the world was far more dangerous than he had first thought.*

But he decided that the judicious thing to do was to think it over. Pray to Iona. He wasn't certain whether she was a saint anymore, but that didn't matter. She was all that he had. Iona. That and the thought of Telia being by his side, providing strength, courage, and discipline.

September Snow was not a goddess. She died a natural death, a *martyr's* death. That was like saying that everything the New Rebels believed in was a cruel hoax.

Chapter Fourteen

AEON AND PALLAS MADE IT peacefully across the waters without incident. They decided to adopt the manners of the monks on Skellig Michael, to travel across France wearing scant clothing, with no possessions, carrying on their persons barely enough to eat. They decided to take on a life of severe vagabondage.

This was to be their noble experiment. The sheer absurdity of the idea made them deliriously happy. It drove from their minds a miasma of darkness, a sense of impending dread.

They thought the experience might actually be fun. It seemed such an improbable thing—*fun*? They knew that traveling in such a manner was riddled with hazards, but they decided that everything they'd done up until then had been extremely dangerous anyway, so why not try to amuse oneself along the way? Why did everything have to be so grim?

Heading out, Pallas, however, couldn't keep a suspicion to himself. He hadn't shared the doubt with Aeon up until then, but now that they had left the islands behind, he decided that it was necessary. "Aeon, for all their supposed self-sufficiency, the monks on the Skellig rocks—I don't think any of them should be alive."

"Yes?" Aeon asked. The expression on his face suggested he anticipated Pallas's doubt. He looked like he shared a similar thought.

"None of it fits," Pallas continued. "They shouldn't have been able to live as they have. Something's wrong. Something doesn't add up."

"How they managed to survive as long as they have?" Aeon asked. "That's your question? On those two small islands? Improbable, isn't it? I have asked myself the same question."

Pallas sniffed the air. He pinched his nostrils. He held his breath. "They should have died of starvation a long time ago. I should never have had a chance to talk to them. That's the crazy part, I should never have had a chance to see them. I should still be naive and ignorant about September Snow, about Iona, about their true histories, and all the rest."

Aeon rubbed his fingers together. "The first time I saw them, all of this was confusing to me too. But then someone in Ireland explained it to me. They had a benefactor. The benefactor was a kingdom in the far northwest, farther north than the north of Ireland. In the middle of the northern portion of the Eastern Sea. This is the unseemly side to the story. The believers, gullible there, supplied them with foodstuffs. Boats were dispatched. Deliveries were made twice a year, grain in good times, millet in bad. But it was enough. Intermittently, they even included a delivery of second-hand clothing. The monks fished whenever they could, but there was too much acid in the water. And they collected seaweed of course. They also robbed birds' nests. That is dangerous work, many a monk fell and died trying to steal an egg from a lofty, isolated nest, with a mother bird fluttering over her nest trying to defend her young, trying to peck the monk's eyes out. So that was not enough to survive on.

"The monks provided the northern kingdom with a soothsaying once a year. He put on quite a show. He convinced the kingdom's chieftains that his soothsaying prayers guaranteed good crops, therefore guaranteeing the kingdom's security. It was a racket, a sham, a ploy. But all that the monk Angus the Elder said to you about September Snow, and Iona, and the rest, was legitimate. That's the important thing. I swear to you it's the truth! That's why they're living there. They are the holders of a deeper truth. Their soothsaying stratagem was only a sideshow phenomenon, compromising their principles only for that other thing called survival."

Pallas nodded his head. "Your explanation explains a lot. Angus the Elder had no reason to lie to me. You have no reason to lie to me. That helps explain their present predicament. So what happened to their benefactors in the mysterious kingdom in the far north?"

"Five years ago, it collapsed. Crops failed miserably. *Four years in a row there was utter darkness.* Implosion of everything. It was as if the land returned to what it had been. The eruption of volcanoes—Iceland and its volcanoes—blotting out the sun. They were still trying to grow grain. Grain? They couldn't even grow hay, much less millet. Bad time to be in the soothsaying business. That kingdom had kept those monks alive with deliveries of food for five or six generations. During the good times, the monks' numbers swelled from barely 14 to over 60. Then the food deliveries stopped."

"What's going to happen?"

Aeon preferred not to answer the question, but he knew he was obligated to do so. He bit his lip. "You're thinking, I'm sure, that the monks are going to die. I'm sure Angus the Elder knows this. Maybe a tiny handful of them will survive. They did so in the past. What will they do when their robes are gone? What will they do when the gruel is gone? What with all the acid in the water, the sea is partially depleted of fish. What will they do when only the birds will provide? There is no one else to provide for them. The times in Ireland are worse than they've ever been. They won't survive on seaweed alone. A diet solely of seaweed will destroy their innards."

"I'm glad you told me," Pallas said at last. "I won't ask again. In light of this, this experiment in severe vagabondage of ours, is it likely to work?"

Aeon broke into a huge grin. "I know it will! Trying it out for the first time, I'd rather try it out in France, *not on the other side of the water, and not in the far dark north, that's for sure. You're right, that place was scary.*"

At some settlements, Aeon and Pallas begged for food. But the doors were invariably slammed in their faces. Conditions were harsh. But the farther south they traveled, the more good luck they experienced, bringing in just enough to keep themselves from starving. In between the odd handout, they subsisted on wild berries, roots, and mushrooms. With his scant clothing, Aeon couldn't impress the locals as he had been able to do in the past. Promises of future compensation didn't work when Aeon tried to barter or borrow. After all, he looked like a beggar. Even when people recognized him from the past, he was no longer a merchant, a man of substance.

Aeon and Pallas knew that they had to come up with a different strategy or they would have to go back to the old way of doing things, which meant they would be at the mercy of thieves.

By accident, Pallas discovered he had a knack for storytelling. Having not eaten for three days, they stopped in front of a broken-down farm outside of Pontivy. They considered breaking in and stealing, but they had made a pact that they would never do that. An old farmer resided there. Cautiously, they knocked on the door. The farmer was impressed by Pallas's strange, defective-looking, milk-white eyes. He told Pallas he would give him a bowl of porridge if he could tell him a good story. Such a dare! Pallas was so hungry he agreed. He put his heart and soul into it.

Pallas told the farmer a story from more than 500 years in the past, about Tom Novak and Iona in the desert of Mexico, and how they survived when the chips were down. It was a story that Angus the Elder had told him, about an education Iona received at the age of eight from a blind Indian who was supposed to be able to impart a special knowledge. Pallas added a little flair, just to make the story more compelling, although it was hardly necessary since the bare facts made the story compelling in itself. Pallas also knew something about the countryside firsthand, having once traveled down to northern Mexico with his friend Matthew, so the physical details of the terrain were not all guesswork. The farmer loved the story in itself, especially the fact that it came from the new world, but more importantly, he enjoyed the experience of the storytelling too.

But the farmer hesitated, as if he were wavering. Anxiously seeing the prospect of food receding, Aeon stepped in front of Pallas and started to dance. He danced madly. He forced himself to do a jig that lasted two whole minutes, moving his feet frantically, all the while, smiling humbly. "That's over the top," the farmer observed. He was so impressed by Aeon's willingness to subject himself to such humiliation that he rewarded both Pallas and Aeon with a large bowl of porridge. The farmer forced the two to eat the food without the use of utensils, armed only with their hands, each seated on the ground. They just tilted the bowls back and channeled the food in, guiding the semi-liquid ooze with their fingers. After they gulped down the food, the farmer allowed them to bed down for the night in his corn crib.

Pallas thought he'd try to repeat the experience. Outlandish as it seemed, had anyone tried to survive by means of storytelling? Hunger was the flintiest and harshest taskmaster. But Pallas learned from his earliest mistakes. Don't just knock at any lonely door and beg, you will invariably be turned away. But meet people where they congregate and offer them something in return. He found that people relished happy endings, even if the tales involved hardship, disaster, or calamity. With his early semi-successes, his confidence grew. Slowly, over time, he enhanced and elaborated on his repertoire. He ended up acting out the stories as payment for food *and* lodging! Sometimes people would let the pair of them sleep in their main room by the fire. Some of these events actually turned into elaborate affairs, where people came from miles around just to attend a performance.

For the most part, Pallas told conventional stories about September Snow and Iona, but he added touches of glamour, flair, color, drama, humor, and human struggle—endearing the stories even more to the listeners. And his successes were all the greater because he was willing to tell his stories even if the assemblage was three starving people who could repay him only with a turnip, a radish, and a cup of tepid water. That's when Pallas's strange, defective-looking, milk-white eyes really lit up, and odd-looking to these people his eyes were.

The two, Pallas and Aeon, decided not to go directly back to the northern Alps. They ended up taking a more circular route. In one sweep, they dipped down to the south of France. They even crossed over the mountains of the Pyrenees for a month, entering briefly into Spain.

Pallas was amazed at how much he enjoyed himself along the way. A three-month round trip turned into an eleven-month journey.

Aeon enjoyed himself also. Towards the end of it, he came to see himself as Pallas's road agent, even though he remembered his crude, humbling beginnings, where he felt compelled to mimic the trained monkey in order to earn his crust in the form of a watered-down porridge.

They also found that the farther south they traveled, the more prosperous the people were. In isolated pockets, they found displays of plenty. In villages there were real shops run by children with crates on display: filled with apples, lettuce, cabbage, leeks, and bunches of garlic, radiant in the sun. Farther south they heard reports that the Gaia-Domes had hung on tenaciously to their port facilities and their farmland, especially around the southern rim of the Mediterranean basin, but especially of late, they were having difficulty surviving.

To return home, the two had to start heading north. They knew that the good times couldn't last forever. Because of their extraordinary luck up until that point, they came to be lulled into a state of complacency. Success softened their tough exteriors, dulled their sharpness. They were slothful, and they had a tendency to drop their guard too often. One day, they walked too long and darkness caught them unprepared. They entered a measly village in a neck of a dark, impenetrable forest, where the residents seemed *too* eager to be friendly. When they smiled, they bared their teeth in a strange way. Both Aeon and Pallas felt an unease. There was the inexplicable sensation that something was wrong, but they couldn't put their finger on what was off kilter. It was late. They were bone tired. They had traveled a long way. They had gotten used to being offered accommodations at the drop of a hat. They were not surprised when they were offered accommodations again. They decided to take a chance. They could have pressed on to a place Aeon felt more familiar with, but when they were offered a warm broth containing plenty of meat, potatoes, and carrots, they couldn't turn it down. They were now, by Aeon's calculation, less than 125 miles from home. Everything had come out golden so far, they were on the homestretch, what could go wrong? Six or seven more days and they'd be in the clear.

When Pallas told the people of his storytelling abilities, they all beamed with delight. With an almost excessive wave of enthusiasm, they requested that he give them a talk.

Pallas had delivered 120 storytelling sessions in 280 days, sometimes to a crowd of a 100, but more typically to a smaller audience, 10 or 15 people, or maybe 25 or 30. But a quarter of his talks were addressed to a lonely farmer or to a lonely farmer's wife, or to three or four stragglers standing alone in a fallowed field. The group that had been assembled in the main hall for him was typical, about 15 grownups of mixed age, probably representing most of the adults in the hamlet, but there were also six very young children present, who sat at his feet in the front. The presence of the children with their eager, upturned faces made Pallas feel more comfortable. Pallas reeled off his established repertoire, almost as if he were in a state of semi-unconsciousness.

When the show was over, the host offered alcoholic drink. Against Aeon and Pallas's better judgment, they drank more than they should. And usually they drank to excess only when they were in a place where they were *certain* they were safe.

In the past, Aeon kept Pallas in check, or Pallas kept Aeon in check. But this time they were both eager to drink. Seven days at most from home? To be sure, they were in a forest zone unknown to Aeon, coming from a direction that he had never tracked before, but how much could go wrong? *They were too close to home.*

They awoke in the morning, experiencing such painful hangovers that they knew a powerful drug had been placed in their drink. They found themselves in a dark, cold place with very little light. Their hands and their feet were bound. When their eyes adjusted, they realized they were in a windowless cellar. In the center of the cellar was a cage, five-feet high, five-feet wide, and ten-feet long. Hunched over, they were locked inside the cage.

Twice a day, they were fed food scraps. Once a day, a bucket of water was lowered in, then an empty bucket taken out.

Aeon was so angry at first. He had remained so utterly baffled. Why were they being kept in a cage? Originally, they had been greeted as such highly honored guests.

Then Aeon remembered when they first entered the hamlet. There were signs all over the place. He had been so stupid. How could he have overlooked the tell-tale signs? First of all, and most importantly, there was a primitive sculpture of a bear, hacked with a stone axe out of a tree trunk, at the entrance to the hamlet. Inside the homes, in multiple places, there were bear images on the floorboards, and brass or clay figurines of bears on tables. In the headman's cottage, there was a twelve-foot-long painting of a bear on the wall, so bold and prominent and extravagant, with browns and yellows and swirling oranges and reddened eyes. It was as if a troubled artist had painted the image. In the main hall where Pallas spoke, there was a collection of bear claws hanging on the back wall. There had been a large pot hanging over a large pile of wood, and a meat-hook hanging on top of it, Aeon thought it had been for preparing bear meat. Why else had the pot been placed outside, and not located inside a home? Before entering the main hall, he noticed it next to one of the side houses. At first, he hadn't paid it any mind. Now, too late, he realized the significance. *There were all kinds of signs of bear worship, but there wasn't any evidence of bears, living anyway.*

Two decades before, an Oggaci elder, long since deceased, had warned Aeon about villages like this. They existed in the most remote forests. Everybody in the outside world thought they had a perverted ritual about hunting bear. They worshiped the beast. But what if they had run out of bears? What did they have to replace the sacred bear meat with?

Pallas awoke. He was wondering what the contraption was that they found themselves locked in. Before he could ask the question, Aeon answered it for him. "It's a bear cage. And a bear hasn't been in it for a long time."

In the corner of the cellar, Aeon saw a heap of bones. At first glance, he thought nothing of it. Bones of dogs' legs, donkeys ribcages, elk, chicken, deer, bear. The bear bones seemed to be the oldest. Then he noticed something that made him sick to his stomach. He realized that mixed in with the others were human bones. Substitutes.

"Either they'll eat you first, or they'll eat me first, and then they'll eat you later," Aeon said.

"What are you talking about?" Pallas asked.

"Do you like to eat bear?"

"What?"

"Do you like the taste of bear?"

"Not particularly. There are very few bears where I come from. Strange subject to bring up under the circumstances."

"We wandered into the wrong hamlet."

Aeon remained silent.

"Is there any way we can get out of here?" Pallas asked.

"Perhaps," Aeon said. "They're not cannibals *per se*. First of all, they cook their food. If given a choice, they prefer bear meat. Their totem is bear, not humans. In this, they're like pigs. Only *in extremis* do pigs wallow in their own feces. If given a choice, they prefer to wallow in mud. Mud derived from fresh water. They prefer mud, that is, bear, to humans, that is, feces."

"What the hell are you talking about, Aeon?" Pallas asked. "Are you hallucinating?"

"Mud's the answer."

"What? Given the promise of mud! Explain this to me!"

Aeon looked calm. It was as if he were in possession of a divine spark. "By mud I mean bear. We *have* bears. They roam in the mountains, in the Alps, above the Jura, above our settlements. We don't hunt them anymore. Why should we? What if they need to hunt a bear once a year, or once every six months, for religious purposes? At the price of setting us free, I'll propose that we give them access to our hunting grounds. They can hunt bear until their heart's content."

"You think that'll placate them?"

"Depends on how much they want to hunt, doesn't it? And they'll have to carry their bears back with them over 125 miles, which is probably an impossible task. Or they will have to kill the bear and carry the carcass on a pole, which is still a ridiculously long way to go. Or they will have to kill the bear and cook it in the mountains, and bring back pieces of bear meat with them. That might work. Or maybe they'll just need to bring a bear's head, or a bear's skull, or a bear's claws, back with them, to prove the kill."

"You mean they may agree to set us free?"

"You have any better ideas?"

"No."

"Do you have any idea how many people there are who pretend to be believers in Gaia, and who are not, Pallas?" Aeon asked. "Wise up. Let this be a lesson to you."

"So what are you going to do?"

"Take them to the hunting grounds, show them what they can have, and while this is going on, they'll keep you as a hostage, guaranteeing their safe return."

"Aeon?"

"What?"

"You're going to have to sell them on the promise of a future."

"I know. It will be the greatest sales job of my life. But I have hope."

"Why?"

"When I first met them, I told them my name. That was a minor mistake. But then I told them I was an Oggaci. That was an even more grievous breach in confidentiality. That was an *unpardonable* error. That's why we're in the cage. And my guess is that they know we have bears up in our mountains, and they're going to want to hunt them. This has been a set-up. This was a trap. And we've walked into it."

Chapter Fifteen

AEON ASKED TO SEE the headman. He was let out of the cage and escorted to the headman's house.

An hour later, Aeon was escorted back to the cage.

A look of buoyancy and optimism shone in Aeon's face. "My intuition was right!" Aeon said. "Good news! Given a choice, they prefer not to devour us. They just want bear. And I don't have to show them the hunting grounds in the Alps, they're already familiar with them. They know that bear roam freely there. My big mouth got us into this mess, but I think I can get us out. But it's going to cost me a dear price. Yet, nonetheless, I think we're safe."

"What's the catch?" Pallas asked.

"Either you have to stay here as a hostage to guarantee the hunting ground's security," Aeon began, "Or."

"Or what?"

"I'll have to replace you with two members of my own family," Aeon said. "Two small children. To act as hostages. For the first three years. To be renewed by two small children, from Mantou's family, or from some other family, for the next three. So on and so forth. Best deal I could get short of armed conflict."

"That's unacceptable," Pallas said, shaking his head. "I refuse to let this happen."

"Happens all the time," Aeon said, pushing Pallas back gently with his hand. "Price we pay for living as isolated tribes. Hating our enemies. Fearing our neighbors. Living in darkness."

"Perhaps I should stay with these people as a hostage anyway," Pallas said in a reasonable voice. "The Oggaci have done so much for me, I'm obligated. I need to take responsibility for something. At least for the first three years. I'll stay."

"Absolutely not," Aeon said, shaking his head. "Out of the question. It's not your problem. It's my mistake. I'm facing this wicked choice because of my poor judgment. I'm responsible. It'll be my family, or my brother's family, who'll make the first sacrifice."

Twenty-five days later, when Aeon returned with his brother's children, identical twins, both of them seven years old, Pallas realized the same thing could have happened to him when he had been a child with the Cundi, back on the Colorado plateau. At least when it came to certain things, there was an assumed loyalty to one's tribe, a collective's hold on its members. In return, there was the collective's responsibility to its members. The two worlds of Aeon and Pallas weren't very different after all.

Aeon seemed exceptionally anxious and weary. With Pallas's release, he deposited the two children with the headman. They guaranteed that they'd teach the boys to farm. They promised they wouldn't keep them in the cage all the time. When one of the boys was allowed to roam freely, only then would the other be locked up to guarantee the other's return.

"Best deal you could get?" Pallas asked.

"Yes," Aeon said. He affected a nervousness that made Pallas deeply concerned. "There's an army afoot. They are moving up from the south. We must get back to the Oggaci as soon as possible. The children will be alright. I've promised that I or a proxy will look in on them once every six months or so. We have so many bigger things to worry about."

Chapter Sixteen

ALL THIS WOULD HAVE MADE Aeon's and Pallas's arrival at the Oggaci settlement bitter, but then the unexpected occurred which compounded their bitterness in a multi-dimensional way.

The settlement had been set ablaze. Corpses were strewn everywhere. Many of the bodies had been hacked to pieces. In the center of the carnage, on a grassy hill, along with other flayed and skewered bodies, Mantou was staked out, on a raised platform, impaled on a six-foot-long spike. The spike traveled along his spine and came out at the bottom of his neck. His head lolled to one side. His skin hung in flakes, as if peeled off like the skin of a banana, torn from his arms and his flanks.

Fires were burning everywhere. Some of the corpses were bodies of the enemy, but the vast majority of them were Oggaci, and half of those were non-combatants.

Pallas saw the crushed body of the old man Cacttus. He looked like a little child, curled up. Pallas remembered that in life he had subsisted on bean curd soup, turnips, and carrots. He looked like a rag doll, a right leg snapped behind his head, his eyes protruding unnaturally. The look of lifelessness in Cacttus's eyes distressed Pallas incalculably.

Pallas wondered why everything had turned out so badly. Aeon walked around the killing field as if he were ready to explode with fury and indignation. Being so close to home, they had thought they were safe.

The two searched for survivors. From the evidence of the destruction, apparently no one had been spared. The victims included women, older children, toddlers, infants.

Aeon gritted his teeth. He knelt on the ground and heaved a sigh. Then he became subdued and quiet. At last, he got up and wandered around aimlessly, restlessly, off kilter.

Aeon continued to roam around for the remainder of the day. It was as if he needed to bear witness, to take it all in, as if it were his punishment for not being there to defend. But the sheer magnitude of the destruction was too great and he was numbed. He could not find the bodies of his own immediate family. (He didn't know whether that was a good thing or a bad thing.) He collapsed again. He then sat motionless on the ground. He closed his eyes. Then somehow he snapped out of it. By the time the sun was setting, he became focused.

He looked at Pallas. Pallas was standing beside him, not having too great a distance separate them. During the entire day Pallas had not uttered a single word, not wishing to interfere with his friend's grief.

"I can't conceive who'd do such a thing," Aeon blurted out at last. His voice was low and guttural, but it didn't sound strangled or labored. "We have had enemies. But in recent times, no one has been bent on our total destruction. Maybe that's why our guard was down."

Pallas thought about the possibility that the Gaia-Domes may have been involved, but he kept his views to himself. Were there any signs of Gaia-Domes' participation? They had a reputation for being despicable, even worse, chaotic and unpredictable, especially when they had fallen on hard times. They'd been known to react to the slightest provocation with a massive display of firepower.

Aeon shook his head, as if all along he had been reading Pallas's thoughts. "We haven't provoked anyone. Over and over, we've bent over backwards to be peaceful. I'd rather deprive two innocent boys of the glorious part of their childhood than fight, even though we could finish off the forest Bear hamlet with a party of 200 warriors. Their only absurd luck was that they held you as hostage. How could they know that you were more valuable in our eyes than the combined worth of the entire Oggaci council? The Gaia-Domes have not operated north of Naples or very far north of Gibraltar for more than a century. What could be their motives? Their military action has always been directed to the south, or the east, or the west. They have always stuck close to home. Besides, there is nothing we have that they could possibly want. Aside from our food stores, our walnuts, our leather goods, what is there to fight over? A division of spoils? In the past, they'd written us off. We haven't even existed to them for a long time. *What were they doing here?*" he finished with a pit of rage reverberating in his throat.

"Yes, but, what if they were desperate?" Pallas asked.

"Like what could be the reason?" Aeon asked. "What could turn them into such blood-thirsty, cruel, murdering, marauding savages?"

"There must be an answer," Pallas said. He felt embarrassed. *What could be the answer?*

Aeon tried to clear his head. "With all this death, there must be survivors. Someone who could tell us what happened."

"It's a mystery, isn't it?" Pallas said. "In the mean time, we'll dispose of the dead. We can't bury them. There are too many. Perhaps we should build one huge bonfire, and burn them all. Including the enemy, there must be nearly a 1,000 corpses."

Aeon found the idea of cremation vile. For the enemy, perhaps that was okay. But he wanted to bury his own. Pallas understood. But Pallas said, "Reducing to ashes is the best course. Among the New Rebels, we always treated our dead respectfully—with burial. But it'll take too long. Before we've had time to dispose of the corpses, disease will break out. If there are any survivors, they won't be able to come back here, not for a long time. We must think of the living. And I agree with you, there must be survivors, even if there are just a handful."

It took Pallas a while to convince Aeon of the expediency—the necessity—of cremation. Then a group of twenty survivors showed up. They had hidden in a clean part of the bog, using reeds as straws for breathing underwater. They weren't able to explain what had happened during the chaos and mayhem of the attack, they just said: "Out of nowhere, the attack occurred. Who were they? Why did they attack? We don't know. That's all we know." They were able to help with the mass cremation, however. The job, nevertheless, took longer than Pallas had calculated, even with all the extra help. It wasn't until the end of the fourth day that they had been able to burn 75 percent of the bodies. Some of the enemies' weapons were lying on the field and the types of weapons suggested that the enemy was related to the Gaia-Domes, but none of the dead were wearing specific uniforms. It was that strange disjuncture that added to the mystery. One thing was certain, they had horses. There were a few carcasses scattered around. Aeon still was uncertain if his family was among the dead. Many of them had been so badly mutilated and so many of the body parts had been intermingled, he didn't know if his next of kin were among the cremated or not.

In the cremation business, the one exception they made was Mantou. In a full ceremony, they buried his body. His grave became a kind of testimonial, a monument to all of the slain. The morning after, Pallas sat at the gravesite. What struck him the most was he was able to watch a large spider spinning her web over the grave from branch to branch in a sunbeam. *While the struggle for life and death—death and life—tumbled over each other, Gaia also continued.*

While the twenty survivors completed the final cremations, acting on a hunch, Aeon and Pallas visited the old sacred island located in the middle of the bog. There something positive happened. They found refugees hiding underground. To Aeon's amazement, his family was intact. There were eleven other families, including five pregnant young women and the mother, sister, and grandchildren of Mantou. The group of 77 had escaped to the sacred place during the middle of the battle, before it had reached its full intensity. The survivors told Aeon and Pallas that Mantou and his most reliable warriors had taken a stand on the grassy knoll, allowing the others just enough time to escape. Aeon and Pallas found the families hiding in an earthen tunnel buried deep beneath the main fort. The tunnel was old, in a state of great disrepair, and it had not been used since the time of Aeon's great-great-great grandparents, when the Drangoes' eastern army had attacked the settlement. Aeon had almost forgotten that the tunnel had even existed.

But the survivors couldn't shed any light in helping to solve the mysteries: Who were the attackers? Where did they come from? Why did the attack occur when it did? Ultimately, what was the motivation? "We were just attacked," they said. "That's all. Their intention was to kill everyone. The only thing we're certain of is they wanted everyone dead."

Seeing his mother, sister, and young nephews and nieces, Aeon rushed forward to embrace them. His relief was profound. "You're alive!" he shouted, unable to hold back his tears. He let his grateful tears fall on his mother's hands. He was also glad he had followed Pallas's advice, having taken the time to dispose of the bodies before the survivors had time to return to see the torched settlement. The sight of the carnage would have been all the more horrible for all of the surviving families. Before they crossed back over the bog, to the decimated settlement, Aeon thanked Pallas again for his sound judgment. When the twelve families plus Aeon and Pallas returned to the burnt out buildings, there were nearly 400 people waiting for them, people who had lived mainly outside the settlement, who had fled deeper into the hills, who had managed to survive the carnage as well.

The horses were posted in a long line of 50 on a ridge overlooking the burnt-out settlement, their breath visible in the early morning hoary frost. Even Aeon, no military man, could detect that they had been ridden into a lather. Wave upon wave of visible heat could be seen coming off the animals' hides. All of the mounted soldiers wore impressive military tunics, and the one in the middle with the stout regal bearing, wore an elaborate hat fringed with black crow wings. The black crown was flared back, making his impressive beard appear fiercer, standing out, glistening white. After ceremonially positioning themselves on the ridge for fifteen minutes as if to display their military prowess, the chief of the Vorungi, Mester, led the horsemen down the hill in single file, their horses cantering on display, as if on parade.

At first Aeon's heart was in his throat, he was initially terrified. Then he eased up and he almost relaxed.

Some of the survivors wanted to run away—they were in a state of panic and fear—but they were also too stunned and way too immobilized to act independently. There was no way they could defend themselves against such a force. Besides, they looked up to Aeon now. After the near decimation of the counsel, he had taken the mantle of leadership.

Aeon's second reaction was one of guarded suspicion. But Mester, as the horses made their descent, gave Aeon a definite peace gesture, holding his fingers high over his head and controlling his horse by pinching his knees. Mester, at 250 paces, made clear his intentions by making *the gesture of the bowl*, the universal peace symbol of Gaia. The gold in Mester's teeth glistened as he smiled conspicuously, in a way intended to allay Aeon's fears.

Pallas turned to withdraw but Aeon stopped him from departing. "Stay put. Don't move. I want you standing here right beside me." Following his command, Pallas took his position beside Aeon. "Mester wants us to think he actually *believes* in Gaia," Aeon said.

As he rode, Mester stopped making the bowl symbol, dropping his hands to regain control of the reins of his horse.

Mester rode up to address Aeon. He must have known that Mantou and all of his warriors had been destroyed. "We are here not to take advantage of your recent misfortune, Aeon. They attacked us right after they attacked you. But we knew what had happened here, so we were ready for them. You bought us time." Looking around the burned out settlement, Mester added, "I see you've cremated your dead. Good thing too! Or you could have killed most of your opponents, at the same time killing yourselves, with the plague."

"Who was it?" Aeon asked. He didn't observe the niceties of diplomatic protocol, which were lost on someone as plain-spoken, shrewd, and determined as Mester. Aeon came straight to the point. "Who were *they?*"

Mester's horse reared up, then backed up two steps, before Mester could reply. He took a moment to steady the horse. "Rogue elements—mercenaries—of a once powerful army. They were once stationed at Hippo, guarding a large number of Gaia-Domes in North Africa. But the Gaia-Domes have collapsed everywhere. Except for a small outpost in Alexandria, none are left."

"The pestilence came up from the south?"

"Of course. They traveled up the Italian peninsula, burning and killing as they went, pillaging not for loot or spoils, but for food. From our reports, we know they made a beeline for us."

Aeon looked skeptical. "Mester, stop playing the fox. You expect me to believe that? Why cross the Alps? Only idiots would do that. If they were driven by hunger, they would have stayed close to home. Makes no sense to come north, at least, not this *far* north."

Mester made a circular motion with his finger at the side of his head, to indicate the questionable nature of the mercenaries' mentality. "Exactly! You put your finger on it! But hunger does strange things to desperate men's brains. Dreams of food in the north. Acting on rumors that turned out to be falsehoods. Farther north you go, the less food there is. We know that, but the rumor mill in Italy must have been up to its usual tricks. 'Don't stay here, there's more food farther away, keep going.' Deception as old as the hills.

So they rode north when they should have gone west. Should have headed for the southern rim of France, or better yet, Spain, or, at least, Morocco. They took the wrong turn. When they realized too late their mistake, they became more desperate. They just funneled themselves into a trap."

"They must have been desperate to do what they did to us," Aeon said in a low voice.

Mester shrugged his shoulders.

Aeon looked carefully into the chief's eyes. He tried to plumb for hidden meanings. But Mester's face was unreadable. He was hiding his true feelings behind a mask. The chief's horse pawed the ground nervously, as though capable of remembering the battle that it had participated in less than twelve days earlier. Did the horse prefer Mester as his master, or his previous master?

Aeon wanted to plead that the Oggaci would have welcomed the opportunity to act as auxiliaries in a battle against the invaders, they just needed to have been asked, but it was too late. He was certain that the horse the chief rode was acquired from the vanquished enemy. With a sinking feeling, Aeon was adding up the betrayals. Even the horse looked a little embarrassed.

Mester shrugged his shoulders. "If it is corn you need, you know, in order to survive, well, during the upcoming winter months, we'll give. We can provide seed-corn for your next planting if needed also. We don't expect any return payment or compensation. We don't think they're coming back. We killed every last one of them, just as they tried to kill every last one of you."

The Oggaci had survived 500 years in a hostile environment, through stealth, hiding, cunning, deceit, only to be defeated in this way. This was how a tribe was erased from the memory of the planet. The Vorungi chief had the delicacy to not say the obvious, that the remains of the survivors of the Oggaci would be subsumed into the larger tribe, probably within a decade. Like all aggressively expanding tribes, the Vorungi would expect nothing less than fealty and fawning devotion from the weak. What was left of the Oggaci could never make it on their own, certainly not in that tough neighborhood. Who would protect them from the Drangoes, for example, now that they had been *invited* across the river?

"If we could unite under our leadership all the five tribes, there is so much the Vorungi could do," Mester said.

"Like what?" Aeon asked. "Conquer the world? Improve the purity of Gaia?"

Mester brought his lips together bitterly, then leveled his eyes. "For a defeated leader, you speak rather audaciously, don't you?" He spoke with just a hint of malice. "End thievery. Boost trade. Give businessmen a chance. Allow trade to flourish. *Something a businessman like you, Aeon, can understand.* I know how gifted you are with words. Don't overstep, Aeon."

Aeon was dying to retort: "The ambitions of a would-be emperor." Instead, being diplomatic, he said: "The ambitions of a wise leader. The wishes of a practical man."

The apt phrases had the desired effect, bringing a smile to Mester's lips.

Just before Mester and his warriors rode away, he brought his horse right up to Aeon. Mester held his horse so close to Pallas and Aeon, Pallas could *feel* the horse breathing down his neck. Aeon could have placed his hand on Mester's horse's pommel. Standing in his saddle, Mester adjusted his sword. Then he bent down. Then he bent forward. He whispered into Aeon's ear: "Look, I'm going to marry our families together. But for the rest, they're as good as our slaves." He smiled. "*But as far as slaves goes, lucky slaves!* For the men, the army, eventual death, but an honorable one, alas, with the end of their bloodlines. For the women, not field work, but work as house slaves. In such a capacity, they might marry well, and if they do, they can do well. The women can come to rule their husbands." Suddenly his eyes fell on Pallas. "Who or rather... What's *that?*"

"What?" Aeon asked.

"Who is this bewildering-looking man-boy with the strange, scary-looking eyes, and my horse is licking his neck? I swear he isn't an Oggaci, a Faschonti, or a Sasho. Did you buy this creature in one of your travels up north, at some far, far away fair?"

Aeon grimaced. He introduced the stranger to Mester. "This is our guest, Pallas. He is from the New World...from the New Rebels. You've heard of *them*? Sent to us by their most illustrious and distinguished religious shaman. To study with us. He's been here for more than ten years." In a low voice, Aeon added, "We don't trade in slaves or children, Mester, you know that."

"Oh I forgot," Mester said in a sarcastic voice. "The keeper! With the useless moldy books, papers, and senseless crap from the Time of the Great Worldwide Catastrophe! You can afford to support a court amuser from some faraway place?"

"It's more complicated than that," Aeon said. "And the New Rebels are a much larger group than you'd suspect. I'm sure the whole world will come to appreciate that truth soon enough." He had grown tired of the tedious conversation.

Mester hacked. Placing his hand below his eyes, he glanced at the ground and spit out a gob of mucus. "In the olden days we exposed babies with degenerate eyes like that on a hillside, for wolf-pups to devour. Small wonder you won't find Vorungi with sickly eyes! We keep a purer strain, Aeon." He extended a glacial glare at Pallas. "Pal-*las!*" he said in a disgusted voice. He was in no mood to talk about Pallas, or about the New Rebels, or about the New World.

Pallas did not know why he had been directed to stand so close to Aeon. Aeon had insisted on it. But he was able to overhear the entire conversation. He thought when it came to the power of might, Northern Europe was no different than the Colorado plateau, perhaps even worse. Pallas was reminded that not everybody liked his eyes, or found them charming. It was a cruel world.

As Mester turned to leave, over his shoulder, he reminded Aeon, "Don't reject our offer out of hand. Corn for the taking. *Bend your knee a little, just a simple gesture, and we'll save you from starvation.*"

▶ ▶ ▶ ▶

Pallas spent the next six months helping the survivors get back on their feet. Finally, he turned to Aeon and said. "It's way past the time for me to make my departure. I'm long overdue in Escalante. I can't wait longer. I need to return to my homeland. I should have left almost a year ago."

"I know," Aeon said. "You've been patient, too. I know. You've stay longer than the agreed upon time. Of course, we'll see to it. I plan to escort you to Calais personally."

"No," Pallas said. "No. You stay with your family. You've suffered terribly. You've endured too much. Mester will be back, and he will have expectations. I hope there is some way that you can keep your freedom and independence."

Aeon would have none of it. "A deal's a deal," he said, shaking his head. "We promised to bring you back to Naxos safe and sound, and we will." Aeon cracked a wry smile. "Besides, conditions being what they are, I may cross what you call the Eastern Sea—what we call the Atlantic Ocean—and travel two-thirds of the way across your continent just to find a new home with the New Rebels. Would your tribe of the Cundi be that different from my tribe of the Oggaci? The idea of marrying into the Vorungi leaves a taste of bile in my mouth. Maybe I could bring my family over as well."

Pallas knew that Aeon didn't mean what he was saying. He was not being serious. It was just idle talk. He knew that Aeon knew that it would have been not only irresponsible for him to leave the Oggaci when they were flat on their backs, it would have been an unpardonable betrayal. In this, the Cundi and the Oggaci were alike. Clan and loyalty were of the highest value.

Pallas told Aeon that he could find his own way home. He told him that his company wasn't necessary. But Aeon would have none of it. And Pallas was glad that Aeon insisted on accompanying him. Aeon still had excellent contacts along the way and Pallas was certain he might not make it back to Calais in one piece without Aeon's guidance and connections.

When they crossed through the neck of the forest that had frightened Pallas so much twelve years before, he again told Aeon the story about the wolf. The first time Pallas had told the story he was eighteen-years-old. Now he was almost thirty-one. Pallas was no longer frightened. In fact, he was so self-assured and bold he wondered why he'd been frightened the first time. So, this time, at the end the story, they both laughed. It was the laughter of veterans, old grizzled survivors of shared campaigns. They felt they could have fought a team of wolves themselves, defeated them, and afterwards eaten them.

Aeon sighed heavily. "We'll never make it on our own. We'll have to knuckle under to the Vorungi. They can take their time in swallowing us up. That's why Mester let us up so gently. The remnants of the Oggaci will no longer be. My great-grandson will think of himself as a Vorungi. Who knows what will happen to the old books. We may be able to preserve a small handful of them, but the rest will be lost. I must try and negotiate a better deal with our old enemies. If trade improves, maybe some of our people can work independently in leather goods. Not just the strong, but perhaps the clever too, may survive. And the monks of the Skellig islands, they'll die out. They've lasted this long, but that has been a miracle up until now. You must bring back to your people the alphabet, the building block for a written language. I'm sorry we've lost in the burning our gifts to you: the written copy of the alphabet, the poetry of Ulm, the prose of Ingeline. Imagine. Visualize. Keep it in your head. I know that you will write something important for the future. Go now, Pallas. Go now, and prosper."

"Prosper?" Pallas asked. "I have no such hubristic ambition. I'll try to survive. Don't you think that's enough? I think it's quite enough." Pallas took on a familiar tone of detachment and passivity, the tone of a scholar. "But I'll try to write too. So long as Naxos will allow me."

"So long as Naxos will allow you," Aeon repeated. "The old master, the old controller."

"Let us bear down all sorrows," Pallas said. He didn't mean it as a salutation or as an ornamental utterance, he meant it as the literal truth. He gasped. Pallas gave Aeon the Gaia salute.

"Yes," Aeon said.

They hugged each other. They then hesitated, then, a pause, then they broke into laughter. They jumped up and down. With their hands on each other shoulders, they circled each other. Up and down, they jumped, round and round, laughter was more important than erudition and protocol. They only stopped frolicking when they reached the point of near exhaustion. Staring at one another intently, they pounded hard on each other's shoulders, like soldiers, like comrades, like survivors, like brothers. They both laughed. Pallas departed.

Chapter Seventeen

PALLAS FOUND A SHIP. It wasn't hard to do. It was an old-fashioned sailing ship, with three masts. On it, he crossed the Eastern Sea. There were twenty crates of oranges in the ship's hold, five crates of iron ore, and pepper and saffron. There were spices that had never been seen or used before by the inhabitants of the Colorado plateau: nutmeg, vanilla, and cinnamon. There was also a ton and a half of sugar!

When searching for a ship, Pallas made inquiries about his old captain and his "revolutionary" steamship. He quickly learned the sad, terrible news that the steamship had been lost. The story Pallas was told was that the captain had decided to make a hazardous voyage that included navigating Cape Horn in winter, five years earlier. The captain's mission was to pick up copper and highly prized tin—and a Chilean wine, undoubtedly the *extra* bonus to make the hazardous trip more palatable—on the southwest coast of South America. The ship must have sunk in stormy seas in the far south.

In Calais Pallas discovered there had been more ships' traffic than ever before. He had plenty of ships to chose from. Pallas had a *choice* of five ships, all of them heading for the new anchorage at Manhattan in New York.

Instinctively, Pallas chose the ship transporting oranges, spices, and iron over the one carrying leather goods and pomegranates, or the one carrying primitive nails, sturdy canvas sails, and hammers; or the one hauling bird manure and artificially manufactured nitrates; or the one transporting "new brides" from Africa and Scandinavia, a category of human beings so wretched they were basically only one step above chattel slaves.

The five ships departed on the same day. They formed into two groups for safety and tried to stay in sight of one another during the voyage. They managed it most of the way, until a huge squall blew off the Grand Banks, scattering all of the ships. All but one arrived safely at port. The ship carrying the "new brides" was lost at sea during the storm, apparently with all aboard perishing.

Ship traffic in the north Atlantic had increased three-fold since Pallas had made his first crossing, but all the dangers were still in operation. Pallas retched and vomited his way through the entire storm, so sick he was barely able to work, going topside to reef in sail, mending torn canvases below deck, and on long shifts, manning the bilge-pumps in the lowest bowels of the ship. But continue to work he did. Like the rest of the crew, he was glad to see the ship pull through the storm.

What Pallas found when he arrived on the East coast of North America surprised him. An outpost of the New Rebels, well armed and equipped, occupied the ruins of Manhattan Island. They traded with Pallas's ship, a ton of the New Rebels' excellent grain for six crates of oranges, and they took some of the iron too.

A New Rebel captain observed Pallas as he was escorted into a small citadel, an edifice built from the scraps of an abandoned Gaia-Dome.

"I've been under orders to await your arrival!" the captain exclaimed in the way of greetings. Pallas recognized the captain as having been one of his classmates, when they had been children. "You should have arrived a year ago," the captain added. "But I was told to expect you anytime. The Oggaci? You lived with them? Since you were late in returning, we didn't know for sure if you were still alive! We've heard mixed reports of havoc, renegade army intrusions, and minor tribal invasions throughout the plain of Europe. I have orders from Naxos, chief vice-president of the executive council, to devote all my attentions to your welfare. However, that won't be necessary, as you are under orders to depart immediately."

"Depart?" Pallas asked in a breathless voice. "I've just arrived! If I am to depart, what is my point of destination? And what's this business of *executive councils*? I thought they were called committees? Civic committees. And isn't that what they did, 'execute'?"

"You're to be escorted posthaste to Escalante," the captain said. "Teams of relay horses will be provided for you along the way. You've been away for nearly thirteen years now. Everything has changed."

"And are the Gaia-Domes all gone?" Pallas asked. "It looks like some of them have been dismantled."

"Gaia-Domes?" the captain laughed. "I haven't heard that one in a long time. Nobody calls them Gaia-Domes. They're *dome* relics. They're kaput. The last dome surrendered eleven years ago. We've locked down practically all of the dome relics, commandeering their materials. The committees, civic and otherwise, have been renamed executive councils."

Pallas was eager to learn all the news. "I can scarcely believe the changes."

"You've been away so long!" the captain exclaimed. "For me to convey anything to you, perhaps I should treat you as if you were a time traveler. We have outposts everywhere, new bases of operation, from coast to coast. We inhabit all points. Plans are being made to make the high ground west of Chicago, or a place east of St. Louis, or above the ruins of Cincinnati, the new capital. Or perhaps we'll carve a new capital out of the wilderness, halfway across the continent. People wanted to make the conjunction of the Mississippi and Ohio Rivers the new capital, but the location is hopeless, subject to frequent and violent flooding. Maybe further west? Things have changed, Pallas! Escalante has grown. But it's too isolated, too remote from the new trade routes. The old holdouts from the dome relics serve us now, providing administrative liaison, know-how, technical expertise. Especially *technical expertise*. They're building a new road that will stretch all the way from the Eastern Sea to the Western Sea. If we could just improve our written communication skills. That's why our reports are so spotty, we have to use runic script. They've added one more letter to the alphabet, P, making a total of 14 letters. They were considering also adding the letter "Q," but as it would have only helped with dome relic words, they changed their minds."

"That's thirteen years' progress?" Pallas laughed. "The letter P? The alphabet must be completely scratched, reformed," Pallas said. "Administrative liaison? What's that?"

"Oh, I guess that's a term we borrowed from the dome relics. We've borrowed a lot of words from them. It's from them we received the term *executive council*. They're changing our language."

"But apparently not the written part yet. You're Ajax!" Pallas said, his mind flashing to a distant memory recognition. "Didn't you beat me up in the third? I was eleven. You were three years older than me. You had freckles on your face. The freckles are almost all gone now."

"Yes!" Ajax replied. "But you're mistaken, I didn't beat you up. I was prevented from doing so. You were such an inviting target, being so much younger, therefore punier, than the rest of us."

Pallas smiled. "I remember. We were in class. I had been transferred up three times to the third. Sure, Peloreus taught us. The fool. I was so much smaller than you. You must have been a half a foot taller than me."

Ajax gushed. "Pallas the brainiac! That's what we called you. Now it's coming back. How could I forget? You were much younger. Even though we sat in the back together, I knew Matthew. Matthew put the squeeze on me. Matthew was the toughest kid in class. *The enforcer*, that's what we called him. He wouldn't allow any funny stuff. You drove us crazy. Your constant blabbering. Chirping. As a talker, you were indefatigable."

"I bet you I didn't know what I was talking about," Pallas said. "Muddy pants know-it-all, that what I was. I was the one who was a complete fool. That's how I see it now, looking back." Pallas thought back. He reminisced briefly about a couple of stand-out mottoes and high-lighted aphorisms that had been taught to them that were trite enough for a schoolmaster to drum into his students, but also just barely meaty enough to catch the attention of a deep thinking philosopher.

"Poetry boy!" Ajax exclaimed. "That's what we used to call you. Even as we taunted you, we secretly adored you. You were small, like a minnow. Yes, I remember, you recited elders' poetry. With such brilliance! With such command! *But that didn't prevent you from claiming you were going to be the greatest poet the world will ever know!* The word poet to me is synonymous with the words small and puny, because of you."

"Is my mother still alive?" Pallas asked.

"No," Ajax replied. "I regret to tell you. She passed."

"And my father? What was his fate?"

"Gone too. Immediately after you left. There was an epidemic twelve years ago. You went to Europe, so you missed it. Must be strange having been away so long. What was your time among the Oggaci like?"

"Yes, well no, doesn't matter," Pallas murmured. "So my parents are dead?"

"Yes," Ajax said, nodding his head. "They were among the first to go. The epidemic came quickly. But we were lucky, it didn't last long. Naxos saved us. *Make no mistake, he quite literally rescued us.* Changed our filthy habits. Changed our entire approach to hygiene. Issued decrees on what he called 'preventive cleanliness.' Now that I think of it, preventive cleanliness was another term from the dome relics. We had to bathe once a week. By decree! Even during cold winter months. Do you know had hard that is? Naxos made sure there was strict enforcement of the law. We placed indoor plumbing in public places. Naxos built thousands of public baths. Because of Naxos, more than a third of our houses now have indoor plumbing. Riding on his accomplishments, he was elected to the newly formed Executive Council and did he lord it over them. He may be chief vice-president, but secretly he runs the show. Trash removal. Special garbage disposal. Every week. We send out huge packs of scavengers whose only job is to haul away garbage. We pay them to collect and take away that which is worthless! Do you understand? They're paid to dispose of things that are of no value! Under strict orders from Naxos. We are made to show respect to them! Ever since the implementation of Gaia changes— 'implementation of Gaia changes'—a whole set of decrees, there I go again, an old dome relic term. Population shot up. Everybody wants to join us. Naxos wears two hats now, one hat civic, one hat religious. He negotiated the end of the Gaia-Domes. He organized the subjugation of the remnants of the dome relic's rulers. We have a thriving presence now in the ruins of San Francisco, in the debris of Los Angeles. We use old—dome relic words now. We don't even speak the same language we did. We don't communicate the way we used to."

"Is Telia alive?" Pallas asked.

"Who?"

"Telia. She was seventeen when I left. She'd be thirty now. Of the Montes family."

"I think so. All her family, except her sister, died in the epidemic. I'm pretty sure."

"Is Matthew still alive?"

"Matthew? Of course. Hasn't moved away from Escalante. Matthew is a kind of leader. No, he refuses to call himself that, he insists on the moniker *non-leader*. He calls himself non-leader spokesperson. For the dispossessed, for those thrown on the rubbish heap of life, for the poor, for the aged, for the sick, for the orphaned.

Matthew drives Naxos crazy."

"Of course Matthew drives Naxos crazy," Pallas said, "Matthew represents all the people Gaia used to represent. I could have predicted that this would happen."

"Matthew is still technically a member of the Forandi Order," Ajax continued. "Does he completely associate himself with them? I don't think so. On multiple occasions, the Forandi have asked him to become their leader, but he has refused. He has partially divorced himself from them. He lives completely on his own, in a single-room dwelling in 'old town.' Naxos calls him *The Forandi Renegade with a Purpose*. I think Naxos doesn't like him, maybe hates him, but he also grudgingly respects him."

"Of course," Pallas said, smiling openly. "Matthew is not a leader. That is Matthew writ large—that has always been Matthew, precisely. Ajax, is Telia Montes still in Escalante?"

"I don't know. Matthew might know her whereabouts. He has dealings with people like her. *New rebels* among the New Rebels. Started as a joke? Now more serious."

Pallas realized it didn't matter. He was going to be in Escalante soon. "What's happened to the New Rebels?"

Ajax shrugged, "You've been away too long! We're self-sufficient. We're stronger. All the tribes, even on the other fringes, have allied with us. The Outosh! The Carbeni! We're paid homage from Cartagena in the south to Abraxos on the Bering Sea. Our numbers doubled with the collapse of the dome relics, doubled again with the release of the last of the dome-relic slaves. Therefore quadrupled. We established ourselves from the tropics in the south to the frozen north. The New Rebels commanded 95,000 fifteen years ago. Today, there are three and a half million of us. Naxos says that within eight or nine years we will double. We have established outposts in the Caribbean, in the Pacific, in South America. We even control a helioplane, bequeathed to us from the dome relics. Naxos treats it like it's his property, like it's his private toy. *Even though he can't get it to fly.* He can get the dome-relic people to administer things—installing indoor plumbing, building roads, constructing aqueducts, making concrete—but he can't get them to fly the last remaining helioplane. He gets his monks to push it around for him. Anyway, we've taken over practically all of the New World!"

Chapter Eighteen

IF PALLAS EVER THOUGHT he had a chance to hug Telia Montes, and pour kisses on her, or at least perhaps see Matthew first, before he'd be required to attend a formal audience with Naxos, his guards made it clear that that wasn't going to happen. He was escorted directly to Naxos's "palace." Naxos himself called the modest four-story residence, equipped with hot water and a flush commode, his *Ecclesiastical Investiture*, a borrowed old dome-relic term. In Escalante, Pallas was treated by the guards as *Novice Notoraire*, meaning a recently ennobled personage without title. That was another old dome-relic term.

Yet Pallas hadn't been noticed by the townspeople, practically none of whom noticed or cared he'd left thirteen years before. But nevertheless he was closely watched.

Before leaving the capital of the New Rebels so many years before, Pallas was an obscure young man. He could have come and gone as he pleased. With relay teams of horses, Pallas traveled 60 plus miles daily, making the return trip to Escalante in thirty-two days, a remarkable accomplishment for a 2,150-mile journey. He noticed a dramatic improvement in the quality of the roads along the way.

He also noticed other striking changes. Escalante was six times larger than when he'd last seen it. A building boom was going on, pushing out the expanding border. The valley had filled with people. And the housing had not just expanded outwards, buildings were going *up*, some of them in the new center of town were an unprecedented four and five stories high. Pallas wasn't sure that he liked what he saw, but he also knew that there was no turning back.

Pallas was brought to Naxos's office. It was markedly different from the previous one, a modest one room austere arrangement. From the reception area Pallas had to be escorted down a blind corridor, devised to keep the residence mysterious. At the front entrance to his office, Naxos greeted Pallas. He was wearing no outlandish hat or garish gloves, as was customary in the Gaia-Domes, but his coat was quite fanciful, with gold trimming and piping and an elaborately ornate collar. Naxos received Pallas with open arms. It was a gesture of informality that took Pallas a little by surprise. And when Naxos ordered the guards to leave, without uttering a word, just a nod and a slight tilt of his head, Pallas thought he could at last relax.

Why did Pallas feel a need to impress Naxos? Because he still saw Naxos as a benefactor, as his good father figure? Or perhaps because he felt the need to justify being away for thirteen years? Or because he felt the need to show that he had changed? Maybe all three reasons.

"*We need a formally written declaratory language!*" Pallas said. "Before we can do that, we need an alphabet! A real alphabet. With 26 letters, old style. Or 30 letters, dome-relics style. Alphabet. Alpha Beta. A's and B's... I learned in New York that they added the letter P to our runic alphabet. Bravo! After 480 years, people can read my name and pronounce it without the slurry speech impediment of a proxy letter T. Pallas, not Tallas! That's progress, isn't it? We're building roads, canals, cities, a new road, a new canal, a new city, every month, so I've been told, but more can't be done without a proper mode of communication, a *written* language. I'll do the work! Put me to the task."

"Yes, I will," Naxos replied. "I'm assigning you to this immediately. Sending you to the Oggaci was the right thing to do." He rubbed his fingers together in glee and in anticipation. "And the timing's right. The timing's perfectly right. We'll get you started straightaway."

Pallas decided to be even bolder. "*Were those guards necessary?*" he asked. "You know I'm to be trusted. You make me feel like I'm an interloper, coming from an enemy camp."

"What?" Naxos asked. He was baffled, or gave the impression of being baffled. "What are you talking about? You're highly valued. We have to be so much more careful these days..."

Pallas glared at Naxos. Naxos had to stare Pallas back down for a long moment. Standing before him, Pallas was no longer an eighteen year old, he was a full-grown individual. Pallas exuded a brashness that reflected confidence.

"Guards accompanying me?" Pallas said. "What am I now? That was never done in Andromenus's time. Isn't that how the Gaia-Domes, or rather, I mean, the dome relics, used to conduct their business? A grandmagister never left the protection of his dome without a retinue of protecting—*also imprisoning*—bodyguards? They were there to protect His Personage, but they were also there to make sure the grandmagister didn't try to run away or hide. We used to have contempt for those cowardly practices in the day. Remember Naxos? That contempt was one of our ways of establishing our sense of superiority over the Gaia-Domes, excuse me, dome relics."

"You compare yourself to a grandmagister?" Naxos asked. He laughed. "Oh, you're so sensitive! You're a traditionalist now! World has changed? Let's have our meeting first, then we'll discuss all other things in good time. The dome relics have taught us about plumbing! They provided technology so we could build an aqueduct. Bringing spring water from the headwaters of the Paria! Without it, no building boom in Escalante, I can assure you."

Pallas began to protest, but Naxos waved his arms erratically, almost as if they were windmills, in the air. He said, "So much to do! So much to do!"

The next thing Naxos insisted on talking about took Pallas by surprise. Naxos didn't demand a formal report. He didn't inquire into the state of Pallas's health. There were no questions about education, writing, language. There was a passing question about the state of trans-Eastern Sea transportation, and the political conditions in Europe, but the third thing Naxos talked about was Andromenus, his predecessor—as if fifteen years hadn't passed since his death.

"Everything I've done is for him. Everything is in his name. I call this the 'Andromenus Age.' Allow me an opportunity to explain why."

"*What?*" Pallas asked dumbfounded. "*What in Gaia's name are you talking about? Andromenus? What's he got to do with it? The man's been dead and moldering in his grave for a decade and a half!*"

When Naxos finished his lecture, which took an hour and a half, Pallas had not been fooled by Naxos's exegesis on Andromenus's legacy. Everything Naxos had done, the dangerously corrupt absorption of the remnants of the dome relics, the modernization of the New Rebels' organizational structure, the breath-taking and rapid expansion of the New Rebel realm, now stretching from coast to coast, was in complete contradiction to everything Andromenus's thinking represented. Andromenus stood for keeping life-styles low key. He stood for purity of Gaia, justice, equality. He especially stood for purity—purity for its own sake, purity through cleansing, purity through chastisement, purity through burning, purity through exile, purity—as an afterthought—through justice and equality. If that meant keeping everybody barefoot and primitive, and keeping everybody in the dark, then so be it. That was pure too. But Pallas said nothing. He realized that upon his return he had stepped out of a time machine.

"So, you agree with me?" Naxos asked. "The days of living in caves are behind us?"

"Yes," Pallas whispered. "Of course." He meant it to sound sarcastic, but it came out sounding serious. He added, "Let illumination and hygiene lead the way."

Naxos shook his head affectionately. He looked at Pallas fondly. "Oh, you have a way with words. I like it. Could not illumination through electricity be a form of cleansing? To end corruption. To end impurities. Oh, I like that. That's neat. Would not Andromenus be so proud?"

Pallas smiled.

Then Naxos talked about the new educational mission, and the new writing project. He talked about Pallas's central role in both of them. "You'll be in charge of all the schools, naturally, and all the writing projects that should develop. We'll build a whole new department (*department*—another word borrowed from the dome relics) around you. We can spend twenty times, thirty times, as much money as before."

Pallas gasped. Was he happy? Was he elated?

Naxos became most animated as he spoke. His eyes glowed. "But there's something bigger than those two things, big as they are. We want you to write the Foundation Document for Gaia. The official one. Up to and including today. That is to say, up to and including Andromenus's legacy." In a hushed voice, Naxos added, "You are not to talk about me. You are not to mention my name." In a louder voice, he concluded: "The evolution of The Unseeing Watchfulness of Gaia into the New Rebels! We don't even have to call ourselves rebels anymore, do we? *What are we?* The Gaia-Domes are gone. We've lost our chief enemy and our rival. That's why we need a foundation document. You'll be in charge. You'll be solely responsible."

"You mean like—not to commit a blasphemy, of course—a Bible?" Pallas asked.

"As you wish. Though we would like you to call it something distinctive, an absolute departure from antiquated religious traditions. The foundation document shall exist on its own. It should begin with Gaia year one, presumably, and take into account the years up to 519 A.G., the year of Andromenus's death. Or perhaps we should start thirty years before 1 A.G.? That would include what the world was like before Gaia began? What do you think?"

"You mean beginning with the unfolding of Gaia, the birth of September?" Pallas asked. "*The former world before Gaia?* That's tricky. Theoretically speaking, we could begin even further back. The birth of Tom? That would be dangerous. Everything before 6 A.G. is educated guesswork. Everything before 2040 A.D., seventeen years earlier, is outrageous guesswork. Do we wish this to be the telling of the tale of outlandish mystics and buffoonish heresiarchs in the dream life of an early Gaia religion? By the way," Pallas added, "I've heard you have some dome-relic personnel in Escalante?"

"Yes! There's one in particular I wish to introduce you to. Their scholar. He prefers to use the title *special magister*. Five hundred years ago, there were *special magisters* in the dome relics. Now I think there's one or two left. We got one of them. He was stationed in Cincinnati, then before that, New York. His parents were stationed at a port in North Africa for many years when he was a youngster. Some time during that time, when he was a teenager, they inhabited for several years a city completely covered in sand in the Levant. I know you'll find him interesting."

Pallas was expected to say something, but what could he say? Silence was better. He was going to share power with the highest administrator of the Executive Council. He needed to speak with grace, caution, and circumspection.

But Pallas had to reply. He had to say something. He couldn't just leave the room in silence. So he decided to say something cryptic, allegoric, deliberately vague: "Truth will conquer. Truth will win out. Truth will come out of truth."

"That's it?" Naxos asked, looking disappointed.

"Yes," Pallas said at last. "Like I said."

Chapter Nineteen

RUMORS WERE CIRCULATING among the Obsidian Order. Pallas was the toast of the religious part of the town. The members knew they were on the verge of a powerful shake up and change. In the corridors of power of the Obsidian Order, and among all the orders of the Gaian religion, including the Forandi, when Pallas walked by, heads turned. He was seen as the man on the way up.

But word of Pallas's return had not yet reached the commercial or military parts of the city. And most certainly, it had not percolated down to the poorest parts of town.

And it was in the poorer districts, in the toughest neighborhoods, Pallas found Telia. And in Pallas's search, it was only in the neglected *encinas* and endblocks where Pallas recognized the old remnants of the Escalante he had once known. All the other parts of the city had been changed, as if the architectural planners and civic authorities had dynamited the dull, twisted lanes and rutted dirt tracks, and laid out a power grid in its place.

Pallas turned a first corner, a second corner, and a third corner, was he nearer to his old family's shack? His old residence? He couldn't tell. The neighborhood had changed. He saw a young man, rawboned and angular, spiritless and vapid, looking as dimwitted as any human being could. He was clutching a clay jar of home-brew, rot-gut beer by the neck. Then Pallas saw him cradle the jar in the crook of his arm. He was caressing it, like it was a baby.

The prospect of the young man ending his life in such an unnecessary way, perturbed Pallas more than a whole division of rambunctious mice, rats, and lice, or the overhanging cloud of melancholy that seemed to shroud the old neighborhood.

Pallas instinctively turned his gaze in the opposite direction. That's when he caught sight of her.

Telia was twisting her skinny body out of the slender grilled side exit, under the tattered cloth banner of a large orphanage's archway. She was carrying a long, thin loaf of bread under her arm, (to donate to a beggar?) and in each hand two empty buckets, one narrow and chipped, made of pitted wood and disintegrating rope, the other deep, broad, made of shiny metal and iron hoops.

Pallas recognized her instantly. She looked both forceful and radiant, as if she had aged only seven or eight years, not thirteen. As before, she was quick and agile (in spite of carrying two buckets and a loaf), and of course there was the tell-tale air of independent-mindedness and a menacing hint of courage. How could a "girl," so bird-like and petite, appear so forceful and intimidating, by the grace of her fluid movements alone?

Pallas wanted to reveal himself. But he wanted to do so to maximize surprise. He wanted to creep up behind her and throw his arms around her. Then he thought of something more devilish, albeit immature. With his stuffiest Obsidian Order demeanor, using his most arrogant voice, Pallas crept out of the darkness and shouted in her ear, as if addressing a street waif: "Hey! Water girl! You live around here? You carry water?" Telia froze, back turned. "Your arms and legs are filthy. You look like an orphan. Are you married to an old man with a broken nose and an advanced case of incurable sun poisoning? I'll buy you from him! You want an easy life?"

Telia turned and swung with all her might. She hoped to hit her ridiculer in the face. In the nick of time, Pallas ducked. Using a one-two punch, she swerved and swung with both buckets, both times missing Pallas's forehead by inches. Caught off guard by the attempt at a double blow, reeling back, Pallas sprawled backwards on the ground, using his heels to try unsuccessfully to inch away. Having dropped to her knees, with a look of somber terror, Telia crept beside him and attempted to jam the heavier metal bucket into his face. With a murderous look in her eye, Telia was ready to shove the more lethal metal bucket into the back of her pursuer's head.

Pallas cowered defensively. He was pushing the bucket back haphazardly, using his flailing arms. Only then did Telia recognized a semi-familiar face—*then she knew it*—it was a faintly aged version of an otherwise totally familiar face. She dropped the second bucket where she had dropped the first. "What have I done!" she smiled, at last her hands empty. "I'm killing my love."

Now that was funny, but Pallas's ensuing outburst of laughter only raised Telia's hackles.

So instead of recoiling from her handiwork, Telia redoubled her efforts. She took the only other potential weapon she had left, the long, thin loaf of bread. She searched like a blindfolded man, with her hands gliding over the filthy, rutted, dirt track, with her hand she at last secured it. She held it aloft and jammed it into Pallas's stomach. She stabbed once, twice. She twisted the bread-loaf as if it were a knife-blade. The bread loaf flaked and crumbled. With laughter, clutching his shoulders, slapping his face, pounding his shoulders, laughing even more, Telia's face was inches from his. Her breath suggested just the hinting aftereffect of garlic, but her neck bore the deliriously pleasant and robust smell of rosewater. "And you come to me. At last! Like a thief in the night! What kind of man are you! *You're a monster!*"

Raising himself, Pallas pressed his lips to hers. He reached out, trying to enfold Telia's arms into his own. Reaching forward, he kissed Telia again. "I love you. At last! I feel like a happy man! You're just the way I remember you."

"Only in your clutches," Telia said, at last welcoming the ardor of Pallas's embrace. "Let go," she said. But what she really meant to say was: 'Don't let go.'

She was too flustered to get the right words out.

After embracing each other for what seemed like an eternity, Telia disentangled herself and rose. In a deliberate and willful caricature of pretending to act prissy, dainty, and feminine, Telia straightened out her toga, a style of dress usually worn by men. "Stay here," she said. A little later, she returned with two more buckets, both of these wooden and fairly well beaten up. Telia handed them to Pallas. She picked up her own two buckets. "Come. Follow me. You know how to carry water, don't you? Shock the neighborhood. Be a man seen carrying a bucket of water. The pump serves 3,000 souls. You wouldn't recognize your own home in this place. You wouldn't recognize your own life in this changed city. But like an old toothless hag, you can at least port water. Now you know you are home!"

Retracing their steps from the spigot, Pallas wanted to ask Telia a million questions. He started with one: "How did you get the job?"

"*Oh, now it's a job? Whaddaya think?*" Telia asked sarcastically. "They'll not allow me to be truly educated. They worship women, but they don't teach them anything of a higher level of significance, unless perhaps if they are merchants' wives or daughters, or administrators' wives and daughters. Women of a lower caste are members of a male household—worse than being outcasts? Like beasts of burden are member of a household—*shelands*. I'm a misfit. You sure you want to be seen by society at large as being in too close an association with me?"

Pallas was at first silent. It pained him to hear Telia speak in the manner that she had. But he knew he had to say something.

"The lack of women's education is a big problem, I admit," Pallas said in a self-embarrassingly pedantic voice. "That's always driven me crazy. But you exaggerate." Pallas tried to continue, but Telia interrupted him. She put her hands up.

"Of course I exaggerate. Can't you use *exaggeration* to make a point? Can it not be, what you call, a rhetorical device?" Telia's testiness turned into anger. "Your surly monks won't even teach me and my kind our sums and useless runic letters. You did, of course, on the sly. I thank you for that. You risked being clapped in irons for teaching a girl her maths and letters, and only thirteen points of lettering at that. They'll elevate a born woman into being a goddess. They'll declare another woman a saint, as long as she's been moldering in the ground for 480 years, but I'm not allowed to do anything more than carry water. Have you ever wondered about that anomaly? To answer your question, Matthew got me the job! And I'm lucky to have it."

Telia's forthrightness disarmed Pallas, as did the power of her words, combined with her unruly, unselfconsciously androgynous appearance. But that had always been Telia.

"This is pitiful," Pallas offered lamely. "Don't be angry with me. I can take you away from this. I am going to be set up grandly. Naxos has made promises."

"No, I share the hidden secret burden of the New Rebels."

Pallas cuffed Telia affectionately on the chin. "This is worse than pitiful."

"No, this is the all-conquering, all-victorious New Rebels at their best! Armed with Gaia. Oh, excuse me, did I say that right? Armed with the true and absolute greatness and graciousness of Gaia, or some such nonsense!"

Telia gave Pallas a wide-eyed look. In an ironic moment, she acted like a cipher, scholar, educated person. "Irony is only good in short bursts, otherwise it represents complacency, if not complicity, in one's own oppression. I know everything. I suppose Naxos is offering you a plum. You're taking it, of course."

"You know everything," Pallas said. "You always did. I can never surprise you."

Later that evening, they sat down together in a dark nook of a tavern. Pallas told Telia all the things that happened to him: his journeys across the Eastern Sea, his travels across Europe, his time spent with the Oggaci. Pallas dwelled a long time on his sojourn with Aeon, when he told long narratives, about September Snow and Iona, and other stories too. But he cut short his account of the secret knowledge he learned among the monks on the Skellig islands off the southwestern Irish coast. Pallas did not want to talk to Telia about any subject that could have potentially involved the topic of heresy. He did not dare risk it.

"Tribalism exists everywhere," Pallas said at last. "Some of the butchery and barbarism of tribalism is worse in Europe than it is here. And when they are not frightened to death of others, shunning all outsiders and foreigners like they, or their ideas, are lice, carrying some dreadful disease on their person, they fight each other to the death like mad dogs."

"But they did listen to you when you told stories."

"Yes they did. There were moments of peace. People love stories. Stories that are well told are more compelling than facts. Before there was science, stories were the way we explained the world. After science, stories still exist. Stories will always exist."

Matthew was not taken by surprise at Pallas's sudden return, a messenger from the Forandi Order, (old classmate), and a different messenger from the Obsidian Order (also an old classmate), within an hour of each other, had informed Matthew that Pallas had concluded his long sojourn and had already had an audience with Naxos.

Among the old classmates, the 52nd class of 519 A.G., in spite of differences their paths may have taken, there were still bonds of fidelity. And to be able to break the news in the form of an announcement about the youngster, the whiz kid, the intellectual prodigal son, who had done so well, it was impossible to refuse the honor of letting the other prominent alumnus, Matthew, know!

Separately, Matthew asked each messenger to speculate on what Naxos had promised Pallas. Even though they were members of different religious orders, they both answered using the same words: "Whatever it is, Naxos promised him something great."

A third old classmate came to visit Matthew four days later. It was a military escort, assigned to Naxos's ecclesiastical office. He had more information but he had not made the connection between the old classmate Pallas of age 16, and the new Pallas of age 31. All the officer said was, "Naxos's been dazzled beyond belief. Place's humming. People are shifting. Things are shaking up. A whole new building has been assigned to the new man already. He comes from out of nowhere and BAM!! Whoever he is, he's big. Who is this man?"

"You don't know who he is?" Matthew asked, incredulous.

"He's new from abroad." The escort smiled, as if he really did know everything. "Pallas Missette."

Matthew asked the officer if he remembered who Pallas Missette was. He shrugged.

"Three years junior? From the days of our old classes? Oh, think hard, you lout!"

"That shrimp?" the military officer asked with his mouth agape. He was taken aback, putting two and two together. "Pipsqueak. He was the class know-it-all. He could regurgitate everything. He memorized everything! He memorized all the oral narratives! Teacher's pet. He's one and the same? He's been gone forever. *I thought he was dead.*"

"Well, he's not. He's grown up. Same pinched nose, same narrow shoulders, same tapered wolverine-face, same sad-looking, bitter blue, eyes-looking-like-ghostly-milk-holes. You should forget whatever it was you *think* you remember about him! Because, I can assure you, in Naxos's office, it will help fortify your career. Pallas is on the way up. Do you get my drift?"

▶▶▶▶

The next day, Pallas paid Matthew a visit, five days after his return.

"I know you had to visit Naxos, and of course Telia first, before visiting me," Matthew began. "It looks like Naxos has you busy already. Where is it? Your alphabet? Have you decided how many letters the New Rebels are going to have? Twenty-six? Like the Latinate? Or 30? Like the dome relic. Your parents are dead. Your brother left for the West many years ago."

"What has become of you?" Pallas asked in a sentimental voice. "Living like a monk out in the middle of nowhere, among the left behind, among the outcasts, among the poor."

Matthew shouted, "*I'm a monk!* The world's changed. I haven't. It's all one big tent. The Forandi Order, against my advice, even they've agreed to place their headquarters next to the Obsidian's, even though it's one-sixth the size. Naxos has concentrated everything under one roof. I've insisted on continuing to reside in old town, or what used to be called old town, now they call it 'reeky,' or 'mangy rabbit's roost,' or some other caustic, cutting epithet."

Matthew laughed. He looked at Pallas gently. "Those many years ago, remember? I told you we would still be alive. Time goes by, but I was right. The first time I realized I was a monk was when I started living in the real world. *Among real people.*"

"You found work for Telia in an orphanage?" Pallas asked. "I'm very grateful to you for that."

"So you found her on your own? Without any help from me?"

"Yes. I intend to marry her."

"Of course. You should. At first, the Mothers of the orphanage were frightened of her. Work that nobody wanted to do. Finding work for others that nobody wants to do. That's what I do. Did you know that there is a new rich merchant class in the town now? There was a period of time where Telia had to hide. The hunt for outsiders, nonconformists, and Gaia deniers, had grown too intense. She had to work like a fiend, hide like a cat, scurry like a rat."

Pallas had so many questions to ask Matthew he didn't know where to begin. Matthew was the way Pallas remembered him, but he still looked like a powerful street tough. He had cuts around his eyes, on his cheeks, on his chin, on his hands, abrasions around his knuckles, he even had scars on his scalp. He *looked* like a street thug, like a brawler. But that created an incongruity, a counter-intuitive distinction, that might have helped to explain Matthew's undeniable charisma.

Matthew, who joined the only religious order actively embracing poverty, humility, *and* obedience, was known among all his peers as the greatest enforcer of them all. This made Matthew an oxymoron: a *militant* Forandi, an iconoclastic Gaian, perhaps even a holy fool.

Pallas asked Matthew to rise. Matthew did. They hugged. Then they hugged again.

They talked for five hours. Pallas spent the night. The next day they talked to each other for another six hours. Matthew brought Pallas up to speed on the politics of the new religious power. Pallas brought Matthew up to speed on his travels to Europe and his life among the Oggaci, and their tragic demise.

Matthew said, "The expansion of Escalante began by accident. Everything happened too fast. But even the authorities now know it was a mistake. The civic powers should have gravitated to a more sustainable location a decade ago. Something near old St. Louis. But with the cycles of flooding and drought? Too dangerous. One moment the Mississippi River is almost a dry patch, next it's a torrential flood plain. As trade grows, especially overseas trade, there's no reason why New York won't become a primary hub again. The only thing left for Escalante to do is to be a religious center. The merchant class won't want to stay here, and why should they? They know they'd be better off along the coasts, or alongside a canal, where there is trade. Most of this growth has been mindless. The environment can support this stupidity for a few more years, maybe for a couple more decades, but definitely not for 50 years. I can assure you, Naxos knows this. He's building for the half century. He's building for the century. That's why he needs you."

"I don't need this now," Pallas said in a grave voice. "What happened to Telia's family?"

"You didn't ask Telia?"

"I didn't want to disturb her. You know her temper."

"Her parents died in an epidemic. Just like your parents did. Perhaps it's just as well. Harsh thing to say but I say it. Her family was always seen as strangers—outsiders. If her parents hadn't died in the epidemic, they would have been blamed for it. Telia's sister couldn't stand the daily suspicions. She just took off without any plan, ran away. For all we know she's dead. Telia was smarter. She went underground. She made herself invisible. How she managed I don't know. I helped her a little in the later years. I helped her even more, recently. With the explosion of growth, I finally got Naxos to allocate a small amount of funds for the maintenance of orphanages. That's one of the things I do. I was able to squeeze a small trickle of money out of the coffers of the Obsidian Order, who, as always, get their funding directly from the pilgrim trade. But they don't squeeze farmers anymore, instead they provide services for the new merchant class, which is far more lucrative. I got Telia a job working in one of the more obscure orphanages, three months ago. She's had to tough it out. But she's a survivor."

Pallas thanked Matthew.

Matthew hesitated.

"What's the matter?" Pallas asked.

"I'm of two minds. I have an urgent need to unburden myself. There's something more I need to tell you. But I'm afraid to disclose the information."

"Why are you afraid?"

"You might overreact. Then I'll be filled with regret at my mentioning it. I'm afraid of what you might do when I tell you."

"You haven't even told me what it is," Pallas said in an irritated voice. "Whatever it is, I'll follow your advice. As always. I promise. I will do whatever it is you tell me to do. I won't overreact."

"But you haven't heard what I have to say? Why so trusting?"

"I trust you," Pallas said. "The world's changing. I have to trust someone. I trust you, Matthew."

"But what if you overreact? What if you can't handle it?"

"Oh, get on with it," Pallas sighed. "I can take anything you can dish out."

"Your father came to me just before he died."

"Really? He envied you, you know. Although the word envy would have been too complicated a word for him to have articulated. What with his pea brain. And his total loathing of education. Actually, he envied everybody. Sometimes I think he envied a mangy dog for his fleas. He envied you, but he also hated and despised you, Matthew. There were times when he wanted to kill you. He wanted to kill a lot of people. Fear of the consequences was the only thing that stayed his hand. He wanted to kill me. But without me to torment, what could he have done to occupy himself? That was the one thing that saved me."

"It was after you set out on your visit to the Oggaci when he came to visit. You hadn't been gone five months. Your father came to me because he was dying. Your mother was already dead. The epidemic was killing thirty people a day. His impending death must have changed him. Within minutes of seeing me, he completely broke down. He spoke to me. Did you know that Naxos came secretly to visit your father?"

"I did not know that."

"Yes, he did that. That's what your father told me."

"Why would he do that?" Pallas asked. "I was nothing at the time. I was three years younger than you! My classmates called me names."

"That was part of your father's confession to me. When he banged on my door, he had a fairly serious fever raging. He was semi-raving. The stress of confronting me in the middle of the night with the truth probably only hastened his death. He said that Naxos gloated—egged your father on. He said, 'Keep beating the boy. Don't kill him. Don't maim him. We'll get his Obsidian teachers to try to get you to back off. But don't completely back off, back off some, but only some. Sharpen his wits. Build his character. Build his hatred. Build him up to a full head of steam.'"

"Get out of here." Pallas shouted. "What are you talking about. Take me for a fool."

"Naxos told your father to keep beating you. He told him it was good for you. He told him it was good for your *character development*. Your father said that Naxos sanctioned this."

"Why would Naxos do such a thing?" Pallas asked. "Naxos was on record as being opposed to corporal punishment in the schools. He was opposed to it in the police barracks. Hell, he was even opposed to it in the prison cells. He's a reformer. He prides himself on being a reformer."

Matthew shrugged his shoulders. "I thought you'd react in a self-conflicted way, that's what you do when your confronted with something extraordinarily difficult to swallow. You reacted the way I thought you would. Naxos is a manipulator. Why should he not be, he's an administrator. He likes to be in control of things. Especially when he identified your early development, your early potential, he had ideas for you way before you were allowed to know it. I think his behavior was the stroke of a mastermind. Naxos did it so that he could eventually save you from the wrath of your father...in the end. Then you would be at his mercy. You would be grateful to him. Eventually, your father would stop the beating but just in the nick of time. Then Naxos would be *your surrogate father, your new father, your good father, the father you always wanted to have.*"

Matthew allowed the information to sink in.

Pallas didn't show anger or regret. He looked calm and reserved. He had overreacted at first, but he calmed himself.

"What should I do?" Pallas asked. "Should I confront Naxos with the truth?"

"No. Absolutely not. It will only make matters worse. Play your game the way you always have. Trust in yourself. You need to keep these matters between us."

Pallas was silent. But Matthew could see that he was slowly coming to a like-minded conclusion. Pallas finally nodded. "I'll do as you say."

"Good!" Matthew said. "And this is to prove a point. Because you overreact. There's more about Naxos. This part you won't believe! Of course you remember the Wise Ones during the time of Iona and Kull, during the crisis time of the rebellion? There were twelve of them? Beginning with Dominic. Then there was Elsie. I remember those two. They were the most important ones. I can't remember all the names. But the last one was Ambrosia? I'm sure you can name all twelve, and recite their biographies."

"Of course," Pallas said. "At least what we know. I'm to write about them extensively. Some of their lives could be fodder for great stories. Even the more obscure ones..."

"Dominic was the most favored. Elsie was the second most favored. Some of the earliest runic stones were named after them."

"Yes, yes," Pallas said impatiently. "You could say I'm an expert on the subject. It was Ambrosia who directed Iona and Kull to the secret hiding place, to the mountain, in the middle of the Nevadan desert. Seven of the Twelve died during the struggle fifty years before, during the counter-attack and the Gaia-Domes repression. Four died within the first ten years after the victory over the Gaia-Domes's army in the desert."

"Of the original twelve, that left only one survivor," Matthew said, nodding his head energetically.

"Yes," Pallas said. "Ambrosia."

Matthew continued. "If you may recall, of the original twelve Ambrosia was the only one who bore a child of her own. Naxos is claiming to be the 27th descendant of Perum, Ambrosia's daughter. He says this gives him an exclusive religious pedigree."

"Oh, he's gone too far," Pallas said in a calm voice. "Iona and

Kull deliberately did not have any children so that there would be no development of royalty or an aristocracy among the New Rebels. It's the foundation motif of our system. That was part of the wisdom of the Original Twelve. Ambrosia was the youngest of them. When Iona and Kull allowed members of the Unseeing Watchfulness of Gaia to bear children again, Ambrosia was the only one of the Original Twelve who was young enough to do so."

"You know that?" Matthew asked. "You're certain of the facts?"

"Yes," Pallas said. "That has come down from the Oral Tradition. I could get an elder to corroborate the information if necessary."

"But the elders have been silenced," Matthew said. "Or subdued. Or co-opted. *Nothing's been written down yet, of course.*"

"I'm supposed to write the Foundation Document of those times, of our founders," Pallas said. "I know people who will attest to this."

"Well, there's going to be something in there about Naxos's pedigree, Ambrosia's daughter. You'll see."

"You mean Perum?"

"Yes, Perum. Naxos's the 27th descendant of Perum, according to Naxos. You'll see. Naxos has already announced it to the Obsidian Order. He's trying to establish the lineage with the civil authorities. Naxos's religious pedigree, going back to Ambrosia, to the Original Twelve—*through*—Perum's ovary."

"Balderdash!" Pallas said. He nodded his head with firm resolve.

"You haven't even started writing that document yet, Pallas, and look at the problems you're going to face. These problems, they're going to sprout up like so many beds of mushrooms after a hard winter's rain. It's going to get worse."

"I'll face far larger problems than Perum's descendants, that's for sure," Pallas said with a note of contempt. "I'll handle this. I'm planning on it getting rough. I'm prepared."

"I believe you, Pallas," Matthew nodded. "I believe you."

Chapter Twenty

PALLAS BEGAN WORK immediately. He found a printer who operated in the city who made a reasonable living printing handbills and accountancy labels for the new merchants. These new high rollers had become the printer's steady clientele for ten years running, but out of necessity they had to use the old runic alphabet—which limited the business. The printer had been a resident in the domes—in fact he had brought his printing press from the domes, carrying it with him, piece by piece, on the backs of his former slaves, who then became his new employees. Pallas told him, "The handcuffs are coming off. We're going to be using a real alphabet very soon."

The printer was delighted to hear the news. "At last!" he exclaimed. "Using a runic alphabet is like painting in black instead of using a rich palate." The printer spent the entire afternoon explaining to Pallas how his printing press worked, how he was able to acquire paper, how ready he was to make the changeover. "All the advanced electronic communication systems collapsed 150 years ago, when the power grid became unreliable. Dome by dome, when they lost electrical current, they lost files. Electric data shims were useless. They went to the Gutenberg model, using a mechanical printing press during the 75-year power drought. Afterwards, the hiatus had lasted too long to retrieve the data. We couldn't reboot."

Pallas hadn't a clue what the printer was talking about. "Data," "files," "shims," "retrieve," "reboot" were all words in an arcane jargon that the former Gaia-Dome personnel were busy introducing into the New Rebels' language. But he completely grasped the efficacy of the mechanical press the printer had shown to him.

Pallas had the printer issue a summons that were posted on every street corner in the city. Naxos had meekly suggested that they ease the public into the new language by incremental steps, but Pallas nixed the idea. Pallas explained to Naxos: "The runic alphabet is finished. It's primitive. It's pointless. In fact, it has always been primitive and pointless. The more extreme the change, the better. Nobody will miss the old system. Except for the old religious scribes who will be put out of work. Nobody reads their stuff anyway." Naxos raised no more objections, happily deferring to Pallas's judgment. Once Pallas received Naxos's nod of approval, everything moved like clockwork because funding suddenly became available.

The postings were such a novelty, people cried out for more copies so that they could paper their blank walls with them. The greatest application of a form of primitive advertising: wallpaper! By this sheer accident, by this fortuitous occurrence, it turned out to be an unexpected public relations triumph. *Of course, not educated in the new alphabet, only those educated in the dome relics could make out what the summons said, and so the only ones who understood the documents were former magisters and their subordinates. But it didn't matter, people were hungry for change, the time was ripe for change.*

They posted thousands of them, just in Escalante alone.

Pallas decided on a 28-letter alphabet, a compromise between the 26-letter Latinate, and the 30-letter dome relic alphabets. He had been taught by the learned among the Oggaci that a couple of letters had been added to the original Latin. One of the letters had been a W. He couldn't remember what all the letters were, but he knew it happened during the early Middle Ages, 2,000 years ago. Oral communication is a living thing. Speech changes with time. Without a written language to anchor it, speech changes even faster. Why couldn't he add a couple more letters to accommodate the growing number of people who were going to use the alphabet?

He issued more summonses. Pallas composed the first missives in his own hand, as it were, but within three months Naxos and the Obsidian Order got into the act and started issuing their own directives.

The dropping of the 14-point runic alphabet happened with breathtaking speed. Pallas turned to establishing a system of instruction for the new alphabet. He immediately acquired 500 acolytes for that purpose. Eighteen months later, the number grew to 2,000.

Everything was ready within a few months. This involved a rapid expansion of activity. Pallas discovered that he had an uncanny ability to delegate authority. Once the alphabet was on the verge of being disseminated, as if Pallas was channeling the administrative spirit of Naxos, he directed with a bold and robust hand. A whole new department was up and running within a matter of months. Pallas poured fire, devotion, and fervor into the creation of this department. He put in 18-hour days. Once the department was able to stand on its own Pallas slowly slipped away. He could initiate with clarity of vision, but once the project was established, he moved on, which was what a competent administrator was supposed to do.

Nine months exactly after the opening day of the changes, Pallas had more or less decoupled himself from all the day-to-day operations of the education system. There were so many new young people able to take up the slack, there was no shortage of skilled labor. They were all eager to work. In fact most of them were profoundly inspired by the project. Without Pallas's initiative, they would have been consigned to the dreary repetition of a calcified runic education, something they had been very happy to leave behind. And Naxos was able to get the ratepayers to bankroll the operation, convincing them how vital the revolutionary changes were for the future success of all forms of business activity. The new merchants even started educating their daughters in the new alphabet with private tutors. Pallas was shocked at how many words were coming from the former masters and the former slaves of the domes. A good forty percent of the new written words emanated from this group, and not just technical terms either. But Pallas realized he shouldn't have been surprised. These people, or at least the former magisters, had been familiar with the 30-letter dome alphabet and therefore had an advantage.

Once Pallas had cleared himself of all of his obligations, with Naxos's seal of approval he began writing the first words of his tome. He set himself up in an office adjacent to his home. At first he called the piece the Foundation Document. But he soon realized that wouldn't do, it had to have a different name. The title was important, so he decided to take his time and not come up with anything hastily.

In Pallas's initial draft the story began with the five-and-a-half-year-old child Iona reuniting with her mother, September Snow, in Gaia year Twelve. In the 12,000-foot-high desert outpost of Bolivia, in the rain-shade of a high Andes mountain, the action began. Anything to keep away from controversy.

Everything occurring previous to that was designated as BEFORE GAIA. Gaia at THAT moment had changed everything.

When Naxos asked him why Pallas wanted to start the document in the odd year of 12 A.G., and not 1 A.G., the dome-relics commencement of the new calendar, Pallas replied, "The dome relics cast their calendar. We embraced it wholeheartedly. It was called the beginning of the age of Gaia. But it wasn't Gaia. In fact, it was its exact opposite. It was the oppression of Gaia. Anything that begins earlier than 12 A.G. will result in dealing with events and people that were encrusted with ambiguity and controversy. To include that part of the narrative will lead to wars and doctrinal disputes for years to come. To preserve the memory of September Snow, we must paint the Gaia-Domes as the evil figures in the narrative. You can't get around that. I know we have many former dome dwellers living among us now, both former masters and former slaves, but it can't be helped. To make this thing work, even on a fundamental level, we must make the Gaia-Domes and most of their inhabitants the unmitigated villains of the piece.

Naxos acted as if he was unimpressed. "But 1 A.G. is the

beginning of the age of Gaia. Everyone in the world knows that. It's the beginning of our calendar!"

"Where do you want me to begin?" Pallas asked wearily. "Twelve years earlier? Twenty-five years earlier? Why not one hundred years earlier? Create a controversial storm that nobody will know how to stop. Do you want Regis Snow in this piece? He really existed, you know. We adamantly deny the existence of Regis Snow almost as much as the magisters of the dome relics used to deny the existence of September Snow. Yet he existed. His existence has always been awkward for our telling of the story. That's why we've tried so hard to ignore him. Why would the man spend the greater part of his life building something that would cause the deadliest oppression in the world? And he was a scientist. The worst bugbear of the past. Leading scientist, most successful scientist, world's greatest scientist. Every bone in Iona's body went in the opposite direction of her father. Teaching survival. Teaching orphaned children about the great collapse, how to live in caves. The legacy of Regis Snow and the Gaia-Domes was always seen as bad."

"But they don't deny the existence of September Snow now!" Naxos reminded Pallas.

"No. They can't. They wouldn't. They've been conquered, haven't they?"

"What difference does *that* make?" Naxos asked in a haughty voice.

"It makes all the difference in the world," Pallas replied calmly. "Conquering a group of people is not the same thing as getting them to come to us freely, without being under duress. Nothing can take the place of a heartfelt conversion, no matter how powerful are our armies. If you don't understand that, there's no way you can understand the transformation by Iona of a bunch of dejected and frightened orphans into a disciplined band of survivalist-warriors called The Unseeing Watchfulness of Gaia. I can emphasize the timely influence of Tom Novak too. The pedagogic part, at least. And I can talk about the role of Kull. That was extremely important too. That might help."

"Alas," Naxos mumbled. "Alright. Write your Foundation Document beginning in 12 A.G. We'll figure out what happened before 12 A.G. when we get to the end. After you've written the later parts first. It will be easier that way. As far as I'm concerned, you can make Tom Novak Iona's father."

"If I really want to be on the safe side," Pallas protested, "I should begin the narrative even later, with September's ascension in 20 A.G. Everything after that is less controversial. Gaia-Domes are still the bad guys, even then, don't forget that. There's no way I'm going to get beyond the fact that certain aspects of the past are going to be controversial."

"Right. Everything after that is less controversial. Begin there. We'll make up the most controversial part at the end. After you've written the main part. Just get on with it."

So Pallas wrote his story straight through and it took him three years to do it. From Gaia year 20 (2071 A.D.) to Gaia year 519. That's when the trouble started.

Chapter Twenty-one

TELIA AND PALLAS MARRIED one week after Pallas initiated his educational reform. Telia set up house for Pallas immediately afterwards in what was considered to be the third nicest part of town. The leadership of the New Rebels provided Pallas with a generous stipend and a reasonable salary. As a wedding present, Naxos threw in the complete payment for the modest house, and at the birth of their first daughter, Pallas was offered a seat on the Executive Council. (Pallas accepted the gift payment for the house gratefully, but shrewdly declined the gift of the seat, figuring that distance from the center of power was better for securing some measure of independence and autonomy.)

In quick succession, Pallas and Telia had four children. Nine months after their marriage had been consummated, Telia gave birth to their first child. It was a daughter. They named her Aura. One year later, Telia gave birth to a second child, again a daughter, who was named Teanna. One year after that, a third child was born, again a daughter. They named her Vivianna. Then, two years later, Telia gave birth to a son. Then, at Telia's insistence, they quit having children.

Pallas and Telia had a big fight over the naming of the son. Pallas had insisted on Gaia names for the naming of the daughters, but as a compromise, Telia was allowed the choice of naming any sons. When a boy was born, she wanted to name him Moses or Abraham, names from her ancient great-great-grandparents' generation, but

Pallas resisted.

"Those are biblical names," Pallas said. "As far as I'm concerned, they're fine names, but, as you know, they're frowned upon. You want to revisit on the head of your son the taunts that your great-grandparents received, the besmirching that was experienced by your great-great-grandparents? It will simply make life more difficult for him."

"But our dear friend Matthew has a Christian name," Telia said. "His family got away with naming him that."

"Yes," Pallas replied, "and he's got scars all over his body to prove the problems of having that name. Look at all the trouble it put him through. And he's a Forandi! Matthew fought with his fists for over two dozen years to acquire that balanced leverage point where his personality was able to cope with anything, just as he's been able to deal with all other forms of adversity. I won't saddle my children with a burden that could invite derision, scorn, even worse, ostracism. Telia, you can teach the children anything, but their personal names are their public faces. Names are the windows to the world. Your parents named you Telia, against their own grandparents' wishes, simply to *protect* you."

They couldn't agree on whether to name their son Prometheus or Proteus, so they settled on Pontus: *Bridge*.

"But you agree I have the right to teach the children whatever I wish?" Telia asked. "You agree to that, right?"

Pallas nodded his head with enthusiasm. "Absolutely. I've always felt that way. For all I know, what you teach them will be far superior to whatever I have to add. This is absolute, Telia. I've given you my word."

This reiteration of a promise given so many years before, before Pallas had even gone to live with the Oggaci, seemed to satisfy Telia more than anything else.

Occupying such a new prestigious post, of course, required Pallas to change and adapt from his previous life, but the change in their lifestyles affected Telia even more. She was no longer forced to live by her wits on the streets of Escalante. And she was so much in love with Pallas, she was happy to make the transition. She liked the idea of making a break with her past, especially in light of the fact that she had learned that her sister had died in terrible circumstances. Living under the rule of a bunch of *edgelanders* and outlaw barbarians, living just beyond the fringes of the New Rebels domain, she had taken her own life.

When Telia's parents died from the epidemic, it perhaps saved them from an even worse fate. Telia was the sole survivor of the family. Her past life had been one of suffering and want, now it was one of comfort and ease, allowing her to easily fill the role of a young mother.

But although by making a commitment to Pallas she had turned her back on her old life, Telia was extremely careful about her relationship with her newly, cosseted world. Telia insisted that Pallas and she not integrate themselves into the New Rebels hierarchy: *she wanted their lives to be separate.* She insisted that they attend as few parties and social events as possible, including mixing with the hugely successful merchantmen, traders, and "commercsears" who had infiltrated into the local social scene. There was to be as little intermingling as possible. Telia opposed Pallas having any extra religious or political ambition whatsoever. This extended itself to the commercial world as well. Telia was absolutely vehement on this point. And Pallas was more than happy to abide by Telia's wishes. He was of one mind on this—which became known as *Telia's rules.*

Pallas saw power as a means to achieving a specific goal. He just wanted to set up an educational system, then once it was ready, quietly slip away from it. He had no attraction to "the thing of power" itself. He secretly craved returning to a life of obscurity. The role of isolated scholar suited him perfectly.

Telia had been so happy when she saw that Pallas had the

strength to turn down Naxos's offer of a seat on the council, on the occasion of the birth of their first daughter. Perhaps, this was why Naxos tolerated Telia's role in Pallas's life, because secretly Naxos himself admired Pallas for his loyalty to his "inner principles," and had offered the gift only as a means of testing him.

And Naxos never pressed Pallas into taking a more public stance, because the lower the profile Pallas kept the less threatening it was for Naxos's own exercise of power. If Pallas had chosen to use the setting up of the educational system as a springboard to even greater avenues of power, in the long run, Naxos would have to have had to pay a dear price, because it could have provided Pallas with an independent power source. But Pallas wasn't interested in that. He was interested in scholarship, and in something that had been forgotten, except perhaps in the memorization of the Oral Traditions: the exercise of creativity.

So Telia's hidden agenda dovetailed with Naxos's explicit agenda, and by virtue of that peculiar alignment, there were no overt conflicts between the two.

And the writing of the Foundation Document went on slowly and laboriously. It was something that Pallas regarded as the most glorious thing that he could possibly accomplish. And to accomplish that goal meant embracing a life of solitude, isolation, privacy. All went smoothly yet laboriously.

Thus Pallas and Telia managed to keep to themselves, and Telia was able to devote herself to the upbringing of their children. The children represented the future. And she was determined to instill in them an appreciation of deeper human values, values that she had secretly been taught herself. So, as a couple, with these approaches in mind, Pallas and Telia rarely entertained outside guests. They were loners. Once Pallas was occupied with the task of writing the latter portions of the Foundation Document, he found it that much easier to live a life of seclusion. On the few occasions when they did entertain, it was almost always Matthew, and usually him alone. He came now and then, especially when he began to become attached to the children.

But we are ahead of the story.

Two years after the beginning of the writing of the Foundation Document, Pallas received an unexpected visit. The man standing at the threshold of his home had a flowing white beard, which made him look like an antiquated religious scholar. That was *familiar.* But there was something otherwise strange about him. Upon closer inspection Pallas realized the stranger wore the cloak of a Gaia-Dome magister, a cloak that might have once been regal and majestic, but was now tattered and aged. The cloak was closer to being a stitched-together bunch of rags than a finely woven piece of raiment. But the man carried a plain walking stick, dark brown in color and four feet in length, which was uncharacteristic of a Gaia-Dome magister.

Pallas paused at the door. Aside from Gaia-Dome personnel Pallas watched being strung up in the central square so many years before, the only other ones he had ever laid eyes on were well fed and beefy. But this man was gaunt and thin as a stick. He was tall, his complexion fair, his face pale. Twenty-five years before, just wearing these clothes in public could have landed him in incarceration, or worse, he could have been attacked by a mob, and strung up lynch-style. But now, apparently, it made no difference. Apparently, he was safe. *The world had changed.*

The stranger's smile was cordial and friendly, and also a little self-deprecating.

The man handed Pallas a faded, yellowing handbill. Pallas looked at the faded piece saying: "Announcement." Pallas recognized it, but was momentarily baffled by its significance.

"I ripped this off a telegraph pole four years ago," the stranger began. "I believe it was the first of its kind to be nailed up in public. It's worth mentioning because I was the only person in the vicinity who could *read* it. You'd be surprised at how many people asked me to read this message to them. But you would have been even more surprised at how many people *did not ask me to read it*. They were quite stubbornly devoted to ignorance and illiteracy. Paradoxically, they also saw the announcement as precious. The handbill was an odd piece of art to them, something they'd never seen before and therefore of great value. To them, it was a talisman, strangely akin to, and strangely different from, the 'ancient artifice of advertising.' Maybe that's why they tacked these bits of announcements up as floral design, to cloak their otherwise blank interior walls."

The stranger smiled smugly. He doffed his hat. It was as if he were offering to an outsider an insider's joke. But Pallas remained baffled. "Advertise" was a word Pallas was well familiar with. He had seen it repeated in some of the old books the Oggaci hoarded. It was also a word commonly used by ex-Gaia-Dome people. Via that route, it had been smuggled by convergence to street-lingo into the New Rebels' vocabulary.

Pallas read the faded handbill. It was just a notice stating that schools would soon be opening in the neighborhood. People could not "read" the notice. But what could you do when you're setting up a new alphabet, without depending on antiquated antecedents?

The first handbill was a mistake. The next notice was written in the old runic alphabet, announcing the new alphabet, then eventually, *much later*, new notices were printed and posted in the new alphabet, with hope of igniting even more interest in the new idiom. After a couple of years, newly minted school children were able to read the handbills.

"What are you talking about?" Pallas asked absentmindedly. "Do I know you? I don't get out much these days. I've become a bit of a recluse. Let's start with what constitutes the usual beginning among the un-introduced: Whom am I addressing?"

But the stranger stubbornly refused to introduce himself. He continued. "The horse before the cart you'd prefer, understandable, but no." He bared his teeth in an odd smile. "For some time now, I've observed you—from afar. I knew you were the first New Rebel to use this new language, but only recently have I learned you actually *created* it. We already had a similar written language before—in the domes—but in a sense, you created a new one. In the new written form, separate from the old runic alphabet, you added verbs." The stranger smiled broadly.

When there was no reaction from Pallas, the stranger became even more animated.

"Like in ancient history!" the stranger exclaimed. "Get it! The Phoenicians—traders— spread their alphabet throughout the Mediterranean, sometime over 3,000 years ago. Their writing arrived in Greece. Several of the Phoenician consonants encoded sounds not used in Greek, and at that point an unknown genius took a momentous step: He converted these unneeded letters into vowels. *Changed history!* The new Greek vowels eliminated nearly all the ambiguity of a consonant-only script, and thus enabled mastery of the alphabet by young people, even children as young as five. Several hundred years later, literacy in Athens approached a third to a half of the male citizens. For the first time, written language was widely shared among the population."

"I suppose there's a point to all this?" Pallas asked. "*What is this? A history lesson?*"

"Of course. And you're intrigued by it too. I know you are. You've accomplished the same thing that I'm talking about. Did you know that on the road to get here, a distance of just under two miles, I passed four small schools and two large ones, with the exception of one, thrown up temporarily, without solid walls, improvised, constructed of wood and thatch, made for the purpose of teaching younger children, but also older children, some teenagers, some near adult age, the offspring of ordinary people. Ordinary people! Not just schools catering to the elite. I know in some ways you've given up on the eldest inhabitants who shun change, but those schools of yours are going to change the universe."

"What?" Pallas asked. He stood at the door with his mouth agape. He was baffled. "Do I know who you are? Have we been introduced? Besides, they're not my schools. I haven't had anything to do with them for a long time. They never were *my* schools."

The man emitted a good-hearted trill of laughter. "And you lived for so many years among the Oggaci?" He regarded Pallas carefully. "Oh yes. Naxos told me about it. Those survivors—the Oggaci—now they remind me of another history lesson. From a different era, perhaps? The lagoons off the northern extremity of the Adriatic coast? During your brief stay in Europe, you must have learned something about those ancient bog lands. The history? Frightened, desperate men who hid in those lagoons that eventually became Venice? Refugees from more inland cities, fleeing successive invasions of Huns, Goths, Lombards, what not. Nomadic marauding clans, 2,000 years ago. Those marshy islands, plagued by fog in winter, choked with insects in summer, made a good hiding spot. Not only were they hard to reach, they were so grim and inhospitable, there was no point in raiding them. Just like the Oggaci with their tiny islands in the swampy mess—in the Jura, at the foot of the Alps! Of course, those fabled Venetian islands, now they're gone. Fifteen feet under! Covered by the encroaching sea! But there's still a skyline of second story, third story, even fourth story buildings—hundreds and hundreds—a myriad of shocking edifices sticking out like ghosts. In the near ground a damaged lighthouse, in the background, a leaning bell tower, next to it a cathedral hulk—slowly crumbling. Otherwise, so many structures gone! Although that was not to be the Oggaci's fate. You saw their exposure to vulnerabilities. What the remnant of the renegade North African Gaia-Dome army did to those poor people! Naxos told me what happened. Not before you cracked the language code."

Pallas had once been so important in the eyes of so many in Escalante, it had become second nature for him to conduct himself with ease. He had gone from obscurity to being an important man, but now he had largely dropped back into obscurity. But now he was uncertain. He had been thrown off his game by this strange-sounding chatter by this strange-talking man.

"I confess," the stranger said, "this progress—educational reform—you've initiated, has been phenomenal. A primitive people crawl on their hands and knees for 450 years, living in darkness—*literal* darkness—cave darkness, in a slouch of superstition. Then in less than one hundred years, they explode onto the world stage. Then after that, a man comes along and *literally wills* an alphabet into existence. Young people's minds change. You have created readers. Now for the first time they have in their possession a written language. They may have nothing of significance to read, official documents, edicts, religious hogwash, uninspired propaganda, but they are, nonetheless, readers. Yes? No?" Again the stranger smiled.

Pallas was overwhelmed by the man's recklessness, brashness, articulation.

Pallas was about to reply when from the back room a baby emitted a cry.

The stranger reacted with a further act of effrontery, almost crude in its effectiveness. "Time it takes—from conception to birth—for an embryo to go through gestation. Nine months? A miracle. Don't you think? Your son perhaps? How old is he?"

Pallas glared back. "That's my eight-month-old daughter, Teanna, you're talking about. I love her. Just as I love her mother. I have another daughter, Aura, who's almost two years old. The three of them mean everything to me. There's another one coming along. They are what I have in the world. You're lucky it was me and not my wife who answered the door. She would have sent you away. She would have clunked you on the head for your arrogance. She's harsh. Harsher than me. Not partial to displays of wind-baggery. *You regard yourself as knowledgeable of ancient history?* You speak in a way that suggests you know things that no one else in Escalante knows? Who are you really?"

"I'm the miracle man."

"I've had enough of this," Pallas replied impatiently. "Leave. I'm getting the police. At first I was a little intrigued, but now you've tested my patience beyond endurance."

"No, no," the stranger protested. "Wait. They actually used to call me the Magus."

"Sorcerers, magicians—out of fashion," Pallas said. But something held Pallas back. Had Naxos put the stranger up to this? Or was this Matthew's idea of a sick joke? Had his Obsidian brothers sent the stranger to Pallas on an errand? That's what Pallas suspected. To get Pallas to say something stupid, dangerous, and be quoted on it later. That was the sort of nefarious thing that the Obsidian Order was capable of doing.

"No joke," the stranger continued. "As I told you before, Naxos was supposed to have introduced us but he *forgot to do so*. I am, or was, ten years ago, a special magister. I'm a holdover from the old regime."

"I already got that," Pallas said. "I see your clothes..." Vaguely Pallas remembered having a conversation with Naxos at the point of which he had been given authorization to begin his educational work. He remembered how intrigued and eager he was at the prospect of meeting a real live magister, perhaps a repository of knowledge of a certain kind. Pallas remembered.

Pallas's interest perked up. "You were the one who had been to Europe as a child, right? I vaguely remember. You were the one who had been to the Middle East?"

"Yes, yes," the stranger replied enthusiastically. "I'm not just a magister. I come from a long line of scholars. I was the last great special magister. As a joke, the grandmagisters used to call me their miracle man, or, on occasion, the Magus. I am the oral repository of ancient religious knowledge: Zoroaster of the Medes and the Persians, Confucius of China, Buddha of India, Mani, Aramaic-speaking and Persian-speaking from the East, but still deeply influential underground in the West. Seminal figures in the history of religion. There were others: Jesus Christ, for example. I'm sure you've heard of him. And then, of course, Mohammad. I'm the old point man to this path of knowledge. But also later knowledge. Middle-period India. China. Japan. The Roman and Sassanian Empires. Mayan, Toltec, and Aztec civilizations. Early and late periods of Medieval Europe. The Enlightenment ..."

"So you're a dome-relic *relic?*" Pallas asked.

"Yes indeed," the stranger nodded. "Perfectly expressed. According to your way of speaking."

"Wait here," Pallas said. He hesitated, then he realized he needed to demonstrate a little more hospitality "On second thought, come in and sit down." The stranger stepped silently into the room. He stood a little awkwardly. Pallas offered him a chair. He sat. The stranger nodded his thanks. Then Pallas turned and murmured, "You wait right here. Don't move. I won't be long."

The stranger looked up. He sat in the hardback chair in the middle of the room, looking mildly perturbed, glaring up at the Gaia Earth art hanging on the wall.

As he tried to appreciate the paintings, he thought of what his great-granduncle had said on the subject: "Art was the trace of man's passage on Earth." But to this observer the sad and pathetically crude etchings were the equivalent of throwing night soil on the wall. The stranger preferred the splendor and glory of Renaissance art.

Judiciously, he decided to keep his non-New Rebel opinions of art to himself.

Then he heard sounds coming from the back room. He listened. There was an exchange of words. This went on for several minutes. On occasion, he could hear the sound of a baby's voice, but this time there were no sounds of crying, just the sound of cooing, followed by the comforting sound of laughter. The stranger strained his ears. He couldn't tell for sure if it was the mother or the daughter who had initiated the cooing sounds, but most of the time he thought it was the daughter. The mother's and daughter's voices sounded in sync. It was like they were engaged in a kind of pre-verbal talk. The pre-verbal interplay caused the conversation between Telia and Pallas to calm down, to become unemotional, in the end it was almost like everything was in a whisper. The stranger thought, those girls of Pallas's were going to have a new language, and they were going to have an opportunity to be brilliant.

Pallas reemerged from the back room. "It's time for my youngest daughter's nap. My other daughter is already sleeping. Let's go for a walk. Do you like to perambulate?"

"What?" The stranger asked, looking befuddled. "I beg your pardon. I haven't heard that term used in a long time. Per-am-bul-ate? You mean amble?"

Pallas's pace of mind had morphed quickly from one of guardedness and skepticism into one searching for external objects of curiosity. He grabbed his cloak. "I think better when I walk. I can ask questions better that way too. This is an invite. Accompany me. Let's walk together." Pallas regarded the man now in a favorable way. "My study is next door but I use it strictly for writing purposes. I prefer not to entertain guests there. I hole myself up inside there. I rarely receive guests now. I've gone back to living a life in obscurity. I like to walk. I like to live a life where I can go unnoticed, you know, be anonymous. *Do you not think that that is not wise?*"

The stranger smiled. "I lived through the last dying gasps of the Gaia-Dome empire, I suppose I can stroll through anything." He took one last glance at the Gaia Earth paintings hanging on the wall, thinking: such a defilement of aesthetic taste! He grasped his walking stick firmly in his hand, and said, "At your service, Pallas! Sweet Pallas! Lead the way."

Chapter Twenty-two

AT PALLAS'S INSISTENCE, they walked for some time. Pallas peppered the special magister with a battery of queries. For the most part they were practical questions, dealing with the special magister's last days in his Gaia-Dome, dealing with the history of the Gaia-Domes in general. Pallas was breathlessly eager for information. What had been the Gaia-Domes' strengths? What had been their weaknesses? At the end, why did they collapse so precipitously? Pallas remembered his conversation with Naxos about the special magister. As Pallas walked, asking these questions, walking at a robust pace, the special magister struggled to keep up with him. He shuffled his feet. He pretended to smile good-naturedly. Pallas then asked him questions about his experiences as a child and as an adolescent in the Mediterranean and in the Middle East. The special magister fielded the questions as best he could.

"But we were so deeply disappointed with what we found," he continued. "There was so little to see. Perhaps you too had heard some of the stories from those ancient times. First there were the ancient Egyptians and the ancient Sumerians, then of course, the Jews, a fractious and quarrelsome people, who fought among themselves when they weren't taking on outsiders. Then later still, much later, Christians. Later still, Moslems. But there was nothing there. Or at least, nothing of recent habitation. With the notable exception of a few goat herders, an occasional camel caravan, salt gatherers, the place was under-populated. My parents and I toured the area, but what was there to see? Can we slow the pace down, sir, just a little?"

The special magister continued to stagger as he walked. "As for Europe? My parents were stationed in North Africa. In a Gaia-Dome in Tunisia. Aside from a trip to southern Spain, and a trip to Sicily and the toe of Italy, Europe was completely out of bounds. But I visited some of the Greek islands, and later, the Adriatic coast. I was sent there when I was eighteen. Once we were in the northern Adriatic waters, we didn't dare touch land. Stared at the landmass, from the sea. The trip up the north Adriatic Sea was a bit of an undertaking. Where Venice once stood, the bent-back hulk of a cathedral, dark, and the upper stories of leaning, sagging buildings. A damaged lighthouse. A leaning bell tower. A few sticks and pillars standing straight up in the air. Otherwise, most gone. From the Gaia-Dome point of view, all of Europe had been overrun by barbarians, two or three hundred years before. But we had heard rumors about the Oggaci. *The survivors from the old days.* We heard about them too. Oh yes, we did."

The special magister tired more. He asked if he could stop and rest. Finally, Pallas agreed. So they stopped and rested together on a park bench, right in the old square, in the oldest part of Escalante.

"I admit to having gaps of knowledge," Pallas replied, "about that time, but there are some things I do know." Instead of being agitated, Pallas spoke in a thoughtful voice. He was almost getting used to this stranger, this Gaia-Dome magister. "More than anything, according to the Oral Traditions, the Gaia-Domes destroyed the truth about the past. They erased most of their records of the horrible things that they did. Billions died. Hundreds of millions were enslaved. But they electronically papered over all the inconvenient facts. After the year 2051 A.D., of the old calendar, is when they began to falsify. Until 180 or 190 A.G.—After Gaia—the first one hundred and fifty years or so were falsified. A totalitarian regime of conformity, mythmaking, and historical fabrication was created."

Pallas frowned. "No mention of September Snow? No mention

of the impossible mission of Iona? The heroics? The bravery? No mention of the candle that refused to be snuffed out?"

"Well, yes, of course! But your metaphor is wrong. Your ancestors learned to live in total darkness. *Without candles!* They stayed in caves during the day. They only went out at nighttime. There was a period when they had amazing night vision. They had abilities that have been completely lost to you now. They—that is to say, your ancestors—were too much of a threat to the Gaia-Domes. How could September Snow and Iona have existed? They could not exist! *Tut-tut!* That's how it had to be. That's how I was forced to remember. *But I was allowed to remember things that were earlier.*"

"But what is the point of you telling me this now?" Pallas asked.

"Because I was one of a long line of the last people to come over to the New Rebels too. We paid lip service to the idea of Gaia, but in our heart of hearts, we never believed in the doctrine. We never believed in the good Gaia, or in the bad Gaia, we believed in being repositories of the antecedent heritage. That's why we were able to adapt to the New Rebels so easily. True believers in Gaia who lived in the Gaia-Domes were true fanatics; they took cyanide rather than surrender to the forces of the New Rebels. And also, they hated losing all the conveniences that their slaves afforded them. They refused to accept any of the changes. I never believed in Gaia. The special magisters were to be the upholders of all of the old heritage, so, for example, that's why I know so much about the now vanished city of Venice. Do you know, what a great center of learning Venice once was? For painting? For music? For poetry? For civilization in general? Marco Polo, on his way to China, started there."

"What's your name?"

"Like I said. I've been called the Magus."

Pallas didn't want to go down that path again. He was angry. "I insist you stop treating me like a child. I never wish to hear you breathe that word, *Magus*, again. We are a primitive people to be sure, but I am not so primitive. Understood? I will ask you only one more time. What's your name? We are a people who believe in Gaia.

We believe in September Snow."

"Lloyd," the special magister admitted. He made a semi-impressive attempt at appearing to be humble. He shrugged his shoulders. "I am Lloyd, sir. I am at your service, sir."

"Lloyd?" Pallas asked. "That's your name?"

"Lloyd." For a moment, the ex-special magister's face flushed with pride. "I was named after my father's great-uncle, who had followed an unbroken line of twenty direct descendants of Lloyds. Through my celibate great-uncle, you might say I come from a long line of special magisters." But all that preeminence was of no consequence to Lloyd today. On reflection, he wished he had not mentioned the pedigree of his ancestors. The New Rebels loathed anything that might lead to the one thing they hated the most, a heredity-based power structure.

"Lloyd?" Pallas asked. "And with the knowledge you have, you call us primitive?"

Lloyd realized he must change his tack if he was going to give a favorable impression. After all, he had to remind himself, the New Rebels were his absolute lords and supreme masters now. "There are many things beyond my ken, I admit," Lloyd said. "But there are many things within the range of my knowledge that I can inform you about. I can tell you about Euclid and the mathematics he discovered 2,600 years ago. I can tell you about the infancy, the beginnings, of Christianity. I can tell you in detail how it progressed from being a crude, primitive cult, in a backwater province, to being the state religion of the mightiest empire the world up until then had ever known. I can tell you in detail about the collapse of that very same empire. The only thing that kept Rome from going completely under, at least in the West, was a business-run, survival-at-any-cost, institutionalized Christianity... I can tell you about the strange strands of inter-confessional rope—Judaism, Christianity, and Islam...whose adherents, when not humble, or involuntarily humbled, were usually fanatics! Yes, unfortunately, more times than not, fanatics. So many instances of intemperance! I can tell about the Dark Ages. I can tell you about the progress of the Late Medieval Period. I can wax lyrical about Dante's Florence. I can recite poetry describing the glory of Cervantes' Madrid. I can draw a splendid picture of Shakespeare's London. I can rhapsodize about Voltaire's Paris. I can draw a cold analysis of Goethe's Frankfurt-on-Main. I can draw a picture of Tolstoy when he resided in St. Petersburg. I can tell you about the Age of Discovery. I can tell you about the witch hunts, the inquisitions, the superstitions, stories that will make your hair stand on end. I can talk to you about the Age of Enlightenment—the Age of Democracy, but compared to what happened before, and what happened afterwards, these were tiny slivers of time, brief moments of...*what?* Freedom? Perhaps. I can tell you about the Newtonian diplomatic and military calculus of 400 years where nation-states emerged to close the Middle Ages. I can tell you about the global man in the street who watched 200 million deaths in war during the 20th century, endured dizzying and difficult technological change. Then in the age of the super-information, and simultaneously, the age of gross inequality, listened indifferently to the Earth groan under the incalculable burden of population and extinction. People danced a death-like dance, while all the time amusing themselves to death. We, that is to say, my ancestors, could hold to the veracity of the record of everything before 2051 A.D. That was our Faustian pact. That was our bargain. Before my ancestors agreed to join the Gaia-Domes. They were allowed that one concession. They could carry it in the deeper parts of their heads. That was the tradition I came from. That was the main reason why the new Gaian calendar was created in the first place, to make a complete break with both the recent past and the distant past."

"Intelligence?" Pallas asked.

"Yes, that's one word we used to describe it."

"Do you have any *written* records of that period, the period before 2051 A.D.?" Pallas asked.

"'Course not," Lloyd replied. "Except what's in my head." Lloyd rapped the side of his head, displaying a freakish smile. "Once they existed. No more. They were all held in electronic data shims. International Archives up until 2387 A.D., or 236 A.G., whichever calendar you prefer. But they're lost. Remember, we were the ones who held absolute belief in the efficacy of every new incarnation of technology that emerged. For that reason, we had no written backups. No parchment backups. Program in electronic data shims, yes, but nothing else. We held them that way for 200 years. Then electricity was destroyed. During the last great Black Out of 236 A.G. We survived with a chronically unsteady flow of electricity for 75 years. Too long! When our grid was finally brought back up, too late. All lost. That's when we started our own oral tradition. You think Naxos sent you to the Oggaci just because he feared sending you to the Gaia-Domes would corrupt you? Those stupid 'books' the Oggaci kept like talismans that were supposed to hold an arcane truth: collections of churlish photos, cheap paperbacks, cloth-bound romances, which I'm sure you spent years poring over. Don't worry about how I know this. Our spies were sent to find out if the Oggaci had anything of value. You must have known how useless those pots of pulp were? Advertisements of a fruitless age of navel-gazing and hedonism? Jumbles of advertisements for women's wear, but not a single copy of the Bible!"

"But you had records," Pallas interrupted, "even if they were just bare-bone ones, of the years before 2051 A.D.?" Amongst the worthless "books" that the Oggaci had preserved, Pallas knew there had been legitimate pieces of *parchment* documents, but why waste time caught in an argument about sources? "Do you have any information about Tom Novak, for example? Any information about his three books?" Pallas asked.

"Why would I know anything about these so-called lost books?" Lloyd asked. "Would they have been in the electronic data shims? Even if you got their dates of publication right? But, as I explained, they're all lost now."

Lloyd was impressed by Pallas's surprising depth of knowledge on such an arcane subject. "How did you know anything about the early life of this fellow Tom Novak?"

"From the Oral Traditions," Pallas said. "*Everything* we hold dear comes to us from the Oral Traditions. Twenty years ago, I memorized practically all of them. Fortunately, I've been known to have a knack for memory."

"Sorry," Lloyd said. "I wish I could be of help to you by giving you information about this Tom Novak in his early years. But I can't."

"This is driving me crazy," Pallas said at last. "You see, I've been selected to write the Foundation Document. Perhaps you heard something about the project from Naxos?"

"You're truly the wisest choice for writing this Document," Lloyd said, speaking in an earnest voice. "You don't have to worry about the Gaia-Domes having their own version of events popping up out of nowhere. Except for what a few of us still have in the coconut, it's all gone. You should be grateful for that. There had been a glut of data, *then fizzle*, practically nothing. You realize that this Document will also be the record for the remnants of the Gaia-Domes as well? I don't think you realize that you carry a much larger weight of responsibility on your shoulders than you think. It's not just a document, nor is it just a chronicle. Your job will be to create something new, something powerful, something that will unite all of us."

"It doesn't matter," Pallas said. "You can't help me. It's the period between 2051 A.D. and 20 A.G. that matters. Those twenty years. That's the hardest nut to crack."

"So you're okay with beginning in the year 20 A.G.?" Lloyd asked. "That's when you want to start? Starting late, aren't you?"

"September Snow's ascension into Gaia, of course," Pallas said. "It's the logical place to begin. The beginning of Gaia's immortality, if you will, metaphorically and practically."

"So you want to begin with a miracle?" Lloyd asked. "The Gaia-Domes tried to work a miracle back then too. The miracle of science. Regis Snow and the nuclear-powered wind machines. A geo-engineering fix to move climate change and global warming in the direction of a human advantage. A Promethean use of science. But you can't take on the role of the gods with complete impunity. At some point your liver will be eaten by a vulture. That's what happened to Prometheus. That's what happened to Regis Snow, too. No wonder September Snow was made into a goddess. She took you down the road of un-technology *and* anti-technology. She turned you into survivalists by having you turn your backs on the scariest aspects of science as it was applied by the Gaia-Domes." Lloyd became very quiet. It was as if he'd fallen into a trance. But it didn't last. After a while, he smiled inwardly. He tried to keep a straight face, but he couldn't. When he tried to keep a straight face again, he completely broke down.

"Miracles, miracles," Pallas replied. "Why not? What's wrong with beginning with a miracle?" Pallas stopped himself. "Wait. It's not a miracle? Wait a minute. It's a sacred text. It's a sacred event. It's a sacred event in the history of our religion. *It actually happened.*"

Lloyd thought hard before giving a reply. Again, he had to suppress the urge to smile. "The best reason we have to believe in miracles, Pallas, is the miracle that people are prepared to die for them. That's another reason why I've been called the 'miracle man.' It's not a term of endearment, it's always been a decoy, a term of irony. The man who studies the ancient history of religion, that's me. I understand you have been given the mission to write this Foundation Document. I understand. But after all this time? After all these years? What's the point? The truth? You really think this dubious character, this phantom scribe, existed? What was his name? What did you call him? Tim Novak?"

"Tom Novak."

"Whatever. September Snow never ascended into Gaia. Whatever you wish to call it, it's the end result of a myth. This history is all gray area. It always will be gray area."

Pallas momentarily became aware of the bench they were sitting on. He experienced a new level of acute consciousness. They were in Escalante. They were smack in the middle of the land of the New

Rebels. He had been a successful member of the Obsidian Order for approximately eighty percent of his 34 years. Gaia was not a theory, it was a grim and harsh reality. Pallas turned to Lloyd. "If you wish to patch up your relationship with Naxos, moreover, if you wish to live among us as a people, you had better stop talking like this. As primitive as you think we are, we have evolved beyond killing people for their beliefs. But people are still sent into exile for stating the heretical belief that September Snow did not ascend to Gaia. They still exile people for claiming that September Snow is not a goddess. For that matter, they still exile people for claiming that Iona is not a saint and is a goddess. Gaia-Domes are no more. Your special privileges have been revoked. You can get away with your cynicism with me, of course. I'm willing to entertain all sorts of ideas, fanciful or otherwise, but out there in the real world, I admonish you, *be careful.*"

"How did you know I was out of favor with Naxos?"

"Why else would you pick this exact time and place to try and wheedle your way into my good graces?"

"Oh, you're wickedly good," Lloyd said. "And you're such a powerful observer. I believe it. You've seen right through me. For the moment, it's true. Naxos is displeased with me. But that will pass."

"And you're quite a flatterer," Pallas said in a quiet voice. "But you will be of no use to me if you're dead. Which you will be, if you keep talking the way you do. But in a certain way, with your knowledge of the very distant past, you could educate me. You could inform me. I'd be appreciative if you did."

"Of course. And I'll tell you something that isn't intended as flattering." Lloyd said. "Since you are so keen on knowing the truth. Your writing this Foundation Document? What a nightmare! I would prefer to be dead than be in your shoes. You have no idea what forces you are going to go up against."

Chapter Twenty-three

AFTER THE BIRTH of Pallas's and Telia's fourth child, Pallas put Naxos off over the completion of the Foundation Document. There had been setbacks in setting up of the language program. Pallas used these setbacks as a pretext to procrastinate and delay the project. Time after time, he was drawn back into the practical world to help with the education project, but he always kept a low profile, as close to being as invisible as possible. He even went back to help with the final polishing of the codification of the written language. He ended up spending slightly more than half his time on the education project, slightly more than one quarter of his time on the written language, and ostensibly 20 percent of his time on the writing of the Foundation Document. He had scarcely time for his poetry. But by this time he continued to recede into the background, letting others take both credit and the limelight. In his background role, especially when the New Rebels realized they needed to "universalize" the education project to include, not just the younger generation, but their willing mothers and fathers and uncles and aunts. So he ended up doing some work on the adult's educational program, but that was it.

And this was where Telia took an active role in the education project as well. It was she who pushed to include—for the first time—girls and women. In fact, it was because she convinced Pallas of the absolute need to include females (and Pallas was able to convince

Naxos of this need too) that she gave unstinting support to Pallas's project. With regard to the education of women, Telia became the face of that campaign. She moved out into the community to wage her own campaign. She was able to get Matthew to collaborate with her to extend courses to the younger girls, to their mothers, even to their grandmothers, especially in the poorer districts. That had become her mission.

Once the new written language became a living thing, and not just an exercise for a revolutionary educational program, problems arose. Some of these problems Pallas should have foreseen. For one, more and more of the words used by the former personnel of the Gaia-Domes kept seeping into what had once been the New Rebels' purer use of language. The practitioners of the old runic alphabet resented *all these changes*. Correctly or incorrectly, they blamed the introduction of Pallas's new alphabet and the new written language for the spread of the so-called "word spoiling," or "phrase corruption." The New Rebels as a group had grown so quickly, it was almost like they were being assimilated by the outsiders, rather than the other way around. But this pace of change, some of it unplanned, some of it unexpected, caused Naxos to believe ever more strongly in the necessity of having a complete Foundation Document. Also, Naxos had reasoned, there was no better way to prevent new heresies from sprouting up. The Foundation Document would also forge a brand-new national identity, and perhaps even more than that.

A runic alphabet teacher—who, like most of his contemporaries, had been made redundant—unexpectedly paid Pallas a call. Pallas remembered the old teacher from the days of his childhood. But like all the others, he remembered him as, at best, a mediocre and uninspiring teacher of Runes, but an excellent teacher of some critical Oral Traditions.

The old teacher knocked at Pallas's office door. Pallas had been bent over his desk struggling mightily to write a first draft of a controversial part of the Foundation Document. He was suffering from his most recent nemesis: writer's block. (Did Tom *know* that September Snow was going to become immortal? That wouldn't make sense. If Tom did, none of Tom and September's conversations would have made sense. Gaian religious doctrine was often fundamentally different from how the characters were evolving in the document.)

Pallas got up from his desk and came to the door. He looked favorably at the prospect of being able to take a break from staring endlessly at his last fragmented, uncompleted sentence.

Pallas was struck by how much the old man had aged. The last time Pallas had seen him, Malmud had been one of Naxos's assistants at a ceremony. At that time, even with the graying of his beard, Malmud had handled himself on the dais very well.

Out of politeness and courtesy, but also giving honor where honor was due, Pallas offered Malmud a chair. Pallas even offered to brew a cup of asparci root tea for him. (Pallas knew that the old man didn't touch alcohol. In fact, the old man fanatically opposed all forms of spirit imbibing. As he rose from his chair, Pallas casually flipped his clay jar of *drago* into a drawer. Pallas practically never drank alone, and rarely drank with anyone else either, especially not members of the Obsidian Order. The one exception was with Matthew. Even then, it was on rare occasions. But he kept the clay jar of *drago* in his office, just in case.)

The old man angrily rejected the offer of the chair. He also said no to the cup of tea.

Malmud's rejection of the tea was discourteous. It showed lack of manners. But Pallas refused to read too much into it. Age had taken the edge from Malmud's voice, which sounded silken but thin. The old man's eyes and cheeks were sunken deeply. Pallas didn't recall ever seeing him so thoroughly distraught.

"Malmud," Pallas said. "My old teacher. Kind of you to come. What is the reason for this unexpected visit? I remember you as someone who guided me in my formative years. How can I be of assistance to you?" Pallas was purposefully laying it on thick. Truth told, he was scandalously patronizing the old man.

"The world has gone to hell," Malmud said. "All is woe. All is falling into a state of corruption. All is collapsing. The anti-Gaia devil has us by the throat."

"Anti-Gaia devil?" Pallas wondered. The use of the word devil sounded almost shocking, but Pallas tried to put a brave face on it. Devil-fear had been part of the older religious mythologies, but technically had not been part of Gaian thinking, *at least not until the most recent eighty years.* Pallas made an effort to smile good-naturedly. But when he saw the expression on his old teacher's face, he realized he needed to take the matter more seriously.

"Now we can't always stick to the old ways," Pallas said. "The world we know is changing. For good? Yes, I think so. For good."

Pallas had become all too familiar with the laments and grumbling of elderly people, especially those who were in their late seventies or early eighties, but it was almost always the old men who objected the most obstreperously to the new regime. The older women in general seemed to embrace the new changes more readily. Telia's intercessions had made a difference. The merchants' daughters and wives, persons of means, had long before acquired private tutors, so Telia's campaign was directed almost exclusively at the daughters of the common people and the urban poor. To his great pleasure, Pallas realized that Telia had blossomed into a consummate campaigner. And she had no problem bringing her oldest children with her on her campaigns. Pallas stayed home with the youngest girl and the baby boy when she went on tour.

"And this will never do," Pallas added, shaking his head. "As much as we have our druthers, we must embrace the changes. How else are we going to face new challenges, challenges we ourselves could never have thought of facing just a generation ago. As was practiced in the past, do you want to lock up girls in their cribs at home? And why should a boy whose only opportunity before had been to be a shepherd, or a smith's apprentice, not be something different, something new. Be a teacher! Be an administrator! Be a pioneer on the threshold of so many new technologies. A former pigsticker can now become a sanitation engineer. We've only had partial electrification for two years now. Do you want to go back to coal-kerosene lighter? Not the ways of the Gaia-Domes!" Pallas warned. "Walking machines. Or as the former Gaia-Dome personnel call them, bicycles! What a vast improvement on walking. I know Andromenus would have approved of these new-fangled wheeled contraptions. And I believe that some day, with the explosion of the written language, people will start to use their second names as well, not just informally among close friends."

Pallas had to remind himself what an old rascal and a thorny iconoclast Malmud had seemingly become. He should have been more careful, but he couldn't help himself.

"That doesn't matter anymore. I did not come to debate with you about this. I don't recognize the town anymore. Practically all of the administrative posts that are created in the outer zones are being taken over *exclusively* by ex-dome personnel, or by sons of ex-dome personnel. These former traitors and their offspring are even grabbing up important administrative posts locally! Ten years ago, they were banned from holding such posts, now they swarm over them. They're sneaky, pushy, conniving, bad mannered. They're not to be trusted. I can't adapt to the new language. If I *could*, I wouldn't. My former students shun me. New students have nothing to do with me. They scorn me, revile me, heap insults upon me."

After standing erect for a few minutes, Malmud's feet were hurting him. He was more than fidgeting. Now he was finding it impossible to stand. And because of his arthritis, his hands were starting to hurt him too. Standing, he wanted to appear dramatic in the eyes of Pallas, but instead he looked like an object of pity. He had turned completely red in the face.

"Change is inevitable," Pallas said in a friendly voice. "You always communicated better in Oral Tradition than in runes anyhow.

You should be proud of that. What difference does it make? We all have to retire eventually. You sure you don't want to sit down?"

Finding the discomfort and ache in his feet too much to bear—in a pique of fury—Malmud surrendered to a chair. Pallas helped him take his seat. "You taught me an important lesson Malmud," Pallas whispered. "*Chronicle Of Kull's Fight With Clive The Sub-Magister.* Remember? I'm sure you do. At the time, it was so little known. And these other poems you taught me. Beautiful! Truthful! *Pre-Gaia, The Collective Souls' Torture As The Best Mind In The World Was In A State Of Shock?* A rarity. Do you remember it? I used that poem as an inspiration for a piece of my writing in the Foundation Document. Of course, I had to tone it down. I had to be careful what words I chose. Tom could entertain ancillary doubts, be befuddled by marginal bewilderments, but not express a sentiment of full-bore, full-tonal skepticism. Oh, if only I knew more about Tom. Perhaps there was something in the Oral Tradition that you'd forgotten—forgotten to tell me—after all these years? You can tell me now. Do not look upon yourself as being less than what you are. During your time, you had knowledge to impart. You should be proud. And you seem to be able to remember some things?" Pallas added with enthusiasm.

The admission of the severe memory loss on the part of Malmud should have been a flag for Pallas, but he didn't give it it's due. "We've set up a home for people like you," Pallas said in a soothing voice, changing the subject. "It's out in the desert. You can mingle with others like yourself. True, conditions are primitive, but I've heard, for the tough at heart, conditions are tolerable. *You're tough at heart.* Corn deliveries are steady. Naxos, brilliant administrator that he is, has seen to that. Electricity and running water may never come to the desert and I doubt they'll come in my lifetime, or even my son's lifetime, but among old friends, like-minded people, maybe you'll at least be able to restore your memory."

The old man shook his head. "Without memory, I'm an empty husk. Allowing the dome-relic people to mingle with us is destroying us, just as surely as your written language will destroy us. Our runic language is useless now. But it kept us safe from impurities. It also forced us to keep our faith in the Oral Traditions. Purity is important. I believe there are toxic elements in the air, causing harm. Those former Gaia-Dome slaves with their *pills, their chemicals, all of their self-euphoria-inducing toxicities*. Today, electricity is worshiped. It's worshiped more than Gaia. Yes, it is! It's more than a convenience. It's a replacement for Gaia. What does it mean? We've become corrupted. An otherwise fleetingly exposed sandbar of lucidity—sticking up, now sinking down, sinking down—beneath the opaque, unbroken surface of obliviousness. That's me. Right now. In my brain. Right now. At this moment. Passing." Malmud twitched. "Passing. I'm frightened! Pallas!"

"Well, that's arguably *what?*" Pallas asked. "It's something to consider." Pallas was completely unable to empathize with his former teacher.

"Okay," Malmud said. "Goodbye. You can drink now if you like." Where the energy came from, Pallas didn't know, but Malmud had suddenly tapped into an inner source of energy. He revived slightly. Staring straight ahead, he exited the room. He went out into the street.

In terms of traffic, between the bustling hours of dawn to dusk, it was a slow time of the day. For foot traffic and the increasing walking-machine traffic, *bicycle traffic,* it was even slower. The timing of the event could not have been accidental, it had been well planned out in advance. Before arriving at Pallas's office, Malmud left a large canister of kerosene on the street corner. (Or rather an accomplice, someone much younger, perhaps a former student, deposited the can there for him.) The canister was so large it looked like it could have held almost four gallons of liquid. After leaving Pallas's office, Malmud walked to return to the canister. He picked it up and carried it with him. He had to hold it with both arms, grasping it to his lap, walking frog-legged. Every three steps he stopped. Then he put it down. He took a breath. He carried it to the edge of the street. Ceremoniously, he sat down on the edge of the intersection. Then solemnly he brought his forefinger and thumb together and touched his forehead, then he brought his forefinger to his lips, his chest, his abdomen. In an act of complete supplication, he got on his hands and knees and let his forehead touch the ground—once, twice, thrice. But he couldn't complete his personalized Obsidian Order prayer. He said the first two words: "I believe..." Then he stopped. He'd forgotten the rest.

Malmud said to himself: "I'm not worthy. I'm dirty. I'm disgusting. That's why I rage over the absence of purity."

Malmud grasped the canister. He poured the contents all over himself. Sloppily, a significant amount of the kerosene slid onto the street. He exercised the task with delicacy and finesse: it was as if he had completed practice exercises a dozen times before. He liberally splashed the kerosene on his legs and feet, on his abdomen, on his stomach. Then he repeated the process. Now with the canister being significantly lighter, he splashed the remaining contents on his upper arms, his chest, his neck. In the end, holding the canister aloft, over his head, he released the last gallon of liquid. He was completely soaked. There was so much kerosene that it spread out on the surface of the pavement, completely surrounding him as he sat. He counted to ten. A triumphant smile came over his face. In spite of his severe memory loss, he was able to count to ten! On the worst of days, his affliction being so terrifying, he barely made it to five. "Ten!" he shouted. He lit the match. He set himself on fire. He went up in a roaring flame.

Malmud had converted himself into a human torch. The flames leaped up five feet, for an instant of three seconds, swoosh! seven or eight feet, over his head. During the first two minutes, it was a bright flame. Then the flame subsided a little, but continued to burn.

Pallas heard shouts and even shrieks coming from the street. He came out to see the cause of the commotion and arrived as the fire was still engulfing Malmud. *Through the film of flame Pallas could still see something.* The old man had been battered, small, frail, old, but now his head was sunk down—caved in—lying on his chest, and he was already more combusting material than flesh.

The authorities arrived fifteen minutes later. When they came, they put the fire out. Later, they sent a team of scavengers in to clean up the mess.

Pallas sat in dread in his office. For months, he feared a repeat of the self-immolation. But it never came.

The incident did not help Pallas get over his writer's block. He worked very little on his Foundation Document for the next six months.

Finally, Telia returned home after a long tour of literacy campaigning. Pallas explained to her everything that had happened, not for once thinking to spare any of the grisly details. She listened carefully. And with alacrity she came to a judgment. "Malmud's suicide was solely the result of a medical condition, his severe memory loss. All the changes that happened to Escalante caused his dire need for purification, but those changes were neutral and inevitable. Electrification? Ridiculous. Ex-Gaia-Dome people diluting our precious language? Nonsense. The more words we have—the richer and broader our vocabulary—the better. Just as your introduction of a new alphabet, and a new written language, had nothing to do with it. As a man who recited the Oral Traditions, memory was the one thing he was most proud of. And with good reason. With his memory loss, he lost the ability to recite. That's what drove him to depression. And that's what drove him to suicide. You shouldn't feel guilty about anything you did. You didn't do anything wrong."

"But he seemed to blame me for everything."

"Ridiculous. You're too sensitive. He was like a man who walks long distances daily. His life depends on being able to walk, not just as a means of conveyance, but for sustenance, for livelihood, for physical health, ultimately, for peace of mind. And one morning he wakes up and discovers he has no shoes. Bad enough, you'd think. But then he wakes up the next morning and discovers he has no feet. Or use of feet. For an Oral Traditionalist, that's what profound memory loss would mean. *Through a glass darkly.* Just as catastrophic. Under such conditions, suicide makes sense. More a relief, than a burden. But why he would choose to commit suicide in such a ridiculously dramatic fashion? Now that does pose an unsolvable mystery, doesn't it? I guess we'll never know the answer to that."

Pallas worked on his Foundation Document for three more years, with ambiguous and sporadic results.

Periodically, Naxos would pay Pallas a visit. "Is it finished?" Naxos asked.

"No."

"When will it be finished?"

"Soon."

This exact exchange was repeated every six months or so, over a period of several years.

Then, finally, Naxos gave Pallas an ultimatum. Pallas had started working on the document in 532 A.G. He had completed three-quarters of it, the section from 20 A.G. to 531 A.G., by 539 A.G. He had also completed the preamble, from the time of September Snow's birth (est. 2023 A.D.), leaving the interval up to the year 2040 A.D. Lloyd had been able to give Pallas some great material about the Eleven-Years-War, between 2040 A.D. and 1 A.G., so he had written a rough draft of that period as well, by 543 A.G.

All that was left was the section before 1A.G. and 20 A.G., a 300 page section. Pallas had written several drafts of it, but none of it could have been threaded together to form a coherent whole.

Naxos told Pallas that he was to complete the document by 545 A.G., in one year's time, or the project would be permanently taken away from him.

It had been an empty threat, there was no one in the wings to take over (except for Lloyd, and Lloyd was out of the question), but Naxos tried to make himself sound convincing.

Pallas sat down and began to write the most difficult part of the document. In a frenzy, he completed it in 350 days, just in time for his oldest daughter, Aura's, eleventh birthday. Pallas's son Pontus was exactly the same age as Iona had been, five and a half, when she had met Tom, when he completed the document.

Pallas called the completed document *The Blessings of Gaia*. Pallas was six months away from celebrating his forty-sixth birthday.

Blessings: a passing nod of acknowledgement to the older religions, THEY WERE RELIGIONS; but gaia, the here and now, which would last forever.

The beauty of it was that there were fifteen-year-old children, sixteen-year-old children, even seventeen-year-old children, who had spent almost their entire lifetimes with the new language. They had no knowledge of the old language. They did not even know what the old runic alphabet was. Now, soon, they would have something really important to read.

Maybe as many as a third of the older generation took to the new alphabet and language. But all of the families of commerce, all of the military officers, and, most importantly, all of the administrators adopted the language with enthusiasm. (It was embarrassing that all of the former Gaia-Dome personal, with the exception of a specific number of ex-slaves, had also learned it.)

The single group who absorbed the new alphabet and language with the most elan and brio were the fifteen-to-forty-five-year-old daughters and wives of the new merchants. These young adults, and many of their older sisters, and even some of their mothers, were the first to hire and take lessons from private tutors. They also formed Reading Societies. Some of them even formed and linked together Literary Associations. Apparently these women hungered for a new cultural experience. Pallas's pre-Gaia-Dome printer was getting a large number of pre-orders for the Foundation Document. The printer didn't even know for certain how he was going to fill all of them. This literary explosion was the real revolution. Pallas was looking forward to see how it would all play out, but more importantly, how the guardians and protectors of the Gaia religion, most prominently the Obsidian Order, were going to handle it. He felt confident for the most part, but he still harbored nervous reservations and unsettling qualms. He had to remind himself that Naxos had taken him by surprise before. He realized that this might be the most difficult stage of the writing: the waiting.

Chapter Twenty-Four

NAXOS SUMMONED PALLAS to his office. He pointed to Pallas's Foundation Document. It sat in a pile at the edge of his desk, a stack of loose-leaf parchment seventeen-inches high.

"Magnificent," Naxos said. "*Absolutely splendid!*" He looked at Pallas with an expression of warmth. Naxos knitted his fingers together and placed them in back of his head, forming a headrest. He casually leaned back in his chair. Pallas couldn't remember the last time he'd seen Naxos in such a relaxed state, so uninhibited. It unnerved him and made him feel queasy.

"I knew you could do this," Naxos said. "I knew you had it in you. Goodness! Thirteen years in the making! Think of it. Eighteen-hundred pages! I'm not complaining, to be sure, the length's reasonable. No, actually, the length's more than reasonable. Think of it, thirteen years you lived among the Oggaci, then, thirteen more years, you wrote your opus. Twenty-six years in total. Your life's been so extraordinary. The thought of the document gives me gooseflesh. It will stand forever." Naxos smiled.

Was Naxos being merely rhetorical? Pallas wondered.

Pallas was already showing evidence of a receding hairline. In the previous twenty-six years, he had aged thirty-five. From the weariness of being a father? From the work of being a scholar? He sat down in the nearest chair. He attempted a tentative smile.

Pallas didn't rise to the bait of Naxos's flattery. Nonetheless, he couldn't constrain his desire to show off some of the scholarly lore Lloyd had taught him. Breaking the silence that now filled the room, Pallas cleared his throat and said, "Virgil, the Roman poet, after dozens of years of work, believed he never completed his poem, *The Aeneid*. He was such an artist, a purist, on his deathbed he was bent on destroying his slightly imperfect opus, because he hadn't, in his mind, got it right. But Caesar prevented him from doing so. If Caesar had acted differently, we might never have heard of Virgil. Virgil borrowed so much from the early Greeks. From Homer especially. Lloyd taught me so much about the writers of old, especially the writers who wrote before 2051 A.D. Even more so, the writers who wrote before 1040 A.D. Even more so, those writers who wrote before the Common Era, in 'B.C.E.' The farther back in time you go, the more knowledgeable Lloyd is. He's like a walking encyclopedia, especially on the subject of antiquity. He really knows his stuff."

"You meet with him often?" Naxos asked. "He's filled your head with unorthodox thoughts and strange ideas?"

"What can be dangerous about ancient history? I allow him to teach me some of the old, lost memory, yes. On a regular basis."

Naxos pretended to take delight in hearing this, but he wanted to stay on point. "But your Foundation Document, your *The Blessings of Gaia*, is not written as a poem. It's written in a more accessible form: prose. And the best part of it is the action stories. They are so dramatic. Also entertaining. I couldn't put the manuscript down. Sure, there were some dull parts—there has to be some history, right? But most of it is so interesting! Your reworking of the South Utah Cave stories was brilliant. I completely endorse your perspective, your version of the events. You play pretty cavalierly with your rendering of the stories but I say, that's good! And one of my favorite parts was how you described how the grownup orphans of Iona and Kull spread out to live in caves across the breadth and length of Mexico, and also into Central America, and into the deserts of the north. Most of the Wise Ones were killed, or otherwise met their death in some ghastly or macabre way, during that time of great peril, but you, an optimist, also depict it as a time of great opportunity. How close The Unseeing Watchfulness of Gaia came to being destroyed by the Gaia-Dome armies, and more specifically, by their relentless search-and-destroy missions! We have forgotten, or I should say, I had forgotten, how much time our ancestors actually spent living in caves. They really did learn to see so incredibly well at night. They weren't just cave dwellers, they were, not by choice, but by necessity, nocturnal creatures. Where did you get the ideas for that?"

"The ideas?" Pallas asked. "They came from the wealth of the Oral Traditions, of course. But the form and style of the writing came from other sources. But especially, from one source of inspiration."

"What source was that?" Naxos asked.

Pallas smiled. "When I was a young man, something special and totally unexpected happened to me. I traveled around parts of Europe after my studies with the Oggaci. These travels lasted for eleven months. During that time, I found myself telling stories everywhere. It was as if my walking aspects and my talking aspects were in near synchronicity. Stories were bread. As a traveling speaker, I was in high demand. And people loved to hear my stories, especially tales that included pieces about personal exploits. People wanted to hear about the trials of Iona, they wanted to learn the truth about September Snow, they thirsted for details concerning the Twelve Wise Ones. Even earlier stories weren't too far distant for them."

"Well, we come to the heart of the problem, don't we, Pallas?" Naxos said nervously. "Because we can never let you describe Tom Novak and September Snow—their relationship—the way you did when they were on their way from New York to Europe. Or when they were on their way from the Himalayas to Antarctica. Or when they were on their way from Bolivia to Mexico. Too intimate! They are way too familiar with each other. And we can never let you describe Iona the way you did, when she was growing up alone as a child, with Tom—in Mexico. But you got September Snow's ascension into heaven exactly right. And Iona's ending with Kull was beautifully written."

"But these are small problems," Naxos said, waving his hand in the air. "These can be resolved by making small changes. They are rectifiable."

"Yes?" Pallas asked.

"There are still larger problems, however."

"Yes?"

"The problem of September Snow's relationship with the Gaia-Domes. The problem of Iona's relationship with the Gaia-Domes. The problem of the Unseeing Watchfulness of Gaia's relationship with the Gaia-Domes."

"They are all one and the same," Pallas said. "The Gaia-Domes were evil incarnate. Our ancestors were fighting them. It was a life-and-death struggle. There was no basis for neutrality, unless you were the odd hermit living alone in the desert. I portrayed the events exactly as they occurred."

"You make it out as if all of the people, practically all of the people, even, what did you call them? Suits? Middle-middles? Upper Minds? Even some of the slaves? Who lived in the Gaia-Domes, were the bad guys."

"They were, weren't they?" Pallas said. "The internal slaves in the Gaia-Domes were kept in submission through the use of chemicals. They and the others were also given material incentives to cooperate, no—cooperate is too weak a term—they actually *collaborated* in what was ultimately mass genocide. The only good slaves were the ones who were working under even worse conditions outside the domes, the ones The Unseeing Watchfulness of Gaia eventually liberated."

"No," Naxos said. "You speak too broadly. You speak too strongly. There was only one type of bad guy. The top leadership. The top dictators. They were the bad guys. They were the only bad guys that could possibly have existed. The rest of the people inside the domes were dupes, or more properly speaking, victims. In fact, practically all of the people were victims. Everyone below the grandmagisters, with the exception of a few bad magisters, were victims. We must change September Snow's relationship with the Gaia-Domes."

"It's not the truth," Pallas protested. "September Snow was a martyr. *To the cause of freeing the Earth from the predations of an ignominious, Promethean-like, world-wide, scientific experiment. September's actions were the only thing that prevented that mass genocide from being completely successful.*"

Naxos grew angry. "September Snow ascended into Gaia. She was not a martyr."

"I meant that September was only symbolically a martyr," Pallas whispered in a quiet voice, gently side-stepping the bigger issue. "You know I believe in Gaia. But I fear you may have been too heavily influenced by Lloyd in your thinking. Technology may or may not be a neutral thing. But we have to treat the past with reverence. *Technology did almost destroy us.* Technology did not save us. *At least not then.* Caves did."

"I may or I may not be under Lloyd's influence," Naxos said. "But it's the only way we are going to find peace in the world we live in today. What's more important to you? The truth? Your Foundation Document? Or progress in our age? Peace in our time?"

"The truth."

"You only have to change, at most, 300 pages, out of an 1,800 page document. Be sensible. The rest of it you don't have to change one iota. Can you see through to do that?"

Pallas's face turned ashen. "But it's the third most important—*perhaps the second most important*—300 pages of the story."

"But you must." Naxos was adamant. "It will be under my supervision, of course. But I've assigned Lloyd to reassess the rewrite as well. You're dismissed. That's all."

Naxos studied Pallas's face carefully. Pallas was deeply upset. He was in an agitated state. It was as if he were too frightened to speak; yet simultaneously, he was also too frightened to remain silent. He stammered in an inaudible voice, "I don't know what to say."

Then, in a squeaking voice, "But you're asking me to convey a false impression."

Naxos shook his head. "We've creaked along with the Oral Traditions for more than 500 years. You expect us to creak along longer? The newest generation refuses to learn the old way. With the new alphabet, you've liberated them. You're the one who's created a splendid, beautiful language. A written language."

"You've asked me to create a legend," Pallas said. "Preserving legends, even worse, creating them, is not the purpose of written language."

"*A legend?* What's that?" Naxos asked. "Lloyd showed me with absolute clarity that legends often express religious truth—with vigor, focus, beauty—with their own form of truthfulness. *These legends* express truth with an all-comprehending understanding!"

"I can't do this," Pallas said. "I can't."

"Well, think about it," Naxos said in a mild voice. Then he immediately changed his tack. He said, "No. Clarification. Don't *think* about it. Our mission, Gaia's mission, insofar as we understand it, is to continue to work as a group. *To survive.* What's the point of looking to any future if we aren't surviving? Without our ancestors' survival, would you have a chance to write a story. Any story? Your imperative is to pass on the knowledge of the one true Gaia faith to all future generations. That's all."

"Even if that one true Gaia faith includes elements of willful fabrication, deliberate falsification?" Pallas asked. "*A legend?*"

"Too finicky," Naxos said. "Too tidy. Imperatives have a lower bar for finding the truth. That's what makes them imperatives. Without a memory—a preserved memory—we are ghosts. Accept this. There is not that much that you have to change. Resolve to accept this."

Chapter Twenty-Five

"DON'T GET YOURSELF needlessly worked up," Lloyd said. "Be reasonable. I'm only here to help. The actual writing of the Foundation Document is, from beginning to end, yours. If you cooperate, you'll receive full credit for the work. You only need to reinvent a measly seventeen percent of the book. Seventeen percent! What cost is that to you? I'm only here to facilitate that."

Pallas remained silent.

"Let's be fair," Lloyd said. "You've already revised different sections of the book, haven't you? So what difference does it make if you do a little more?"

"What?"

"'Course you have. No coyness, Pallas. You don't think I wouldn't notice?"

"I don't know what you're talking about," Pallas said in protest. "You are taking great liberties—dangerous and unwarranted privileges. You should readdress yourself to your station here. You're just here to serve as an advisor."

"You know exactly what I'm talking about," Lloyd said. "I'm your advisor. Providing you take my advice. September Snow never ascended into heaven, you boob. She was never seen by the original Unseeing Watchfulness of Gaia as a goddess! Iona was never a saint."

Pallas was awestruck. He was speechless. After a long moment, he regained his speech. "How can you speak like this? How dare you?"

"I may be the only other person in this town who knows this truth besides you. But I do!"

"This is an abomination," Pallas said. "Sacrilege. Heresy. Where did you come up with this?"

Lloyd grew bolder. "Oh, it's dangerous alright, spare me the pieties. I've been listening to a steady spew of pieties for more than ten years now. My great uncle, my namesake, Lloyd the Celibate, remember when I talked to you several years ago about him? He visited the two small islands, Skellig major and Skellig minor, off the coast of Ireland himself. Like I'm sure your voyage was, it was perilous. He got there about forty years before you did, in 490 A.G. Even as a young man, less than thirty, he was a powerful scholar. He had a profound thirst for knowledge. That forced him to make dangerous—very perilous—journeys. You can get around in the seas these days much better than people realize, even with primitive boats. He told me about Ireland, what truths he learned there, before he died. The monks? The bearers of the secret truths about September Snow? I know you secretly visited the islands yourself."

Pallas tried to scoff. "Even if you told Naxos, or the elders of the Obsidian Order, they wouldn't believe you."

Lloyd thought for a moment. "Yes, that's true. They would have no reason to believe me. It had never occurred to me to use this for purposes of blackmailing you. I'm being sincere now. It would never have worked anyway. Me? A former special magister? They'd have skinned me alive. And it doesn't matter. But, all the same, I know the truth."

"But how did you know that I visited the islands?" Pallas asked. "I have kept that secret from everyone. I've even kept that secret from my wife—-to whom I tell everything! I've also kept the secret from Matthew. I've kept it buried deep in my heart. Like my poetry." Pallas put his face in his hands.

Lloyd's face lit up. "Just reading your manuscript I could tell you were twisted and tormented writing about September Snow's Ascension. Yes, you wrote the section. And you wrote it lovingly, brilliantly, with fervor, with devotion, with passion. But it was hard. *It didn't come easily.* I could tell. It must have been the hardest thing for you to have written in your life. Because you knew, in your heart, it wasn't true."

Pallas buried his face in his hands. "HOW DID YOU KNOW?"

"Remember when I first met you? Remember when we were taking that walk? Remember when we were talking about my skepticism about September Snow's Ascension? How arrogant I was? You said so yourself."

"Yes," Pallas stammered impatiently. He couldn't hide the fact that he was flummoxed. "Why remind me?"

"The words you spoke didn't give you away, not straight away," Lloyd continued. "But the expression on your face suggested something hidden. I had doubts. What really gave you away were a few things in your Document that you could only have learned from the monks on the Skellig islands in Ireland. You slipped some of their commentary in. I'm sure Naxos didn't notice that, but I did. You could not have learned them from the Oral Traditions. That much I figured. Then I nailed it."

"And what were the things I said?" Pallas asked. "The incriminating evidence?"

"Could September's body have been buried at sea? So there would be no grave to revere in the future. If September ascended into heaven, there's no reason why the Gaia-Domes would have had to destroy all their records of her existence. That's what happened to Tom's body. And his records. You knew more about Tom than you ever could have learned by traditional means. You ask the questions, but you don't provide the answers. As if she ascended? But would Tom have believed that she had ascended? Of course not. But then, he was of the older generation, and by virtue of that fact, he had been hopelessly corrupted by all those retro influences you took such care to avoid. If anybody had read the Document and knew the truth, it's as if you couldn't resist trying to give them a nudge to create for themselves a speculative cover. You can't be truthful about Tom's character and make September's ascension work, so you fudged it."

Pallas was silent. At the moment, he feared speaking. He was afraid of what he might say.

"There are still some people left who know the Oral Traditions better than you can imagine, Pallas. Not all of them have immolated themselves. You must be careful. We better take great care with this."

Pallas was silent.

"It's going to be a great Foundation Document," Lloyd said. "And I love the fact that you are insisting on calling it The Blessings of Gaia. Eighteen hundred pages long! There's just a few things we have to clear up first."

Pallas stared into space.

"We can do this," Lloyd said. "It's less work than you think. It involves fewer changes that you think. Trust me."

For the first time, Pallas got drunk on his own. Never before had he had something on his mind that he couldn't talk to Telia or Matthew about. The only person he could talk to was Lloyd, and so, in his office, alone, he got himself drunk. He wanted to anesthetize himself. At one point, he even thought about Malmud. With tears in his eyes, he felt shame. But it was an inchoate shame. Was it the shame of betraying an abstract idea of literature? Or was it the shame of betraying his religion? Or the shame of betraying both? He wanted to shirk all thoughts along these lines, get his mind off both subjects.

Even though he was suffering from a severe hangover, the

next day Pallas visited his printer. The printer had finally recreated a machine from the past. He had announced his "reinvention" to Pallas two months earlier. At their last meeting, the month before, the printer had enthusiastically asked Pallas to come by and check out his "new contraption" as soon as he was able to visit. "It's almost done. It will be completed in a week. Come." He had named it a key-walker.

"We can eventually upgrade it," the printer said enthusiastically, when Pallas visited him. "When electricity becomes more reliable. But for now it's just a manual key-walker." (Why did the printer call it a "key-walker?" Because you let your fingers do the walking.) "Well, here, give it a try," the printer said. "I think you'll enjoy it. I tried to put most of the letters where they'd belong, but basically it's a guessing game. The letters and tabs were made out of metal, or bone, by necessity, but the box itself, the carriage, the roller, the space bar—I made out of wood. Actually, it doesn't matter where the letters are put, just so long as the key-walkers are put in the same place. This one is just a kind of prototype. I wanted you to be the first to try it out. I saw a picture of one in a magazine folio collection when I was a young man in the Gaia-Domes. It was called not an electronic apparatus, but an *electric* typewriter. One ran on electricity. This one's manual."

Pallas played around by hitting the tabs. First he hit a letter too softly. He adjusted. Then he hit one too hard. He adjusted. Then he got it right. Pallas started with only his index fingers, but within thirty minutes, he was using most of his fingers. An hour later, he was using all his fingers, including his thumbs. After playing around with it for five or six hours, he was able to "key-walk." He discovered he had to memorize where most of the letters were, especially the vowels, if he wanted to key-walk, with any accuracy. He preferred the vowel keys, because they were made of bone (they were elegant). The consonant keys were made out of steel. Eventually, he even tried key-walking with his eyes closed—touch alone. Pallas decided to try key-walking something very quickly. He remembered what Lloyd had said to him when he first met him: "It's necessary. Your job will be to unite us."

As an experiment, Pallas tried to key-walk the phrase as quickly as possible. He even closed his eyes, touching blind. But he key-walked too rapidly. Using his pinkies in an unskillful manner, he got two letters in reverse. It came out: "It's necessary. Your job will be to untie us."

Pallas gasped. Unite had been changed to untie. Then he smiled. An entire thought could be actually reversed with a single letter reversal.

He placed a new piece of paper into the wooden roll of the machine. He keyed the phrase again. This time he kept his eyes open. He got it right. "It's necessary. Your job will be to unite us." Pallas murmured to himself, in a low voice: "I must do this? For the sake of peace?"

The printer smiled boldly, proud of his new contraption.

Chapter Twenty-Six

IT TOOK ONLY FOUR MONTHS to rewrite the objectionable passages. Lloyd and Pallas worked on the revised portions, fifteen hours a day, six days a week. It required fifteen revisions. Each of these was submitted to Naxos, who received them with enthusiasm. Of these rewrites, nine were minor changes, but six involved major alterations.

Tom was no longer the man he had been in the first document. Pallas couldn't even recognize him in the storyline anymore. When it came to September Snow, there was now no skepticism about her divinity. Tom was a firm believer in Gaia, from beginning to end. And that was the end of it.

And the inhabitants of the Gaia-Domes, 99.999 percent of whom were innocent dupes, or long-suffering victims, forced under duress to do the vicious and horrible things that they admittedly did, had been misled by a series of grandmagisters, twenty in each generation, they were truly the evil ones. By the end of the final draft, during the last rewrite, Pallas got so drunk that he felt the urge to throw up. This resulted in an involuntary act of projectile vomiting.

For several months Pallas had been scarcely able to keep his food down. He lost weight. Lloyd had been keeping him so well-oiled with alcohol during the final months of the rewrite that Pallas either appeared to have a serious drinking problem, or in fact did have one.

Pallas was miserable. During the little time he spent with his family he argued with them. Many times the bickering and quarreling turned bitter. Pallas was uncharacteristically short-tempered, too often over the smallest, pettiest, and most trivial personal matters. At one point Telia found Pallas so unreasonable and impossible that she took to the road, pushing the ideals of universal literacy and taking all their children in tow. "I'm packing my bags," she said at last. Naxos, at his most manipulative, bent over backwards to facilitate Telia's travels, even putting the military and the nascent diplomatic corps at her disposal, something totally unprecedented. So, for the first time ever, she was able to cross not only West, overland, but also sail to a half dozen of the southern ports of South America. Naxos did everything, regardless of expense, to get Telia as far away as possible.

Six months earlier, Naxos sent Matthew on a special mission to the East Coast. He was sent two-thousand miles away and given large sums of money to set up orphanages and recruit for the Forandi Order. For the first time ever, Matthew was able to recruit according to his own subjective parameters. Matthew ended up milking the project for two and a half years, the longest journey he had ever gone on.

As a result, for five hundred years thereafter, the Forandi Order on the East Coast was known worldwide as the most autonomous and independent religious sub-order in all of the New Rebel Gaiadom. Recruits flocked there. But eventually, between 1050 A.G. and 1097 A.G., they were brought back into line, forced within the boundaries of mainstream orthodoxy.

At the time Naxos made his decision, he wasn't about to leave anything to chance. He didn't care what price he had to pay, and therefore he had given Matthew something that he would never have otherwise given him, a free hand. By doing this, he ensured that Pallas would be alone during the time of the rewriting of the document with Lloyd.

And when Telia and the children did return two months after the last rewrite had been completed, Pallas didn't look like a father or a husband, he looked ash-faced and aged. He looked utterly defeated, as if he were awaiting his execution.

Naxos was so frightened and anxious about how Pallas might react to a mass printing that he decided that he would leave Pallas's name off the masthead. There was to be no mention of Pallas's authorship, in fact there was to be no mention of any authorship at all.

It was Naxos's intention that *The Blessings of Gaia* would be a holy script, whispered by the spirit of September Snow into the ears of anonymous foreign scribes. It would be understood that they took an oath never to reveal themselves or the nature of how the revelations had come to them. Thus, Pallas, the actual author, was to remain forever unheralded and nameless.

For most of the years Pallas spent writing the Foundation Document, he had sought isolation, privacy—most importantly, obscurity. As a final protection against Pallas's more recent unpredictability and tendency toward volatility, Naxos decided, in a final act of supreme will, to give Pallas what he wanted. Pallas would remain obscure.

But the release of The Foundation Document was postponed once again because of Lloyd's last minute intervention. And in the meantime, Pallas was supposed to have disappeared without any public notice or comment. What Naxos did not figure on was that the recently returned Telia was to be the primary agent toward that very end. If Naxos had planned it out himself, he could not have organized the unfolding scenario better. More than just being the object of an urban legend, Naxos was the last great manipulator of the Obsidian Order. There would not be another one quite so powerful for another five hundred years.

Chapter Twenty-Seven

TELIA WAS ANXIOUS to talk to Pallas. "What have you done?" she asked.

"I've created a monstrosity," Pallas said. He told her the complete truth. He didn't leave out embarrassing details. Like an earth-rimed dam that had burst its banks, he spilled everything. He spewed forth a long continuous deluge of unburdening.

Pallas explained what had happened fourteen years earlier when he had visited the monks living on the island of Skilleg Michael, off the coast of Ireland. Of the controversial views of Angus the Elder. Of the true nature of September Snow's absence of divinity, and also of Iona's true identity. He explained the bitterest part. He explained the falsification of the Gaia-Domes' role in the attempt to destroy the Unseeing Watchfulness of Gaia. The only good thing was that the story about Iona had been left alone and everything before 1 A.G. and after 20 A.G. (excluding the last 26 years of Tom's life, and the means of his demise) had been left intact.

"So in a nearly 600-year-long cycle, only 20 years were altered, not counting Tom," Pallas said at last in a resigned way.

"You must disavow this work," Telia said. "All of it. You must do this."

"They won't let me do that," Pallas replied. "In fact, it's worse than that. There are courtly women, merchant wives, daughters, military officers' wives, administrators' wives, ready to read my work, and view it as if it were the absolute truth, as soon as it is released. There are members of the Obsidian Order ready. There are members of the Forandi Order ready. There are former slaves of the Gaia-Domes, former Magisters, former Suits, former Middle-middles, former Upper Minds, former illiterates of the inner cities of the realm of the New Rebels—thanks largely to you—ready. There are impoverished peasants living in isolated hamlets—ready. There are shepherds living alone near mountaintops—ready. There are ploughmen who during the day are behind the plough, but at night, perhaps by light of a lonely candle or a primitive kerosene lamp—ready. Perhaps the Oggaci, if they have not yet been crushed by their stronger neighbors, will read the book. Perhaps there will be nonbelievers of Gaia—generations from now—who will have a vague notion and an inchoate idea of Gaia, and will read, come to a different view, perhaps even a conversion. My printer says that my book will set off a revolution. But it doesn't matter. I have been ordered to leave. Exile. My book will remain behind. But I will go."

"Then we, your children, all of us, must go into exile with you," Telia said in a voice that was firm.

Pallas had an unexpected impulse to laugh. But he suppressed the urge. He was glad. He knew he would no longer touch another drop of alcohol so long as he could look into Telia's eyes. She was his rampart and strength. She was his love. Upon Telia's arrival that morning, Pallas swore he'd straighten out: quit drinking, total abstinence.

Lloyd, whatever his incomparable charms, was never going to turn him back into being a graceless and useless drunk that he semi-was, *and also semi-pretended to be.*

Telia, just by her being, was Pallas's light in the darkness, guideline to the truth.

And in that moment Pallas realized that there was no one in the world who reminded him of Iona more than Telia did. Telia was far from the personification of Iona, but she was the modern-day equivalent of Iona. Telia was, in Pallas's view, the repository of

Iona's strengths, including the one strength that all the new technologies, amenities, and creature comforts were doing so much to defile, obscure, and annihilate: the courageous stand against abusive power. That was Telia all over. That had been Iona all over once, too. Yet the New Rebels, under the leadership of Naxos, would do almost anything now to silence Telia, even kill her. Pallas had no doubts what the Obsidian Order was capable of. Pallas knew Telia's tenacity, and her stubbornness not to be used, not to be suborned. For her own protection, they had to go into exile. But he couldn't tell her about his poems, that was one last truth he kept hidden.

"Telia, I know you want to do this," Pallas said. "But why should our own children have to suffer?"

"We will suffer as you have suffered," Telia replied. "For Gaia. For the truth."

And Pallas and Telia and the four children, after a discussion that lasted eight hours, all agreed they had to leave. The children were unable to give much input, being so young, but they were told what to expect in fairly realistic terms. The difficulties and dangers were not glossed over.

After the talk with the children, while they were lying in bed together late at night, Telia said to Pallas, as though they were continuing a previous conversation, taking up where they had last left off: "The ability to adapt is one of the reasons for the survival of the human species. We have gone over this again and again. The absolute truth now. This is the message of our history as a species."

Pallas nodded in agreement. "Yes, I get it. That is my conclusion too. But what if humanity adapts to those very things which will destroy the species?"

"In that case," Telia said, "we mustn't let ourselves be contaminated by the general insanity. That's what The Unseeing Watchfulness of Gaia was all about. *Containment. Isolation. So that there would be something to hope for in the future."*

Pallas looked guilty. Sensing that, Telia continued to say what she was thinking.

"The Unseeing Watchfulness of Gaia embraced the darkness of the caves so that it could separate itself from the darkness of the rest of humanity. It did so for over three hundred years. Remember, my family joined the group much later on."

"But why does everything feel so wrong right now?" Pallas asked in a state of perplexity and total exasperation.

"Because whatever the Unseeing Watchfulness was then, it is not what it is now."

"It's staring me right in the face," Pallas said.

"What was the most important thing that Tom ever said?" Telia asked. "Engraved on a Runic stone that they could not erase. 'All history is philosophy, and all philosophy is religion, all religion is literature, and all literature is art, all art is music, painting, dancing, and all music, painting, dancing are the heart, brain, hand of man and woman, through all of time.' Didn't you once tell me he wrote that on a small scrap of animal skin? He gave the skin to Iona when she was 13, just before she began her journey across the Forbidden Zone. The message, rotting slowly on the decaying animal skin, was transferred finally onto a runic stone, many, many years later on."

Pallas felt love and devotion and awe. He was so grateful that Telia was at his side. "You're one of a kind. Did you know that? Just like Iona was one of a kind."

"Iona was one of a kind, but I'm not Iona. I'm not a true Gaian. I'm a Jew. A Jew, Pallas. I intend to raise my children as my ancestors did. The only person I told this to is Matthew. He accepted it with compassion and love and understanding. He accepted it. You've always kind of known this, or at least you strongly suspected it. I let things slip out when we were alone. That's another reason why I didn't want to commingle with the bigwigs in the establishment. Though we never really talked about it, I didn't want to hurt your chances for success. Sustaining secrecy is so much easier when you keep it up around the clock. That's what my parents taught me. But now I'm declaring it outright. Now I'm telling this to you now. So if you have any druthers, any reservations, any caveats about the decisions we are making about our exile, you can ask me now." With those last words, Pallas was perfectly happy. During the rest of the night, nothing further passed between them.

In the morning, Pallas said, "If you're a Jew, Telia, then Matthew's a Christian, and I am a follower of Gaia. But we're all friends."

"And you've figured that out completely on your own, haven't you?" Telia laughed. "He's kept that secret pretty well hidden, hasn't he? We can't be the only ones, living secret lives, but we're the only ones you know. And all those poems you keep inside your head? I've often wondered, what secrets do *they* conceal?"

If Naxos had planned this outcome, it could not have come out better for him. Matthew was 2,000 miles away. As long as he was busy and preoccupied with his project on the East Coast, he could not pose a threat. Only Lloyd insisted on having one last meeting with Pallas, before the entire family went into exile. Lloyd wanted to have one last chance to explain to Pallas why he was making the wrong decision. He was going to use every argument that he had at his disposal. Of course, Lloyd didn't know Telia well enough, there were still secrets about her, but he thought it was worth a try.

In his arrogance, Lloyd thought he could return Pallas to his cause, creating through a back door a Gaia-Dome semi-ascendancy.

Chapter Twenty-Eight

"I ARRANGED THIS MEETING because I think it's important," Lloyd said to Pallas. "I know what you're thinking. I know how your mind works. Reexamine your goals. Reconsider your motives. In that light, rethink it right through. *Reboot*, as my ancestors were fond of saying. All I ask is that you look at the cold, hard facts flat on. Absorb. Move."

Pallas loathed it when Lloyd talked in an antiquated cyber-chatter. But how could he help it? He was a product of the former Gaia-Domes. Their final lasting legacy was to be technology.

Lloyd even thought of offering Pallas an alcoholic drink to soften him up. (Not street-vendor drago, but rather a rare serin-laced elixir, that was reputed to have mild to moderate hallucinogenic properties. It was brought in semi-illicitly by brewers from the old remnant Gaia-Domes.) But whether street-vendor drago, or serin, Lloyd knew that'd be the wrong step. He could tell, by instinct, that once Pallas had settled on the course of exile, he had reformed himself. There were even rumors going around in the Obsidian Order that Telia had "straightened her husband out." Offering drink, that fatal step would have been counterproductive. Lloyd knew he had to tread carefully. Sound examples. Biting arguments. *Reason. Deduction.* Attack Pallas's thought processes where they were the most vulnerable, that was the best approach.

"No," Pallas said. "You can't change my mind. I'm going. I'm going into exile. I never wanted to write that document in the first place. Naxos pushed me into it. I did want to introduce the new alphabet. I take great pride in that accomplishment. I also saw the arrival of a viable written language as a major achievement. But I never wanted to write a Gaia story. *The Blessings of Gaia* is wrong. It should never be written. It should be told. Passed down by word of mouth. Only by word of mouth. The Oral Tradition was the best means of conveyance we had."

"Now is not the time to be second guessing from the standpoint of humility," Lloyd said. "False humility, I should add. Stand up and take a bow. Make your claim to a crown. If it is not a religious crown, well then, let it be at least a literary crown. You deserve it."

"No," Pallas said, "that is the truth. I never should have written that crude monster, that rude ogre, in the first place. Making it all the easier the certainty of my going into exile. The Blessings of Gaia is, in essence, a falsity."

"Don't be such a sap for overgeneralization," Lloyd reasoned. "Exile is dangerous. You can't be just thinking about yourself. *Think about your family. Think about your children.* You know what I say is true. Exile is dangerous. It's worse than dangerous, it's almost certain death."

"And living in Escalante isn't dangerous?" Pallas asked. He gave Lloyd a look that sent a chill down Lloyd's spine. Then Pallas struck Lloyd with an expression of complete contempt. "You forget. I'm a New Rebel. In spite of all my sophistication, I'm a New Rebel. Maybe not proud of my father, but proud of my mother, and proud of my grandparents. Yes. Old-fashioned. Not one of your types. Where does it come from? I never figured that one out—it's like a mystery process: facts, process. All that machine-like meta language. You're a bunch of scrapers and bowers. You were too obedient to your first bosses, now you want to toady to your new bosses. Grandmagisters? Obsidian Order? What's the difference? None of us can compete with you. We're not congenitally equipped. No wonder Matthew took the chance to go to the East. I don't blame him. He's back on the frontier now. Upon her return, Telia put stiffness in my spine again. I do not seek Naxos's protection from anything anymore. He's been manipulating me for decades now. Enough! My father's been dead twenty-six years now. Should I allow him to still have a hold on me from the grave? I'm done with it. I'm on my own. Exile? So what! It will be an honorable death. *And an honorable death for my wife and my children if need be."*

Lloyd saw that it was worse than he thought. He immediately saw that there was no point in pursuing a conciliatory gesture. When a New Rebel said he "liked something," or he said, "it felt good," it meant he was prepared to die for it. New Rebels could be so stiff-necked when it came to primitive notions of courage, especially when their pride was at stake. That was one of the reasons Lloyd admired Naxos, and could never admire Pallas.

Because Naxos knew how to manipulate people. He knew he could never win the New Rebels over with counter-ideas alone. He knew he also had to go at it slowly—baby steps—getting them accustomed to creature comforts, bread, circuses, the ease of modernity, the most subtle corrupter of them all: sloth; rebooted with a powerful punch of manufactured need. Former Gaia-Dome hydraulics engineers operating in Escalante? Change for the good? Change forever! Water supply, plentiful water, democratically distributed, that was the new Gaia! Practically nobody could resist that. It was too powerful. That wasn't the evil of the old Gaia-Domes operating, that was something good, for a change. That's what Lloyd was thinking. But that kind of thinking wasn't going to work with Pallas.

In spite of his all-paid-for house and his manifest security, Pallas was too much the independent-minded, too much the ascetic, too much the seeker of truth, to be brought over like that. *He was too interested in the truth, when comfort and ease should have been all that was necessary.*

Lloyd knew he had to take a different tack. What about history? That was the one thing Pallas admired about Lloyd. That was Lloyd's strength, his deeper pool of knowledge. His knowledge was his best card.

Lloyd knew the first example from history he could offer Pallas. "You don't think they didn't change some things when they wrote the Bible?" Lloyd asked, squinting his eyes.

"You're talking about Jews now, right?" Pallas asked. "The ancient Israelites? I remember you gave me an extensive history lesson about them. I've even tried to talk to Telia about the subject. She instantly tells me to keep my mouth shut. Mention *Jews* in her presence and she's ready to attack with a stick." (Pallas had no compunction about telling Lloyd the truth about Telia's secret, especially because it was now going to be the secret of his children as well.)

"Yes," Lloyd smiled. "Remember my report on the Jews! On the other peoples of the book? Pushing monotheism over touchy hangover practices of worshipping their neighboring tribal gods? Judaic xenophobia and particular-ism over universalism? They even had Moses writing the early books, as if that was possible. How could Moses have written Exodus? Could Moses have written about his own death? My point? Your redactions in *The Blessings of Gaia* are not unprecedented. You changed the script to match the needs of the time. So what? They got the story, and when I say 'they,' I mean there were probably a multitude of them, maybe over centuries, all anonymous, a joint effort. And they got the story pretty much right. *But how did they know this? Didn't they have to pick and choose between different versions? Could they not have made stuff up?* Why do you have to get so uppity about it. A wrathful God? Yahweh? A brutal tribal people? Israelites? Jews? By the way—Israelites? Jews? They're not the same thing. But they got the basic story right. Even as late as the sixth century B.C.E., Hebrew was written with only consonants. No vowels. It wasn't until the Septuagint was written—in the third century B.C.E., by Palestinian Jews, seventy-two the mythology has it, in seventy days—the legend has it, in Alexandria, Egypt, that these Hebrew scholars started using vowels. *But in Greek. That must have changed everything. Changed the way it was written.* Here's the thinking of the traditionalists: 'You write with vowels the way

Greeks do, maybe you're beginning to think the way Greeks do, too.' Bah. Blasphemy! And other impious utterances about sacred things. Like those sixth-century anonymous writers during the Babylonian captivity, and even more, like those third-century writers in Alexandria. Like them, we let you temporize all you wanted. We just wanted a little something in return."

"The Bible is a dead letter," Pallas said. "That's why we need *The Blessings of Gaia*. That's why this question is so serious. Having done some things wrong in the past, for the wrong reasons, doesn't make it right for the future. I don't buy your argument. Aside from you showing off your erudition, what could be the relevance of the 'B.C.E.' Jews, or the early Christians, for that matter, to the Foundation Document?"

Lloyd frowned. He looked down. "Well, you had to mention that. What's the mark of a good teacher? A teacher who produces a student who surpasses him. Alright, I lost points on that one. I have a better historical metaphor. The New Testament Covenant business."

"Aside from you showing off your erudition, what could be the relevance of the early Christians to the Foundation Document?" Pallas asked.

"There you have it!" Lloyd exclaimed. "My very point. Christians! So you think they had the story all wrapped up from the beginning? If Jesus was a Jew, and he was a firm believer in the Mosaic Law, both of which were true, how could he ever have seen himself as being the Son of God? Him? A God-man? That was a Roman ideal! That was a Greek *idea*! Emperor Augustus saw himself as a God-man! Romans! Let's jump ahead, three hundred years. The Roman Empire, in all its splendor and glory, embraces this grotesquely weird and utterly bizarre superstition of charnel houses and god-killings and then they worship this pathological loser, who had been put to death in the most despicable way a Roman could imagine: crucifixion. And now you have the incarnation before the resurrection, and so long as there isn't any second coming, an institution called a Christian church that just needs to keep it going. And this business of the Virgin Mary! Parallels between the old Roman-Greek-Egyptian Mother of a deity and our *September Snow* is so outrageously ironic and so bizarre I can't keep a straight face while I'm talking to you... "

Pallas was angry. He wanted to scream. But he didn't. He restrained himself. "I don't know what Matthew would have thought of any of these things, but I don't think it would make sense to him anyway. I don't know what kind of Christian you'd call him, but he doesn't care about any of this. Does it matter?"

The conversation had gone in a direction that Lloyd had not wanted it to take. Pallas was over-touchy and defensive. Pallas seemed incapable of seeing the world in the present being what it had been in the past. "Okay," Lloyd said in a soft, yielding voice. "I got one more. One more argument. One more. It's a better one. You'll appreciate it. All I ask is that you listen."

"It's only because of our long association that I endure this," Pallas said with resignation.

"One more," Lloyd said. "Then I'm done. Galileo Galilei. 900 years ago. Hear me out. The true hero of all the believers in science. But in his own time, he too reneged on the truth. To save his own skin. But afterwards, everyone knew he was right. He *thought* he understood about gravity. And he knew from Copernicus, his scientific predecessor, that the Earth revolved around the Sun, not like Aristotle had said, the other way around. Which of course had at the time been the indisputable position of the Church, the Sun went around the Earth, and that the turning of the Earth on its axis accounted for the apparent rising and setting of the stars. Modern astronomy. No less. Why? Because the Church said (imagine the Church being the Obsidian Order at this moment), Aristotle could do no wrong. But Aristotle did do wrong, Pallas. Now this is where everything went crazy."

Pallas stared at Lloyd with an expression of stark confusion on his face. Now this was taking everything a step further.

"Just because Galileo Galilei got this one right, Aristotle is no longer omniscient. Does this, in turn, make Galileo Galilei omniscient?" Lloyd asked. "No. He was a great scientist, but so what. That he knew everything? Because he bettered Aristotle? With Copernicus's help? There were a few far-fetched theories rolling around at the time, about the mystery of what caused the ocean's tides, a secondary question about the nature of the Moon's gravity. It would be an understatement to say that this was a profoundly controversial subject at the time, just like the primary question of gravity was. Some had the audacity to think that tides were caused by the gravitational pull of the moon. Could you imagine that? Which later, two centuries later, proved to be true, through the application of the scientific method. But do you think our true and pure and great scientist Galileo thought such a thing was possible? No. He thought that this theory was preposterous. He thought that anybody who bothered to entertain such a madcap hypothesis was crazy. Maybe they should not be burned at the stake for harboring such heretical beliefs, that would have been too severe, but they should not be taken seriously either by anybody in the religious community or in the nascent scientific community. To Galileo, at the time, to suggest that the gravitational pull of the moon caused the oceans' motion of tides was as crazy as proposing that a cow was jumping over the moon, or that the moon was made of cheese, or that there was a man in the moon, or somebody pasted the moon, like a picture, on the wall of the firmament, *like a fake, human delusional creation*. All these beliefs held sway at some time or another. What is the truth?"

Lloyd looked at Pallas carefully. "People in general, no less scientists, will always get things wrong. And in the face of it, eventually with time, the truth will win. There eventually will be a corrective. So what's the moral of the story of Galileo's science? Believe in the future, Pallas, *your* future, *Telia's* future, your children's future. Recant. Save your skin. Maybe not in your lifetime, Pallas, maybe not in two centuries, maybe not in a thousand years, but eventually, have faith, the truth will win out. In the meantime, you've written a superlative story. Stand up and take a bow."

"Truth is the truth," Pallas said. "What is not true, is not true. I stand by that. That's my truth."

"Indulge me one more time," Lloyd said. He couldn't conceal the desperate expression on his face. He knew this was going to be the last throw of the dice.

"No," Pallas said. "Enough. Your time's up."

"It won't be about history," Lloyd pleaded. "It's not about the past. It's from the future."

Pallas raised an eyebrow. Now he was curious. He hesitated. "Alright," Pallas said. "But I'm warning you, this is it. Say your piece."

"Can't you see that your Foundation Document is just a made up story anyway! Like Matthew? His Christianity? End of time? Does anybody believe in that story anymore? The Earth is going to heal itself in the long run, no matter what September did. This is the truth. *The truth!* No matter what you said. What difference does it make? As far as the Earth is concerned, the Earth is going to shrug off humankind and go its merry way. It doesn't matter to the Earth whether it's killed off 89 percent of the people, or 99 percent of the people, or 100 percent of the people. People have been around for what? A half-million years? The Earth is going to do what it needs to do to fulfill its needs. A few thousand years later on, even tens of thousands of years later on, or even a million years later on, there's nothing new in geological time. Once every one or two or three million years, an asteroid or a comet hits the Earth and produces a crater 5 to 30 miles wide. It involves the release of the equivalent of anywhere from 3-trillion tons to 18-trillion tons of explosives. The damage done would be significantly less than, or potentially greater than, the damage caused by the climate change and global warming caused by humans five centuries ago. Because of our own limited perspective, your story is just hubris. September didn't save the Earth (no human or collection of humans could ever do that), she saved humans. Yes, the truth, Pallas! Did she save the Earth? She didn't save the Earth. She saved a few humans. After eight and a half billion died, more or less, give or take, over 550 years, so what! A huge human population crash is no big deal. Before there were humans, or even pre-humanoid prototypes, the Earth had gone through at least six mass mega-extinctions. They lasted for hundreds of thousands of years, some maybe a million years. An extraordinarily large asteroid crashing, a mega-volcano spewing lava and ash for ten thousand years, massive warming, sudden freezing: all told, six extinctions. Like falling dominoes, certain species and plants die, causing others species to subsequently die. This last human catastrophe wasn't even a quarter as disastrous as one of these typical mass extinctions. *Humans are not that important.* Go with the myth. September's a goddess, because she saved humans. Your ancestors, that's all. Humans are condemned by some human trait, by some strange indeterminate human gene, to mythologize themselves, demonize others, and make certain individuals greater than they are. (Whether they bring God, gods, or goddesses into the equation, is another thing, I won't go into that.) As you admitted to yourself, you were halfway there anyhow, when you agreed that September Snow was a goddess. A little harmless mythologizing of the human stuff will allow science to take root again. I know that might sound paradoxical and even counterintuitive, but I know it's true. All the same: I HAVE BEEN A GREAT STUDENT OF HISTORY. That's why I'm so sanguine about the proliferation of that truth called The Blessings of Gaia. It will proliferate. A few small white lies told now will allow for more possibilities in the future. You fudge now so that the truth can be told later."

"Truth is the truth," Pallas said. "What is not true, is not true... That's my truth. You don't believe in anything. You believe in what is expedient. You believe in what works at the moment. With your catalog of examples, Jewish writers of the Bible, Christian apologists, Galileo. You have proven nothing except showing how human absurdities on occasion win out. I'm not trying to prove any scientific theory. I'm trying to tell the truth. If you take us out of the picture of the Earth, nothing else works. Everything dissolves into nothingness. It is us not playing Gaia! I'd rather be inaccurate as all hell, and still be true to all that. You believe in nothing."

Pallas sighed. "Our truth is prosaic, provincial, provisional, humble. Our way is to a smaller piece of the truth. But that smaller piece is a fuller truth. Your way is to the larger truth. Although I do not question the logic of your particular knowledge, I question the logic of greater knowledge-in-general—that reaches too far." Pallas paused. "You win the debate. But you don't convert me."

"You're just too religious for your own good," Lloyd said. "Skepticism, an adherence to an objective platform of observation, the scientific method, will get you closer to the truth than myths about living into eternity. Even if that myth only extends to September Snow. Ritual can become too mechanical, a matter of rote repetition, you've been fighting against that all your life, until life is breathed back into it with the fresh urgencies of a prophet... Be that prophet! Embrace the Document! Meet your destiny!"

"Again," Pallas shrugged, "I can't refute your arguments. But it comes down to something else. Because evil—historical evil—of the Gaia-Domes, trumps all. If we do not acknowledge the existence of that evil, can we give any credence at all to any human knowledge? In any context?"

"Evil is relative," Lloyd replied. "I've studied history. It will always be."

"If that is so," Pallas said, "what I say will always be irrelevant. Remember, you lost to the New Rebels. The Gaia-Domes, after 550 years of an uneasy stalemate, in the end, lost the war. You are trying to make our otherwise resounding victory into a Pyrrhic victory. By picking up the crown that you found lying in the gutter. By coming in through the back door that Naxos opened for you just a crack. With the Foundation Document, or that is to say, with your *redaction* of the Foundation Document. I can't prevent you from doing that. Can one not be skeptical about religion—and also be skeptical about science too? Can one not be skeptical about oneself?"

"And you're so stubborn," Lloyd shot back. "I've given you all this time in trying to help you. Naxos's hatred of Telia knows no bounds. He blames her for your intransigence. If the only way to kill her is to kill you, he will. This exile, this won't be like any other exile, Pallas, please, Pallas, I swear to you, I'm telling you the truth, you're going to be sent to a dreadful place. I'm trying to save you."

"But why?" Pallas shouted. "Wait now!" he interrupted. His intent was to defend Telia's honor, no matter what, under all circumstances. Pallas was not afraid of what was going to happen to him. He didn't care. "Telia believes in the power of truth. Just like I do. That's all she's guilty of. She's not a threat to anybody. Nobody, except me, listens to her anyway. I know where this place is they're going to send me. *When I was seventeen, when I was doing Naxos's dirty work, I scrubbed clean four words from a Runic Stone. It had been there, now it's not. I'm now paying for that crime. I dishonored Gaia. And I also desecrated a historical heritage.*"

"Well, isn't that the point?" Lloyd asked. "Telia! As long as she's breathing and influencing you, Naxos sees her as a threat to him." Lloyd paused. "The place you're going to? You say you know what's there?"

"Naxos is doing what he thinks he's forced to," Pallas said in a trailing voice, ignoring Lloyd's question. He decided he was not going to answer it, under no conditions was he going to reply.

For once, Lloyd could see that, yes indeed, Pallas *had* apparently grown a backbone.

"Well, of course, he's doing what he's forced to," Lloyd replied in a sarcastic voice. "What do you expect? He's a member of the Obsidian Order. Like yourself once was, Pallas. Now, because of your beloved Telia, you're forever going to be seen as being beyond the pale, as being an incorrigible renegade."

Pallas realized the conversation was over. But he said one last thing. "I joined the Obsidian Order when I was seven years old. My father forced me. Later, Naxos secretly enforced, secretly facilitated, not my earlier beatings, to be sure, but my later beatings, at the hands of my father. And at that time, Naxos was pretending to act as if he were my protector. Matthew told me all about this. Just before my father died. My father confessed this truth to Matthew. All of the manipulation that Naxos did."

Lloyd looked as if he was bored. He was studying his fingernails, or more specifically, he was examining his fingernails' rims, to detect if there were even the tiniest smudges of dirt. There were none. His nails were clean. Lloyd looked dutifully satisfied. He didn't look up. As if transfixed, he continued to stare at his grime-free fingernails. "When I think of all the things I've seen in the last few decades, Pallas, I find myself applauding the works of my species. What we are capable of is astonishing. We're such good toolmakers. Like circus performers—better yet, like trained seals, like all the circus animals traveling in their cages—on the face of the planet, we do our tricks." He paused. "As long as there are desires that are impossible to satiate, Pallas, there will always be belief systems—religions—that will stand in their stead. After all these years, that is the truth you've never been able to understand. Well now, go into exile. I give up. Go die."

Pallas mumbled in a voice so faint and humble that he clearly didn't care if Lloyd could hear him or not. "You understand the past better than I do, that is, the historical truth. But I have a higher opinion of humans than you do. And if that is all that Gaia stands for, then I'll stand by that."

Chapter Twenty-Nine

WITH PRACTICALLY ALL the occupants of the town preoccupied with their business interests, and the comings and goings of their own affairs, Pallas's family left, without fanfare, without anyone in Escalante taking notice of their departure. They had been ordered to pack light, limiting their belongings to six 40 pound sacks. Pallas's family was escorted by a heavily armed patrol of twenty (arsenal included laser guns), all of whom were mounted on horseback. The family, along with a few precious belongings, traveled in a light wagon. The escort guard took them all the way to Deseret, the old intersection point of Pallas's earliest travels.

As it had been during the time of Pallas's solo trip when he was eighteen years old, Deseret was a way station at the beginning of the Nevadan desert. Then a smaller patrol consisting of seven mounted troops took them a further 150 miles into the desert. At one point, the guards decided to take an extended break, which involved two overnight rests. Pallas recognized the place where they decided to stop immediately. As if it were the day before, he remembered the family who had lived there. It was where Pallas had secretly recovered from his wounds, twenty-seven years before. To Pallas, the memory of the scene was stirring.

The farm, if you could call it something that grandiose, had long since been abandoned. The buildings, especially the outbuildings, were nothing more than moldering ruins. The main building was utterly beyond repair. In the old farmhouse there were two places where the roof had completely fallen in. A covey of doves lived in one of the two broken-down sections. Of course there were no signs of Raine, Bhamini, or Myrina. Was Myrina still alive, Pallas wondered? He tried to make the calculation. If she were still alive, she couldn't be more than forty-one or forty-two or forty-three.

Pallas looked inside to see if he could find the elk skull mounted on the wall. But no, the wall where the skull had been hung had collapsed. A few splinters of wood and a few pieces of reeds lying on the floor had once been part of the roof. There were the broken pieces of wood that had once been a chair, now lying in a clutter in what had once been the main room. Mixed among the pottery chards were bits of glass and tiny pieces of cloth.

Pallas was given the freedom to wander around without an escort. He walked the entire periphery of the farm, looking for mementoes and perhaps the potential for a gravesite. There were neither. (As to the fate of the last inhabitants, that was a very bad sign.) He even tried to wander out to the spot where he had been saved by Myrina, on the desert flatland, but the terrain was only vaguely recognizable, and he could not find the spot.

Pallas had hoped he could find something that would remind him of the past: a remnant of a doll, an ornament, a broken cooking utensil, anything, among the piles of the ruins, but there was nothing. Or almost nothing. In a far corner, in the back of the building, under a crumbling wall, he found something that was totally mysterious and completely out of place. It was a functional walking machine chain. And it wasn't rusty. It had been well-oiled, five feet long, looking like a shiny, skinny snake. It was coiled up in a tight circle, all by itself. *How strange.*

Pallas picked it up. Grasping it, pulling it end to end, he stretched it out with his arms. Then he looped it around his arm and carried it out to where the patrol troops were lounging. He showed it to Lieutenant Aries. "Look! A walking machine chain. How did it get here? There are no signs of any walking machines out here, or even in Deseret. Finding an abandoned horse bridle wouldn't cause me to bat an eye, but a newfangled apparatus from a walking machine? *Where did it come from?*"

Lieutenant Aries did a double-take. "Walking machine? Oh, I get it, you mean bicycle. That's what you're holding in your hand, a *bicycle* chain." The officer smiled. "You'd be surprised. There are a few uses you can put to a bicycle chain. It's a sharp-toothed piece of metal. And it's been oiled recently, maybe a few months ago. You say it was just lying there in the dirt?"

"Yes," Pallas said. " May I keep it?"

"What for?" Lieutenant Aries asked in a bored, tired voice. "Never mind. What difference does it make? 'Course you can keep it. What harm could it do?"

Maybe it wasn't such a great enigma after all, Pallas thought. A patrol had gone by, probably a few months before. A trooper had been carrying a bicycle chain with him in his pouch, something with a sharp cutting edge (something a mud-hut farmer would have known how to put to good use), and the trooper had accidentally left it behind when the troop pulled out.

Scanning the surrounding vista, Pallas already knew what he was going to use it for.

Pallas asked Lieutenant Aries, "What is the story about the cannibals?"

"You mean in this part of the desert?" the Lieutenant asked. "There was a complete eradication project back in 530 A.G. They're all gone. They all died out fifteen years ago."

Pallas had a thought-prayer: Give thanks to Gaia. One less cause to fear for his children.

Exactly ten days after Pallas's family departed from Escalante, Lloyd stormed Pallas's and Telia's old quarters at the head of a team of youthful shock troopers. They were a phalanx of Obsidian Order initiates, armed with hammers, sickles, knives, sledgehammers, screwdrivers, and shovels, as if they had been sent in to accomplish an exorcism in the form of an exculpating religious search. Under Lloyd's command, they stripped the vacated building. They tore the floorboards up. Using sledgehammers, they pounded in the walls, looking for hidden cavities between the pieces of drywall. Armed with a multitude of shovels, they dove into the dirt. In the backyard, in the front garden, every inch along the side walls, every inch within the enclosing walls. They searched the attic, rifling through every box and storage bin they could find. They stripped bare armoires, chests of drawers, kitchen and dining room compartments, cupboards. They ripped apart old, discarded clothing that had been left behind, broke dishes, hurled pots and pans across the room, and emptied the corn cob recycler, to see if anything was hidden inside.

Having exhausted their search of the first floor and the attic, they finally searched the basement.

At last they found what Lloyd was looking for. Buried under a 125 pound granite rock in a corner of the floor, in the dankest and farthest corner of the basement, underneath a stairway, they found a strongbox. Lloyd had four of the strongest initiates crouch down and dig it out. They dragged the box upstairs and placed it on the kitchen table. Using a pair of sledgehammers, they snapped open the flinty old lock and spilled the contents onto the table.

There were a collection of twenty leather bound pouches. In each of the pouches were thick, sturdy envelopes, and in each of the envelopes was a poem, perhaps two, in total about a thousand envelopes, holding a collection of 1,500 poems. The envelopes were bundled together in groups of twenty, and each bundle had been placed inside a separate leather-bound pouch. The pouches must have been inspired by the Oggaci method of book preservation, Lloyd surmised. Ten of the bundles were labeled "personal," four marked "literary," four labeled "religious," two marked "political." Lloyd smiled. He recognized that Pallas had chosen an Aristotelian categorical rubric to organize his papers, a modified form of organization Lloyd had taught him himself. *A back-handed compliment.*

Upon quick and cursory examination, Lloyd randomly took some of the poems from the different pouches—different bundles of envelopes—and started to examine them. What a find. After thirty minutes of this, Lloyd dismissed the wrecking crew. He realized he had hit a goldmine.

Just a small section of a literary part was a formation of lists and the concentration on what Pallas's poetic imagination perceived as essential. Pallas's concentration process simplified the quantity of human figures, reducing them to just a few vivid and vital, ideal figures. Lloyd saw the pattern. It replaced the crowd of phenomena with a few symbolic acts. Vast stretches of time were fused together. These poems were going to be the logical outgrowth of the Oral Tradition for the people. These literary poems were supposed to act as an intermediary between the old Oral Tradition and *The Blessings of Gaia* document (thus partially subverting *The Blessings of Gaia* document by providing an alternative written codification of the oral traditions).

Oh, how devilishly clever, Lloyd thought. Pallas had been thinking two steps ahead.

Lloyd read two sections of the "literary" poems, and also perused a portion of the "personal" poems. What he found there was scandalous! Pallas had pulled out all the stops.

It took Lloyd six hours to peruse just thirty percent of the "personal" poems. The vast majority were written in the new alphabet of course, but a much smaller number of them, the earliest ones, were written in old Runic text. The earliest ones, on yellow paper, had dark blotches. What did these blotches signify, Lloyd wondered? (As far as he could tell, they didn't exist anywhere else.) At first, Lloyd thought they were dried pieces of food, leavings from someone who had been hastily eating as he scribbled. Then Lloyd realized the colored spots were remnants of dried pieces of blood—Pallas's blood. Oh, these were poems of an awkward child, someone who had just experienced a mighty beating, written in a youthful, *horribly* shaky hand. (This conflicted with the legend that Pallas never wrote down any of his poems when he was a teenager or a young boy, though he insisted he hadn't.) The latter poems, of course, had been written with a steadier, more mature hand. Taken down from memory, Lloyd wondered? Undoubtedly.

Aside from the few exceptions, Lloyd surmised that probably Pallas had kept the reminder of his youthful poems stored in his head—memorized—for twenty years, perhaps as long as thirty years. Then he brought them back up and wrote them down, when conditions were safer. All facilitated, of course, by his fabulous memory.

Lloyd spent several days carefully selecting and reading Pallas's poems. He became so fascinated he ended up reading all of the personal poems, most of the literary ones, and all of the political and religious ones. There were even ten strikingly written environmental poems, composed in an antiquated secular idiom, thrown into the mix.

Several days later, with the accompaniment of two young Gaian initiates, Lloyd brought Naxos out to take a quick look at the pile of contraband.

"Pallas had been busier than I thought," Lloyd said, laughing. "All these poetics! There's almost as much material here as there was in the original Foundation Document."

Naxos stared at the pile dumbly, apparently unable to fathom what to make of the find. He shook his head, less as evidence of consternation, more as evidence of incomprehension.

"Maybe the poems," Lloyd said, "were far more important to Pallas than the Foundation Document ever was. But this explains much. His initial reluctance to go into exile. His seeming willingness to change some of the manuscript. It had all seemed too easy at the time. Now we know the truth! He needed more time to collect the poems together, even though he had probably written down the lion's share of them as many as seven years ago. Why did Pallas give the appearance that he was giving in so easily? He was buying time. Frankly, I think he even partially faked the heavy boozing so he could throw me off the scent. The poems were the things he didn't want found. The Foundation Document was secondary. This I knew: Pallas preferred to write in poetry first and foremost, not prose. What was the name of that poet Pallas learned about during his sojourn with the Oggaci? Ulm. I think that was his name. Pallas thought that Ulm was a genius. I think that Pallas modeled himself after Ulm. It was reputed that Ulm had written all of his poetry between the ages of 16 and 21! A very young poet indeed! Pallas talked about Ulm when he was drunk. Probably blurted out more than he realized. Probably thought that as long as he was only talking about Ulm, he was safe. That's why I knew he'd hidden his poems, or at least, raised some very serious suspicions. Did Pallas really care about the Foundation Document itself? Can we know? Well, he did care about his poems.

"Some poems here say that September Snow was never a goddess. He also penned devotional poems to Iona. And in the private poems sections, he wrote such loving, even worshipping, poems to his wife, Telia. That was a surprise! Some were quite boastful. Sometimes I got the impression that the two of them, Iona and Telia, were more or less interchangeable. At least in Pallas's eyes they were. Scandalous!"

"Why would he hide his cache here, of all places?" Naxos asked, looking at the opened strongbox with the broken lock and the piles of papers arranged around it. "If he had committed so many of them to memory, why not write them down later? Why not write them down after he had gone into exile?"

Lloyd shook his head. "Taking them with him would have been the same as destroying them. Where he was going was virtually a death sentence. I told him as much. He didn't know we were going to provide him with horses, a wagon, barrels of water, an abundance of food. A chance. No, he thought he'd be dead in three months time, or at least before the end of the first summer. He hid them there for Matthew to find. And to keep them for safety's sake.

Perhaps, if any of Pallas's children should survive, Matthew would have had some of the personal poems to give to them later. There were several poems addressed to his son, Pontus. In a thoughtful way, Pallas addressed the question of his mother's Jewish heritage."

"I don't get it," Naxos said. "How would Matthew have been able to find the cache? And why the leather pouches?"

"Oh, I'm sure Pallas left a note giving directions and instructions for Matthew. But now all Matthew will find is a repositioned granite rock, and an empty hole, two feet deep. As for the leather pouches, who knows? They're designed to last for 250 years, maybe longer. Maybe Pallas had an alternative plan. Or if not a plan, a hope?"

"So you were suspicious? And you just *knew* he had buried the poems?" Naxos asked.

"Like I said," Lloyd said. "Ulm." Lloyd knew that he was appearing cryptic, but he didn't care. *How could a passionate poet ever hide forever his cherished creations?*

"So what do we do now?" Naxos asked. "You say the poems are seditious, too...adventuresome?"

Lloyd laughed. "Oh, they're adventuresome all right. Most of them are seditious. Even the milder ones are disrespectful, irreverent, or impertinent. Or deal with improper subject matter. We must burn them all."

"All?" Naxos asked. "Are you sure? Isn't that drastic?"

"Cautionary. With regards to Pallas's poems, there must be nothing left. Apparently, Pallas loathed his father. He had good reason, he was beaten repeatedly, every once in a while, he was beaten within a few inches of his life. In the early years, he respected you, even loved you, but later that turned negative. It seems he wanted to distance himself from you, but couldn't. That would help explain why he became so reclusive. He apparently was resentful because you forced him to desecrate a runic stone when he was young. There were other things he mentioned that I won't repeat. He saw through your vanity, though."

"Did he *really* write about that?" Naxos asked. "It happened so long ago. I'd almost forgotten."

"You mean the rune stone desecration? Yes, Pallas wrote about *that*. That's when he became aware of how much he had submitted to your corruption—or to a wider and deeper corruption."

"The ingrate."

"He loved his mother," Lloyd continued. "He wrote lovingly about tortured and abused women. He could never figure out why the whole Gaia religion was based on the worship of women, or at least on the symbols of early womanhood. His mother's life had been a vale of tears. In anger, in righteousness, he wrote about that too. It's all in there."

"On second thought, shouldn't we save a few of his poems?" Naxos asked. "The innocuous ones anyway. For posterity's sake? For the archives? With no more runic alphabet, this could be the beginning of the archives."

With deliberate sternness, Lloyd shook his head. "No, we in the Gaia-Domes used to go through this sort of chicanery every fourth generation or so. The last big occurrence was 200 years ago. The Orion Heresy. It spawned a massive witch hunt. I used to be able to sniff out dissenters and traitors—all the time, in my own day. Of course that was on a much smaller scale."

Lloyd paused. "There's another reason. In a deeply emotional and drunken state Pallas once confided in me that *The Blessings of Gaia* should be destroyed. Forever. He said we should stick to the Oral Tradition, like Homer's *Iliad* and *Odyssey*. Before the Greeks began using their alphabet, they memorized everything. In light of that fact, by destroying his poems, I am only fulfilling Pallas's deepest and purest wishes."

"You really are a piece of work," Naxos murmured beneath his breath, but he wished he'd taken the words back as he said them. He spoke now out of a sense of irony, not out of a sense of anger, or even regret. "With Pallas's departure, I need you now more than I ever did before. That's the reason why I put up with you. You really think you know *everything about the world*, don't you, Lloyd?"

Lloyd smiled.

"So, very well," Naxos added, "although, a tidy loss it will be for our future scholarship. I wish there were some way we could preserve a memento, a tiny piece of memory, of Pallas. We owe him *that* much."

"No," Lloyd said, shaking his head. "No. Not this. If you don't come to regret it later, the men who follow in your footsteps will."

Lloyd directed the two Gaian initiates to scoop up all the poems from the table and bring them out to the courtyard. Each of them carried only two small bundles of papers, small handfuls each. They carried the papers with solemnity, walking slow with self-conscious pride. Dutifully, the two insisted on taking part in equal measure. Lloyd stood back, quietly laughing. Then Lloyd and Naxos conferred in low voices. They watched the pile of paper on the paving stone grow. The so-called most favored initiate deposited the last bundle. He did so with a religious gesture, it made the wonk-like, officious Naxos feel jealous of the young man's flair for acting. Oh, how Naxos wished he knew how to move with splendor, elegance, grace. He was too much the flat-footed administrator to perform a credible spiritual role in a Gaia ritual.

The most favored initiate (ironically, his name also happened to be Pallas) then was given the honor of striking the match. He rolled-up a piece of paper. He directed it to the sacred taper, lighting paper, slowly, with pomposity—solemnity. He stepped back. The fire traveled from one stack of letters to others, and the fire heaped up, the ashes whirling around in the wind. The pile of 1,500 poems, along with their sturdy, thick envelopes, burned.

"Well, that's the end of that," Naxos said.

"Not exactly," Lloyd replied. He cleared his throat.

When the task had been completed, Lloyd took Naxos aside and said, "The Foundation Document—*The Blessings of Gaia*—we're not finished. It must be redacted again."

"Again?" Naxos asked. "For the love of September, I thought we were done with it."

"There were problems that in the first and second rounds of redacting I neglected."

Naxos looked surprise. "Wait, stop. I thought you said it was done. You promised. That was part of the deal." He became angry. "I don't like changes this late in the game, Lloyd."

"It must be re-redacted one more time," Lloyd replied in a flat voice. "Reading some of Pallas's poems, you see, convinced me of the necessity. Pallas was too clever, he must have hidden more things in there than what I was able to see. Nobody reading it now will notice it, but a scholar in the future, in the distant future, might be able to tease out some of the truth. *Pallas was so clever.* Oh, his poems, especially his literary ones, show how clever he is. It's like performing surgery on a cancer. We've already cut out the corrupting material, sure, but we need to cut a broader sanitary collar too, around the scarred area. To be on the safe side."

"You want to *rewrite* Pallas's work?" Naxos asked in consternation.

"Damage his most cherished piece of art?" Lloyd asked. "You kidding? Send me into oblivion! Cut off my hands! *I sketch primitively—while Pallas photographs with his mind's eye!* Nothing could be further from my mind than to hamper Pallas's genius. No, no...little has to be rewritten. What needs to be done is subtle, more in the way of reforming the foundation of the subtext, Pallas was, excuse me IS, a writer. *The Blessings of Gaia* is beautiful. It's as epic as Homer, as tragic as Sophocles, as engagingly human as Shakespeare, as monumental as Dante. Pallas writes with a passion only associated with the greatest of artists. He is a true aspirant in the vineyards of creation. There are places where he applies humor too. Considering the darker aspects of his semi-tragic personality, that's an achievement! Most parts of his work are fun and effortless to read. The writing is for the most general and widest readership. It's a masterpiece. Anyone who pens such a work should be proud. Redacted. That's all. Perhaps some reshuffling for consistency's sake. Relax, look, nothing, unduly, ah, aha, it seems, well, no worries, ahem..."

"Get to the point," Naxos commanded. "How much do you need to cut? You should have told me about this before, Lloyd! I don't like being blindsided. How much?"

Lloyd came prepared. He brought from his breast pocket a long, slender piece of paper that resembled a shopping list. He unfolded the paper in the middle. Then he dipped and fished with his other hand a pair of bifocals from the bottom of his lower coat pocket. Retrieving them he placed them on the brim of his nose. Clearing his throat, he read: Six percent of the section taking place between 1980 A.D. and 2040 A.D.—*housecleaning*. Fifteen percent of the section taking place between 2040 A.D. and 1 A.G.—*more cosmetic than substance.* Seventy-five percent of the section taking place between 1 A.G. and 20 A.G.—*serious change.* Sixty-five percent of the section taking place between 20 A.G. to 46 A.G.—*serious change.* Thirty-five percent of the section taking place between 46 A.G. and 71 A.G.—*serious change.* Five percent of the section taking place between 71 A.G. and 122 A.G.—*small change, just housecleaning.* The rest, right up until 534 A.G., right up until the near present time, no change. It's all fine after 2185 A.D. No changes." Lloyd put his laundry list back into his pocket. He took his bifocals off. His eyes narrowed.

Naxos tried to speak, but he was so irritated and tongue-tied, he couldn't get the words out.

Lloyd interrupted Naxos before he could speak. "Now Naxos. Look. Regis Snow died in 10 A.G. September Snow da...da, excuse me, ASCENDED—begging your pardon, ASCENDED—into the Great Unknown in 20 A.G. Is that okay? Tom died in 46 A.G. Kull died in 80 A.G. Shortly thereafter, Iona died. All these dates, except the first one, the one concerning Regis Snow, will be included in the final draft. Pallas never would have changed some of these sections, no matter how subtle or compelling had been my promptings. Once I was certain he was going into exile, I knew I had to do this. Some things still have to be taken out. The sections have to be taken out, or severely curtailed, or no one will believe that just the very top leadership of the Gaia-Domes, maybe 20 people, 50 people at most, each generation, were responsible for the greatest crimes, the greatest misadventures, the greatest disasters, the greatest injustices. Or as Pallas has described them in one condemning phrase: 'the greatest single disaster of a near mass genocide to have ever occurred.' With our first revision, the book went from 1,800 pages to 1,570 pages. Now it will be pared down to 1,300 pages. Just a shave. Not a hair cut. When you consider the 595 years covered, plenty of material, plenty still left to read, a very fine book." Lloyd paused for a moment, so that his words could have the greatest effect.

Naxos was silent.

"There are reasons for this, the new calendar began in 2051 A.D." Lloyd continued. "But The Unseeing Watchfulness of Gaia had been stuck in the old measurements of time from before. They kept to the old calendar, although that was by default, since they didn't use any calendar to speak of. They were in the dark, quite literally and figuratively, for 390 years. The New Rebels started using the Gaia calendar in 448 A.G. I think that was when our emissaries secretly visited your predecessor, the head of the Obsidian Order? Clotus? Wasn't that his name?"

"Clotus the Meek," Naxos corrected. "Not to be confused with Clotus the Guardian. Or Clotus the Pious. Clotus the Guardian lived 241 years ago, Clotus the Pious 310 years ago. Clotus the Meek was the fifth—that is—fifth Obsidian leader, going back in reverse time. That is, fifth, if you include me."

"Right," Lloyd nodded. "Part of a long illustrious line. Clotus the Meek. Pallas was right about one thing, you really do need to acquire last names, if for no reason than to avert confusion. We know it was Clotus the Meek because that's when the first Runic Stone was dated. As the predecessor's predecessor of my predecessor explained through them to me…"

"Then there will be unity among us all?" Naxos asked. "At last. This is peace then. This is harmony, right?"

"Yes," Lloyd sighed. "With these changes done. Then there will be unity."

Naxos didn't take too long to think on it. He decided to put it to rest. "Well then, what are you waiting for? Begin. I want it wrapped up and published by early 548. No later than that. Okay, late 548. Okay, early 549. On second thought...maybe we should wait longer. Pallas will have been gone for two years by then. He kept a low profile anyway. Did you know he attended only one Covenant Day celebration in the last twelve? Even then, he refused to sit on the dais. When we forced him to, he insisted on sitting at the very rear and he left the ceremony early. Especially during the last seven years, he's been fiercely reclusive. It won't be hard to phase him out."

"Do we assign another author?"

"What?" Naxos asked. "I don't know what you mean."

"Do we assign the Document the name of another author?" Lloyd asked. "We can't say that Pallas wrote it. Even less, we can't say that Pallas Missette wrote it. We could make a name up. Say it was written down by an outsider from across the Eastern Sea, from New York, say *he* was Pallas. A different Pallas, of course."

"And what do we do when we have to produce this author, this Pallas?" Naxos asked. "No. No author. Just say the work was inspired by September Snow. No author worth his salt is so indecent or arrogant or lacking in grace as to attach his name to such a sacred document. Have you ever heard of an author ascribing his name to a Runic Stone? Utter blasphemy."

"No one will believe that," Lloyd said. "In this age, it won't fly. *We have to do something.* Especially among the old dome-dwellers. Yes, I know they're difficult. But they have to be considered."

"What do I care about them?" Naxos shrugged. "So what? What difference does it make? In 500 years, in 750 years—all will believe. It has been written, right? That's all that counts. In the meantime, everybody has his or her Foundation Document. We could stress that *The Blessings of Gaia* was written by people from a faraway kingdom. They refused to give their names. For piety's sake, for the sake of modesty, they insisted on remaining anonymous. And then the document will be inspired by September Snow. *Which it shall be.*

Because we say so."

"And Pallas?" Lloyd asked. "What about him? What finally happens to him?"

"What about him? Pallas abandoned us so we'll abandon him."

"Well, you have to hand it to Pallas," Lloyd said laughing. "You asked him specifically, indeed demanded, your name not be mentioned in *The Blessings of Gaia*. On that score he followed your commandment to the letter. No citation of merit. No eulogy to achievement. Not even a passing allusion to a teensy-weensy accomplishment. Nothing. The document ends with Andromenus. Andromenus's Legacy. Andromenus, the leader everybody liked and so many revered. Your humble—and undoubtedly spiritually legitimate—predecessor. 519 A.G. How not to end it? At least in this, I admire you your modesty, Naxos."

Lloyd returned to the small domicile Naxos had set up for him. He went into his breakfast nook, an alcove that he had converted into a study. But what was the point of having a study? The Gaia-Domes had left not a single book of literature for posterity. Not a single book of prose, not a single line of poetry. Nothing. All they had left were some terrible examples of governmental practices and policies, and some wonderful pieces of technology. Technology had been the last best hope of the Gaia-Domes—the one and only weapon left in their otherwise depleted arsenal to try and gain entrance into the world of the New Rebels. And Lloyd and his fellow former Gaia-Domers used that weapon to the maximum, to their greatest advantage.

In the far-distant future, people would think of the Gaia-Domes as something completely different, vastly different, than what they actually were.

Separate from his earlier, superficial, *pro forma* declaration, after one year of "exhaustive study," Lloyd formally embraced the Gaia religion of the New Rebels. He did it with all his heart. He did it with such a powerful display of fervor that nobody could have questioned his sincerity or integrity.

Having declared his new faith in a grand ceremony, Lloyd joined the Obsidian Order. Six months after that, he became Naxos's official right hand man.

At this point Lloyd and Naxos were getting on in age, way past the mid-point in their careers. But they managed to work together as a team for another sixteen years. As a consequence, the Obsidian Order in particular, and the Gaian religion of the New Rebels in general, went through many changes. The changes were great. And most of these very same changes lasted many, many centuries. But not all of them lasted forever.

Naxos couldn't leave it as Lloyd had left it. He had his reservations. When he returned to his office after having watched Pallas's poems burn, he wrote a special directive that was addressed only to the echeloned and titled leadership of the Obsidian Order. It said: "Pallas had to leave us. His ordeal of deprivation may seem to be a waste to some, but to our Obsidian Order it must be seen as a moving reminder of the redemptive qualities of duty and perseverance. We must remember all the sons and daughters of the Unseeing Watchfulness of Gaia. For that reason, Pallas must not be consigned to the dust heap of complete oblivion. I make now here the authorization that thirty-seven years hence, in the year 582 A.G., our new alphabet shall be called the 'Pallinate,' in honor of the memory of Pallas. If only one of my directives is honored in the future, let it be this one. Thirty-seven years hence, for all generations to come into the future, our alphabet shall be known as the 'Pallinate,' for ever and ever. As I issue this, so shall all future heads of the Obsidian Order issue this. According to the order of September and Iona, as it is within my power to extend, I do extend this."

Chapter Thirty

AT THE SITE OF Raine's abandoned desert farm, Pallas's family was given a detailed map, two barrels of water, a generous fifteen months of rations of food, a sturdy, little wagon, and most importantly, two small but able ponies. They were told where to go. It was a distance of 139 miles to their new desert place, a bit to the south and west of Iona's shrine, in the heart of the desert. It was west of the Desatoya Mountains, a crescent-shaped, arid range rising to 8,000 feet, also known as "the forever barren mountains."

In such a freakish and hellish landscape, even the heartiest were expected to just barely survive.

Speaking on behalf of the family, speaking in declarative sentences to set the record straight for the entire world, Pallas intoned: "We do not feel shame. We hold our heads high. We know that what we are doing is decent, honest, and worthy, worthy of any who claim to be followers of Gaia, worthy of all who claim to be Gaia-lovers. We go in truth. We go with it. Well, it's ours anyway. The truth part. Even if it's only our truth."

"Well, you better go with some preposterous notion of truth," Lieutenant Aries snickered with a sneer. "You know this farm is derelict, right? You think it's dilapidated? You think it's a wreck? Well, wait till you see where you're going! If you think rattlesnakes and scorpions are the kind of creatures worthy of bestowing friendship, well then, you're in luck! Patrols, like ours, will visit you once every three months, or once every six months, or once a year, but at undisclosed times. It's just sand. But if you can keep your horses alive and use them to transport water from the mountains, not the Desatoya Mountains mind you, which are barren ten or eleven months out of the year, but the mountains farther to the east, you might make it. Also, if you are able to hunt game in the eastern mountains which rise to 10,000 feet, and in a couple of places, 11,000 feet, maybe you'll survive. For a while. You won't be able to grow anything in the desert, except maybe creating a tiny fenced-in garden, and only then it will have to be nurtured by water you bring from the mountains. You can stay in the mountains for short periods of time, for short trips, but you must live in the desert, or you'll risk being reported, and if you are reported, you'll be executed. Those are the terms of your exile. The art of monitoring exiles will be improved. It will be perfected. Believe me, you'll be monitored. We will have a way of monitoring from the sky in a few years, thanks to the dome relics' technology. They can't even fly a single helioplane now, but soon they will be able to launch a satellite with eyes in its head to see and watch you. Just give us the right kind of technology and we'll become the masters of the world. *Oh, the world's changing and it's changing fast, Pallas.*"

"It doesn't sound so bad where we're going," Pallas said, smiling. "My family is brave and strong. And you've given us a lot of provisions. That must have been Naxos's doing."

"Naxos and Lloyd jointly agreed," Lieutenant Aries corrected. "Apparently, they both decided to let you live...for a while."

"Listen, listen to me," Lieutenant Aries added in a softened tone. "You're going to make it through the winters with ease. You're also going to make it through the shortened autumn months and the shortened spring months. That won't be the problem. What's going to kill you are the summers. The summers last forever, five or six months out of the year. One bad year, this year, the next year, the year after that, will do you in. No exile has ever lasted more than four summers out there. How will you keep your ponies watered? That will be more than a challenge. There'll be other challenges as well."

"Come what may, better than Escalante," Telia interrupted, spitting her words out in a vengeful-sounding voice. "Let's be going, Pallas. What are we waiting for? A sign? From where? From the head of the Obsidian Order? We'll be free from all of that gibberish and utter nonsense at long last. No time to lose."

Before she shook the reins vigorously to signal the pony to move, she turned to the officer and gave him a nasty stare. "What do you offer, Lieutenant? Perhaps you should say to us: 'Bear down all sorrow?' Indeed, like daughters and sons of Gaia, 'do we bear down all sorrow?'" Telia gave a harrumph, followed by a sarcastic cry. "No stirring riposte? No stinging reply? At last! No words? When Andromenus had been our leader, he recited that phrase and it meant something. *Now the sentiment's been degraded.* It's a desecration. It's an Obsidian Order prayer, in other words, a non-prayer. It's been added to 'THE CANON OF THE 100' prayers. If I say this stupid, moronic prayer often enough, if I say it with enough phony exuberance, should that give me a dispensation from the corn tax? No. They'd tax beasts of burden in the field if they could. They'd tax orphanages if they could make a penny out of it. They'd tax dung and the dung beetles who harvest it, if they could turn it into gold. To be freed from these slimy, sponging religious dictators, that would be cause for celebration!"

Telia took a breath, held it in, let it out. "Since we're going into exile, I can speak my mind at last. I'm a Jew! Praise Covenant! Praise Yahweh! Praise all the prophets! I'm a Jew! I'm a Jew! I'm a Jew! We've been around...what? 5,000 years? That's something to be cheerful about, isn't it?"

Looks of bafflement and bewilderment crossed the faces of the soldiers.

With the exception of Pallas and Matthew, and a little more vaguely and circumspectly, her children, Telia had been silent on the subject of her true religion for most of her lifetime.

"Already, I can smell the cleanness of the desert!" Telia shouted robustly. "I can smell the wholesomeness in the air!" Mockingly, pleadingly, pretending to inhale, she made the motion of breathing in deeply. Her eyes flitted with joy, but there was a rising undertone of sarcasm in her voice. "No foul excrement of religious sanctimoniousness out here. No sir! We're too far away. The devotion to technological force—as evidenced by the old Gaia-Domes—ends in a solipsistic blind alley, ends in a worshipfulness of selfhood. We've vanquished the Gaia-Domes, so we've been told. But have we actually conquered them? Maybe in the process of subduing them, they have secretly subverted us? To what degree has this happened? How are we to know? But we're so far away! Free at last! I bet you don't even know what a Jew is! Have you ever seen one before? Maybe you have, but you didn't know it when you did! We're always hiding!"

Addressing Pallas, Lieutenant Aries pronounced in a stern yet steady voice, "You should address your wife's lack of chastity and decency. Her outrageous behavior, sir, is inelegant. It is unGaia-like. You should correct her. I've no idea what a Jew is... *Are you a Jew, Pallas?*"

Telia continued to hold back on the reins. She turned to the lieutenant one last time and said, "Like Tom Novak preached: 'All history is philosophy, all philosophy is religion, all religion is literature, all literature is art, all art is music, painting, dancing, and all music, painting, dancing are the heart, brain, hand of man and woman, throughout all of time.' Now those words—these *ideas*—I can abide by. I can cherish them. They should be part of a framework of a larger heritage. These words are bigger than Gaia, bigger than the entire world!"

The lieutenant shrugged. "Tom Novak? Trouble! They say he might have been corrupted by pre-Gaian ways. He might have been a carrier of a virus. From the distant past! Sometimes they say that's why he said those inexplicable things, those indecipherable words, those words of praise for the evil one from the deep and distant past...."

"You've got it all mixed up, Aries," Pallas said, smiling. "You're out of your depth. I learned this from Lloyd, you can live a lifetime and never meet a Jain, a Buddhist, a Hindu, or a Jew. There's so precious few of them left! Even harder to find a Christian nowadays, isn't it? Can you even find one now?"

"Can we go now, please. All you people do is talk!" the four children pleaded from the back of the wagon. On their hands and knees they stuck their heads out through the oil-skin curtain, just behind where Pallas and Telia sat. They sounded like a Greek chorus. They loved their mother, but they knew that if she was given half the chance, she'd harangue Lieutenant Aries forever. Then they began to sing. It was a beautiful song. It was a Gaia song. It was a song that had been intended to unite everyone, filled with piety, devotion, and truth. *It was what the children believed. It was what they'd been taught to believe. It was a song that filled the air with Gaia, and with tenderness.*

Their voices trembled like silver tongs in the air, saving Pallas, Telia, and Aries from more useless and pointless argument. The lieutenant was moved by the children's song. Alas, he couldn't say "Bear down all sorrow." He'd be charged with hypocrisy by Telia for the use of that careworn expression, so in lieu of saying: "good luck," or "try not to die," both expressions inadequate, he said nothing. But he was sorry that they had to part the way they had. The children's singing had touched him in his heart. He waved to them and said, "Go now, go now, please...go." He didn't enunciate the words, he barely murmured them under his breath. But he waved.

Pallas and Telia had agreed before setting out that they'd share the duties of driving the team. Once on the trail, Aura, their oldest, at fifteen, was going to be trained to take the reins. Eventually, all the children, would be trained to become experienced teamsters.

On that first day of departure, Pallas was so transfixed, focused, and obsessed with the question of how they were going to not perish, he couldn't understand his children's shouts and snatches of songfest—bits and pieces of which—wafted from the back of the wagon. But these sounds clearly comforted him. In Pallas's eyes, his children were easily more valuable, more important, more esteemed, than his wife's life, or his own corrupted and imperfect life.

After the first two days Telia observed their trek with her own brand of stoic quietude. Every time Pallas stole a glance at Telia to glimpse her profile, her expression revealed no hint of second guessing, no doubts, no remorse over their momentous decision. Pallas could see Telia had the bit between her teeth. "Stubborn as a mule." "Strong as an ox." These were terms of endearment that came to Pallas's mind. In the face of danger, as unflinching as an ox, Telia was the strong one. She was going to be the strong one for all of them. She was always going to be the strong one. As *bizarre as it might have seemed, she wanted this to happen. Telia looked as if she was prepared for death, for anything, for everything.*

And to Pallas's satisfaction and relief, the ponies proved to be strong, resilient, and well-disciplined. (They might not have a snowball's chance in hell to survive, Pallas wondered, but he sent up a prayer of hope to that effect!) The ponies, unstintingly, soldiered on. They managed to hold up stolidly under the strain of a combination of difficult terrain and wafts of heat and sun, imperious and stoic to the ascending whirlwinds of dust.

In all, the small-like beasts pulled together. There was hope.

The family too, soldiered on, as any family should.

After traveling twenty-two miles during the first two days, at the end of the second day, as if they had planned it all out with perfect timing, they reached the crest of a fairly high ridge. What a coincidence! They stopped at this point, realizing they were going to enjoy a panoramic view. They got out and stood in a line, linking hands. Together they stared due west. Light faded. There! The sky lit up in a streaked-golden, glorious sunset.

Chapter Thirty-One

PALLAS AND TELIA'S FAMILY pushed their way across the desert floor. It was a slow, monotonous journey, yet their progress was steady. It was still early autumn. But winter was fast approaching. That would be the best time to travel. They could take their time. They had plenty to eat. There was no shortage of water. There were a series of perpendicular mountain ridges, running on a north-south axis. And when they crossed these higher ridges, they found something they had not planned for or expected: there were places where the ponies could forage and even water.

At some spots, at the very height of the ridges, they had an unobstructed view, extending at least ten or fifteen miles, sometimes even as far as twenty miles. Each view from each subsequent ridge afforded a magnificent vantage point, a resplendently blue sky, a panoply of iridescent azure splendor. And then they'd reach the crest of the next mountain range, maybe 5,700 feet, or 6,200 feet, or 6,700 feet, (one time 7,200 feet!) and, coming up over the lip of the mountain ridge, they'd see down into the next wide, gently sloping valley, stretching out ahead, ten miles out, or even twenty miles out, to the next mountain range. *Ugly country, pretty views. And at the top of one of the crests, there was so much forage for the horses they decided to stay for an entire two days and two nights.*

After five and a half days of traveling like this, Pallas noticed something that surprised him. It was located in a two-foot deep depression, just to the left of the trail, at the bottom of a gully. Near the edge of the dry wash, there were three scrawny dwarf trees: they looked like children with bowed heads bent to form a circle, causing them to form what looked like a triad of hand-grasping children. There were also six bunches of creosote bushes, fragrant with life (Pallas could smell them), four clumps of almost rectangular-shaped dangerous poison weed, and other scant vegetation. Pallas wasn't sure what the names of the other odd-looking vegetation were, but they had green shoots branching out from their stems. Pallas was looking more carefully than usual because he was looking for potential forage for the ponies.

At first Pallas thought it was a clump—but of *what*? Pallas wasn't sure. Something about the bundle disturbed him. He decided to take a closer look. He got down from the wagon. In the passenger seat, slumped on her side, Telia stirred. Waking, she asked in a drowsy, semi-somnolent voice: "Is there a problem? Have we stopped?" But Pallas remained silent. Finally he mouthed in a gentle voice: "Nothing. Go back to sleep." Taking a few steps Pallas abruptly stopped. He realized the oblong shape that seemed at first to resemble a partially filled gunny sack was the moldy figure of a human. Pallas approached to get a closer view. At least two years dead—more likely two and a half or even three years dead, Pallas figured. Most noticeable of all was the skull, protruding from a thick, disintegrating collar, an inch-and-a-half wide at the bone of the neck—a cravat, crumpled under the skull's chin—and below a multitude of bones—wrists, hands, fingers—sticking out from threadbare sleeves. Hints of other bones could be seen through the tattered, weathered, disintegrating clothing. *Who* had he been? Why had he been traveling alone? Had he been a pilgrim, wandering a hundred miles off the main pilgrim trail. Had he been an exile? Had he been an East-West express rider? Had he been a soldier? His clothes vaguely suggested soldier's clothing, but there were exiles who'd been known to wear a soldier's blouse and matching pants, a common enough practice going back a decade or two. Telia was now completely awake and minding the horses as they eyed some potential forage that was too close to a clump of poison weed. She pulled the reins in sternly preventing them from getting their mouths close to the dangerous food. She was going to admonish Pallas for leaving the horses unattended, but she saw him staring down so intently at the ground that she decided not to disturb him. Then Pallas turned and asked Telia if she thought it was better if the children examined the corpse for themselves.

A strange request? Not at all.

Telia came down from the wagon. Having secured the ponies by tying them close to one of the dwarf trees, Telia wanted to get a better look herself. She had a slightly different take on the mysterious body. "Could have been anyone," she murmured, taking Pallas's hand. "He's not from your religious order, that's for sure. He could have been a member of an outer tribe even. Could have been an exile from the Gaia-Domes—for all we know." She then corrected herself. "That's impossible. Gaia-Domes have been gone for more than a dozen years. *Who is he?*"

"And Gaia-Domes never used threats of exile as a method of social control," Pallas said. "They executed their dissenters at the first sign of insubordination. Just a small, quiet, but public act of defiance, then retribution and quick death. This man had nothing to do with any Gaia-Domes."

"Right, all the same, could have been anyone," Telia murmured. "Of course the children should do an examination. There's valuable information here. We shouldn't hide anything from them. They must know what to expect. They must face everything, *as it exists*." She nodded her head in a practical way. "Look, his boots aren't cracked! I bet you they fit you, too! You're so lucky, Pallas!"

"It's very dry here," Pallas noted. He decided to make an examination of the corpse before allowing the children to join them. Pallas checked the pockets. The trousers had deep pockets, similar to the kind that a soldier might wear. What were the contents? There was a watch (broken), a compass (bulky), a four-inch-tall toy rag doll, two dozen kernels of planting corn, and crammed into the biggest pocket, a small (dead in Pallas's view) apricot tree sapling. Pallas didn't need to see any more. He shouted out the children's names. Then with an added sense of urgency, he yelled, "Come on! Come see this. On the double! At once!"

The last three articles clinched it for Pallas. They confirmed for him that the deceased had been an exile. He must have had at least one daughter (viz. the doll), and a place, or an idea of a place in his imagination, where he could plant his corn and his apricot tree. *Why was he alone? In this place? Why was he separate from his family?*

Pallas took the corpse's boots for himself. Placing the soles to the bottom of his feet, he could tell, both in terms of length and width, that they were almost perfectly matched! The socks were unsalvageable though—the right one had been stuck to a long piece of rotted flesh all along the instep, the left one was only marginally cleaner, and was snagged on a spur of bone.

Pallas gave the kernels of corn to his wife. She nodded happily at the gift. Although Telia was more or less an urban girl, she was a competent farmer. She'd know what to do with them.

Pallas watched dazzle dance in Aura's eyes, their oldest, as he handed the corpse's broken watch to her (the closest thing she'd own to a piece of jewelry). With his knife Pallas plied buttons away, almost all of which were gaudy and ornamental, from the corpse's shirt, pants, and coat. He gave the buttons to Teanna, their second oldest. She looked satisfied, but also a little disdainful, but not in a rude way. (Teanna's nature mirrored her mother in this, they both expected little, and rarely indulged in extravagant or unrealistic fantasies.) Without thinking Pallas handed the doll to their youngest daughter. Vivianna knitted her brow. She looked perplexed. She knew she wasn't likely to get everything she wanted. But she pressed anyway. Pallas added several lines of silver piping from the corpse's collar. She continued to look displeased. Pallas added the corpse's visor cap. That brought a brief, albeit cold, smile to her face. (If any of the children might have been "high spirited," that is to say, a little spoiled, it was Vivianna.) She stuffed wads of cloth and strips of linen around the brim of the cap, wearing the stupid oversize cap wherever she went for the next fourteen months, until she lost it when she had to fetch water in the middle of a galloping windstorm.

Pallas gave the compass to Pontus. He was happy. When nobody else claimed it, Pontus insisted on taking the apricot tree sapling as well. In Pallas's opinion, the sapling was beyond saving. Pontus didn't mind. So Pallas gave it to him, but added a warning: "No one's going to share their water with you for this dead plant, you understand. *If you want to try to revive it, that's fine. That's your business. You must use your own water though. Agreed?*"

"Fine," Pontus said. He, like two of his older sisters (the exception was Vivianna), had always been agreeable to the establishment of reasonable rules.

The compass, aside from boots and corn, the only piece of booty both useful and functional, weighed a hefty ten ounces. "Three cheers for the inferior technology of the New Rebels!" thought Pallas, "a tribute to our clunky application of science."

After they examined the corpse, Aura spoke first. "The stiff's dry. Where you see an inch of skin, it's as dry as parchment. Sun's absorbed almost all the bodily fluids. Given a similar sort of circumstances, same would happen to me. Afterwards, would my clothes be so ill-fitting? He has such a macabre smile on his skull, like he's telling us something, and he's in on the joke. What actually killed him? No mystery. Lack of water. What else could have done it? Tree falling? Meteor strike? Helioplane attack? *Snakebite?* That's a thought… that could actually be plausible. Plausible, yet also unlikely. No. Verdict is in. Lack of water."

"It wasn't due to an attack of a predatory beast," Teanna offered. "Not here! Dehydration or heat stroke was the immediate cause. Either one. Take your pick. Basically he baked to death."

Nodding, Pontus confirmed his concurrence with Aura and Teanna's analysis. In contrast, Vivianna, on the sly, stuck her tongue out at both Aura and Teanna. She then turned to her mother and gave her her most irresistible smile. She followed that up with a haughty, tight-lipped expression, in the end refusing to comment one way or another.

Like Pontus, Telia agreed with Pontus and Aura's analyses. (She ignored Vivianna's contrarian naughtiness.) From Telia's point of view, Gaia had no time for mercy or sentimentality. The children were looking at death the right way, at a cool objective remove. Gaia could go on about doing what it was going to do, all the same, humans lived or died on their own. Too many people had died in the past 500 years for her to be seduced by idle theories underpinning a use of prescribed prayer petitioning for Gaia's so-called protection. On the other hand, it was not the wrath of Gaia that killed the wanderer either, it was the indifference of the universe. But if you could get along with nature, in spite of all that, all the better. Was Gaia love? It was not. When it came to death, Gaia was cruelty and a harsh, glaring, perishing sunburn.

Less than ten minutes after leaving the corpse behind, Pallas shouted: "*What's wrong with me? Whoa! What's the matter with me? Have I lost my mind? What am I doing?* Mother! Mother! My goodness! My goodness! We must bury the body! Have I forgotten my most sacred vow?"

Eyes popping out, looking overwrought, Pallas began to turn the wagon around. To complete the process, he had to guide the thin wooden wheels carefully over dozens of uneven bunches of sagebrush and even over a couple of fairly large rocks. This was difficult, causing the wide turn and circumnavigation almost fifteen minutes to complete: just to get the ponies and the wagon turned around. The horses didn't want to turn back. They were obstinate about changing direction. But under Pallas's stern command, they at last responded.

Even Telia was trying to figure out what was going on, still baffled and mystified.

"We must go back!" Pallas said in a panicked voice. "We bury everyone. Even the poor! Even the indigent! Where is our shame?

Are we not members of a like-minded species? If only for that reason, we must! Even if it's for a stranger. Even if it's for a three-year-old rotted corpse. He might have been a man of honor! Might be a distant relative! If not, so what! So what if he's from a different tribe! Or even from an outer tribe! We bury the dead. Or am I wrong?"

All in the wagon didn't ponder for a second being contrarily. The children, and of course Telia, had seen corpses before, but not this far away from home. Nobody had quite remembered seeing Pallas in such an overwrought state. All were silent. Until Pontus piped in.

"Providing we have a spade, right dad?" Pontus said. His remarks were met with relief. "Right? Do we want to scratch the earth with only our fingers? With only a digger stick? No!"

"Provided we have a proper implement to dig earth," Pallas agreed. "Must be sensible." Pontus's stab at humor seemed to provide balm for Pallas. "Or in lieu of that, watered ground. And a fine digger-stick! At least, our hands. If there are plenty of them. Water. We're not in danger. We're not under attack. Certain conditions must prevail. *We bury.*"

Conjuring up a memory from the past, Pallas still had only a semi-relieved expression on his face, but he felt better. "I made a promise to myself many, many years ago..." he muttered under his breath. But he didn't complete his thought. He decided not to tell his family the story of the three cannibals he met on the trail, when he was seventeen years old, and their unburied carcasses. With his index finger he daintily touched the ridge of scar on his side, which had healed so long before, but was still there as a reminder.

There was another important lesson here, Pallas explained to them. They didn't bury the stranger for his sake. They did it for their own sake. To prove to themselves their own humanity. *To prove, after 500 years of imposed depravity, they still had common decency.*

Not one word about Gaia. No "religion." Over the grave, just a moment of silence.

Reversing the team and the wagon once more, they continued

westward. They climbed an occasional mountain ridge, but the floor of the desert was home most of the time. If they hadn't had to stop to provide forage for the horses, and if they hadn't stopped to bury the corpse, they could have gotten to their destination in seven day's time. Instead, making 14 miles a day, it took them ten days. On occasion there were clouds overhead, which provided a little relief from the sun.

They found a gap in the Desatoya Mountains, 2,500 feet below the neighboring ridge line. Then, on the floor of the barren desert near the western side of the Desatoya Mountains, they arrived. The abode was actually much larger than the primitive hut that had been described to them. (Why exaggerate the negative? Perhaps just to make them feel a little more exposed and vulnerable than they actually were.) It was a windowless five-room, mud-floor, mud-wall, mud-roof hut, with slender rough-hewn boards for support. But it did have a front porch.

For Pallas and Telia this desert exile experience was going to be a trial. They were already well into their forties and already set in their ways.

For the children—between ages 11 and 15 years—this was going to be something different, it was going to be their "home." Maybe some of them might have a chance for a long-term survival. Maybe not. It all depended on how well they adapted.

Protecting the two barrels of water from evaporation was the most important thing. Pallas found a place in the shade with a marvelously preserved protective black plastic cover. When unfolded the piece of plastic was thirty feet square. Pallas had never seen a piece of sheeting that large before. Pallas hadn't even seen tiny pieces of plastic in the desert. Plastic, being very, very old, and being very, very durable. It had been scavenged from an abandoned Gaia-Dome, Pallas figured. If he could dig a hole deep enough, and double-wrap it with the plastic sheeting to form walls, all he would need would be eight lengths of wood for the hole. Pallas could store the water without using the barrels. What a lucky, freaky, one-time break.

Pallas was in a state of ecstasy! Already! Once the water was preserved in the plastic and pole-lined hole, Pallas could use the two empty barrels to gather and hold more water, thereby doubling their water-storing capacity in one fell swoop.

From a survivalist's point-of-view, Pallas assumed Naxos and Lloyd could not have guessed how lucky the family was going to be. All because of someone leaving behind, perhaps a year before, perhaps many years before, it could have been an old army patrol, a long piece of black plastic sheeting and some beanpoles! If one had been superstitious, one could have thought that something, perhaps even a higher being, was looking out for them. Even the otherwise skeptical Telia was a little taken aback by the lucky break. But for her, and ultimately for Pallas too, luck was luck—that was all. No hand of Gaia did they see in this good fortune. That would have been too primitive a thought. But they were glad for the break anyhow.

After they had drained all of the water in the barrels into the hole, figuring out how to take the empty barrels not to the Desatoya Mountains (which were too barren), but to the mountain ranges 60 and 75 miles to the east, was now the most important thing. There was plenty of water in the northern end of the Shoshone Mountains, winter and spring, and plenty of water in the middle and northern end of the Toiyabe Mountains, all year round. Closer by, sometimes there was water in the so-called Reese River. It was normally dry five months out of the year, and otherwise just barely a trickle a few inches wide, and in many places corrupted by undrinkable chalky saline. So the two mountain ranges were the best options. Their primary survival depended on that. All of Pallas's and Telia's thoughts were concentrated on that one goal.

And to achieve this goal, this they endeavored to do.

Chapter Thirty-Two

THE CHILDREN WERE DISTRACTED. Pallas was mildly concerned. Telia felt a greater intensity about the matter at hand. None had faced this kind of situation before. What were they to do about it? It was a dilemma. Should Pallas take Pontus with him immediately to the mountains to retrieve two barrels of water, and while they were at it gather firewood for cooking, and also gather extra firewood to fend off the coming winter's cold? Or should they cut holes in the mud walls of the hut to make windows right away, or, as Pallas put it: "Establish 'freedom-loving portals' for their children to view the world through."

"Are you kidding?" Telia asked in an acid-reeking, sarcasm-dripping voice. "Water! Therefore, indirectly, food! Or, on the other hand, freedom, learning, while we're at it why don't we throw in speculative navel gazing? What kind of a choice is that? You call that a choice?"

Telia insisted on securing water first. Water was the basis of life, nothing good could happen without it. Education, and "broadening horizons"—those otherwise esteemed values would have to come later, perhaps much later.

Telia wanted to make sure this descending order of priorities should be maintained.

So in response to the hand-wringing threats and *cri de coeur* moans of impending doom from Telia, Pallas and Pontus refitted the wagon to secure the barrels. They harnessed the ponies. They made ready to take off for the hills to gather firewood and water, while the women beat the hut into shape. They constructed a rudimentary kitchen, cutting a vent into the roof to enable smoke to escape. They also partitioned the floor space into bedrooms (without actually having any beds, they were all going to have to sleep on the floor), and tried to figure out how to maximize shade everywhere. (Figuring out how to make their clothes last much longer without using precious water to wash them too frequently would be a problem they'd have to figure out later.)

Pallas and Pontus agreed to take all the heavily soiled clothing with them to the mountains to wash, now that they knew they were only going to be able to wash clothing once every four or five months, or perhaps more frequently during the hot summer months, when they went to the mountains to replenish their water supply.

Scarecrow-like and stark as it was going to be, this was going to be their new world.

But at the last moment Pallas changed his opinion. He said no. Education couldn't always be the last item on the agenda. And so to assert his new opinion, he unharnessed the ponies.

Telia couldn't believe what her eyes were telling her. "What are you doing?" she asked. "Have you lost your mind? What kind of an example are you setting? You bury the bones of a rotting corpse—a man we do not know, which we all agreed to. Now what is next? Did I stand in opposition to you as we all stood around gazing idly at the beautiful sunset, days ago? Alright, I'll teach the children as we go about our work routines and tasks. I'll have them learn about our heritage as we go about our chores. I'll give instruction. Don't you see? I'm trying to find a place of compromise with you, husband!"

"I don't care if it kills us," Pallas shouted, "we're going to teach our children the value of education. *And aesthetics too!*"

"Aesthetics?" Telia asked in a state of near incomprehension. "You're going to include aesthetics in the curriculum? When did you become crazy?"

"Do we have to live like animals?" Pallas asked. "No. We don't. We will teach our children the value of perspective."

"Perspective?" Telia asked.

"That's right," Pallas said. "Perspective. Gaining it. I'm not crazy. Don't make the children think I'm demented, I'm not."

"Well, it sounds as if you're crazy, husband!" Telia screamed. "If you persist in this manner, I'm going to kill you. YOU'RE DANGEROUS. YOU'RE DEMENTED!"

"Well, you better accept the fact I'm demented," Pallas said, "because that's what I am."

With that, smiling gleefully, Pallas whipped the bicycle chain out of his satchel. He uncoiled it lovingly, slowly, as if it were a braid of gorgeous hair, rather than a metal mechanical part. He ordered his son to follow him and they vigorously started boring a hole in the wall. Energetically Pallas and Pontus took turns at the work. They pierced the dried mud with a digger stick, working fiercely, and little by little, they produced a notch in the wall, boring a hole in the dried mud. It took them a good piece of time to dig from one side of the wall clear through to the other, the walls being eighteen inches thick. Finally they pierced all the way through. They exclaimed their victory.

Then Pallas set out two vertical plumb lines and attached two horizontal lines with string, to form the shape of an imaginary oblong box. They attached the bicycle chain to a piece of string, and fed the string attached to a metal tube through the hole, little by little, and with Pontus standing at the exterior of the house, and Pallas standing inside, they fed the bicycle chain through the small hole. To protect their hands, they wrapped them with pieces of cloth. Then they each grasped one end of the chain and, with all their might, sawed through the soft dirt, cutting a four foot long line in the wall, traveling an inch at a time, twenty seconds for each inch. It was a laborious process. Turning at a right angle, they cut up another three feet, following the plumb line. In this fashion, they produced a four foot by three foot "box" in the wall. Pontus came inside to join his father. Then, pushing with their shoulders, from the inside, the soft dirt tumbled like an avalanche onto the ground outside. The task took six hours to complete. From time to time, Telia would come back and stare at them as if they were aliens, as if they were strange apparitions who had arrived from some distant planet.

"At last!" Pallas shouted. He stuck his head out of the gaping hole that was eventually to become a window. His grin was huge, stretching from ear to ear. He looked like an absolute fool. With clinched fists, her hands folded sternly at her waist, Telia looked like a hugely disappointed taskmaster. So angry, with a look of fury in her eyes, she looked like she wanted to seize a club and hit Pallas's head with it.

"Your bicycle chain. For what? Windows? You're crazier than I thought. You! You must've planned this weeks ago. I knew you were up to no good. You and your stupid bicycle chain!!!"

"Voila! A 'broadening-of-the-horizons' window!" Pallas said. "For our children! *Aesthetics!* Pontus and I will do three more windows, all around the house, facing all four directions—north here, and east, west, south. After Pontus and I come back from the mountains after retrieving water, of course, I don't want to give you the impression that I'm totally irresponsible. But if you don't commit to perspective, in some way, in the beginning, when will you commit to it? When will you achieve it! That's the message we must teach our children! Before we teach them any other lesson."

"Why have walls at all?" Telia asked in a cutting voice. "These windows are only going to make our house hotter in the summer, colder in the winter. They offer no practical advantage, in fact, quite the opposite! What are we going to use to cover them with? Canvas? We don't have any. Plastic sheeting? Oh, I suppose we could dig some of that up. *Another miracle.*" She shook her head admonishingly, but the look on her face had softened. It occurred to Pallas that in spite of Telia's sharp tongue, he had charmed her with the sheer audacity of his absurd pageantry. He had curbed her wrath with the sheer effrontery of his quixotic performance.

"There's nothing practical about this, you know, Pallas, but I sort of get the point of it," Telia said, relenting at last. Tears welled in her eyes. Her voice which had been brittle, softened. "Okay, I get it. This is how our children will remember us. Let them remember us for this. It may kill us. But *something* will kill us anyway. Not sun poisoning. Not snake bite. No, not at long last, dehydration. Nor, as if it were an even longer-term death sentence: starvation. I guess it might as well be aesthetics." She made a sound that was partly a laugh, partly a strangled sob, but the larger part was laughter. In spite of it all, Pallas had apparently won Telia's heart.

Pallas realized why he loved Telia so dearly. He was devoted to her stubbornness too.

That night they prepared and ate a ceremonial dinner. The children decorated the table. They festooned it with their prettiest tablecloth. They also brought out an ample supply of the "good" candles. The family ate from their generous larder of provisions. Divvying out larger-than-usual portions, they ate a meal of beans, rice, water of course, and for dessert, equal portions of raisins, dried apple wedges, and dried orange slivers.

"Tonight," Telia said to Pallas. "Tomorrow night. And the night after that. You and Pontus may stay before you go to the mountains. *And you will leave in no more than three and a half days time or I will kill you!*... But before you depart, I will tell the children the true story of their ancestry, of their heritage. It's high time they learned the truth."

Chapter Thirty-Three

THREE DAYS AND ELEVEN HOURS later, Pallas and Pontus made their first trip to the mountains. During the next twenty-four months of their exile Pallas and Pontus or Pallas and one of the other children went to the mountains for water and firewood, and sometimes to engage in hunting. On that first trip, Pontus got a chance to plant his apricot sapling, at a spot 8,000 feet elevation that was well watered and shaded. By the fifth trip, which was Pontus's second trip, the sapling had grown into a small tree. It had prospered.

The entire family learned how to survive in the desert. When it was the appropriate season, they planted a garden which gave them just enough vegetables to keep them healthy, and just enough beans to keep them from starving. Growing water-intensive crops like rice was impractical, of course. Sometimes Pallas was able to bring back some small game from the mountain trips, and even a fish or two! On two occasions he returned with venison. The provisions that had originally been given to them ran out within eighteen months, so there was no more dried fruit to be had. But Pallas found several sources of pinon nuts, and although the picking and gathering was laborious, several times he was able to harvest a goodly amount! It was all about arriving at the right time of the year. It was amazing how long the pinon nuts could last, once harvested.

But even with all this gardening and gathering going well, it wasn't enough. On the desert floor itself, hunting and gathering was well-neigh impossible. It was Telia who truly saved the family's lives. When conditions had become existentially desperate, she single-handedly revised the Timbisha Shoshone Indian practice of gathering mesquite bean pone, which had been passed down to her through the lore of her great-great-great-great-great-grandparents. Any place there was a tiny amount of water on the desert floor, there were Mesquite trees. The trees grew in places that were otherwise completely unsuitable for agriculture, they required no cultivation and they were easy to harvest. Telia gathered the mesquite pods when they ripened between June and September. She ground the pods into a flour. Mesquite flour was not only nourishing as an everyday diet, it was food that could sustain them when there was no other food source. By adding water, the dough could be rolled out thin and cooked over the coals like tortillas. This mesquite flour had a pleasant caramel, nut-like flavor and had more protein than most grain flours. When there were no vegetables and beans to be had from the garden, and there was no meat or fish or nuts to be had from the trips to the mountains, during the toughest of times, during the most difficult months, at the height of the summer, the family subsisted on mesquite flour tortillas. So long as they could bring water down from the mountains, that and the pods from mesquite trees were *the only things* that made a difference between life and death.

When a New Rebel troop came out for the sixth time to inspect the settlement, the lieutenant in charge said, "Since you had plenty of provisions to last you the first eighteen months, and you figured out how to bring water down from the mountains, we knew you would probably last a year and a half, maybe two. What amazes us is that three and a half years on, you're still surviving. No one would have guessed that would have been possible! And you have windows in your house that are facing in all directions! Where did you find the wood to cover them up from the cold in the winter and the heat in the summer?"

"My son Pontus found planks of wood and some rusty old nails in an old mine shaft in the mountains," Pallas said. "A bit of a miracle, I know. I'm worthless at carpentry. Pontus isn't much better. It was Telia who was able to fashion the wood and nails to create those sturdy frames and shutters. Great windows, no? She's the miracle-worker. We can improvise."

"You people are incredible!" the lieutenant admitted. "But at the beginning of next year, there is a new rule you must follow. This has come from the very top. Two males can't any longer be away from your settlement at any one time. Also, there must be at least four people here at the settlement at all times. Failure to comply with this rule will result in immediate death. That means the entire family. No subject to review. Breach of the regulation will result in summary execution. I wish I could report differently but it's the new rule. Pallas, I'm being reassigned. My replacement is all regulation. More than that, he's a sadist and a cruel murderer. Watch out."

"Obsidian Order must have their teeth in it all the way by now," Pallas said.

"They're running everything now. There's no check on them."

"Why have you still not brought me a copy of the Foundation Document?" Pallas asked. "You know I want to read *The Blessings of Gaia*. You promised me last time you would."

"They keep delaying the publishing. Everyone's dying to read it. I've heard it has beautiful prose. They keep delaying it. I don't know why this is happening."

After the troops had left, the children asked their mother what the new rule meant. "It means they never expected us to last this long," Telia said. "It means they expected us to be dead by now. If we continue to stay alive for another year, maybe a little longer, they'll be looking for an excuse to snuff us out. What else could it mean? Do you agree, husband?"

"Yes," Pallas said mournfully. "Paranoia isn't always stupid nor is it always foolish. They're delaying the publication of *The Blessings of Gaia* until I'm dead, I'm certain of this. Why else would they delay? They're waiting for us—or at least me—to die."

"Why didn't they kill us in Escalante?" Pontus asked. "Why go to all the trouble of sending us out to the desert, if all they wanted was for us to die?"

"Good question, son. They wanted us to die at the hand of the desert, not by their hand. I think that, up until now, that has been their way of thinking. That's changed. They never counted on your mother having knowledge of the mesquite. That was their big miscalculation. Who back in Escalante would have thought that the mesquite was the one reason we'd survive out here!"

"Up till now we've beaten them," Telia said. "They'll kill us now, husband."

The children looked on with wondering eyes, but they had all been toughened before (maybe with the exception of the occasionally mischievous Vivianna, who had been hard to discipline and correct). As a group, they looked impervious. They did not look frightened.

Yet Pallas insisted that he and Telia take their conversation outside, so they could speak freely. They ended up walking three hundred paces away from the front door. "Why are you being so fatalistic?" Pallas asked. "Why are you being so resigned. That's uncharacteristic of you. You're a fighter! *You've always said you could beat them!*"

"Not this time," Telia said. In a sad voice she added, "I'm a realist. This is it."

"That's all you have to say?"

"That's it. It's the end."

"That's it?"

"Maybe we can save one or two or three."

"One or two? Three?"

"Our children." She laughed bitterly.

"I forbid you to speak like that," Pallas said. "We're not dead yet! You're scaring me!"

"I put it to you, husband. When has forbidding me anything been effective?" Telia asked. "Maybe one of them will have a chance to survive. Maybe one."

"I forbid you to say that."

"I'll figure it out. I'll do it. I'll do it for all of us. I'll figure it out. It's a luxury for us now to even think some of us can survive. *You cannot survive. I cannot. Alas, most of our children cannot.* But we may have a choice."

Chapter Thirty-Four

BECAUSE OF THE NEW RULE, Pallas and Pontus knew that this was going to be the last trip that they were going to be able to take together to the mountains. The rule wasn't as crushing as it could have been, they at least had another three months of grace. Pontus was four months shy of his fifteenth birthday. Aura had just celebrated her nineteenth. Teanna was eighteen. Vivianna was seventeen.

On this trip Pallas and Pontus took a different route. They traveled several days before they got to the foot of the Shoshone Mountains, forty miles north of their usual route. They passed through a wide canyon that narrowed more and more as they went. At one point, Pontus looked up and noticed a series of impressive petroglyphs—some were just six inches long and wide, but a few were several feet long. They were carved onto the surface of the towering overreaches of the basalt. The images were geometric, consisting mainly of interchangeable patterns of florid swirling lines and circles. Most of the basalt rocks were brown in color, some black, a few were a distinctive greenish-black. The old scratch marks really stood out on the surfaces of the greenish-black ones.

"Yes, I knew," Pallas said. "I took this route for this reason."

Pontus's fascination about the scratch marks was overwhelming. Pallas ordered the horses to stop. It seemed like a good idea to give them a rest. It wasn't actually too hot, barely 80 degrees Fahrenheit, so the horses didn't require shade to make the most of their break time. To get a better view of the petroglyphs, Pallas descended from the wagon and climbed up the gentle rise of the canyon. Pontus followed his father eagerly, his own steps right behind his father's steps, careful not to slip or fall in the loose shale and the rocks.

After walking alongside the canyon rim for about three hundred yards, Pallas saw even grander examples of the art. This time the swirling lines and circles were more distinctive and elaborate, larger, with complicated patterns. "This is a great find!" Pallas shouted. Stepping up close, he showed Pontus the scratch marks, tenderly touching them with his fingers.

Pontus was bewildered by what he saw. "What are they?" he asked his father.

"Records of Indians," Pallas explained, taking in his breath. "Indians passed through here." He fingered the surface of the rocks with a sense of thrill and awe. "I don't know why I call them Indians. Actually, they're records of a *nomadic* people who traveled through here. I doubt very much the people who made these marks actually lived here. That is to say, settled here. How old are the marks? One thousand years old? 1500 years old? My guess. Maybe older."

"I see them...*but what are they?*" Pontus asked.

"Oh," Pallas replied smiling, nodding. "Their presence. Establishing their presence. Beyond that, who knows what the marks mean? Communication?" Pallas shrugged. "Don't know. Many of our people, the New Rebels, come from the mix-blood Indians of central Mexico, southern Mexico, and Central America. Your mother is a rarity. She came from a line of Sephardic Jews dating back three millennia before their forced conversion to Christianity in Spain in 1492. Half a century later, they came to the New World. As had been their practice before, Telia's ancestor's hid their Jewishness under a facade of Roman Catholicism — initially in Spain, then in Mexico. Fifty years later, after their initial arrival in the New World, they traveled to the northwestern fringe of the province of New Mexico, all the time secretly hiding their faith. Three centuries later, they arrived at the desert. A century and a half subsequent to that, they intermarried with Timbisha Shoshone Indians. Where did my family come from? That's all lost in time. I've no idea."

Pallas began to scramble down the hill. But before Pontus could follow him he noticed an eye peeking out from between a chink in the rocks. *What was that? Pontus wondered.* Then there was a pair of eyes from the fissure. The eyes were large. The entire creature then came out and stood prominently on a rock, not moving. It was as if the creature was sunning itself.

"Come back," Pontus shouted to his father. "Come back quickly!"

His father turned and scrambled back up the hill.

"What's that?"

Pallas looked. "Goodness. Never seen one of these... They're usually so shy. It's a big, fat chuckwalla!"

"A what?" Pontus asked.

The creature was close to two feet long, if you included the tail. It had a hard, tough hide of gray glistening scales, looking more like an ancient reptile than a familiar desert lizard.

"You know these things are rare, don't you?" Pallas asked. "Your mother would know what to do with it. The Piute and the Timbisha Shoshone knew what to do with it! Eat it!"

What surprised Pallas the most was that this reputedly shy, elusive creature was brazenly parading itself in front of them, seemingly nonplussed and unafraid. Or maybe it was because Pontus and Pallas were a good fourteen feet down below him. Or maybe his kind had not seen humans for so many hundreds of years that he had severed his memory stem from the sense of danger that humankind represented.

"The only way you can catch one is to come up from behind, *actually from above*, and drop a noose around his neck," Pallas said. "If he has enough time to scramble back into the rocks, he wedges himself in and puffs himself up, and in that strange condition of extreme bloat, there's nothing you can do to pry him out."

"You've never seen one before, Father?"

"'Course not. This is the first I've seen."

"But you know about them?"

"My Uncle Xandry, when he was a young man, not only saw one, but caught one. Happened many hundreds of miles from here, much closer to home. My uncle's friend saw it from below, and my uncle caught it by approaching from above. He used a noose. Strange. I remember my uncle mentioning it wasn't a hot day, maybe a day like today? Could that be part of it?"

As they scrambled down the hill, they looped back down to where the horses and wagon were situated. Several hundred yards from their destination, Pallas noticed a horizontal slit in the rocks. Upon closer examination, Pallas realized the slit was an opening to a cave. The rim above the slit kept the rain out, and therefore kept everything inside protected and pristine. If Pallas narrowed his body, he could just barely slip through the cave opening. Excitedly, he beckoned his son Pontus to join him. A good twenty feet inside was a small circle which could just barely accommodate three or four people at one time. Six rusty cans lay around the circle. Pallas had stumbled onto an ancient camp.

"Look at this, son!" Pallas said. "Another rare find!"

"I've seen these kinds of rust-metal objects before," Pontus noted. "Closer to home. I even knew someone who collected them, ones that had not been too oxidized or too dissolved or too disintegrated. He found them in the back of a cave, and in the back of a deep overhang. If you look in the right place, you can find them. They're not so rare. Though these, in spite of their brown rust markings, look in better shape than the ones my friend tried to collect."

"Hah, but have you been able to figure out how old they are?" Pallas asked. "No, of course you haven't! How could you? You haven't the information to do so. But I am one of the extreme few who has that information. I learned it from the Oggaci in Europe. I learned it from a man named Cacttus. Let me show you."

Pallas arranged the six cans in a straight line. Two of the cans were rusty through and through, the tops, middles, and bottoms were uniformly rusty. Pallas said: "These are church key cans. Probably beer cans. The church key can was opened using a separate metal apparatus, and it created an indentation at the top of the can." Pallas showed Pontus the marking. "The church key can was introduced in 1930 A.D. It was highly popular throughout the world, but it was phased out in the 1980s. The other four cans have aluminum tops, so they're not rusty, but still shiny, as you can see. The newest pop-top can was introduced in 1975 A.D. It lasted the longest. It lasted until the beginning of the 2050s, right up until the end of the Eleven-Years-War. In the Gaia-Domes, it had an after life, some say until 25 A.G., but that is speculation. You see the innovation, the aluminum pop-top stays on the can, right? The church key can lasted 50 years. The latest style aluminum pop-top lasted 75 years, or maybe longer. So among these six cans we have two well preserved examples of each of the three types. Do you realize how rare that is? What date does that tell you the cans came from? That is to say, what was the date they were deposited here?"

"How do you know this?" Pontus asked with a look of incredulity. "You're a walking textbook of ancient knowledge. How do I know you aren't just making this up?"

"Just answer the question. The question involves a lesson your mother would approve of, combining mathematics, arithmetic, and history, maybe even a bit of pre-history."

"Between 1975 and the 1980s. About 625 years ago."

"Exactly," Pallas said, smiling. "You've learned my lessons well. Well done. Now you are what could be called an archaeologist. And I love how I've been able to teach you how to back-read time."

"You're not making this up? You're not manufacturing it out of your imagination?"

Pallas shook his head. "No. I wouldn't lie to you, son. No."

"But how could you have known all about the cans *and* their dates?" Pontus asked.

"Among the Oggaci," Pallas said. "I lived with them more than thirty years ago." He smiled. "Cacttus, a scholar, a kind and gentle elderly man, found a book for me about cans in the archives that had a special section dealing with innovations about can construction in the Twentieth Century. The book was dated 2003 A.D.—or 2003 C.E., Common Era—if you want to get all Lloyd-esque about it. But the book was about changes that had occurred in beer can construction 30 to 40 years before that. Apparently, collecting beer cans was popular 625 years ago. That's why there were books about the subject. Now, as to why the Oggaci had *that particular* book in their archive, I'd never be able to figure that out if my life depended on it."

Pontus was speechless.

"So," Pallas said, "here's the archaeological part of the story. The persons who were sitting cramped around this tiny campfire ring, drinking these cans of beer, did so around a campfire built about 625 years ago. Why were they there at that specific time? Because earlier in the day, before that evening of relaxation, they were looking at the petroglyphs on the basalt cliffs. Enjoying themselves, no doubt. Why else would they have been here? There's nothing else here to see but the petroglyphs. And the petroglyphs dated back at least 750 years before the beer-swillers, maybe even 1,000 years before them."

"And all this time the chuckwalla's been—waiting? Waiting for us to arrive, Father?"

"A damnably sentimental and romantic way of looking at things, Pontus, your mother would say. She would not approve." Pallas roared with glee. He watched Pontus out of the corner of his eye, hoping to get a sign of his son's complicity. Pontus shot a smile back. Pallas let loose his joy. "You got it then," Pallas said. "That romantic gene. Like I do. The chuckwalla survived the climate change—the Gaia destruction—because he lived in caves. Well, not exactly in caves. But in a kind of cave. Inside the indentations of the rocks. In the worst of times, some of our ancestors mimicked them. And that's how they survived. Even in a small cave like this. Perhaps."

Pontus was very happy. "You've explained everything to me. You always explain everything so well, Father. These *strange*, strange stories you tell! I completely agree with you. I mean, I agree with your notion of romanticism. I also agree about the sentimentality. Let us celebrate our discovery of the chuckwalla!"

Pallas dearly loved all members of his family. But he couldn't hide his favoritism. He especially adored Pontus. "A romantic. Don't disclose that side of your nature too readily, Pontus. I've tried to bury the truth of my romanticism deep inside me. But your mother always saw through me every time. Our ancestors sacrificed all that they did, so we could afford to experience a little romanticism in our lives—which is another way of saying: elevate our concerns so that they are above the level of hardscrabble survival. What's wrong with getting our heads out of a deep mire of misery, out of a slough of banality, out of a depression of tedium, every once in a while? After all these years, how should I arrive at any different conclusion? Let's go gather water so your mother and your sisters can survive. And experience some romantic feelings too. Why not be romantic about nature? About aesthetics? About the nature of how the Earth exists? Why not? What could be the harm in doing that? Isn't that also a truth about Gaia? Writing the Foundation Document, writing *The Blessings of Gaia*, that meant nothing to me."

Pontus interrupted Pallas. "Are you resentful, do you feel an injustice had been done to you, when they took your name off *The Blessings of Gaia*? Surely that must have been difficult."

"Rather a relief. What difference does it make? That isn't modesty or humility speaking either. It took a horrible burden off my shoulders. If my ideas came from another place, if I was just serving as a conduit for a belief—or a blessing—from some other place, then that's good enough for me. Why not let the book be an anonymous inspiration from Iona? From September? Why not? Does it matter?"

Pontus could see a look of resignation in his father's eyes. He didn't like it. To Pontus, the look seemed like an acceptance of death.

"Writing my poetry, writing the truth of my soul, now that meant something to me," Pallas said. "That's my truth." But as Pallas said this, he was laughing.

Chapter Thirty-Five

THEY RETURNED from the mountains with water, two barrels full, and a little bit of wood that they were able to collect up past the 10,500-foot level.

Fortunately, all six members of the family were present and accounted for when the patrols showed up the next time. This was a lucky break. The new lieutenant arrived with the troop, and he introduced himself. He was strongly built, looked incredibly tough, with fierce-looking eyes. Unlike his predecessor, he made it abundantly clear at the outset he was capable of committing any multitude of acts of abomination and indecency, but more to the point, any number of acts of brutality.

"I wish you owned a dog," he declared to Pallas with a devilish glint in his eye. "I'd shoot the creature in front of you. Then I'd force you to gut it. Then I'd force one of your daughters to wear the hide around her neck as if it were a collar, as if it were a furwrap. Each one of your daughters could take her turn. That would be entertaining. Then I'd force your wife to squat in the dirt and eat the carcass raw. The only thing she'd have to devour the creature with would be her hands. Just her hands. And her teeth. Break a rule."

Pallas was speechless.

"My father, like his father before him, and his father before him, was raised in a Gaia-Dome. I'm proud of that. It's a good heritage. *I was technically raised both inside and outside Gaia-Domes...*

Beginning at the age of thirteen, my father taught me special skills. I bet you can guess what they are. I cracked my first skull when I was 12. I won't tell you what I did at the age of 14, but it involved a dentist's drill and a pair of eight-pound tongs."

"At least up until recently, according to the rules of the Western Army, your recruitment would not have been permitted," Pallas said in a low voice.

"I've heard tell you were a complete know-it-all," the lieutenant snapped. "A real smart-ass. I'll visit your place anytime I want. At sunrise. Just before sunset. In the dead of night. When you least expect me to show up, there I'll be. You might as well put an extra plate on the table, just in case I might make an appearance. That's how much I'm going to be all over you. By the way, the protocols of Western Army recruitment process were changed three months ago."

The world of Pallas and Telia and their nearly grown up children had changed irrevocably.

Pallas and Aura made the next trip to the mountains together. The time after that, Pallas and Teanna. And the time after that, Telia and Vivianna. It had gotten to the point that only Telia could manage the unruly Vivianna on these trips. Even without Vivianna wearing her stupid-looking visor cap, Telia still had to whip her ill-disciplined youngest daughter into shape.

A year and a half after the imposition of the new rule, Pallas decided to make a trip to the mountains on his own. This arrangement was unprecedented, but Telia thought it was high time that he did so.

In the late spring of 553 A.G., Pallas decided that he would travel farther than he had traveled since their resettlement. He wanted to go 95 miles farther north into the Toiyabe Mountains, all the way up to the southern rim of the mountain overlooking Iona's sacred shrine.

Pallas had been seventeen years old when he had last visited the shrine, it had been a solo journey, and he thought that he'd make a similar journey to commemorate the thirty-four years that had passed since that time. If something terrible happened, all of the children were now of an age where they could more or less fend for themselves. Even Pontus, the youngest, had proven capable of taking care of himself. He had traveled all the way to Lake Tahoe in the Sierra Nevada in the west, all the way to within 175 miles of the Snake River to the north, all the way down to within 175 miles of the north rim of the Grand Canyon to the south, riding on one of the ponies.

Pallas would have made this trip sooner, but it would have involved leaving the wagon at a base camp, and since there were no roads, even primitive ones, going north from that point. He would have had to ride one of the ponies, crossing difficult terrain, adding an extra eleven days to the journey. He figured, why delay the trip any longer? He was at an age where if he didn't go now, he probably would not have been able to go later.

For a number of reasons, he felt everything was closing in on him. Telia had noticed that each time the troops came now to visit them they were more formal, direct, severe, seemingly disappointed when they counted heads and realized there were four members of the family present and at least one of them was male. It was as if they knew, or expected that at some point, there would be a slip-up.

When Pallas left, both he and Telia had a premonition that something bad was going to happen. They both were very formal when Pallas made his departure. Telia stared in her husband's direction long after he left, making the children nervous.

"That crazy lieutenant visits us fifteen to twenty times a year, what can we expect?" After the last statement, she didn't continue to voice her thoughts, but her children could tell by the look on her face that she was having thoughts, and none of them were good.

Immediately after Pallas's departure, Telia sat her children down. She decided to gather them around the east-facing window, Telia's favorite. On some days you could even make out the sharp, pointy outline of the Desotoya Mountains from there. She decided to tell them a story that she had never told them before. Up until this point she had been of two minds, but now she decided that she must do so. They were no longer really children. Aura and Teanna were full-grown women, and at the age of eighteen even Vivianna was beginning to show hopeful signs of maturing. Pontus was beginning to grow a patch of whiskers on his chin, just like the ones Pallas had grown when he had turned sixteen.

"Your father is visiting the shrine dedicated to the memory of Iona. It's a good time to tell you something else about your background, something I haven't mentioned before."

Aura was a little suspicious. "Why have you waited until now to tell us, Mother?"

"Because before I didn't deem it necessary to tell you. I've since changed my mind. Now I think it's important."

"Okay," Aura said.

"Beginning in 2051 A.D., at the time of the beginning of the Age of Gaia, your ancestors could no longer survive in the desert. They managed to hang on for another ten years, more or less living in the open, but as they did their situation became more and more precarious. At last they knew that they had to find a cave if they were going to have any chance at surviving. In search of a cave, they traveled many hundreds of miles. They found caves on numerous occasions that otherwise might have worked out, but only if they had been a smaller group. Some of the caves were large enough, but there wasn't enough water. They were searching for a cave complex that would be suitable for a fairly large family—including orphans, stragglers, and refugees from other wandering families that had suffered nearly complete decimation. Therefore, initially, they made the horrible mistake of not dividing up into five or six smaller groups, but now it was too late. Incidentally, the Unseeing Watchfulness of Gaia had been perfectly willing to divide up into groups as small as three or four individuals, if that was what was necessary for survival.

"Before they could find their ideal cave, your ancestors had fallen to the level of abject starvation. The effects of the climate change had grown worse—*far worse, involving terrible, terrible droughts.* They had not anticipated that the change in the climate would be so rapid, so severe. Then the huge outbreak of sun poisoning with the destruction of the ozone layer added to their problems. Out of the original eighteen of them, five had fallen ill and died within a one year period. It was then that the man who had been born in 2014, who was now forty-seven years old, and the oldest in the group, made the great sacrifice."

Telia paused for a moment. Her children were no longer children. They needed to know this.

"The old man (under those conditions, forty-seven was pretty old) offered himself up, and his wife, and the two oldest children, to be eaten. He told the others, 'Drink our blood and eat our flesh, and in doing this you will have enough sustenance to make it to the promised land.' So they did as he told them and nine survivors made it to a cave that was just large enough to accommodate them. There they made certain that no baby could be born until someone older had at first died. The first baby was not born until one of them died in a fateful rock fall. In this way, the group stabilized their population. And in this way, they managed to survive over a period of hundreds of years, never allowing their group to grow larger than nine or ten."

Pontus asked, "Was that part of the Jewish tradition?"

"It was part of no tradition," Telia replied. "It was what they had to do to survive."

"But the old man? And his wife? And the two oldest children? They ate them?" Aura asked. "That is positively diabolical. That was cannibalism!"

"The old man's sacrifice, you mean?" Telia asked. "And the wife's? And the two oldest children's? It was four acts of cannibalism to prevent cannibalism in general. It has been our family's biggest secret all these years. I bet you there were occasions where this happened among the Unseeing Watchfulness of Gaia, but since we've always had such a fearful hatred of cannibals, these types of stories have been generally suppressed. Even in the Oral Traditions. But it's our family's story. Ask your father about acts of cannibalism during times of starvation, I bet you he could relate one or two."

Pontus said, "But with only nine or ten people in the group, wouldn't that mean inbreeding?"

"You're so clever," Telia said. "You're the smart one, Pontus. And you're right, too. They had an answer for that. After the first one hundred years or so, they sought out other groups who were also living in a stark survivor mode. Of course they sometimes had to travel great distances to do this. They exchanged boys and girls with them who would soon be of child-bearing age. By doing this, they did not interbreed. During the later years at least."

All the children were silent.

Then Aura broke the silence. "So you had to tell us this story? Why now? There must be an ulterior motive."

Telia regarded Aura with a look of fierce devotion. "We, the two of us, are going to die, Aura."

"Soon?"

"Yes, my dear. Very soon."

"Some of us? All of us? Mother, please. Mother, say, some of us. Don't say all of us. Please."

"Most of us. Maybe all of us. Time to make a sacrifice. And Aura, when you fixated on your crude notion of cannibalism, you missed the whole point of the story."

"The strong sacrificed themselves for the weak," Pontus said. "That's your point. A reversal of the natural order, or at least, a partial reversal of the natural order. Weak were not devoured."

Telia smiled. "Yes, my moon lover. Yes, my star gazer. Yes, my truth teller. You're just like your father. Both of you are the ones who nearly always get it right."

Two weeks passed until there was nearly a full moon. Pontus had calculated the days. Since the age of twelve, phases of the moon had been a passion with him. Pontus called this interest a passion, not a *scientifically-based* one, but rather an *aesthetically-based* one.

Since their arrival in the desert, Telia noticed her husband had been encouraging Pontus in his pursuit of these bizarre types of aesthetics. Most of the time Pallas did this encouragement in secret, but Telia could sense it. Telia suspected Pallas did it even more often and in greater depth when Pontus accompanied him on trips to the mountains, but she didn't have proof of it. It was impossible to get absolute proof because Pontus didn't need any encouragement. He was filled with an effervescent love of beauty. Telia sensed Pontus was too much of a dreamer for his own good. But what could she do about it?

On his own initiative, Pontus had become an explorer and his explorations did not always entail simply searching for food and water. Once he had turned thirteen, he'd become an expert rider. With a pony he could travel sixty miles a day. The fact that he was skinny, weighing a mere 112 pounds, made it easier on the pony. Pontus could travel great distances even on foot without the benefit of a pony, so why try to stop him? Besides observing the moon, Pontus was an avid star-gazer in general. From the beginning, Pallas had been indulgent of Pontus's celestial fascinations. Telia had tried to be a disciplinarian at first, but then she grew wary of trying to reform Pontus, then resigned. He was incorrigible. The daughters resembled Telia more in their frugality, practicality, and common sense, but Pontus resembled his father more in his dreaminess and expansiveness. What could she do about it? She decided to use it to her advantage.

So it came as no surprise to her when Pontus came up to her and asked permission to walk to the nearby sulfur hot springs that night to soak. He was still small enough, just barely the size that could fit snugly inside the slit of the narrow, tiny pool. He wanted to gaze up at the full moon as it transited the night sky, all the while submerged in the hot water. One last time before it was too late.

He was shocked when his mother agreed. "'Course you can. If not now, when? Better now."

Pontus had a foolish grin on his face, a grin that reminded Telia of Pontus's father's grin when he had been young. "It's only for a night. Maybe I should wait until father gets back, in case the soldiers come. But it's now or never. It may be the last time. I'm getting too big to fit into that tiny slit of a pool."

"Go," Telia said. "What will happen, *will happen*. Say goodbye to your sisters before you leave, son."

"Are you certain?"

"Yes."

It was easy for Pontus to walk the ten miles to the spring. He arrived just as darkness was falling. He stripped down and submerged himself in the briny, sulfur-filled, rotten-egg smelling water, looking up at the gloaming of the darkening sky, waiting for the moon to show. He fell asleep for a good two hours, but when he awoke, there it was, the moon resplendent and full, hanging overhead. Away from the doldrums of exile, away from the boring routines of a daily grinding life, away from the tedium of endless chores, he was alone. The hot spring had a replenishing effect. He thought to himself: Was it naughty, perverse, or even downright evil to pine for such a thrilling and heavenly experience?

He stared at the moon. His body tingled. It was as if he had escaped, at least for several hours, from the desert, from the detritus of the quotidian. His father had been a poet. Pontus knew some about this aspect of his father's life. But Pontus never had any desire to write poetry, nor did he have any desire to read it. Yet he loved to have his mind swim round and round in this languorous passivity. Just him. And the moon. No Earth. More importantly, so far away from earthly demands. It was as if there was no earthly gravity. It was a form of bliss, but heightened by a sense of edginess and urgency. Oh, this glorious moon! He stared at it. This oceanic feeling went on for hours. And it felt so good. But when the moon had traveled so far across the night sky that Pontus had to turn almost on his side to continue to watch its movement, he suddenly became alarmed. He was suddenly overpowered by an inexplicable sense of fright. It had been a mistake to come out here, he realized now. He had been irresponsible. In his selfishness and in his need to escape, he had put his sisters' lives, and also his mother's life, in jeopardy. Why had his mother allowed him permission to go in the first place? Pontus needed his mother to give him orders! He was too young, too impetuous; he needed to have someone to restrain him.

Without even drying himself off, he jumped into his clothes. There was a film of gray light peeking out in the east, telling Pontus that the sun would be rising soon. If he set out now, he could make the settlement in two and a half hours, if he walked at a brisk pace. Why had he been so foolish? Why had he been *allowed* to be so foolish? This was still a mystery to him.

As he walked quickly, smoke was coming from the dirt-walled hut. He could see it in the distance. Something was wrong. Twenty minutes later, he arrived. The four dead bodies had been laid out in a row, in front of the hut, his mother and his three sisters. Their faces were covered, but Pontus could tell by the clothes they wore that it was them. How soon had the troops left after the execution? Maybe an hour before. Perhaps three or four hours before. Pontus could smell their presence. When he entered the hut he saw that they had rifled through the food, mainly mesquite pod flour and pinon nuts, that had been left on the table.

Why had the soldiers left the hut so abruptly after having executed the four? Where were they? Maybe they had gone out in search of Pontus? Or maybe they'd gone out in search of the missing father? Or both of them. The troops knew that two people traveling together almost always made the trip to the mountains.

Finally Pontus got up the nerve to examine the bodies of his sisters and his mother more carefully. Bullet wounds to the chest, to the heart, executed at close range. Why had they not received bullet wounds to the head? Weren't the troops concerned that one of them might have survived bullet wounds to the chest? How quickly did death come to them? Congealed blood, almost black like a dark purple stain, appeared in the center of each woman's chest. Each of his sisters was shot three times. The bullet holes formed an almost perfect triangular cluster. But there were six bullets in his mother, the same cluster of three bullets to the chest, and an extra bullet to the stomach, an extra bullet to the neck, an extra bullet to the forehead.

PONTUS COULD NOT FIGURE OUT WHY HIS MOTHER, AFTER HER DEATH STRUGGLE, WAS STARING AT HIM WITH HER EYES WIDE OPEN. LET HIM GO. LET HIM GO SEE THE MOON. LET HIM DEPART. WHEN, IN THE PAST, UNDER SIMILAR CONDITIONS, WOULD SHE HAVE ALLOWED IT? WHY DID THIS HAPPEN? WHY DID THIS HAPPEN NOW?

Pallas realized the deaths of his mother and three sisters had been the direct result of his action, of his selfishness.

Realizing this, he wanted to commit suicide. But Pontus also realized death was going to come to him soon enough anyway, once the troops returned to finish the job they had started. Perhaps more to the point, Pontus knew he was under a rigid moral obligation to bury the bodies immediately, as soon as possible. The only thing that kept him from this task was a letter his mother had left for him. It had been hidden in a designated place, the special place where notes were to be hidden in the event of an emergency. Under a smooth flagstone lying halfway between the southwest corner of the hut and the edge of the garden, Pontus found the note. He read it:

Pontus, my dearest son,

As you'll have discovered before reading this, we're all to be dead, all five of us, five of us (yes, this soon will include your father), so that you may live. Before your father left for the mountains, I discussed this matter with him. You need to know that   jointly we came to this conclusion. We knew that if we waited for the lieutenant to decide for us, all of us, all of us together, would die. But your father and I realized there was another way. If we were cagey and cunning about this, well then, at least the youngest might survive. I knew that the lieutenant was going to come. I had overheard a member of his troop the previous month inadvertently let slip out the words: "We are going to return on the night of the next full moon." So you didn't kill me or your sisters. No thoughts of suicide now, son! I've had them—both your father and I have had them—but I forbid you from having them.

When you went to the hot springs to see the moon, I knew that the lieutenant was going to show up and that I would tell him that you had accompanied your father to the mountains. Of course, the lieutenant would be deliriously happy to have a cause to kill us all. (As if he needed a cause, sooner or later, he was going to kill us all, cause or no cause, and this was the only way we thought we might be able to trick him, while we still had the advantage of the "high ground" of timing.) As you're reading this, no doubt the troops and the lieutenant are in hot pursuit of your father and you. Obviously, they are not going to find you, but here's the thing, they are not going to find your father either. He went out of his way to go visit Iona's shrine, one last time, and he timed that visit for this week. (How could I not allow it? After all, it's his religion.) I'm sorry I didn't let you in on this plan, but I knew you would never have gone to the hot springs if you had known what was going to happen.

Son, I ask your forgiveness for my having committed this unpardonable act of subterfuge. This is not your fault. This was planned. This is my and your father's sole responsibility. When your father returns, assuming he eludes the troops, you take one of the small horses and travel as fast as you can to Escalante. It's extremely important that you get there before the troops and the lieutenant get there so you must ride fifty miles a day, or something close to fifty miles a day, and you mustn't stop till you get there. Your father will stay behind and try to detain the troops and the lieutenant as long as he can. He also will tell them that you died in the mountains, viz. the missing pony and the missing you. Will this work? We don't know. All we need to do is to buy time for you. Find Matthew as soon as you get to Escalante, he will send you in disguise, incognito, to the East, so you can join the Forandi Order. You probably don't know this, but before we went into exile, Matthew managed to secure significant and powerful autonomy for the Forandi Order on the East Coast, at least for the time being. We are relatively certain it will be within his powers to make your trip to the East happen. This is sort of complicated, so please son, don't screw it up. If you can get to Escalante in seven or eight days, you're virtually certain to beat the troops back. That's crucial. All this is hanging on your performance, so again, don't screw it up! We know what riding you're capable of when you've set your mind to it! All you have to do is wait for your father to show up. He will. In the meantime, bury your sisters and me, son. I'm counting on you. Don't leave the job for your father. It'll break his heart.

Your mother, Telia

P.S. Isn't it amazing how well your father has taught me how to use this marvelous new alphabet, viz. this letter? You know what to do with this when you've finished it. Burn it.

P.P.S. My dearest, dearest son, we cannot live without you. So live. I command it.

Three days later Pallas arrived riding one of the ponies and had the other pony in tow.

Pallas looked so messy and bestraggled, it was obvious from his appearance he'd been riding for several days on end.

"No ceremony, son. You buried them? Good. They're looking

for me. They knew my routine in the mountains. They must have come across what they thought was the abandoned wagon. I must have been a hundred miles away at that time. I had gone completely outside my routine. I was visiting Iona's shrine and I had taken both of the ponies with me. You know her shrine is still as beautiful and simple as I had remembered it. I visited the runic stone. 'She did not die.' I had scratched the words out. You can't even see the place where I'd scratched the words out, I'd done such a splendid job. There are bits of moss and dirt here and there on the stone, it was thirty-four years ago! Lost my innocence. You must ride away, son. I'll stay here. I'll wait for them. The lieutenant will kill me. That's all they really wanted anyhow. He'll almost be doing me a favor. But I know that there is a way that you can escape! I knew you'd discover your mother's letter. There's not that much more to discuss. Get on your pony and ride!"

Pallas was talking so fast it was as if he were someone trying to regain some self-respect.

"I killed my family...my sisters," Pontus said. "My actions killed them."

"Circumstances killed them, not you," Pallas interjected.

"But I left for the night. I deliberately broke the rules. That's why they're dead."

"They're dead because Naxos wanted them dead. Or Lloyd wanted them dead. Either way, it amounts to the same thing. That's why they're dead. It's your mother and I who bear the full brunt of all responsibility. You have a chance to make it. By the way, your apricots are ripe!"

"But father!"

"No buts. Get on that pony and ride. I command you. You have a chance. The only chance we have is through memory. *Your memory.* Without memory we have no chance. Only you can provide that. Sometimes memory is more important than life. But when you tell your children about us, when you start to establish your own Oral Tradition, just tell them about Telia, keep her ancestry going.

Do not mention me or my authorship of *The Blessings of Gaia*. And for goodness sakes, do not mention any of my ridiculous, vanity-driven poems."

It was at this moment Pontus looked carefully at his father's ghostly milky-white, pin-pupil eyes. For some reason, Pallas wasn't cloaked all over. Perhaps from riding through the brush and trees at the higher elevations in the mountains, the cloth covering one of his upper arms had been torn, thus bearing the skin underneath. The thicker cloth covering one of his upper legs was also shredded. Pontus could see through both the exposed places the surface of his father's skin. He could see the still visible marks, cuts, and scars from the brutal beatings and savage whippings Pallas had received at the hands of his father.

Pontus could see that his father had not led an easy life. Pontus was looking at a man who appeared as if he had been broken, saddened by a powerful grief. But it was more than that. Pontus's father now had the face of someone who was *beyond* the woebegone.

Pallas said, "Remember when I talked to you about the aperture, the special one: the doorway? The doorway is more important than any window can be. Remember me talking to you about the doorway? Remember me talking to your sisters about the doorway? Remember?"

"Yes, Father."

"In a positive way, only precious few of us ever make it through that portal. For the rest of us, it is a doorway we avoid at all costs, until against our will we're propelled through it into an endless dreamless night—to join the vanquished, the vanished, the disappeared, the annihilated, the forgotten. When you talk to your children, just mention Telia. Only mention your mother. Do you understand?"

"But why?" Pontus asked. Tears formed in his eyes. "But why not mention you, Father?"

"I must die here. Telia is my Iona."

Chapter Thirty-Six

WITH PLENTY OF WATER, and plenty of mesquite tree meal-pone and some pinon nuts, that's probably all Pontus needed to make it back to Escalante. But he was going to have to circumvent the settlement of Noobie by five miles, the settlement of Pioche by five miles, and the settlement of Deseret by at least ten miles, and that meant that the trip would take almost a half-day longer than it otherwise would. He decided to ride right over the back of the Toiyabe Mountains, a more direct route, thus saving time, but also a harsher route because there were a few places where there were very steep climbs. He definitely was not going to meet the troops and the lieutenant, at least at the outset of the journey.

And by going that way he could harvest the very first of the fruit produced from his apricot tree. When he got to the five-year-old tree, it looked small and it had grown up a little dwarfed. The elevation was too high, it would have thrived better had it been planted lower down the mountain, but then there wouldn't have been sufficient water there. Pontus had planted the sapling in an indentation next to a tiny "run-off," a melt from a snow-snub located about 2,500 feet higher up the slope.

That first year the small tree bore less than seventy apricots and only half of them were fully ripe. But Pontus enjoyed eating from the fruit of his tree, from the sapling he had planted when he was only eleven years old.

Right away, he ate eight of the ripest apricots himself. He pocketed about twenty others. He fed four of the apricots to the pony. He'd be a dead man without his pony, so he made sure he cut and slit the apricots into halves, removing the pits before he plopped the halves into his pony's welcoming mouth. They were a team. Pontus could stand in front of his friend on the morn of the coldest dawn, nuzzling nose to nose, rubbing back and forth, gently removing the hoary frost off the tough, wiry hairs of the pony's nose. Reaching out, Pontus placed his arms around the pony's neck. He kissed him. He caressed his friend's neck and shoulders. He ran his hand along his slightly curved back until he came to the hindquarters.

Oh my goodness! Pontus remembered his father telling him the story when they had gone out on a water-gathering expedition. It was as if it had been told to him at that very moment! It seemed so real to him! In his mind! It had been one of his favorites. It was about Marjoram. She had been a doctor. She had acted as a doctor and a surrogate mother to the thirteen-year-old Iona, after Iona had emerged from the blistering ordeal of crossing the Forbidden Zone. Marjoram directed Iona to a cave. During this part of the story, Marjoram's burro was introduced. Marjoram was devoted to her burro. She loved the creature so much it was as though she treated the creature like a human being.

Pontus's pony was in great shape. He was like an excellent athlete. Of course Pallas had given Pontus the best of the two ponies, the one most rested, the one with the stronger leg power.

Pontus traveled about half of the daylight hours, and about half of the night time hours, in the saddle sometimes as much as twelve hours per twenty-four hour segment. However, on day three, and on day six, they traveled just six hours, thus giving the pony an eighteen-hour long stretch of inactivity so he could restore some of his stamina and strength.

Pontus journeyed east, then corrected southeast, then corrected east again, then corrected southeast. Pontus and pony traversed the desert floor. They climbed the crest of mountain passes. They crossed the intervening desert valleys. Pallas had provided his son with a primitive map so it'd be easier for him to find freshwater sources. But mostly Pontus didn't need the map. He could just see where the intervening mountains were. He eyeballed where the run-off water would have gathered beneath them and made a bee-line for that. He was good at that. Even as young as the age of thirteen, Telia had dubbed her son the best pony rider she had ever seen.

Pontus was making excellent time. He knew he could beat the troops and the lieutenant by at least two days, and if the troops and the lieutenant dawdled—which they were almost certain to do—he could beat them by as much as a week. But Pontus didn't take any chances. He and his pony galloped across the desert, although in the end the trip took a total of eight days.

When Pontus arrived in Escalante he did exactly as he had been told. He immediately went to see Matthew. He didn't stop first to wolf down a decent meal or have a relaxed sleep and extensive lie-down, two things he profoundly desired.

No. He was a man now.

As he had before, Matthew was living in the poorest part of town. Pontus knew exactly where to find him, his father had provided the details.

Matthew hardly looked up. He seemed absorbed in his reading. He didn't seem at all surprised when he saw Pontus enter the room. "Would it be Aura or Teanna or the naughty Vivianna or you banging at my door? It's you. I'm sure your parents determined they could save only one of you. Who could ride the best? Later on, who could hide by pretending to have become a monk? Who was the youngest? The strongest? Four or five centuries ago, leaders of the Unseeing Watchfulness of Gaia often had to make such decisions too, Pontus, so don't think your parents were alone in having to have done that."

Pontus stared at Matthew blankly.

"A leather satchel containing your father's poems was

confiscated. Alas, I tried to retrieve it. But of course I was too late. Lloyd got there before me. I bet you he read the poems, probably all of them. Could you imagine him poring over them? Lloyd always knew Pallas was a first-rate poet. I'm certain he destroyed the poems after he'd read them. I'm sorry that happened because I know how much those poems meant to your father. You know, thirty-four years ago, I actually got your father to recite one of his secret poems to me. So subversive? It took everything I had to pry that poem from his mind. He wouldn't recite the other ones, but I got him to recite that one. I promised him, then and there, that, if need be, I'd take care of his children. With that promise I tricked him into reciting it. Even to this day I remember all the lines. We were taught so well how to memorize in the old days. They don't teach that skill any more, do they?"

> *September Snow did not die*
> *In an anonymous ditch*
> *On a strange, immutably dark road*
> *Forsaken by all the people, castaway by all the world*
> *Under an ozone-depleted firmament*
> *In a death-knelled environment*
> *On a cruel rock: beyond hope of being repaired Earth:*
> *Mocked by indifference: the universe non-sentient, non-alive.*
> *No! No!*
> *Hail Gaia! Hail Truth! Hail the pinnacles of both paradigms.*
> *For are these two seemingly unrelated IDEAS not the same?*

Matthew regarded the youth standing in front of him. "That's it. Your father composed those verses when he was sixteen and a half. Come to think of it, pretty darn close to your age now. He was a romantic. He took the stuff seriously! He was a fool—in a sense, he got it wrong. Truth and Gaia are not the same."

Pontus stared at Matthew with a puzzled expression on his face.

"Gaia doesn't care about us humans, Pontus. Humans don't

mean anything to Gaia. We live in an annihilating universe. We inhabit an indifferent universe. What is man, alone in this incomprehensible cosmos? Unable to answer that question, that's why, so many years ago, slowly over time, Gaia was converted from being a science—a real science—into being a mock religion, a pseudo-science. The reason why it got so weird and tangled and complicated was because people at the time of Tom's generation, six hundred years ago, got mixed up about what science actually was. 'Science' became a new fangled form of religion. They didn't separate these incompatibles. Equating science and religion was where everything went awry. Tom never got mixed up in that controversy. That's why Tom never believed in Gaia. In the process of evolution, Gaia doesn't care who wins. Doesn't care who survives. Four hundred and fifty years ago, we barely made it by the skin of our teeth. Civilization crashed. It was a close call. Gaia doesn't care who prevails. Human beings? Single-celled sea slime? Your pony? Doesn't matter. Why be so proud about this near-death annihilation? Why not let it go?"

"My father told me in confidence that you were passionately, that is to say, secretly, a Christian."

Matthew laughed. "It's true. But only the ethical part. I was never much concerned about the metaphysical part. 'Do unto others as you'd wish them to do unto you.' 'Love your neighbor as yourself.' That sort of thing. Or as Buddhists say: 'If you're suffering, best way to alleviate that affliction is to find someone else who's suffering, and help them, and by helping them, you help yourself.'" Matthew paused. "Of course, these ethics have existed all through time. Anything new?"

There was silence.

"Pontus, you must understand this. Your father spent his entire life trying to understand the character of Iona. He tried to understand her character by studying old books, listening to old narratives, studying the thoughts of old people, listening to sages, seers, the wise. He didn't realize until almost too late that the key to understanding the meaning of Iona was right in front of him, in the living flesh. The physical presence of your mother. His wife, Telia! All he had to do was imagine what Iona would have been like today, and he didn't need his imagination to do this. All he had to do was look into the eyes of his wife."

"But my mother was betrayed by Gaia," Pontus said in a slightly confused voice. "She was rejected by the New Rebels! Towards the end, they wanted to kill her. In the end, they did! Even earlier on, she was seen as an undesirable, as an outcast, as a pariah."

"You missed everything, Pontus. She was rejected by the New Rebels of 553 A.G., not the New Rebels of 20 A.G. Or the New Rebels of 50 A.G. When they were The Unseeing Watchfulness of Gaia, they might have accepted her. Embraced her. More than that, they might have immortalized her. She might have been seen as an inspiration, as a role model."

Pontus was silent.

"Oh you just don't get the point, do you, Pontus? You're as thick as a brick. The Christians didn't come up with this stuff alone, the Jews had this before them. My grandfather was a Christian. Why was he a Christian? For one reason only. Because he was stubborn about his ridiculous religion. That's the only reason why he was a Christian. Stubbornness! Christianity meant nothing more to him than that it provided a platform from which he could act as if he were an eccentric. He could act as if he were different, as if he were a gadfly. That's why my parents, after my grandfather died, had no difficulty converting to Gaia. They had no trouble jettisoning their father's stubbornness. That's my ridiculous heritage. Thank God, excuse me, thank Gaia, your heritage is so much more interesting. Gaia believes in loving others. Even if it has nothing to do with Gaia. That's why I have no problem embracing Gaia. Why my embrace is not incompatible. Gaia borrowed the ethical commandment from Christianity just as Christianity had borrowed it from others, from its antecedents.

"Your mother told me all about her heritage, *all that stuff*. You are not a Jew by belief, Pontus. You are a Jew by heritage. Religions are not claims to knowledge but ways of living with what cannot be known. Christianity gave birth to savage violence, but, at its best, religion—that is to say, religion in general—have been attempts to deal with mystery rather than the hope that mystery will be unveiled. It doesn't matter what you actually believe, Pontus, but you are to do as your mother commanded. You are to remember her. Not necessarily in the context of a religious heritage. You are to remember her as a link from the past to the future. Maybe none of us are able to live authentic lives. Maybe only September Snow and Iona lived authentic lives. Maybe that's why they are so cherished. Maybe that's why they are so beloved. But we should love those who are living."

"What am I supposed to do?" Pontus asked.

"You're going to join my Order. The Forandi Order. Not the Order as it exists here, but the Order as it exists in the East. You are not going as Pontus, son of Pallas and Telia. That'd be too dangerous. Pallas must disappear from history. The only thing he'll be remembered for is that he was the creator of the alphabet. Naxos promised me that sometime in the future that honor would be bestowed upon your father. Will Naxos keep that promise? I guess I'll have to wait around long enough to find out. Somebody's got to keep Naxos honest. Why not me."

"So far away?" Pontus asked. "So far away? In the East? As a member of the Forandi? What am I to do there?"

"Your father traveled more than twice that distance—as far as you are going to travel, more than that, he even traveled across an ocean, at the age of eighteen. And when he went...he went alone. Traveling was so much more difficult then: it's easier now. I'm going to provide you with a guide. Your mission is so much less difficult than your father's mission was. Your mission is to survive."

"That's all? Survive?"

"Yes, survive. You're also to follow your mother's commandment, whatever it may be. Only in that way, can I relieve myself of the burden of the promise I made to your father, and the promise I made to your mother, and the promise I made to myself."

"Truly, truly, Matthew, please help me. Really, really, what is Gaia?"

Matthew almost exploded in anger. "I don't know! Why do you ask me such a terrifying question? Why don't you try looking out for yourself? Isn't that enough? You want to know what Gaia is? Why don't you try reading your father's book, *The Blessings of Gaia*. That's a start. I've heard rumors it's going to be a fantastic read. The Obsidian Order has given authorization for a huge, supreme send-off, in three months time. They've just been awaiting word of your father's death. They've been waiting for that for several years now! Obviously, you've traveled faster than that word has traveled. Congratulations. That's the only reason you're alive. Everybody's dying for it. Everybody's waiting for it. I've heard people'll be willing to stand in line just to kill for it. The new *Bible*? What a scream. You can fight against propaganda. You can fight against coercion. You can fight against outright repression. You can even fight against brilliant displays of strategy and exhibitions of wily guile. Lloyd's strengths. But I ask you this? Can you fight against indoor plumbing and electricity?"

"You sound bitter," Pontus said.

"You'll be leaving early. Way before morning's first light. Come to think of it, let's call you Iaon: son of nobody. Son of a made up name, if you wish. For safety's sake."

"My father never told me you could be so cynical, Matthew."

"Your father's dead."

The morning was cold. Pontus was forced to rise early. A strong, forceful-looking, determined-looking man of an indeterminate age, but probably in his early forties, with a prematurely graying short beard, was staring at Pontus intently. He was standing in the doorway, his hands folded neatly at his waist. The odd-looking fellow wasn't wearing the robes of a Forandi monk, he was wearing the uniform of some sort of foreign-looking soldier. But he was clearly someone Matthew knew, obviously a most trusted aide. The man was a portrait of toughness, resolution, constancy.

Throughout the night, Pontus had slept incredibly well. He had drifted off to sleep immediately after wolfing down a Spartan-like cold supper prepared for him in the Forandi Order's scullery by an eccentric-looking monk suffering from a serious wall-eye.

Next to the simple Forandi Order bed there was a small window frame with a tiny plate of glass. The glass was completely glazed over. Through the glass darkly, Pontus couldn't see out. At the thought of not being able to see, he sighed. He wanted to wait for morning's light, so he could detect and discern something: perhaps a vague movement of a human figure, or just the swaying of a tree in the wind. But he could tell by the stern and withering expression on his guide's face that their departure was going to occur just as soon as Pontus had hurriedly dressed and gathered his precious few belongings together. Pontus shrugged his shoulders. They'd be heading East? That much was certain. They'd be riding horses? Probably.

Pontus was alone. He was silent. He was frightened.

THE END

the story continues...

Embers of the Earth is Book Three of THE BLESSINGS OF GAIA series
BOOK ONE: *September Snow* (2006)
BOOK TWO: *Runes of Iona* (2010)
BOOK FOUR: *Auger's Touchstone* {forthcoming}

Books one and two of the Blessings of Gaia series

"Robert Balmanno's *September Snow* is futuristic fiction at the very top. It can be placed beside Frank Herbert's *Dune*, Aldous Huxley's *Brave New World* and George Orwell's *Nineteen Eighty Four*."

"A potent —and important— parable for the 21st century."

Order yours today on line, or at your local bookseller!

ROBERT BALMANNO has worked as a library specialist in a Silicon Valley library for 30 years. He is a trade union activist and served as a Peace Corps volunteer in West Africa, working with cattle in small villages in Dahomey (Benin).

Balmanno earned his bachelor's degree in Political Science from the University of California, Santa Barbara and did post-graduate work at the University of Edinburgh in Scotland and the University of London, King's College.